'The careful revealing of clues, the clever twists, and the development of Henning Juul and the supporting characters make this a very promising start to a new series' *Suspense Magazine*

'Superbly compelling ... the characters leap right off the page, and the relationship between them is as twisted and complex as the story itself' *Shotsmag*

'Thomas Enger writes a murderous thriller that begs comparison to Jussi Adler-Olsen or Stieg Larsson. With *Cursed* Enger has proved that he definitely belongs in the top ten of Scandinavian authors' **literaturmarkt.info**

'Unexpected and surprising ... like a fire in the middle of a snowfall' *Panorama*

'Thomas Enger is like a bottle of very good red wine. With time he just gets better and better. *Cursed* is a top-class crime thriller from a top-class author' *Mokka*

'The name is Thomas Enger. Make sure you remember it, because he's a man about to join the ranks of the best crime novel writers of the Nordic countries ... and he has achieved something quite exceptional already with his first novel, *Burned* ... It's one of the best crime novels this reviewer has read for a long time, in a language that sparkles and gleams with strong images, and at a tempo that almost makes you forget to draw breath' *Kristeligt Dagblad*

'Unforgettable ... the interweaving stories are simply engrossing. A masterful debut thriller from an author who happens to be Scandinavian' **Misfit Salon**

'An excellent read ... fascinating' **Journey of a Bookseller**

'An intriguing Norwegian whodunit' **Genre Go Round**

'A fascinating addition to the Scandinavian Noir genre. I look forward to the series unfolding' **Crimesquad**

Cursed

ABOUT THE AUTHOR

Thomas Enger (b. 1973) is a former journalist. He made his debut with the crime novel *Burned* (*Skinndød*) in 2009, which became an international sensation before publication. *Burned* is the first in a series of five books about the journalist Henning Juul, which delves into the depths of Oslo's underbelly, skewering the corridors of dirty politics and nailing the fast-moving world of 24-hour news. Rights to the series have been sold to 26 countries to date. In 2013 Enger published his first book for young adults, a dark fantasy thriller called *The Evil Legacy*, for which he won the U-prize (best book Young Adults). Enger also composes music, and he lives in Oslo.

Follow him on Twitter *@EngerThomas*, or on Facebook: *www.facebook.com/thomas.enger.77* or visit: *thomasenger.net*.

ABOUT THE TRANSLATOR

Kari Dickson grew up more or less bilingually and went on to read Scandinavian Studies at UCL. She then worked in theatre for a few years, and was asked to do literal translations of two Ibsen plays, which led to an MA in Translation Studies. Initially, she worked as a commercial translator, but now concentrates solely on literature. Her translation of Roslund & Hellström's *Three Seconds* won the CWA International Dagger in 2011. She also teaches occasionally at the University of Edinburgh.

CURSED

A crime novel

Thomas Enger

Translated by Kari Dickson

**ORENDA
BOOKS**

Orenda Books
16 Carson Road
West Dulwich
London SE21 8HU
www.orendabooks.co.uk

First published in Norwegian as *Våpenskjold*, 2014

This edition published by Orenda Books in 2017

ISBN 978-1-910633-64-9

Typeset in Garamond by MacGuru Ltd
Printed and bound by CPI Group (UK) Ltd, Croydon CR0 4YY

This book has been translated with financial support from NORLA.

NORLA
NORWEGIAN LITERATURE ABROAD

SALES & DISTRIBUTION
In the UK and elsewhere in Europe:
Turnaround Publisher Services
Unit 3, Olympia Trading Estate
Coburg Road,
Wood Green
London
N22 6TZ
www.turnaround-uk.com

In the USA and Canada:
Trafalgar Square Publishing
Independent Publishers Group
814 North Franklin Street
Chicago, IL 60610
USA
www.ipgbook.com

In Australia and New Zealand:
Affirm Press
28 Thistlethwaite Street
South Melbourne VIC 3205
Australia
www.affirmpress.com.au

For details of other territories, please contact *info@orendabooks.co.uk*

PROLOGUE

August 2009

Daniel Schyman knew that people would talk about this day.

It was one of those days when the grass and bushes by the roadside sparkled. The air was sharp and clear. The sky above the trees was so blue it almost hurt the eye. He knew that, right now, the forest would smell raw and cold, but soon the adders would slither out, unsure about what time of year it was. And the larger animals in the forest would seek out the shade, where they would lie chewing on heather and on the berries that had started to ripen. And when the sun was at its highest, everything would smell warm and dry, and every step in the forest, every startled flap of the wing, would be heard from far away. Just thinking about it made his body tingle.

After Gunilla died, Schyman had struggled to find a reason to get up in the morning. They didn't have any children, nor did they have many friends. The silence frequently kept him chained to the armchair in the living room, from where he stared out at the surrounding fields and countryside with empty eyes, and wondered what more life had to offer a man like him.

Nothing, was what he most often concluded; an answer that made him wonder if perhaps he should follow Gunilla into eternity. But it was not like him to give up, so time and again he had hauled himself out of the chair and decided to devote himself to what he loved most in life. On days like today, he was in no doubt that he had made the right decision.

Schyman turned off the road, leaving the asphalt for the gravel, and slowing down as he drove between the trees. It was almost as though he was holding back so he wouldn't experience everything too fast. When he reached the red barrier, he was surprised to see it was already open, but he thought no more about it and parked in a large open area beside the path that in winter served as a ski track. Another car was already there; it had obviously arrived quite recently – he could still see its tracks in the damp gravel. Schyman turned off his engine, got out of the car and opened the boot to let Lexie out. She had a harness on.

As always, he stood and looked at her, at her tail wagging back and forth, at the light in her eyes. He had paid nine and a half thousand for her, but there wasn't a sum large enough to cover her true value. Lexie was the best beagle in the world – always ready for a walk, always pleased to see him, even when he had only popped out to the shop.

Schyman took out his rucksack and shotgun, a Husqvarna that his father had given him on his sixteenth birthday, and he had used every autumn since. Perhaps it wasn't entirely right to call the man his father any more, given what he'd learned over the past few days.

To think that he was actually Norwegian.

He couldn't imagine what his parents – his *real* parents – must have gone through. What they must have sacrificed.

War was a board game from hell, in which you had no control over your fate, and rarely did any good come of it. Even though Sweden had remained neutral in the Second World War, its people were still affected by what happened. The couple who had brought him up had opened their home to give shelter and help to people they didn't know; and they weren't the only ones. Sacrificing oneself for others was an ideal that Schyman valued highly – it was perhaps the greatest of all virtues.

Schyman no longer felt sad or melancholy when he thought about the people he had grown up with, the people he had called family – mother and father – but in the past few days he had pondered what his life might have been like if they had lived just a little longer. He had been left on his own with the farm and forest when he was only seventeen. The man who had phoned him a few days ago, who was coming to see him later on today, had told him that it was originally intended that he would be told about his background when he turned eighteen. If that had happened, things could and would have been very different.

But he was happy with his life all the same. A little more money wouldn't have changed that much. And he would never be Norwegian. Schyman would stay in Värmland until the day he died.

He looked over at the other car that was parked by the path. Funnily enough, it was Norwegian, too: the letters LJ sat beside the flag of red, white and blue – colours that always made him think of oil and the Winter Olympics. He had never seen the car before and didn't recognise the registration.

Did the owner have a hunting permit?

Perhaps the owner was not here to hunt, even though that was why most people came, especially so early in the morning. In his younger days, he might have tried to find out who had taken such a liberty; it was his forest, after all. But things like that weren't so important to him any more.

Schyman clipped a lead onto Lexie's harness and they started to walk. They had been out hunting every day for the past week and, as always, she tugged eagerly at the lead. He loved letting her take him deep into the forest; he listened to her panting, to the music around him – the twigs that snapped underfoot, the flapping wings of birds taking flight, the wind soughing in the trees, the spongy gurgle of trodden moss slowly rising again.

He didn't usually let Lexie off the lead straightaway. As a rule, it took a while before the hare was flushed out, and sometimes it didn't happen, but that was hunting. Every time, though, was just as thrilling as the last: when he took up his position in terrain where he guessed a hare might be hiding, with Lexie ready to get on its trail any minute. When he knew his quarry was close; when he felt his heart pounding in his throat; when he had to get things just right, everything he had practised, making it all as precise and effective as possible...

That was when he felt alive.

And the silence that followed. The release of tension.

There was nothing better.

⊙

They had been walking for about half an hour when Lexie stopped and pricked up her ears. Her tail stiffened. Schyman, too, heard something snap in the undergrowth somewhere further into the forest. It couldn't be a hare. In the sixty years or so that he had been hunting in the forests of Värmland, he had never yet heard a hare.

He wondered whether he should let Lexie off the lead, but quickly decided against it. Last autumn, a pack of four wolves had passed through his forest. There were more and more wolves in Sweden.

Lexie had her nose to the ground and was pulling at the lead. She held her head a few centimetres above the ground, moved from side to side, pulled, quivered, sniffed and stopped, turned her ears, then moved off again. Deeper into the forest, the ground alternated between clawing heather and boggy hollows, squelching underfoot.

Soon she stopped again.

Schyman called out a hello, but got no answer. Nor did he hear anything. Not straightaway. Not until he heard a click close by.

He turned his head quickly. Spotted the clothes that almost blended in with the surroundings. A green baseball cap. A barrel pointing straight at him from a distance of about twenty metres.

Then a bang.

A powerful force threw him backwards. His rucksack took some of the impact of his landing, as did the lingonberry bushes; and when his head fell back into the soft greenery, it tickled his cheeks. But he couldn't move, he just lay there, listening to the sound of the shot penetrating further and further into the forest.

And then silence.

It didn't hurt, not until Schyman tried to draw breath – then his mouth filled with blood. It felt like razor-sharp claws were tearing at his chest. He felt something warm and sticky running down the side of his stomach. The smell was metallic and pungent.

More snapping branches as the sound faded into the distance. He tried to keep his eyes open, but it was hard to see.

Schyman heard Lexie whining, felt her nose on his forehead, her wet, rough tongue against his cheek. He tried to get up and lift his hand to her neck, but couldn't; instead, he collapsed back onto the heather and lingonberry. Lexie blocked out the sunlight, which was now starting to warm.

He needed that warmth.

Daniel Schyman knew that people would talk about this day. He closed his eyes and felt the light evaporate.

Gunilla, he thought.

Eternity is waiting.

1

'Where is it? Where *is* it?' Nora Klemetsen hissed, angry with herself more than anything else. She didn't have time for this. It was nearly a quarter to eight; the bus would be just around the corner.

She rummaged through her bag to check that her mobile phone, keys and the cards she needed were there. Would she never learn? Why could she never get things ready the evening before?

Nora went into the kitchen, put her bag on the table and bent down. Her scarf fell over her eyes. Impatiently she threw it back over her shoulders, noticing a bit of eggshell and a pen under one of the chairs, breadcrumbs, and a ball of black fluff from the woollen socks she always wore when she was at home.

She straightened up, took off her jacket and the long scarf – it was too warm to wear it in here – and went into the living room. Maybe she'd had it in her lap when she sat watching TV after Iver had left? And then she put it down when she went to have a shower and brush her teeth?

She lifted up the cushions on the sofa, looked under the blue-flowered throw that had managed to conceal the remote control, then got down on her hands and knees and peered under the light-brown three-seater sofa, which she really hadn't been able to afford, before glancing under the table in the corner on which stood a lamp and the radio. But it wasn't there either.

Could it somehow have got under the TV unit?

Nora crawled over; the cold parquet floor hurt her knees, which were already tender from before. She studied the dust and crumbs that were a constant reminder of how long it was since she'd done a good clean, but that was all she could see.

Nora scrambled to her feet, feeling a bit dizzy; she hadn't eaten yet – she always ate three pieces of plain crispbread when she got to work. She tried to think through what she had done the day before. Not much: Sunday papers in bed, brunch on the sofa in front of the telly, an hour's stroll up and down the river, supper with Iver and an evening forcing herself to think as little as possible.

No, she hadn't had it in her hand yesterday.

Nora went back to the kitchen table, turned her bag upside down and shook it hard so that all the coins, hair bands, receipts and dusty throat pastilles fell out – even a mitten she'd been looking for since the spring suddenly appeared on the kitchen table. And then there it was, under the worn mitten.

The ball.

She clasped it in her hand and sat down for a moment, squeezing it and rolling it around and around until all the glitter inside was dancing and whirling about. When it stopped, she saw the heart with an arrow through it, and the imprint of his teeth – as though Jonas had tried to bite it in two, unaware of what the consequences might be if he actually managed to. Glitter and fluid everywhere, on his lips, his sweater, the floor.

It wasn't a ball as such, it was a hard plastic sphere, but Jonas refused to see it as anything but a ball, and so that's what it was.

Nora couldn't bear to hold the thought, the memory, any longer, so she stood up and dropped the ball back in her bag, put her jacket and scarf on again and went to look in the full-length mirror in the hall. She picked off some hairs that were caught on her sleeve, fixed her fringe, straightened her jacket and put the bag over her shoulder.

There.

Now the day could begin.

◉

It was autumnal outside.

Nora had always liked this time of year – when the weather was so grey and wet that the only thing you could do was bury yourself under a blanket and enjoy all there was to do on a sofa. In that way, she was just like Henning. If there was an excuse not to go out – except to work, of course – he would find it: there was a good film or series on TV; it was such a long time since they'd lit the fire; he was in the middle of a great book, or trying to get through all the newspapers he hadn't managed to read during the week.

There was so much she loved about Henning. His sense of humour, his quick wit. But it wasn't just what he said or did, or who he was. It was more something she saw in his eyes. Even though she had short hair and freckles, and frightened everything that moved when she sneezed; even though she reminded people of a toad whenever she got drunk and started to hiccup; even though she got tetchy and slammed the door when he hadn't put the cushions back on the sofa or put away the laundry when it was dry, his eyes never changed. His eyes that said he still wanted her, no matter what.

When Nora was growing up, the walls were constantly changing. Her father was in the army, so it was hard to settle anywhere, hard to make lasting friendships – something she struggled with well into adulthood. Even when she finally did make friends, she wasn't very good at nurturing relationships.

Henning had been everything she wanted: a refuge, a lover, a friend – someone with whom she could share both her fleeting thoughts and her deeper meditations. Someone she could be completely honest with, without having to worry about the consequences. It had been perfect, as long as there was only the two of them.

Then Jonas came along.

To begin with, the little boy had only strengthened those feelings. They were a family. With a capital F. She loved going home, breastfeeding him, watching him grow. But Henning was not a reconstructed man; he wasn't the type to do the laundry and change nappies without being asked, didn't always know what was good for a child or a family. For the first year, in particular, he just buried himself in his work, sleeping in another room at night because he had to be fully functional during the day, and using the weekends and any free time to relax, catch up on the news, and not least, cultivate his sources. Nora had to ask him to take Jonas out for a walk in the pram so she could get an hour's sorely needed nap.

Their love and friendship had faded. In the mornings, in the bathroom, they had passed each other like strangers. They had communicated almost exclusively by text message, and then only about practical, everyday things. The structure she had wanted for her life was crumbling. The walls were starting to move again. Whenever she said anything, he promised he would try harder, but it never took more than a week before he had slipped back into his difficult ways.

The separation was more a cry for help than anything else; that's to say, she'd hoped that Henning would see it as such. Instead, he became angry and sad, and not just a little suspicious – he kept accusing her of having found someone else. She sometimes saw him prowling up and down outside the building she had moved into, cigarette in hand, looking up at her windows.

They managed to work together regarding Jonas. But then came that awful day that neither of them could bear to think or talk about. Nothing could ever be the same again. They both knew that if they had only managed to find a way to carry on living together, Jonas would still be alive. They couldn't look each other in the eye. Divorce was the only sensible option, even though it represented a level of sorrow and defeat that she had never quite managed to accept.

Life carried on, in one way or another, and she had met Iver at a time when she desperately needed to laugh and to think about something other than Jonas and Henning. Iver was able to leap out of bed on a Sunday morning and drag her down to the quay at Vippetangen to catch a boat out to one of the islands. Or take her to a bowling alley; she had never had much interest in ball games, but had to admit afterwards it had actually been a lot of fun. Iver might also read a book to her in the evening, sometimes naked, when there was nothing they wanted to watch on TV.

Almost everything was different with Iver. And yes, he liked her, he even liked her a lot, she was fairly certain of that. But he didn't have the same glow in his eyes. Perhaps it was unfair to compare Iver with Henning, she thought, or Henning with Iver, for that matter, but that's what happened when you started to wonder if you'd made the right choices in life – you asked yourself questions and had feelings, which, after the argument with Iver the night before, seemed even more relevant.

Perhaps 'argument' was the wrong word for what had happened. A prerequisite for an argument was that two people disagreed and gave voice to that disagreement. Iver had said nothing, just mumbled a few syllables into his three-day stubble, and then gone home, without giving her a hug or a kiss or *anything* that might indicate how he felt about what she had just told him.

It was so typical of Iver – to back off when things got serious. There was never a right time to talk about difficult things. And if she did manage to manoeuvre him into a corner, his response was always the same: 'Do we have to talk about this now?' As though the right moment would magically pop up out of nowhere one day.

The fact that he behaved like this was perhaps the only answer she needed, Nora thought. And now that he was back on his feet again, after having been signed off, she knew what it would be like. He'd be working late; his mates would have the beers lined up at the bar; there'd be jobs he just had to follow up – anything to avoid sitting down and talking to her. But he was going to have to say something at some point. Just as she was going to have to say something to Henning.

She had no idea how she was going to manage that.

The streets were damp and leaden; yellow leaves lay in the gutter like dull reminders of the summer that had been. The mornings were still light enough, but there was an ominous chill in the air, a shudder of winter that made Nora pull her jacket tighter round herself. She looked up Uelandsgate to see if the bus was coming, then stood in the queue at the bus stop and checked her watch. Thirty-five minutes until the morning meeting. That meant she needed to come up with something to write about, quick.

◉

'Here, let me help you.'

Nora hurried into the Aftenposten building. Birgitte Kråkenes was bending over with her back to the door as she tried to wrestle a full bottle of water up onto the blue dispenser. Birgitte was the first person people met when they came into the editorial office.

'Oh, thank you,' she said, and turned towards Nora. 'These things weigh a ton.'

Nora was quickly beside her, and together they lifted the transparent plastic bottle, which was wet with condensation, up into position. Birgitte thanked her again and smiled.

As the receptionist, she was always smartly dressed and she had a welcoming, wrinkle-free face that made Nora green with envy. Birgitte's skin had a special glow about it, a hint of summer or something peppermint-fresh – Nora had to dig around in her memory to recall her own skin being like that. The worst thing was that Birgitte was only a few years younger than her and had two children. But Nora couldn't help liking her. She gave everyone who arrived at the newspaper office a pleasant welcome.

'There's someone here to see you, by the way,' Birgitte said, as she sat down behind the reception desk on a chair that didn't creak.

'At this time?' Nora asked, grabbing a freshly printed copy of the morning edition from the pile in front of her, and, with half an eye, glancing down at the headlines.

Birgitte nodded and pushed her dark, chestnut-framed glasses up on her nose. 'He's waiting for you.'

Nora stretched her neck to see. A man was sitting by her desk, his legs crossed and looking around restlessly. He was wearing dark clothes, in a style well suited to his colouring. His hair was longish and messy, black with some grey streaks through it.

'And does this man have a name?'

Birgitte examined the paper in front of her.

'Hugo Refsdal,' she said, looking up again.

'Never heard of him,' Nora commented. 'Did he say what it was about?'

Birgitte shook her head and shrugged.

'Fair enough,' Nora said. 'Nice jacket. Is it new?'

Birgitte smiled and glanced down at her dark-grey blazer. 'New? No, I've had this one for a long time.'

'Well, it's very nice,' Nora said.

Birgitte's smile lasted until the phone rang. She picked up the receiver with one hand and waved to Nora with the other.

Nora carried on walking through the editorial office, an open-plan room that was just as boring and neutral as any other editorial office she had been in over the course of what would soon be a ten-year career as a journalist. There was wall-to-wall carpeting, light-coloured walls, meeting rooms with big windows, and masses of cables and computer screens. The most recent IT bling was a 75-inch TV screen, placed in the middle of the room; it had become a gathering point, especially when the sport was on – which was practically all the time.

She nodded to some of her colleagues, who were already at their desks, ignored the incessant ringing of telephones and voices that rose and fell and focused on the man, who stood up as she approached.

Before she had reached the desk, he said, 'Hello,' and took a step towards her with an outstretched hand. 'We've never met before, my name is Hugo Refsdal. I'm Hedda's husband.'

Nora shook his hand. It was sweaty.

'Hedda?' she repeated, wiping her fingers discreetly on the back of her trouser leg.

'Hedda Hellberg.'

Nora stopped.

She hadn't heard from Hedda since they'd been at college together, when they shared a tiny flat up at St Hanshaugen. Nora didn't think that Hedda had ever worked as a journalist; she had certainly never seen her byline anywhere.

'Ah, yes,' Nora said, at last. 'Hedda.'

Nora had lots of good memories from that time. Every day had been a party, and the world had been theirs for the taking. She had realised very early on that she wanted to be a journalist, whether it was for radio, TV or more traditional media. She had imagined herself covering wars and catastrophes, immersing herself in the problems and asking critical questions, teasing out the truth, becoming a wiser person and maybe even helping other people to become wiser at the same time. She had wanted to mean something to other people.

But reality proved to be very different. The only time that Nora actually heard from her readers was when they wrote to point out that she had got her facts wrong or simply to have a go at her. People had no shame when they could hide behind a keyboard.

Pulling herself back to the present, Nora looked at Hedda's husband, standing in front of her. It was hard to work out what he wanted, but Nora realised that something was amiss.

'Is there somewhere more private we can go?' he asked. 'I don't want to sit here and—'

He broke off as one of the foreign correspondents walked past. Refsdal followed him with his eyes until he was well out of hearing. Nora had the feeling that Hedda's husband might burst into tears at any moment.

'Yes, of course,' Nora replied. 'We can go over there,' she pointed to the room where the management meetings were always held.

Refsdal waved his hand as though to say 'lead the way'. Nora put down her jacket, found her mobile phone and headed over.

'Would you like a cup of coffee?' she asked, over her shoulder.

'No, thank you.'

'A glass of water? Anything else?'

'I'm fine, thanks. I drank enough coffee before I came out.'

Nora carried on towards the meeting room, greeting colleagues as she went, and wondering what Refsdal wanted to talk to her about. He followed, a couple of paces behind, negotiating the chairs and desks.

They entered the IKEA-yellow room with its oblong table in the middle, covered with the day's papers, and sat down, each in a red fabric chair at opposite sides of the table.

'So,' Nora said, leaning forwards, 'how can I help you?'

Although Refsdal seemed to acknowledge her direct question, he struggled to reply. He looked away and focused on something outside the room. He clasped his hands together, only to let go of them again, and then laid them flat on the table.

'Do you know who Oscar Hellberg is?' he eventually asked.

Nora thought about it. 'He's Hedda's father, isn't he?'

'He *was* Hedda's father,' Refsdal corrected her. 'He died almost two months ago now. Lung cancer, even though he never smoked a single cigarette in his life.'

'I'm sorry to hear that,' Nora said.

She had met Hedda's father once, when he came to Oslo to visit his daughter. Because Nora shared a flat with Hedda, he had taken them both out for a meal. She remembered him as a handsome man – attractive and well dressed – and genuinely curious about the people he met. Especially the waitresses.

'It was very hard for Hedda,' Refsdal continued. He picked up a pen that was lying on the table in front of him and played with the top.

'She sat by his bedside day and night for the last couple of weeks.' Refsdal fidgeted in his chair, and held the pen as though it were a knife. 'Even though she knew that Oscar would die, she still struggled to accept it when he finally did. She became more and more detached. We have a son, and she barely paid any attention to him.'

Nora noted that he was talking about Hedda in the past tense.

'She came to me some weeks after he died and said that she wanted to get away for a while – to "rest", as she put it. And I thought, great! Whatever she needs to be herself again.'

Refsdal put the top back on the pen and then used it to scratch his stubbled chin.

'I was a little taken aback when she said she wanted to go to a clinic in Italy for three weeks, but maybe that was what she needed. How could I know? So I thought, OK, fair enough, don't begrudge her those three weeks. We can see how things are when she gets back.'

It took a little time before Refsdal continued. Nora sat patiently and waited, watching his eyes, which seemed to be looking for something on the wall. He didn't blink until his eyes filled with fluid.

'She wanted total peace, she said – didn't even want to take her mobile phone with her. She didn't want us to call her at the clinic, she just wanted to be alone and "find her feet again". She even wanted to take the train to the airport alone, but in the end, I finally managed to persuade her to let me drive her. Which I did, I drove her to Gardermoen, and when I dropped her off, she said that she loved me, that she loved us, our family. Smiled, for the first time in weeks. Obviously, I was glad and thought that everything would be fine. But...'

Refsdal ran his free hand through his hair, a movement that reminded Nora of Iver. He always did the same with his hair, as if it needed an airing every now and then.

Refsdal carried on talking: 'At the end of the three weeks, I went to Gardermoen to pick her up. I even took Henrik out of school for the day so he could be there when his mum came home.' He put the pen down on the table, folded his hands. 'But Hedda wasn't on the plane.'

There was silence in the room.

'We waited and waited, looked everywhere – all over the airport – tried to talk to the people who have the passenger lists and things like that, but they weren't allowed to say anything. So I called the clinic in Italy where she said she was going to stay. And that was when things started to get very odd indeed.'

Nora leaned even further forwards across the table.

'The lady I spoke to said that she'd never heard of Hedda, and that Hedda had never booked to stay at the clinic.' Refsdal played with the ring on his finger, turning it round and round. 'You can imagine what went on in my head.'

Nora nodded slowly.

'I phoned everyone I could think of; asked if they had heard from Hedda. But no one had, so the only thing I could do was to call the police.'

'When did you do that?' Nora asked.

'Eleven days ago.'

Nora regretted that she hadn't brought a notebook with her. 'I don't remember seeing anything in the papers,' she said.

Refsdal gave her an exasperated smile. 'Hedda's family have always been anxious to keep up appearances,' he said. 'They didn't want anything about it in the papers. They thought that maybe Hedda would turn up again, and then there wouldn't be any awkward questions. But eleven days have passed now, and we still haven't heard a word from her.'

'So, in effect, Hedda has been missing for a little over a month?'

Refsdal nodded.

'And what have the police done about it?'

'Well, they've done everything they can,' he said, and exhaled loudly. 'They've confirmed that Hedda did not get on the 09.50 flight to Milan that day, and that any traces of her stop at Gardermoen. No one has seen her since that morning outside Departures.'

Nora looked at him thoughtfully. 'What about the surveillance cameras at the airport?'

'There are hundreds of them, of course, and they're recording all the time. But if the police don't ask for the relevant recordings within seven days, they're deleted.'

'And as she was supposedly away for three weeks, to begin with...'

'...there are no pictures of her.' Refsdal completed Nora's sentence. 'Not from Gardermoen, at least.'

'But the police haven't said anything about her being missing?'

Nora already knew the answer to this question. The police preferred not to involve the media in cases where there was a clear suspicion that the missing person might either have committed suicide or run off with someone else. Media attention always made it harder to come back.

'No,' Refsdal said, and looked down.

Nora thought for a moment.

'Given how hard she took her father's death, the police assume that she's committed suicide, is that it?'

Refsdal lifted his head slightly, then nodded.

'I don't know if Hedda ever told you,' he said, wiping away a little wetness from the tip of his nose with his sleeve, 'but her aunt disappeared as well, sometime in the nineties. Everyone assumed that she had committed suicide.'

Nora recalled that Hedda had spoken about her Aunt Ellen.

'Which is why everyone now thinks Hedda has done the same,' Refsdal said. 'That it runs in the family.'

'But you don't think that's what happened?'

Refsdal picked up the pen again.

'Which is why you're here,' Nora continued. 'You want me to write something about her.'

He looked down again. Was silent for a long time.

Finally he said: 'Hedda and I once talked about smart people.' He smiled tenderly at the memory. 'If we'd ever met anyone we envied because they were so smart.' He shook his head gently, a smile still playing on his lips. 'And Hedda said that she'd never met anyone smarter than you.'

Refsdal looked up at her.

Nora held his gaze, before she suddenly realised what he had said. 'Than me?'

'That's what she said. And I remembered because of your name. You both have names from Ibsen plays.'

Nora was embarrassed, but she flashed him a quick smile, and a memory popped up of one evening when she and Hedda had drunk a lot of red wine and, for some reason, had started to talk about Ibsen. In their drunkenness, they both dug out their copies of *Hedda Gabler* and *A Doll's House* and tried to have a conversation using only the lines of their namesakes.

Happy memories.

'I thought you could perhaps investigate a bit more,' Refsdal continued. 'You knew her, after all. And you're a journalist. You can engage people in a different way from me.'

Nora nodded slowly as she thought this through.

'What do the rest of her family say about it? Do they think it's the right way to go?'

'They don't know that I'm here.'

Nora pushed out her chin.

'And I don't care what they think. Henrik and I are closest to her, we're her immediate family, and we have to find out what's happened to her. If Hedda is dead, I'd like to be able to visit a grave. The rest of the family couldn't disagree with that.'

There was a half-full jug of water in the middle of the table, with a stack of plastic glasses beside it. Refsdal stood up, reached out for the water and poured himself a glass, looking at Nora to see if she wanted any.

'I think that's been there since yesterday,' she said.

'Doesn't matter,' he said, and emptied the glass in a few swift gulps.

Nora carried on: 'Has there been any activity on Hedda's mobile phone or email accounts since she disappeared? I'm assuming the police have checked?'

Refsdal swallowed and sat down. 'Nothing,' he said, drying his mouth with the back of his hand.

'What about money? Did she make any withdrawals before she went missing?'

He shook his head. 'I did ask if she was going to get any euros before she left, but she said that she could sort that out down there. In Italy.'

Clearly a lie, Nora thought to herself. She realised that she was becoming increasingly curious as to why Hedda had lied about a trip she was never going to make, especially as she then promptly disappeared.

'So Hedda has left no data traces from the day you drove her to the airport until now?'

Refsdal shook his head in silence.

Nora activated the screen on her mobile phone and saw that she only had four minutes left until the morning meeting. She took a deep breath and said: 'I'm going to be honest with you, Hugo. On first impressions, I would say the police were right. Not a single email, no movement in her bank account...'

'But her father's death wouldn't have made her that depressed...' Refsdal stood up again. His cheeks were flushed now. 'Oscar had been ill for some time, and not only that – Hedda has a son, and I'm sure she would never abandon him of her own free will.'

Nora looked up at him with sympathetic eyes. 'I realise that you still have hope, Refsdal, but—'

'It's not a matter of hope,' he interrupted. 'I have slowly started to accept that I may never get Hedda back, but I have to find out what happened to her.'

Nora stood up as well. 'So what do you think has happened then? You clearly don't believe she's disappeared of her own free will. Did someone abduct her at Gardermoen, in front of thousands of potential witnesses?'

The first of the managers looked in through the window.

'I don't know,' was Refsdal's muted response. 'I really don't know. All I know is that, when Henrik goes to bed at night and wonders where his mum is, I have nothing to tell him that makes any sense.'

Nora looked at him, could understand how he felt, and yet at the same time couldn't. For two years, she had found it hard to understand that Jonas was dead. And even though she knew that something that was in some way related to Henning had happened, she couldn't get past the paralysing grief. She couldn't bear to think about whose fault it was. It was no one's fault, and it was everyone's fault. Nothing could make Jonas come back, anyway.

She picked up her phone from the table. 'I'm sure I can do a good article for the paper and internet editions. I'll ask anyone who was at Gardermoen that day to come forward if they saw her; and anyone else who knows anything, for that matter. Something might turn up.'

Refsdal nodded enthusiastically.

'But, before I do that,' Nora said and looked him straight in the eye, 'I need to know that you are one hundred per cent certain about doing it. The article will put a lot of pressure on everyone who knows you – your son included. Other newspapers, magazines, television, radio will probably contact you. Are you ready for that?'

Refsdal gave her a hard look and balled his fists so tight his knuckles turned white.

'I'm ready for it. I'm prepared to do whatever it takes, as long as I get an answer I can at least try to live with.'

'Good,' Nora said, and took a step towards the door. 'Do you have a car?'

'Sorry?'

'Did you come here by car?' she asked over her shoulder.

'Yes, I...'

'Excellent,' she said, and put her hand on the door handle. 'Let's go for a drive then. I'll just pick up my camera first.'

2

The clean, shiny Skoda zipped silently down the motorway. Fields flashed by outside the window, flat and brownish-yellow; the trees lining the road over Gjelleråsen towards Nittedal were dark and sad. The sky above was a uniform grey. It felt to Nora as though it might rain at any moment. Yet she longed to be out in the fresh air, to get out of the stuffy car that smelt of old aftershave, away from the forgotten child's sweater on the back seat that made her feel queasy.

Thinking about Hedda helped.

'Tell me about her family,' she asked as they passed a large warehouse, pallets of plastic-packaged products standing outside. Refsdal turned down the volume on the radio by running his thumb over a small ball on the wheel.

'How much do you know from before?' he asked.

'Not a lot, really. Hedda never talked much about her family. But I do know they were pretty wealthy and had some land and gold here and there. They even had a coat of arms, if I'm not mistaken.'

Refsdal nodded, put a hand on the gearstick. His wedding ring made a small *clack* sound.

'They're not aristocracy or anything like that,' he said. 'It was Hedda's great-grandfather who bought the coat of arms not long after the war.' He rolled his eyes.

'You can do that?'

'You can. That sort of thing was important to Great-Grandfather Hellberg. He was a lawyer.'

Nora nodded pensively. 'You said that Nora's father died. Is her mother still alive?'

'Oh yes,' Refsdal replied. 'Unni is still very much alive, no doubt about that.'

The car accelerated a little.

'Oscar and Unni didn't exactly have the best relationship,' he told her. 'They had separate bedrooms, among other things. And they never went on holiday together or anything like that. I don't think she visited him much in the hospital towards the end. She couldn't face it, she said – as though she was the one you should feel sorry for.'

They passed an articulated lorry, with only a few centimetres to spare. Its backdraught made Nora feel that it was about to topple over.

'What does she do?'

'Unni, you mean? Or Hedda?'

'Both, for that matter,' Nora said, and started to pick at a broken nail.

'Hedda has been a wine importer for a few years now,' Refsdal said. 'Her own company. And Unni worked in the family business, looking after the accounts – but now she's a full-time widow. Whatever that may entail.' Again, he rolled his eyes.

'And the family business is...'

'Hellberg Property. They have property all over Vestfold – developing and selling. Hedda's older brother, William, is the director of both departments.'

The car overtook a big Mercedes towing a cream cabin-cruiser. Money on wheels, Nora mused; she couldn't remember the last time she had been on a boat.

'But Hedda was never interested in working there?'

'She might well have been, but Hedda, well, she would rather be her own boss, if you know what I mean. She wanted to try and make it on her own.'

Another memory of Hedda popped into Nora's head. In one of their lectures, they had been asked to write four sentences that summarised the contents of a press release from the Ministry of Foreign Affairs. A Norwegian family had been involved in an accident in

Thailand, and Hedda had insisted on naming the spokesperson from the local police – a name that meant nothing to Norwegians, a name they would forget as soon as they heard it – instead of just saying a spokesperson from the police in Bangkok. When the lecturer pointed out that everyone else in the class agreed, Hedda simply refused to accept it, then stormed out of the classroom and didn't come back until the following day.

'How was her company doing?'

Refsdal waited a moment before answering: 'The wine business is very competitive,' he started. 'She decided to give it a try after a holiday in Italy. She fell totally in love with a wine we had there, but it wasn't possible to get it here. So it more or less became her mission in life to have it included in the Vinmonopolet selection. And she succeeded, but it was dropped again six months later after a couple of bad reviews in the papers. Even though people could still order it, Hedda was left with a lot of boxes that she struggled to sell. They're still standing in a storage space she rents in Tønsberg.'

'I see,' Nora said.

'She's tried to sell it at various fairs, and approached all kinds of hotel and restaurant chains, but you have to *pay* your way into that market. And Hedda couldn't afford to do that.'

'So she didn't get any financial help from the family to get started?'

Refsdal shook his head. 'As I said, she liked to do things her own way.'

The yellow line along the edge of the road was wide, and drew Nora's attention. After a few hundred metres, she forced herself to look at something else; it was as if she was being hypnotised.

'Did she inherit any money from her father?'

Refsdal glanced over at her again.

'I only ask because money, or a lack of money, is often what drives people to suicide.'

Refsdal had his eyes on the road again. He drummed his index finger against the steering wheel.

'Yes,' he said. 'She probably did.'

Nora turned to look at him. 'You don't know?'

He held back for a moment.

'Hedda didn't want to go into details,' he said at last. 'And I didn't feel it was right to pry about money and things like that, given the situation. But even after my father-in-law had died, we talked about the possibility of selling the house and moving.'

'And she didn't say how much she'd inherited? How much she had to play with?'

Refsdal shook his head.

Nora nodded again. She waited a good while before asking her next question.

'What was your relationship like?'

'Mine and Hedda's?'

She gave an encouraging nod. Refsdal took his time.

'Well, it was...' He reconsidered. 'We had our problems, of course, just like everyone else, but we've never talked about separating.'

Nora thought about herself and Iver for a moment. She had never felt any particular joy at being with him, but then she wasn't sure what that word meant any more. She definitely had feelings for him, but how deep did they run? How important were they?

'Hedda had another brother as well, didn't she?'

'Yes,' Refsdal confirmed. 'Patrik. He works for a pharmacy company in Oslo. I reckon he travels more in a year than the prime minister.'

Nora let out a quick laugh.

'And how did the brothers take their father's death?'

Refsdal cocked his head to the left, and then to the right. 'With composure, I would say. Or ... I don't know really, I was more concerned about looking after Hedda. But when they carried the coffin out, they were crying like everyone else.'

He moved back into the inside lane. Nora looked out of the window at the fields and trees, saw several rows of houses in a dip between Olavsgaard and the turnoff to Skedsmo. They all looked the same. As though a child had been given a Lego set and been told to build a town but had only used one kind of brick.

'I need the phone numbers of everyone you think Hedda may have spoken to in the weeks before she disappeared,' Nora said.

Refsdal pulled his fingers through his hair again.

'Does she have a best friend?'

'Kristin Theodorsen,' he said, and coughed discreetly into his hand. 'She lives in Tønsberg.'

'OK, good. Then I've got something to start with.'

They drove for some kilometres without saying anything. Nora looked out of the window again, watching the world pass by. The only sound was that of the wheels running over the asphalt. An airport express train rushed past in the opposite direction. It looked like a furious snake moving with determination.

'You said that there were no electronic traces of Hedda,' she remarked after a while. 'Does that mean the police have looked through her computer?'

Refsdal shook his head. 'Because they don't suspect anything criminal, they didn't check it. I've had a look myself, but didn't find anything of particular interest.'

'Did you check the recycling bin? Old log files?'

He hesitated slightly.

'Please do,' Nora said. 'There might be something that can tell us where she is, or what's happened to her.'

They passed the fields outside Langelandsåsen near Jessheim. Two deer were grazing by the edge of the forest. Nora watched them until they disappeared behind a hill.

Soon they pulled up in front of Departures at Oslo Airport. When the car came to a stop and Refsdal had put it into neutral, he gripped the steering wheel with both hands and looked straight ahead. The car was filled with the noise of a plane landing and the reverse thrust. In front of them, a car boot opened. It was full of suitcases and bags. A little girl jumped out of the car, her eyes gleaming with excitement. She had a doll in her hand.

Nora got out her camera, looked over at Refsdal and put her hand on his arm.

'I know this is hard,' she said, sympathetically. 'But I promise you, it will be a good article. People will read it. So let's just hope that someone has seen Hedda.'

3

The Zippo lighter felt like a friend in his hand. As though it belonged there.

Henning Juul slid his thumb over the spark wheel, slowly to begin with, then in one quick movement. A yellow flame appeared and danced teasingly in front of him.

He looked at it, then closed the lighter.

There was a time when he couldn't even look at flames, when the very thought of lighting a match made him sweat. But he had persevered all the same, every day, until he managed it. And once he had done it, he felt lighter; he could see more clearly, it was easier to breathe. As though a physical weight had been lifted from his body.

Henning flipped open the lighter again, lit it: the sharp sound mixing with the soft drumming on the windscreen. He extinguished the flame. Lit it. Extinguished it and lit it, several times, sat there staring at the dancing yellow tongues while he waited for Geir Grønningen, Tore Pulli's best friend, to appear.

Henning was sitting in a car that he'd found on *finn.no*, and had bought more or less the same day. It was yellow and just the right size, just the right age. He needed a reliable form of transport that would keep him warm when the rain fell steadily, night and day, when people wrapped themselves up in thick clothes and struggled to see how they would cope with the cold months that were rapidly approaching. Henning loved his ancient Vespa, but it was no match for King Winter.

He closed the lighter, put it away in the centre console and turned on the windscreen wipers. Looking up, he caught sight of himself in the rear-view mirror.

'Are you a killer?' he asked himself.

That was what she had said, his mother, the last time he had been to see her. That Henning was responsible for his father dying too young – at the age of forty-four. Henning had no idea what she meant. He couldn't remember much about that day, other than that he went into the bathroom in the morning to find his sister, Trine, sitting on the floor hugging her knees. She looked at him, pointed to the bedroom door and said: 'He's dead.'

How the hell could he have killed his own father? He was only sixteen at the time.

Henning was plagued by so many thoughts and questions, but there was no point in asking *her*, Christine – his emphysema-ridden, alcoholic mother. She had refused to explain herself, just closed down, as she always did when he wanted an answer.

Henning knew that he would have to stock up her fridge again soon, buy her cigarettes and some bottles of St Hallvard liqueur, do the washing up, hoovering, laundry. Trine never went to see her. And now she had escaped to the Bahamas for some peace after the scandal that had forced her to step down as Minister of Justice.

Henning looked away from the mirror. He had enough problems as it was. Sometimes the nights went on forever; he couldn't close his eyes without reliving it all – the smoke billowing towards him and the intense stinging in his eyes; Jonas's screams from the room engulfed in flames; the heat that hit him like a wall; his skin and hair catching fire when he galvanised himself to jump through the angry, snaking, yellow-orange arms.

Sometimes he woke up in the middle of the night, bathed in sweat, the smell of burned hair and skin tearing at his nose. He heard sirens and thought that they were coming to get him where he lay in the backyard, unable to move his body, unable to understand how you could possibly hold your son in your arms and still not be able to save him.

That was two years ago.

Two years since he and Jonas came home after school, lit the fire, had tomato soup and macaroni for supper, with three boiled eggs – two for

Henning and one, minus the yolk, for Jonas – and then did what they always did on a normal Tuesday: played Funny Bunny until Jonas won; did a hundred-piece jigsaw puzzle with the picture of a killer whale and two seals; and then watched a bit of TV. There wasn't time to fit much more into that day. And even though they were indoors, Henning hadn't been able to get rid of the chill in his bones from earlier in the day when he had stood for hours outside a block of flats in Lambertseter where a woman had been found dead.

That was why he had settled back down on the sofa after Jonas had gone to bed, pulled a blanket around him and had one, two, three glasses of cognac, then waited to feel the heat spreading through his body to his cheeks. He'd read a little. The heavy-water operation had always fascinated him, but a deepening sense of warmth and wellbeing meant that his eyelids had slowly dropped. It was practically impossible to resist the sleep that was stealing over him, and so he didn't hear a thing when someone came into the flat and set it alight around half past eight.

Henning had had two years to think about what might have happened if he had only had two glasses cognac instead of three; or if he had had none at all – after all, it had been a normal Tuesday; whether the outcome might have been different if he had been able to find another way to escape rather than taking Jonas with him out onto the balcony as the heat and his melting skin had glued his eyelids together. If he might have managed to hold onto his son's arms a little tighter when he jumped from the slippery wet railing, just after he'd told him that everything would be fine, there's nothing to be scared of, Daddy will take care of you.

Henning opened the car door and stepped out onto Kjølberggaten, where the cherry trees hung their bare crowns between the two lanes. When they were in full bloom in spring, the street was a jewel in the city, and it was impossible to walk or drive down the avenue without being moved in some way.

There weren't many people around, the odd taxi hissed aggressively over the speed bumps and a cyclist spun by, spraying water in an arc from the back wheel. A man was out jogging in only a T-shirt and shorts. You could see his breath. Three Pakistani women, each from a different generation, stood at the bus stop, waiting for either the 67 or the 20. An elderly man was pushing an elderly woman in a wheelchair; their progress was slow. Then behind them, he saw Geir Grønningen, all two metres of him, coming towards him, with a full gym bag over his shoulder.

His black leather trousers sat tight around his thighs, and his white vest was equally tight under the open, black leather jacket. Grønningen liked riding motorbikes, liked to *show* that he rode a motorbike, and it was no skin off his nose if people thought they would rather not meet him after dark.

Grønningen worked as a bouncer at a club full of scantily clad women, and when he wasn't chucking randy, grabbing men out onto the street, he took occasional work as an enforcer. Beating up people who wouldn't, or couldn't, cough up.

The first time Henning met Grønningen, he found himself studying the man's physique – his upper arms, neck, muscles, the bulge of his belly. There were veins on his neck that were as thick as straws. And even though there was something kind and soft in his eyes, Henning quickly realised that Grønningen would never show this in what he said or did. He was too tough for that, too hard.

He was smiling now, behind the beard he had let grow around his mouth, and greeted Henning from a few metres away: 'Blimey, look who it isn't!'

Henning held out his hand, but immediately regretted it when Grønningen's massive paw squeezed his own thin piano-player's fingers.

'You alright?'

'Yeah,' Henning said. 'Not bad. And yourself? On your way to the gym, as usual?'

'Have to, don't I?' Grønningen quipped.

'Still only free on Saturdays?'

'Yep,' Grønningen confirmed, lifting the bag higher on his shoulder.

'Have you got time for a coffee?' Henning asked.

Grønningen shook his wrist and a watch slipped out from under the arm of his jacket.

'Yep, should be fine,' he said. 'Even though it gives me a fucking acid stomach.'

His laughter was deep and rolling. Henning laughed with him and pointed to a door close by that led into an establishment that almost certainly served coffee, as well as local produce from farms with romantic names. Everything about the café said organic, even the table at which they sat down.

Henning ordered two cups of black coffee.

The only other people, apart from Henning and the big man, were two friends over by the window that looked out onto the street; they were deep in conversation, dissecting what had happened at the weekend, no doubt. A radio was playing softly, and outside the buses and taxis whooshed by in a regular rhythm. It was safe to talk. Safe enough, at least.

'So,' Grønningen said, once they'd got their coffee. 'What's up?'

Henning put his hands round the cup, unsure where to start. How much did Grønningen know about his dead best friend's business?

In the days leading up to the arson attack on his flat, Henning had been working on a tip-off about Tore Pulli – he'd been told that he had made his fortune in real estate by illegal means. Henning didn't doubt for a second that there was a link between this story and the fire at his flat. The question was, what role had Pulli played in it all?

Tore Pulli had grown up more or less without parents. They both died in a car accident when he was eleven, and he got involved with the petty crime scene pretty early in life. Soon, he was lured in by the Hell's Angels, so it was inevitable that he ended up with some dodgy friends. When Tore started bodybuilding, he discovered that he had a talent for beating people up, and that he could make a living from it. In the nineties, he built up a reputation as one of Norway's meanest, and possibly most infamous, enforcers – the staff at Ullevål Hospital had even named a certain type of jaw break after him.

When he reached his thirties, however, he quite literally hung up his knuckle-dusters, and started to buy and sell property instead. Lots of people were curious about how he would manage to make the switch. But Pulli put all the non-believers to shame; his company was very successful and he became a rich man – though not without a few raised eyebrows and questions as to whether he'd allied himself with some of his former clients, people in the real estate business who knew all the tricks; how to con people out of large sums of money without getting caught. But, try as they might, the Norwegian fraud squad, Økokrim, had never managed to catch him.

When Henning found out that Pulli still had at least one foot in the criminal world, the hunting instinct in him was awakened. His question was, who was involved in the extortion, and how? Henning's aim was to expose them all and show that Pulli was one of their main players. If Henning had managed to name names and document their methods, it would have sparked a wildfire. Heads would have rolled.

But it was difficult to investigate that kind of thing without people getting wind of it. Henning soon became certain that Pulli had decided to resurrect his former skills and do a job on him. That was why he had had Henning followed in the days leading up to 11 September 2007. Pulli was well known for being thorough, and Henning believed he intended to find out when and where it would be easiest and best to attack.

But Pulli was not the only one who faced prison and considerable financial losses if Henning's snooping led to a published story; so naturally he wasn't alone in wanting to prevent that from happening. And because Pulli had been watching Henning, he must also have seen who broke into his flat on the night that Jonas died. There was even a possibility that Pulli had photographs of whoever did it.

The fire and Henning's jump from the second-floor balcony had changed everything. It took him almost two years to get back on his feet, and he still had partial memory loss.

Pulli, meanwhile, had run into problems himself. He had been sentenced to fourteen years behind bars for the murder of Jocke Brolenius, a well-known enforcer and member of the Swedish League in Oslo. The fact that Pulli was innocent didn't make things any better; and that was why he had contacted Henning – a journalist who he knew was good at digging around. If Henning could clear his name, he promised to give him information about who had entered his building on 11 September 2007.

Henning had succeeded in doing this, but to no avail. Pulli was killed in Oslo Prison before he managed to keep his part of the deal.

Henning visited Tore a few days before he died and saw the effect that prison life had had on the ex-enforcer. He was stooped, as though his fate was weighing on his shoulders. Even though he had lost a lot of weight, he was still a formidable and intimidating figure; his eyes glittered when Henning asked him something he didn't like. Henning was still unable to decide whether he actually trusted Pulli or not.

And now he was dead. Killed with a needle dipped in poison. And there was not much Henning could do except continue to dig. He was aware that Pulli knew the Swedes, and that there was a possibility that Jocke Brolenius had done work for people in the property business – people who Tore knew, who he may even have worked for previously. People experienced in paying their way out of problems, and who knew where to find someone who was willing to kill Tore for money.

So Henning took a sip of his coffee and said: 'I hear there's not many of the Swedish League left in Norway now.' He put down his cup. 'Do you know if that's true?'

Grønningen tried to make himself more comfortable on the narrow chair, and bumped the table so that his coffee spilled out over the saucer and his hand.

'Think a couple of them are still around,' he said.

'A couple of them?'

'Yeah. Maybe more; I don't know.'

Grønningen looked around for a napkin. Unable to find one, he shook his fingers, picked up the cup and took a sip.

'...who are still working as enforcers?' Henning asked.

Grønningen nodded.

'Do you know any of them?'

Grønningen paused for a moment.

'Why're you asking?' he said.

'I need to speak to them,' replied Henning, without offering any explanation.

Grønningen put a hand inside his leather jacket and pressed on his left pectoral.

'You can forget about that.'

'Why?'

'Because...' Grønningen sent the women over by the window a long look. '...Because they don't talk to people they don't know,' he said. 'And if they find out you're a *journalist*...' Grønningen said the word as though it left a bad taste in his mouth.

Henning had known it wouldn't be easy.

'But they talk to you,' he persisted.

Grønningen started to laugh. 'None of them want to talk to me either. Not after what happened to Jocke.'

'But they must have heard that Tore was innocent? That none of his crowd had anything to do with Jocke's murder?'

The door opened, and a clearly new mother pushed a pram into the café. The plastic cover on the pram was dripping. She sat down a few tables away. Grønningen followed her with his eyes, as he ran a hand through his thin hair.

'Don't think I can help you, either way,' he said in a hushed voice. 'Not easy to get hold of the Swedes.'

'But you could try?'

The woman who had just come in lifted a tiny bundle up from the pram, held the baby in front of her and cooed.

Henning pulled his chair in closer to the table.

'When I proved that Tore was innocent, you said that I only had to ask if I needed any help. Well, now I'm asking. I need to get in touch with the Swedes, and I don't know who to ask other than you.'

Grønningen slowly let out a deep breath, then sat there playing with his cup. He looked around the café. The baby at the table nearby was gurgling happily.

'OK, I'll see if I can get hold of Nicklas,' Grønningen said, eventually. 'If he's still part of it. He's just had a baby boy. I'll ask if he can get us a meeting with Pontus.'

'Who's Pontus?'

Grønningen looked around again before answering, in an even quieter voice: 'He's the boss of what's left of the League. If anyone knows anything, it'll be him.'

'OK,' Henning said. 'Sounds good.'

'No,' Grønningen protested. 'Not good at all. You don't fucking mess with a man like Pontus.'

'What do you mean?'

Grønningen leaned in towards Henning, as though he was going to whisper a secret.

'He's cagey as hell, and he's a mean motherfucker. Likes to see people bleed. Likes to see that people are scared of him. Doubt he'll be up for a chat with either of us,' Grønningen explained, then leaned back. 'But I'll give it a try.'

Henning smiled. 'I appreciate it.'

4

Nora sat down at her desk and reached for the open packet of oat crispbread sitting beside her computer screen. There were only two pieces left.

For the next couple of minutes she did nothing other than listen to the sound of her own munching. Only when she felt her blood-sugar levels were at an acceptable level did she open Outlook on her PC and check to see if she'd received any emails. She had, lots of them, most of which she deleted without reading. But one of the emails was from Iver.

She took another bite of crispbread, and then clicked on it.

From: iver.gundersen@123nyheter.no
To: nora.klemetsen@aftenposten.no
Subject: Yesterday
Hi Nora
Sorry to leave in the way I did last night. I didn't know what to say.
Still don't know what to say, to be honest, or what to do, or what you expect me to do. Think I need a bit of time to sort everything out.
Hope you understand that it's not easy for me either.
Kiss from
Iver

Yeah, yeah, Nora said to herself. I understand. But running away doesn't help. Just as she couldn't run away from Henning.

Maybe it is as well to get it over and done with, she thought. She pulled her mobile phone out of her bag and typed in the four-digit password. Finding the most recent text message from Henning she wrote:

Hi, can you meet me after work today? Got something I want to talk to you about. Hugs, Nora.

She immediately regretted how she'd signed off. A hug might indicate that she wanted to talk about something nice.

Henning answered straightaway.

Give me a time and place and I'll be there.

Nora suggested that they meet on the corner of Christian Kroghs gate at four. She soon got an OK back.

Nora put her phone to one side, leaned forwards on her elbows and sat with her hands in her hair, like two wide-fingered combs. She thought about the almost-kiss with Henning at his flat, not so long ago, how the walls had seemed to vibrate around them as they stood there, their noses almost touching, after a goodbye hug that had lasted a little too long. Things could have got really messy; all it would have taken was for one of them to make the first move, step a centimetre closer, and everything would have been different. It would have been even harder then to say what she had to tell him now, in a few hours' time.

'Everything alright?'

Nora sat up and looked straight into the eyes of Merete Stephans, one of the other news journalists. Stephans was almost one metre eighty tall and liked to use her height and deep, masculine voice to intimidate other female journalists who worked in the same field. The fact that Nora worked on her section on the same paper, gave her no advantages. Quite the opposite, in fact.

'Yes, why? Shouldn't it be?'

'Absolutely,' Stephans said with a smile. 'It's just you look a bit peaky.'

'I'm fine,' Nora replied promptly. 'Very well, in fact.'

'Good.'

Stephans still had a wry smile on her lips as she walked over to the nearest Nespresso machine. Nora hated lies, no matter how white they were; and, anyway, she'd never been particularly good at telling them. One look from Henning was all it took to undo her. Fortunately,

Merete was not as observant, despite her grand illusions about her own journalistic superiority – or, as Nora would describe it, mediocrity.

Nora finished the crispbread and looked down at the notepad in front of her. Hugo Refsdal had written down the names and telephone numbers of everyone in Hedda's family, and the number of her best friend, Kristin Theodorsen. Nora picked up her phone and dialled.

'Oh, hello,' Kristin Theodorsen said when Nora introduced herself. Kristin's voice was high, almost falsetto. Nora could hear rustling on the line, as though Theodorsen had the phone wedged between her cheek and shoulder while she was doing something else.

'Is it a bad time to call?' Nora asked.

'No, not at all, I'm just putting on my jacket, to take the dog for a walk. He gets a little, well, excited when he knows we're about to go out.'

'I see.'

'Down! Down!'

Nora heard some eager barks and the scuffing of paws on the floor.

'Sorry about this,' Theodorsen said. 'It's...'

Her voice disappeared again. There were some loud movements, and then calm.

'There,' Kristin Theodorsen said. 'I'm all yours.'

Nora laughed the little laugh she used, and hated, when she was cold-calling.

'Well, I won't keep you long,' she started. 'I understand that you are Hedda Hellberg's best friend, is that right?'

There was silence for a moment.

'Yes, I ... I guess I am.' Theodorsen had lowered her voice.

'I guess you know that she's missing, then?'

'Yes, of course.'

'I'm going to write an article about her for tomorrow's *Aftenposten*,' Nora said. 'And I hoped that you might be able to give me some background. You probably know Hedda in a very different way from her husband.'

'Yes, I guess so,' Theodorsen said, in a stronger voice. 'What would you like to know?'

'As much as possible,' Nora said, and let out a deep breath. 'I'm most curious to know whether Hedda had any problems you were aware of; I mean, other than her father's illness and death, and the fact that she wasn't managing to make ends meet as a wine importer.'

Nora propped her left arm on the desk and leaned forwards with her pen at the ready.

'No, not that I...'

'She wasn't ill, was she?' Nora asked, to see if this would prompt Theodorsen.

'Not that I know of.'

Nora waited a few seconds before asking the next question, giving Hedda's best friend time to think of something. The line remained silent, however.

'Was there anything about her recent behaviour that struck you as odd?'

Theodorsen thought about it.

'Well, obviously, she was affected by Oscar's death. But I don't think there was anything else in particular. Certainly nothing unusual.'

Nora drew a few random lines on the page. 'How often did you meet?' she asked.

'We swam together every Thursday – if she was in town. And otherwise, we met up now and then.'

Nora straightened up a little. 'Did she tell you about the trip she'd planned?'

'What trip?'

'She told her husband she was going to Italy for three weeks.'

'Oh, yes,' Theodorsen said. 'That. Yes, she did mention it. But ... I thought the whole thing was a bit odd. I didn't get it.'

Nora stopped the pen in the middle of a word. 'What do you mean?'

'Well...' Theodorsen hesitated a moment before she continued. '...I don't know how well you knew Hedda, but she's always been a bit stingy.'

'Stingy?'

'Yes. She didn't always find it easy to open her purse. And three weeks in Italy, at the place she told me about – well, that would cost a fair bit.'

Yes, especially as she didn't have much money in the first place, Nora thought, and would have lost three weeks' potential earnings. But then again, she never went.

Theodorsen's comment had stirred another memory in Nora. She remembered that, when they lived together, Hedda had been very careful to make a note of whatever she bought for the flat, and was always keen to settle up as soon as possible, even if it was only a matter of a few kroner. And when they were out on the town together, she was adept at getting men to buy drinks for her.

'What kind of relationship did Hedda and Hugo have?' Nora asked, wiping some crumbs of crispbread from the desk.

'It was good, I think. Or ... oh, I'm not sure. Obviously, in the past six months, everything has been focused on her dad. And her son and work took up quite a lot of her time.'

Nora put the pen in her mouth and chewed it gently. 'There were no other men in the picture?'

Theodorsen didn't answer straightaway.

'I don't think so,' she said eventually.

Her dog barked again in the background.

'Is there anyone you can think of who had a reason to hate Hedda?'

'Do you think someone's killed her?' Theodorsen asked.

'I don't know,' Nora said. 'At the moment I'm keeping all options open.'

Another bark.

'If she had any enemies, she certainly never told me about them,' was Theodorsen's answer.

'Right,' Nora said, and put down her pen. 'If you think of anything later that might be important in relation to Hedda, I'd be really grateful if you could let me know.'

'I will.'

Nora ended the call and sat pondering. It seemed odd that Hedda would take her own life when she had so many positive things around her – a son, a husband who obviously loved her, a job she enjoyed. It was also strange that any trace of her stopped at Gardermoen, and that she should go to so much trouble with her preparations for the trip if what she had planned was to commit suicide.

Nora took out Hugo Refsdal's business card. It described him as a freelance computer engineer and web designer. She dialled the number.

'Hi, it's Nora Klemetsen again,' she said, when he answered. 'I was just wondering: is Hedda's suitcase still missing?'

'Yes,' he replied.

'Do you remember what kind of suitcase it was? Was there anything that would make it recognisable?'

'It was black, unfortunately, like practically every other suitcase. But I think she'd stuck a Norwegian flag on it, or something like that. Perhaps not a flag, but the colours of the flag. A ribbon, if you know what I mean.'

'Yes, I know the kind of thing,' Nora said, as she made a note. 'Was it full?'

'Sorry?'

'The suitcase, did you notice if it was fully packed or not?'

'Yes, it was just as heavy as it always is when she goes travelling.'

'Right,' Nora said, and paused for thought.

If Refsdal was right and Hedda had not disappeared of her own free will, then someone must have somehow lured or tricked her into getting into a car. Or maybe she'd taken a taxi somewhere and paid in cash. Or she might have taken a bus or a train. It was perhaps a little overoptimistic to expect someone to remember a woman travelling on her own with a black suitcase – even if it did have the Norwegian colours on it.

'I'll need a photograph of Hedda – a portrait,' she said. 'Do you have one you could send me electronically? As recent as possible, preferably.'

'I'll see what I can find.'

'Great. Thank you.'

Nora put the phone down, and made the decision to wait before she called NSB about trains, the taxi operator in Romerike, the airport express bus and Oslo public transport – primarily because it would take forever to find out who had been working at the relevant time on the day in question. It would be much easier to do this once she had her newspaper article, which was to be published the next day, as a good starting point.

Instead, Nora used the next hour to write up what she had so far. She didn't need to spend any time on the headline: 'This Is Where Hedda Disappeared', with the question underneath, 'Have you seen Hedda Hellberg?' The photo of a broken and sad Hugo Refsdal standing outside Gardermoen airport later in the article would work perfectly. People would read it; it might even get a mention on the front page.

Nora breathed deeply when she was finished. It didn't take long before she was thinking about Henning again.

She was dreading their meeting already.

5

Henning tried to keep his balance on the loose cobblestones between Gunerius shopping centre and Grønland. He managed it now and then.

He looked at his watch. Twelve minutes past four. Had he got the time wrong?

He checked his phone. No, Nora said four o'clock. Maybe she was caught up with something at work, Henning thought. Normally she was bang on time, unless it was something she wasn't looking forward to. Like a few days ago, when they were going to lay flowers on Jonas's grave. Henning had sat waiting for half an hour outside her flat, before she finally came down on shaky legs and got into the car.

Henning had had the feeling then that Nora wanted to talk to him about something, but neither of them had managed to say much; they just stood there with their heads lowered, crying softly.

Henning spotted her between two roller-skaters, who swerved either side of her. She was walking slowly, with her jacket tight around her body and a scarf wrapped round her neck. The wind was lifting her short fringe to the side, but it didn't matter, Nora looked elegant whatever the weather.

She hadn't seen him yet, and Henning enjoyed being able to watch her from a distance for those few unguarded moments – to see her as she was, as other people who didn't know her saw her. He had to presume they were all captivated by her beauty, just as he was.

When they first started going out together, he couldn't believe it was true. The girls at school had always mooned over other boys; the fact that he was clever and rarely joined in with activities after school didn't help. He'd got used to doing things alone, to thinking only about himself, not having to consider anyone else. He had no idea what love was until he felt it for Nora.

It had made him uneasy and scared at first. It was so unfamiliar. He felt that he was losing control over himself and who he was. But Nora always managed to ease his fear, and gradually he had let go and learned to relax – too much, perhaps. He became himself again, fell back into old habits. What he had learned, too late, was that if you were in a relationship with someone, you couldn't be who you really were, deep down. You had to be considerate. Play the game.

To think that he'd ruined something that was so good. What they had together.

Henning got out his mobile phone and took a picture of her. He didn't know why, he just felt like it. Nora noticed him as he did it and pulled a mock-angry face. They hugged briefly when she reached him, and whispered hello into each other's ear. Then Henning held her out at arm's length and asked: 'Are you hungry? Shall we go somewhere and get a bite to eat?'

Nora didn't answer straightaway.

'I'm not hungry,' she said. 'Or that's to say, I am, but I don't feel like eating.'

Henning looked at her for a couple of seconds, but she avoided his gaze.

'Well, we can at least get a coffee,' he said. 'I'm freezing.'

Nora nodded slowly, still not looking at him. Henning pointed to Den Røde Mølle, which was nearby, so they went in and sat down at a table by the window. The tablecloth had grease stains. The waiter came over with some menus, but Henning told him they only wanted coffee.

He stole a glance at Nora while they waited. She stared apathetically out of the window, as though she was in the middle of a daydream. Once the waiter had put the coffee, milk jug and sugar cubes on the table, she seemed to wake up and pulled one of the cups towards her, put her hands round it and mumbled her thanks.

Her lips were dry, almost cracked. Henning noticed that her cheeks were a little fuller than before, but it suited her. She had lost far too much weight after Jonas died.

'Did you come straight from work?' she asked, without looking at him.

'I'm on leave.'

Nora jolted to attention. 'Leave?'

'Yes, three weeks,' Henning told her. 'They wouldn't give me any more, I haven't been working at 123News for that long.'

'But why have you taken leave?' She sounded surprised, her tone almost aggressive.

Henning picked up the salt shaker that was standing on the table and tilted it.

Her shoulders fell again. 'Does it have anything to do with Tore Pulli, by any chance?'

'Among other things.'

'You don't give up, do you?' she said, with a sigh.

Henning looked over at her. 'No, Nora,' he said. 'I don't give up.'

They sat in silence for a few moments. Henning wondered whether he should tell her about his breakthrough or not. It was she, though, who had asked him to come, not the other way round.

'How are you?' he asked in the end.

Nora hesitated, and then started to tell him about the article she was writing – about the mysterious disappearance of an old friend from college. The story seemed to inject a bit of colour into her cheeks, there was a glow and warmth to her voice. But as soon as she was finished, there was silence again. And, without any warning, her lower lip started to tremble. Her eyes welled up and before Henning could say or do anything, she was sobbing.

He looked around quickly; there were people at the neighbouring table, but they were both engrossed in their phones and didn't notice Nora staring hard at the table as the tears rolled down her cheeks.

'Sorry,' she said, quickly. 'It's just so...' Her voice was hoarse, and she shook her head ever so slightly.

'What is it, Nora?' Henning asked, after a while.

She didn't answer, just stared down at her hands. Henning took a sip of coffee.

'Is it something to do with work?' he asked, and put down his cup. It clinked against the saucer.

Nora shook her head.

'But what's upset you, Nora?' he tried again, after more silence. 'Is it something to do with Jonas?'

'Not directly,' she said, sniffling and blinking.

Henning gave her a long look.

'Is it something to do with ... Iver?'

She didn't say anything for moment, but Henning knew he'd hit the mark, more or less.

He straightened up. 'Nora, I don't know that *I'm* the right person to...'

'And it's got something to do with you as well,' she interrupted, and looked straight at him, her eyes clear and wet.

Henning tried to guess what she was talking about, but failed.

'There's something I have to tell you,' she said, eventually. 'I wanted you to hear it from me, not anyone else. And there's no easy way of saying it, so I'm ... I'm just going to say it.'

The chair felt hot under him. Henning changed position. Nora hunched her shoulders, closed her eyes and exhaled so violently that Henning felt it on his face.

Then she said: 'I'm pregnant.'

6

Aargh, he said to himself, as he watched the ball roll in a wavering line towards the hole. Grass mats were hopeless. You never got a perfect roll, no matter what. They might be good for practising your stroke – the putting movement that hopefully meant the ball rolled straight towards the hole; but it was never the same as a proper green.

Maybe it had something to do with the floor; maybe it wasn't completely flat. The small square of felt – the grass, as they called it in the shop – had some air trapped underneath that made it bulge here and there. And that was never a good thing.

He tried a couple more times, but didn't make the hole. He carried on for another ten minutes, but the times that he did get the ball in the hole felt more like chance than anything else.

Golf.

A bastard of a game, but my God it was good when you got it right. If only he had time to play more, to *practise* more, to do more than just work with idiots who paid him far too much to help them extricate themselves from the problems they had managed to get into. What was the point of life if all you did was work? He should be out there, hiking in the mountains, catching enormous trout in Alaska, doing yoga and awakening his inner chakras three or four times a day. Shouldn't he have achieved a higher understanding, a deeper knowledge by now?

He shook his head. He actually bloody loved the idiots; couldn't help it. What would he do in Alaska anyway, other than get great f-ing mosquito bites that never stopped itching, or be eaten by a hungry brown bear? And there was actually more and more to do, an increasing number of things to look after, traces to erase.

He didn't have blood on his hands, not directly, but he was, to a certain extent, responsible for the fact that some individuals had ended up in the grave a little earlier than they might have anticipated.

He had found himself thinking about the first job a few times recently, without knowing why. It was nearly twenty years ago now, and had all started off innocently enough. His client had said: 'Oh, I just wish she'd die.' Then, after a few moments' thought, he had replied, tentatively: 'If that's really what you want, well ... I might know someone who can help.'

The client had stared at him for a long time, not in shock, more weighing up the possibility that had just been presented. The rest was all about money and execution, and he was good at both.

And so far, he had managed to stay in the wings, where he was happiest, though there had been a couple of close calls. The strange thing was that knowing he might be caught, that he was playing a game, gave his life meaning. It filled him with tension and excitement. The worst thing on earth for him was repetition; the humdrum everyday. He had to have *something* to make the blood fizz in his veins.

Talking of which, he thought ... but then there was a knock at the door and his secretary popped her head round.

'They're ready,' she said.

He nodded and smiled at her, watched her turn and leave. Her skirt hugged her hips, her behind, and her tights were so thin that they kissed her legs, thighs, all the way up to...

He closed his eyes.

Women.

Without a doubt, God's greatest creation; he could never get enough of them. He put the Scotty Cameron putter to one side and went over to his desk, sat down on the high-backed leather chair, pressed a button on the telephone and leaned back.

'Gentlemen,' he said dramatically, his own voice reminding him of the auction scene at the start of *Phantom of the Opera*, the second before the enormous chandelier crashes onto the stage. 'We have a problem.'

'What is it *now*?' a voice taking part in the conference call asked.

'It doesn't look like he's going to let it lie. He's got three weeks off work and is sticking his nose into things that are none of his business.'

A loud sigh emanated from the phone.

'I don't like it,' he continued, closing a three-pack of Pro V1 balls that was lying on the desk in front of him – maybe he would get time for a round at Bogstad Golf Course later on. 'What I do like, however, is to take precautions.'

There was silence.

'So what are you suggesting?' the other person asked.

He put down the golf balls. 'Damage control.'

'At what level?' another voice asked.

'Top,' he replied.

There was silence again.

'I don't know,' said one of the others.

'What don't you know?'

'If we should go that far. We don't know for certain that he'll find anything.'

'And you're willing to take the chance?'

They waited for him to say something. He was used to it. It was always him who had to step up and make them comfortable with his suggestions.

'I don't think we can wait much longer,' he continued. 'And the more he looks, the more people he talks to, the more curious everyone will become.'

The others didn't say anything for a few moments.

'I'm with you,' the first one said.

The other thought a bit longer, before he eventually said: 'OK. But I don't want to see any reports on the news.'

They spent a few minutes discussing strategies, money – the usual things. They always had to go through the motions, even though he knew they would give him *carte blanche* in the end.

As they talked over each other, he clicked onto Golfbox – one of the websites he had saved under favourites. He clicked back and forth and stared at the screen in disbelief. Not a single tee-off time available at Bogstad later in the day. On a normal weekday, too.

'Ah well,' he said to himself and leaned back in his chair. There would always be other opportunities.

7

A man with garlic breath and a beer gut bumped into Nora and mumbled an apology.

She hated this shop. The shelves were too close, the aisles too narrow. There was hardly room for customers or shopping baskets.

She looked down at her own basket. Bread, a bag of rice and two chicken breasts – one for today and one for tomorrow. She picked out a bottle of sweet chilli sauce and then went to wait in the queue for the till.

What had she expected? That he would nod and say, 'I'm really happy for you, Nora?'

Anything would have been better than the empty look he gave her just before he stood up and left. He didn't hear, or didn't *want* to hear her following him, begging him to stop. He simply carried on walking, almost reeling, as though he was drunk and wearing uncomfortable shoes.

So now what? What was going to happen now?

Nora paid and went home, put the food on the worktop, put some rice in a pan, added salt and water, then rubbed pesto onto one of the chicken breasts. She needed to eat. While she waited, she sat down on the sofa with the ball in her hand and channel-hopped between bad soap operas. She didn't think about Henning, didn't think about Iver, didn't think about anything.

The rice started to boil, the chicken started to spit.

What if Hedda was dead?

The thought was shocking. For the two years that they had lived together, Hedda had probably been the most important person in her life, certainly the one she spent most time with. And yet now, twelve or thirteen years later, it was strange how little she felt. How had that happened? Had they argued about something before Hedda moved back to Tønsberg?

Nora shook her head. She would remember an argument. More likely, they had just started a new chapter in their lives, found new friends, new flatmates. Time was strange like that. It smoothed over everything, erased things, made anything you didn't nurture difficult, or worse. Nora had thought of Hedda several times since their college days, but she'd never actually picked up the phone and called her. And the more time that passed, the harder it became.

Hedda had been a good friend. They had laughed a lot together. And, when she made up her mind to do something, she was enterprising and focused. Like the time they decided to paint the flat; it only took them two days. Hedda threw herself into the task and was far more careful than Nora.

She was not the type to open up to people, however. She was curious and enjoyed being with other people, but not even Nora could say she knew a lot about her life. She never talked about her feelings; the furthest she'd go was to say whether she liked or didn't like whoever she'd been on a date with. And she never talked about previous boyfriends. Nora had often wondered why. If, perhaps, Hedda had a problem trusting people, for example.

But was she someone who would commit suicide?

Even though people could change considerably over time, Nora just couldn't imagine Hedda was capable of such a thing. True, she had been living a very different life, but Nora always believed that everyone had something essential about them that didn't change over the years and wasn't influenced by what happened around them. And, generally, Hedda did what she set out to do. The fact that she was determined to make Norwegians like a wine she had fallen for on holiday was yet another example of her strong will and perseverance.

Nora turned the chicken breast in the pan, saw that the pesto had browned, just the way she liked it.

'No,' she said to herself. 'Hedda did not kill herself.'
It just wasn't like her.

8

When Henning opened his eyes, he had no idea where he was or how he'd got there. It took a moment or two before he realised that he was lying on a bench outside the Deichmanske Library in Grünerløka, and that it was nearly six o'clock. He also realised that he must have had one of his blackouts.

He had the last one when Iver Gundersen rang to tell him that Tore Pulli was dead. Henning had gone out, he discovered later, in his slippers, and had then woken up a few hours later with bleeding feet because he had stood on some glass. His neighbour, 78-year-old Gunnar Goma, had found him on the stairs and managed to get him back up to his flat.

The last thing that Henning remembered this time was that he had been sitting in a café with Nora and that...

Oh my God.

Nora was pregnant. Nora was fucking pregnant.

Now that the world had stopped turning, it was as if a wound had opened up in his stomach. Nora was pregnant. And what was worse: *Iver* was going to be a dad. Iver, who could barely look after himself. Who rarely took anything seriously. Who eyed up beautiful women as they passed.

Henning sat up and rubbed his hands over his head. So that was how easy it was, to start again with someone new.

It was a while since he'd felt the need, but now he wanted to drink himself senseless and wake up in a gutter somewhere with a bump on his head and a broken heart.

Or maybe not wake up at all.

He had lost Jonas and Nora; his own mother thought he was a killer; and Trine, his sister, didn't want anything to do with him.

What was the point?

What was the fucking point?

The hunt, he thought. That was the point. He had to find the answers. He couldn't give up before he'd found them.

⊙

Grünerløkka was greyer than usual as he started to walk home. A wet heaviness threatened to envelop him, but Henning didn't care; he actually quite liked the rain. Which was something.

He stopped. There was a buzzing in his inner pocket. He fished out his mobile phone, almost surprised that no one had stolen it as he lay sleeping on the bench. Geir Grønningen had sent him a message. And it wasn't the first one either.

Henning opened the most recent.

How about it? You ready to meet Pontus?

Henning blinked a couple of times, then went back to the first message.

Have managed to get a meeting with Pontus. Meet me at the Lade-gården bus stop at seven.

Henning checked his watch. It wasn't too late. He even had time to go home and have a shower first, get something to eat. He thought it over for a moment. A meeting with Pontus. The Mean Motherfucker.

Henning tapped in his reply: *Absolutely*.

9

Dusk had started to fall over Oslo by the time Henning got off the 32 bus in Bispegata, at the stop that was called Ladegården, even though the old manor house lay a little way off. There wasn't much here to bear witness to any former glory. The bus stop was nothing more than a pole with a sign, and if you wanted to sit down while you waited, there were a couple of concrete blocks that had been left by the roadside. Two portaloos stood nearby.

On the other side of the road, the view to Grønland was obstructed by double-storey portacabins. Huge, yellow cranes stretched up towards the mackerel sky. Behind the cranes, several buildings were under construction.

Oslo was one big building site.

Through the bushes that lined the road, Henning could see the surface of the artificial lake, which had been made to replicate the old shoreline of medieval Oslo. The water had taken on dark evening tones: the surface was completely still, so it looked like oil. Somewhere in the distance a seagull cried; it was joined by others, before silence fell again. There was something lacklustre and flat about the city, as though it was tired of waiting for something to happen.

It was easy to spot the big man as he came sauntering down Bispegata. He was wearing exactly the same clothes as he had been earlier in the day, and although his tread was heavy, there was something light and confident about him.

'You didn't need to come with me,' Henning said, when Geir Grønningen reached him.

'Oh yes, I do,' he replied. 'You can't go to see these boys on your own.'

Henning arched an eyebrow.

'Seriously, you can't.'

Henning looked at him for a short while.

'Where are we going?' he asked.

'In there,' Grønningen said, nodding.

They walked past the portaloos and came into an open, tarmacked area the size of a football pitch. There were dark skid marks on the ground where cars had spun round, burning rubber. Even though Henning couldn't see anyone, he still had the feeling they were being watched.

There was a garage on one side, and behind it, what appeared to be warehouses. A few cars were parked in the marked spaces and outside the closed metal doors. Piles of folded cardboard boxes, great sheets of chipboard, and pallets were stacked up outside – some were empty, others still full and covered in plastic. He could hear voices, but saw no one.

'Do you know what free fighting is?' Grønningen asked.

Henning hesitated.

'It's a kind of martial art where everything's allowed,' the giant of a man told him before he could reply. 'Kicks, elbows. The Swedish enforcers here do it. It's not exactly legal, but that's why they like it. And this is where they do it. Every Monday and Thursday, seven o'clock.'

Grønningen waved his hand around. Henning tried to make out what he was pointing at, but could only see the brick wall that rose up into the sky. The bricks were more brown than red, and here and there the windows were missing.

'A real "fight club", then.'

'Yep, could say that. They beat the shit out of each other but they're still good mates after.'

'And that's where we're going?'

Grønningen nodded.

'Great,' Henning said.

'Hey – it was you who wanted to talk to them.'

They fell into a silence in which all they could hear was their shoes on the tarmac. Henning pushed back his shoulders and breathed in deeply.

They passed a big green Mercedes van that was parked by the fence. The driver's cab was full of boxes and clothes. Grønningen led him to the left of the building, past rusty blue containers, more empty pallets, the door to a sheet-metal workshop, and a roller door, which was grey at the bottom and brown at the top. There was no sign of life. No cars outside, no motorbikes. There was complete silence.

'Are you sure it's here?' Henning asked.

Grønningen nodded and walked straight over to a matt-blue door.

'Have you been here before?'

'Nope, but I know the guy who rents it out.'

Grønningen rapped on the door with his knuckles three times then took a couple of steps back.

The door was opened soon after by a man with a swollen lip and a drowsy expression on his face. He had no hair on his head, but plenty on his face. His fair beard was flecked with blood, which flashed like a warning light. He said nothing, just looked both of them up and down.

'Hi Nicklas,' Grønningen said.

The Swede didn't answer, just continued to stare at them.

'Is Pontus here?'

The Swede smiled. He stepped forwards, looking around, then indicated that they should stretch out their arms.

He searched Grønningnen first – thoroughly. The Swede took his mobile phone.

'You'll get it back after,' Nicklas said.

Grønningen nodded reluctantly.

Then it was Henning's turn. He stood with his legs apart to make things easier for the Swede. Felt his strong hands on his legs, round his ribcage, in his pockets. He took Henning's phone as well, then made a follow-me gesture with his head and opened the door for them. He gave Henning an extra hard stare as they went in. The Swede's breath smelt vile, as though he'd been eating rotting herring.

They were at the top of a dark set of stairs, which led down to a dimly light hallway. Henning could hear muffled sounds from below, then a shout and some clapping and cheering. He followed Grønningen, certain that his footsteps could be heard for miles. The noise in the basement didn't stop, though; in fact, it increased – Henning heard moans and whoops, laughter and cheers, the sound of punches and kicks, bodies falling to the ground.

The room downstairs was like something from a film. It was basic, with great, square beams and a concrete floor. The light came from a single bulb hanging in the middle of the ceiling. It felt as though the floor was covered in a thin layer of dust and gravel, and it smelt of a mixture of raw fruit and sweat. The smell didn't bother Henning. What he saw straight ahead of him did, however. He counted seven people standing in a kind of ring around two men who were in the process of killing each other; at least, that was what it looked like. Both had bloodied faces; one of them had a great gash above his eye. Neither of them was wearing any protection, be it boxing gloves or mouth guards. There were no coaches in the corners, ready to throw them towels or give them a drink from a plastic bottle. The floor was not covered in any way; it was just bare concrete.

No one seemed to care that Henning and Grønningen had come in. Everyone was focused on what was happening in the ring. The two fighters slammed each other to the floor, sat on each other and pummelled each other frenetically. Each punch would have been enough to send Henning sailing, but these men continued to fight, spitting and pulling faces, roaring, hissing and growling at each other, as they picked themselves up from the floor and caught their breath before starting another round. They looked for openings, a tentative kick. Then they locked together again. One got his arms round the other's torso, lifted him up and threw him to the ground. His opponent's head smashed against the concrete. Henning heard a crunching sound. He was sure that the man lying underneath would die.

Then one of the onlookers clapped his hands. And immediately there was silence. The fighters stopped fighting and the ring opened up. The man who had clapped turned to look at the new arrivals.

Henning felt himself shrinking, all the strength leaving his legs.

'So,' said the man who clapped. 'I see we have visitors.'

The man stepped out of the shadows. The single light bulb seemed to shine on him alone. The others drew back. The man had a shaved head, and was bare-chested with tattoos everywhere; and even though he was clearly not the fittest, even though he was as round as he was tall, Henning did not doubt for a moment that he was strong. Very strong. He had a scar on his chest and his shoes – or boots, rather – clicked as he walked. Sharp edges and pointed toes. He stopped about a metre in front of them. Looked at one, then the other, with a callous smile on his lips. He focused on Grønningen. Took a step closer.

'Hi Pontus,' Grønningen said.

Pontus didn't answer. His smile had vanished. His eyes flashed with aggression, but Grønningen stood his ground; perhaps it helped that he was seven or eight centimetres taller than the Swede, who Henning feared might explode at any moment.

Henning noted Pontus's face. He had a scar on one side of his upper lip. A gold tooth. A monster nose. Like Grønningen, he had a goatee, which he had plaited from his chin. Part of one ear was missing. Henning didn't dare think how or why he'd lost it, or what had happened to whoever was responsible.

The others had now moved a step closer, too, but Henning couldn't see their faces clearly. They were watching Pontus's every move. The big brute looked like he was studying every single pore on Grønningen's face.

'Well, gotta hand it to you,' Pontus finally said. 'Coming here like this,' he swung his arm round to indicate the room, 'that takes some nerve.'

'Thanks for agreeing to meet us,' was Grønningen's reply.

Pontus took yet another step closer. There were no more than a few centimetres between their faces now. When Pontus carried on speaking, his voice was quiet and intense.

'Now tell me why I shouldn't give you a headbutt, right here.'

'You can if you like,' Grønningen said, his eyes riveted on the Swede. 'If you think it'll help.'

'Yeah, I do actually,' Pontus said. 'It would help a lot.'

'But it wouldn't bring Jocke back. And I had nothing to do with Jocke getting killed. You know that.'

Pontus looked like he really was considering giving Grønningen what he suggested. They stood staring at each other for a few long seconds, as though they were professional boxers posing in front of a camera.

Then Pontus took a step back, gave an almost imperceptible nod and turned his attention to Henning.

'And this is *the journalist*?'

Grønningen told him it was. Henning swallowed hard, tried to straighten his back, stand tall. He didn't know what to do with his hands as Pontus moved closer. Shaking hands was hardly the norm with these people. He put them behind his back and immediately felt like an old man. Clasped them in front, put them on his hips, stuck them in his pockets.

'I know who you are,' Pontus said, and stopped a couple of metres from him. 'You're the one who found out who killed Jocke.'

Henning tried to answer, but found his throat was too dry. He coughed and tried again.

'Yes, that's right,' he said, and felt proud for a brief moment – a feeling that was probably misguided in the present company. The Swedes stood around them, arms crossed, while they waited for the boss's next move.

'Nice work,' Pontus said. 'Who're you out to save this time?'

Henning thought for a few moments before answering. 'Myself, I think.'

'How come?'

Henning looked down while he considered what to say, how much he should tell.

'My son is dead,' he said, and lifted his eyes to look at Pontus again. 'He's dead because someone set fire to my flat. My theory is that the people who did it are the same people who killed Tore.'

'And so you've come here? This is where you think you'll find Tore's killer?'

Henning nodded. 'The police have arrested someone, but I'm not interested in him. I want whoever it was who ordered the killing. And I think Jocke Brolenius knew who it was.'

One of the others behind Pontus coughed; it sounded more like a bark. Pontus took another step closer and he stopped right in front of Henning. A dark veil had fallen over his eyes.

'You think it was one of us?' he demanded.

'No,' Henning said swiftly. 'I'm looking for someone with connections. Someone with money. Some of you might well have both, but as far as I know, none of you have been in the business of buying and selling flats in the past ten years or so.'

Henning's cheeks were burning. He had taken a step back without realising it, and he was leaning his upper body back in a slight arch to keep as much distance from Pontus as possible. One of the others whispered something that Henning didn't catch. Further back in the cellar somewhere, a drip fell from the ceiling.

'So you want to question us,' Pontus said, taking a step to the side. He twisted round to look at Henning, his boots scraping on the concrete floor. 'And why would we want to help you?'

'Because I found out who killed your mate. You owe me a favour.'

Pontus smiled briefly as he studied Henning with gimlet eyes.

'You hear that, boys?' he asked, without turning away. 'The journo wants to interview us.'

The Swedes roared with laughter. Pontus started to pace again, smiling and laughing. Then he was back in front of Henning.

'OK,' he said. 'You can ask your questions. But on one condition.' He pointed his thumb over his shoulder. 'You have to do it in there.'

Henning followed the direction of his thumb. Pontus was pointing at the temporary ring in which the fighters had wrestled only a few minutes ago. It took a moment for Henning to realise exactly what Pontus meant.

'Pontus, he's never...' began Grønningen

'Shhh,' Pontus said, pointing his finger at Grønningen without looking at him. 'This is between me and my new friend here. That's the deal. We'll stand in the ring and you'll ask your questions.'

Henning looked at Pontus and then at the others. Some of them smiled in anticipation. Henning swallowed, hard.

'But I've never fought anyone before,' he said.

'And I've never been interviewed before,' Pontus replied. 'So we're even stevens.'

The Swedes guffawed.

I'm going to die, Henning thought. *That's for sure.* One punch from those hands and he would go flying, bang his head on the concrete floor and never wake up again.

'He's had two hip operations,' Grønningen tried. 'Three screws in...'

'Are you his babysitter, or what?' Pontus asked. 'He can talk for himself.'

Pontus turned back to Henning again. 'Well,' he said, rubbing his hands together. 'How about it?'

Henning looked at Pontus, saw a gold tooth gleam when he smiled, his rippling chest muscles, the size of his hands. This could be the only chance you get, Henning told himself. He might know something.

Henning took off his jacket and dropped it on the floor. 'OK,' he said. 'Let's go.'

10

BigB put down 'WEBER' and got fifty-eight points, managing, of course, to put the W on a triple word score and to use it twice. Weber? Wasn't that a barbecue manufacturer? So proper names were suddenly allowed, were they?

Nora was still leading by eleven points, but she had lost three games over the course of the evening, and it annoyed her more than she liked to admit. That, and the fact that her phone hadn't rung or vibrated, meant she was irritated.

She had sent a text message to Iver to ask where he was and what he was up to, but hadn't received an answer. He was probably still thinking, Nora reasoned; or he was out with some contact or source. She had sent a couple of messages to Henning as well, saying that she wanted to talk to him, but he hadn't responded either.

Nora played 'BEAVER'. Ten lousy points. She got up from the sofa with a grunt and went into the bathroom. She couldn't avoid looking at the reflection in the mirror – a person she didn't recognise; pasty and puffy in the face, drawn and drained of colour. Red eyes and dead hair.

'Are you really thirty-seven?' she asked her reflection.

She wondered whether she should call her mother; she spoke to her once a week, but really only ever on Sundays. If she rang her now, she would just be interrogated about what was wrong. Maybe she could ring her sister, but she would probably do the same, as they only every talked once every six months or so. All Nora wanted to do was talk to someone she knew cared about her. Talk about safe things.

Fortunately, only her face was visible in the mirror, so she didn't have to see her whole figure. She could feel it already, though: her trousers had got tighter recently. The only positive thing about being pregnant was that her breasts were looking more like themselves again.

For some reason, she felt the need to shower all the time. She had showered in the morning before she went to work, then again when she came home after meeting Henning, and again, now, just as she was about to go to bed; all the smells and heat and food – *everything* seemed to lie like a film over her skin. She *stank*. So she told her reflection to bugger off and took off her clothes, opened the shower door with such force that it banged, and turned on the water.

When it was eventually warm enough, she stood underneath and massaged herself in the flowing heat for a long time. Then she soaped herself, several times, but didn't bother to wash her hair this time, just wet it. She closed her eyes and wondered how on earth she had managed to end up in this situation. The best thing would be if she could just run away from both of them; start again somewhere new when the child was born. Concentrate 100 percent on being a mother. She could manage perfectly well without men.

Quarter of an hour later, she got out of the shower, thankful that hot water was included in the rent, and checked her mobile before drying herself. She sighed. Still no messages. But BigB had been at work again with a new made-up word and was now leading by thirty-three points.

Nora snorted with indignation, dried herself, brushed her teeth, pulled on her dressing gown, then went back into the living room and turned on the TV. She found the matches and lit the candle on the windowsill. A thin, little candle in a thin, little candlestick. The one they used to put by Jonas's place at the table on his birthday. It only took ten minutes to burn down, but Jonas loved those candles; his face took on a special glow when he sat there staring at the thin, little flame.

Nora turned off all the lights, got her bag from the hall and took out the ball. She sat down on the rocking chair and gazed at the candle on the windowsill as she rocked back and forth, back and forth, squeezing and turning the ball so the glitter and flame created a shimmering curtain of gold and silver before her eyes. And soon she felt at peace.

She could go to bed.

11

There was a great roar of expectation. Pontus entered the ring first, with his back to Henning. The man looked like a wall. Then he turned with a smile and spat on his hands.

'Give him one, Pontus,' one of the others shouted.

Henning moved closer; saw the others watching him. Pure glee. *This is going to be fun.* Grønningen said nothing.

Henning could smell the sweat. They were all bare-chested. An intoxicating blend of flesh and tattoos, hair and concrete dust.

'You'll have to take your T-shirt off too,' Pontus said, pointing.

He did as he was told, and dropped it onto his jacket. He heard laughing behind him.

'How much do you actually weigh?' Pontus asked.

'Seventy-one kilos, the last time I checked,' Henning replied.

Pontus laughed loudly.

'And where are the screws in your hips?'

Henning pointed to his left side, pulling down the edge of his trousers to reveal a long scar. Then everything went black – white spots danced and looped in front of his eyes, his groans lost in the noise of the Swedes laughing. He realised that Pontus had kicked him right on the scar. It took all Henning's strength not to collapse. The Swede had his fists up, ready to defend himself, as though he was prepared for Henning to retaliate at any moment. Then the reality of the situation seemed to dawn on him. Pontus lowered his shoulders and arms, relaxed completely.

'First question,' he said, and stopped dancing in front of Henning.

He started to walk up and down instead, thumping his chest and patting his cheeks.

Henning caught Grønningen's eye; he was standing with his left hand tucked under his right armpit, his other hand round his neck.

'Well, come on then,' Pontus said. 'What are you waiting for?'

Henning tried to block out the pain.

'When Jocke was alive,' he croaked, 'who gave him the jobs?'

Pontus started to laugh, and laughed for a long time.

'You think I'm going to tell you that?' he said at last.

Then he made a move as though he was about to punch Henning, which was enough to make him take a step back. The spots danced in front of his eyes again. The gang behind him roared in delight.

'Shit, you're even more stupid than I thought,' the Swede smirked.

Then another explosion out of nowhere. Henning felt the side of his face sting and realised that Pontus had slapped him, as though he was a little girl.

The gang laughed again. Pontus smiled.

Henning clasped his cheek, expecting to feel blood. He didn't, but the stinging was intense and lasted for a long time.

They circled one another.

'How well did Tore and Jocke know each other?' Henning asked.

Pontus put his left ear to his left shoulder and then did the same to the right; his spine cracked.

'How did they know each other?' Henning added.

'One question at a time,' said one of the others watching. Henning got the feeling it wasn't the first time they'd seen something like this.

'I don't know,' Pontus answered. 'But you can ask him about that,' he added, nodding at Grønningen, a movement that caused Henning to make a mistake.

He looked over at Grønningen for a second at the most, but it was enough. Pontus stepped closer and threw a punch that landed just above Henning's right cheekbone. It made a sound, but strangely enough didn't hurt; his face just went numb and the room started to spin. He staggered to get his balance then sank down onto his knees, wondering if this was just a taster.

Some of the others clapped and whooped. Henning touched his cheek, his fingers smeared red. It felt like his face had doubled in size.

He managed to get to his feet and tried to focus on Pontus in the whirl of dust and concrete, but he could only see the outline of something moving. Henning tried to stand up straight, but wasn't sure if he could.

'Who might gain from Tore being put out of action?' he asked, spitting. Red dribble hung from his mouth; he wiped it away with his hand. His sight returned to something like normal. Pontus was still walking back and forth in front of him, his head lowered.

'Us,' he said. 'We all would. Tore was a fucking idiot.'

Pontus came at him again. But this time Henning was prepared; he saw the punch building in his opponent's right shoulder and managed to duck in time.

'Ooooh,' the others roared.

Henning stepped back. The next move was even more obvious, but Henning made another mistake, focusing only the arms. He realised too late that it was only a feint, and when Pontus threw out his leg at a ninety-degree angle, he didn't have time to do anything before the inside of Pontus's foot hit exactly the same spot as his last kick.

Henning sank to his knees and didn't manage to put his hands to his face before the next kick. A high-pitched ringing vibrated in his ears before he hit the concrete floor, face down. His teeth crunched together and everything went black and white, then suddenly: absolute silence. He looked up, his cheek still on the concrete, saw the Swedes laughing and clapping, punching the air triumphantly, but he couldn't hear them. Then he spotted Grønningen standing behind them all.

Henning put his hands to the floor, felt how cold and dusty it was. He got back up onto his knees, spat again. The dust turned red; a cut above his eye was bleeding. Pontus strutted in front of him, bathing in the glory.

Henning had been waiting for a moment like this.

When Pontus turned his back and faced his audience, Henning jumped up, focusing on the great hulk of a man in front of him, feeling his rage, how strong it made him. He didn't care about the pain, he just launched himself at Pontus, got hold of his head with one hand and pushed the big Swede forward. Pontus didn't have time to react and Henning managed to slam him into one of the square pillars holding up the ceiling. The impact of head on concrete caused a flurry of white dust to fall from the ceiling.

Almost without realising what he'd done, Henning watched Pontus stand there for a few moments seemingly stunned, before he turned back towards Henning and sank, bewildered, to his knees.

There was absolute silence.

Everyone was looking at Pontus.

The Swede stared into thin air until his eyes once again focused on Henning, still looking astonished. Henning stood over him, bent double and gasping for breath. But Pontus didn't fall to the floor, he just stayed there on his knees with a confused expression on his face.

The room was silent for a long time.

'I don't know what he's called,' Pontus said slowly, in a deliberate voice. 'But the guy who gave Jocke most of his jobs was some super-lawyer. That's all I know.'

Suddenly a spark flared in his eyes; he grabbed Henning by the neck, pulling him down.

And then there was darkness.

12

When Henning's eyes fluttered open, it was dark all around him. He realised he was somewhere outside the brick building, and that it was evening, night, or early morning – winter or cold spring. He was sitting with his back against a freight container.

He made an attempt to move.

Difficult.

His face felt like a ball, full of air. He ached everywhere, especially in his thigh. It felt like he'd been run over by a house.

Geir Grønningen was standing over him. He had a black eye. Henning closed his eyes again, tried to wet his lips, but couldn't feel them, he just felt the rips, as though he had licked something splintered.

'Are you awake now?' Grønningen asked.

'Don't know,' Henning mumbled, and put a hand up to his face. Couldn't feel a thing.

Grønningen hunkered down beside Henning. The container vibrated as his back hit the metal. The big man put his elbows on his knees, leaned forwards. Shook his head.

And then started to laugh.

'That's the maddest thing I've ever seen,' he said.

'Huh?' Henning grunted, without moving his eyes; he was staring at things on the ground – a stone, a puddle, a branch torn from a tree.

'I've never seen Pontus on his knees. Never even heard of it happening before.' Grønningen ran his fingers through his hair. Then he laughed again, shaking his head 'Fuck me.'

Henning concentrated on trying to recognise some of their surroundings. Could see some spots of light up there somewhere, heard the leaves rustling, a tram accelerating. There was something hammering and thumping, but he wasn't sure if it came from the city around him or from inside his own head.

'You're quite something, Henning.'

A gust of wind gave him a cold kiss on the cheek. Gradually, his eyes managed to focus. It wasn't often that he saw stars in Oslo, certainly not as clearly as now. He tried to find the Plough, but didn't manage it; instead he noticed that there was a half-moon, that the trees on the hill at Ekeberg were dark.

'Think we should get you to A&E,' Grønningen said, and glanced over at him again. 'Reckon you've got concussion.'

'And sit in a queue for hours?' Henning tried to shake his head, but stopped straightaway: everything was turning already.

They sat and listened to the evening, the sound of a train approaching. Neither of them could see the tracks that whined and creaked.

After a while, Grønningen stood up.

'Let me help you up, at least,' he said, and held out a hand.

Henning took it. It was liked being pulled by a ski lift; it hurt in his hips – it hurt everywhere.

'D'you need help to get home?'

'No,' Henning said, holding up a hand. 'I've caused you enough trouble this evening.'

'Wasn't doing much anyway,' Grønningen said.

The seconds ticked by. Then Grønningen nodded and said: 'C'mon then. The buses don't come as often at this time of night.'

Henning followed him obediently, step by step, and discovered how unsteady he was, how hard it was to lift his feet. His head was thumping, he felt sick, but swallowed it down, concentrating on his feet and the ground. Soon there was more traffic around them, and Henning guessed they were at the bus stop. He looked up at the skyscrapers through the dark. The shiny, cold windows reflected like mirrors. And above them, high up on the hillside, the ski jump at Holmenkollen was illuminated, even though it was weeks before the first snow would come.

Even a ski jump brought back the memories ...

'You alright?' Grønningen asked.

'I'll manage,' Henning said.

'You sure?'

'Mmm.' Henning swayed.

Grønningen stood looking at him for a few seconds, assessing the damage.

'OK,' he said, eventually. 'I'm off.'

Henning managed to get on a bus that went in completely the wrong direction, so he had to get off and go back into the centre of town, where he found a tram with a number he recognised – 13. Very appropriate for the day so far, Henning thought as he made his way to an empty seat, not caring about the stares from the other passengers. His head was still spinning, whistling and thumping. He had to hold the back of the seat in front so he didn't fall over.

He took out his mobile and saw that it was late and that Nora had sent him several text messages. He pressed his thumb down on the screen to unlock it.

He deleted all the messages without reading them.

13

In their eagerness to do their job, the desk editors sometimes ruined Nora's copy. They rewrote things, made up titles and created leads that had little to do with the text, mucked around with the pictures and broke up the flow of the language. Nora had yet to meet a journalist who didn't have a horror story to tell; so *desk* was often used as a swearword, and not without cause.

But this time, the editors had barely moved a comma. The article about Hedda had been placed at the top of the print edition's front page, and was just as it had been when she delivered it. And, from what she could see of the screen above Birgitte's head, it had a good position in the online edition as well. But it was only now, as Nora read the words that she had written, that the story somehow became real for her.

Hedda was missing.

It hit Nora in a way she had not expected. She started to cry in front of Birgitte, and rushed over to her desk before the receptionist had a chance to ask what was wrong.

Nora managed to pull herself together before the morning meeting, however. It was decided that she would rent a car and drive down to Tønsberg to investigate a little, talk to Hedda's family and friends, and check the tip-offs the team hoped would start coming in. She had plenty of time. Most people had just got to work and she couldn't expect many leads until after lunch, when they would sit down and have a look at the online papers.

It took her nearly an hour and a half to drive to Norway's oldest town. She parked in a large, open car park outside City Shopping. It was a few degrees warmer in Tønsberg than it had been in Oslo, but there was still a definite autumn chill. The trees on Nedre Langgate were being tossed and whipped about in a cold wind from the canal, which Nora could see just a stone's throw away.

The Hellberg Property offices were next to the shopping centre where Nora had parked, on the corner of Tjømegaten and Nedre Langgate. There was a McDonald's restaurant next door; Nora, who hadn't eaten anything other than her usual three pieces of crispbread, resisted the temptation to wolf down a cheeseburger before walking to the door, which told her that Hellberg Property was open from 10 am until 7 pm on weekdays and 9 am to 3 pm on Saturdays.

A bell tinkled over Nora's head as the door shut behind her; she stopped and looked around. This part of the premises was clearly dedicated to sales. In the window, there were details for a variety of flats – several of them already had SOLD splashed across them in big, red letters. There was a screen on the wall showing a further selection of properties.

Nora had expected the place to be a hive of activity, with buzzing phone lines and voices talking passionately about the west-facing balcony and Italian tiles in the bathroom; for the moment, however, there was only one agent there. He sat hunched over his desk and didn't even look up when Nora came in, just continued to fiddle with his phone. His eyes were glazed.

'Excuse me,' Nora said, taking a step closer.

The man looked up reluctantly, slowly pushed himself away from the desk, put his phone down and then took a few moments to get up. Once he had straightened out his suit and pushed back his shoulders, she saw that he couldn't be more than thirty and was rather short. There was scant evidence of facial hair, and he had a light-blue cravat that matched his suit. His hair was slicked back.

Nora introduced herself and said which paper she worked for.

'Oh right,' the man replied, looking down. 'So it's you, is it?'

Nora walked over to his desk.

'I read your article this morning,' he explained.

Nora looked down at his name plaque: FRITZ GEORG HELLBERG.

'And you are?' she asked, all the same.

'...Hedda's cousin. Everyone calls me Georg.'

Nora held out her hand.

He hesitated a moment before taking it. 'I work for William, her brother,' he said.

'A real family business.'

He let out a quick laugh. 'There are lots of other people who work here as well. I mean, we don't *only* sell property. But William is the boss. The Big Brother.'

Nora gave one of her lopsided smiles, catching the double meaning.

'Well, I'm in luck, then, if I can talk to more than one of you. Is he around? The boss, that is?'

Georg ran a hand through his hair. Nora wondered if it was greasy.

'I think he's in a phone meeting; I'm not sure how long he'll be.'

Georg bent down to pick up an umbrella that was lying half open on the floor, then folded it up before putting it in a stand that housed several other umbrellas bearing the Hellberg Property logo.

Nora pushed her fringe aside. 'Perhaps I could talk to you, in the meantime?'

She took a notebook and pen out of her bag. And even though he still hadn't given her an answer, she asked: 'Did you have much to do with Hedda?'

'Yes, I ... we hung out together when we were younger, especially in the summer holidays.'

He sat down on a chair, making it creak, crossed one leg over the other and leaned back a little, folding his hands in his lap.

'Her father had a summer house out at Hulebakk, and he let us stay if there was room. So that was generally where we met. Certainly before we were teenagers.'

Nora pointed to the chair beside him and asked with her eyes if it was alright for her to sit down. Georg gestured his assent with his hand. She pulled the chair over and sat down opposite him, putting her bag down on the floor beside her. Georg leaned forwards, pressed a button on his phone. The screen lit up.

'When did you last see her?' she asked.

He pushed his phone away and picked up a white T-shirt that lay crumpled on the desk. Nora noticed that it bore the same light-blue logo as the umbrellas.

'A couple of weeks after Uncle Oscar died, I think,' said Georg, folding the T-shirt.

'In what context?'

He put the folded T-shirt back down on the desk. 'It was a dinner at Aunt Unni's, out at Kalvetangen,' he said. 'Everyone was there.'

Nora made a note. 'And how was Hedda then?'

Georg shrugged. 'I guess she was just as normal. I mean, she ... well, of course, she was affected by Uncle Oscar's death; we all were. But I didn't notice anything in particular.'

Nora bit the end of her pen, felt the plastic give between her teeth. 'Did you talk to her?'

'Just to say hello, really. I was sitting quite far away from her, so there wasn't really the opportunity.'

Nora crossed her legs and swung her foot up and down; she needed to treat her boots before the winter, she thought.

'Have you had any sightings yet?' Georg asked.

'I haven't checked my email since I left Oslo. I just drove down,' Nora told him. 'But something always turns up in cases like this. People notice more than they think.'

'So you think she'll be found?'

Nora looked at him. 'Don't you?'

Georg shrugged again. 'I don't really know.'

He picked up his mobile phone again and pressed the top button. The screen light reflected on his clean-shaven cheeks.

'My mum disappeared in the mid-nineties,' he said. 'Most of the family think that Hedda's done an "Aunt Ellen", that she's just disappeared, simple as that – taken her own life. Made sure that no one will find her.'

Georg seemed to be even younger when talking about his mother. Nora could see the loss in his eyes, the vulnerability.

'It must have been awful. For all of you.'

He nodded again.

'Can I ask how old you were when it happened?'

'Thirteen,' he replied.

Nora wanted to ask how much Georg knew about *why* his mother had disappeared, but that wasn't the reason she was there. She could imagine the situation, all the same. First the fear, then the hope, which gradually faded. Then the desperation, the grief. And then, eventually, the certainty that they would never know. Emptiness followed. Nora wondered if the same would happen with Hedda.

She looked around as she thought about what to ask next. On the wall, there was a framed photograph of some men in smart suits accompanied by elegantly dressed women. She quickly spotted Georg. He was sporting a cravat in the picture as well.

As Nora turned her head she saw a tall, thin man who must have slipped silently into the room. He was standing only a couple of metres from them, looking at them intently. Everything about him said 'boss'. Nora realised that this had to be William, Hedda's brother.

'Could I have a word?' he said to Georg.

Georg remained where he was, slouched and glazed. Then slowly he turned his head towards his cousin and pushed himself up with a quiet, but audible sigh.

'Please excuse us a moment,' William said to Nora, with a smile.

'Of course,' she said.

She followed them with her eyes as they left, William in front, Georg walking slowly behind. They stopped around the corner. She couldn't hear them, but could see them in a mirror that hung on the wall by the entrance. William was the one who did the talking, and judging by his body language, he was anything but pleased. Georg looked up at his cousin, his face showing nothing, then he nodded and carried on into another part of the premises. William Hellberg straightened his jacket and then came back to Nora wearing a broad smile.

She stood up and put her bag over her shoulder, but kept her note-book and pen in her left hand.

'Hello,' he said. 'I do apologise. Georg said that you would like to talk to me.'

'Yes, if that's possible. My name is Nora Klemetsen; I work for *Aftenposten*.' She held out her hand.

William gave her a firm, warm handshake. 'Shall we go into my office?'

Nora didn't need to be asked twice. She followed him up a short flight of stairs, around a corner, past a kitchen area and water dispenser, and a large meeting room. William turned at the door to his office and indicated that Nora should go in first.

'Again, I do apologise,' he said, as he closed the door and indicated that Nora should sit down. 'We would rather only the closest family made statements about Hedda. I hope you can understand that.'

'Of course,' Nora said, and sat down on a deep chair with long arm rests. William went around to the other side of the large desk, opened one of the buttons on his jacket, sat down and pulled the chair up to the desk. Even though he was now sitting, he seemed to be twice as tall. The smile he sent her over the table was apparently genuine enough, however.

The room smelt of aftershave. Nora noted that William had a ring on his finger and was wearing a gleaming watch in which all the cogs and workings were visible. He also had a conspicuous scar on the back of his left hand. As though he had been branded.

On the desk there were photographs of a couple of little boys, and a gun dog with a lolling tongue. The room was clean and tidy, with fresh fruit on the table and a small fridge that contained a large bottle of champagne and some smaller bottles of rather exclusive water. A framed photograph of a farm in its blossoming spring glory had been given pride of place on the wall behind William.

He noticed that Nora was looking at it.

'That's Morsevik Farm,' he said, proudly. 'Just after the war, there was a man living there who had lost all his family. He had no heirs and didn't want to stay there any longer. But, as you'll know, allodial law puts restrictions on the sale of farms. It's a complicated thing to understand, though, so he contacted my great-grandfather, who was a practising lawyer at the time, and asked for help. My great-grandfather then realised it might be smart to use his knowledge of property law to make a real business out of it. So he set up a company: Hellberg Property. The rest is history, you might say.' William smiled. 'Would you like a cup of coffee?'

Nora would have killed for three bars of chocolate and a Coke, but she declined the offer of coffee and instead asked if it was right that William and Hedda had spent some time together by Oscar's bedside.

William shook his head.

'We weren't there with him at the same time; we overlapped as one of us arrived and the other left. I wasn't actually there that often, though. One of my sons...' William looked down at the photographs on his desk '...he's got Kawasaki disease. My wife and I have been extremely anxious since John Travolta's son died.'

Nora didn't know much about the illness, but understood their worries perfectly well. She waited a moment before asking her next question.

'I've heard that Hedda took your father's death extremely hard.'

William put the tips of his fingers together so his hands made a triangle. 'Yes, she was very close to Father.'

Nora wondered if she should give her condolences, but then decided it seemed a bit odd so long after the event.

'And what are your thoughts about her disappearance now? Do you think it has anything to do with your father's death? Was her grief too much to bear?'

William cocked his head to one side, and then the other. 'I don't know, really. Obviously, she was very upset, but I find it hard to believe that she took it *that* badly.'

'Stayin' Alive' suddenly filled the room. Nora blushed furiously. She pulled her phone from her bag and ended the call without looking at the number.

'Sorry,' she said.

'That's OK.' William lifted a glass of water that was standing by the phone and took a sip.

'So you don't think that Hedda has committed suicide?'

William put the glass down again. 'Put it this way: Hedda has always been tough, a bit of tomboy really, if you know what I mean. When she was a child, she didn't cry if she grazed herself or anything like that, and she always wanted to do what Patrik and I and our friends were doing. I've always seen her as being someone who can take a few knocks. Which is why it doesn't make sense to me that she'd take her own life. But I can't imagine why anyone else would want to harm her, so...'

'What *I* find a little strange,' Nora started, 'is why she said that she was going to Italy for three weeks, when in reality she hadn't even booked the trip. It was quite clearly a lie.'

'No, I don't understand it either. She might of course have been abducted by some madman. It does happen occasionally, unfortunately. A psychiatric patient, or someone like that.' William looked away.

Nora thought she knew what kind of thoughts and pictures were going through his head, even if his calm, almost impassive exterior didn't betray them. She couldn't think of anything more to ask, so she stood up and closed her notebook.

'Thank you for your time,' she said, and held out her card. 'If you think of anything else that you feel I should know, don't hesitate to get in touch.'

William stood up, and took her card. 'I will do.'

14

At some point during the night, Henning lost count, but when he finally got up a good many hours later, he was sure that he'd vomited at least ten times. It was obvious that he had concussion, and had probably broken a rib or five, but it wasn't so bad that he hadn't managed to have a few lucid thoughts in the hours he'd lain awake waiting for another wave of nausea.

He had gone through all the lawyers he knew who might give enforcement jobs to people like Jocke, and had come up with a likely candidate pretty fast: Lars Indrehaug, the lawyer who had defended Ørjan Mjønes, the man the police had arrested, suspecting he was the brains behind Tore Pulli's murder.

Indrehaug was a good lawyer and a smart man, but Henning had never liked him. There was something about the tall man's arrogance, his aura of invincibility – as though he was the blind goddess's loyal squire and was only doing what duty required of him. But Henning also got the feeling that Indrehaug *liked* being the confidant of criminals, that he enjoyed their company; Henning had attended several court cases where he'd seen Indrehaug chatting happily with his clients outside the court in the breaks. It was only a hunch, of course, and nothing he would take to the bank, but in the course of the night, Henning had decided to look at Indrehaug more closely, to see if he could find anything that linked him to Jocke. And, therefore, to Tore Pulli.

When he'd arrived home the previous evening, Henning had tried to bandage himself and affix some plasters as best he could, but looking at himself now in front of the bathroom mirror, he saw that he'd made a poor job of it. One of the plasters on his temple was about a centimetre away from the cut. And he had managed to put a sticky end on the wound itself.

He looked terrible. His upper lip was swollen, and under one of his eyes it looked like an extra bag had appeared. He discovered that he had to move slowly. His head ached and he was still nauseous.

He dipped his hands in cold water and carefully washed his face. It felt unfamiliar to his fingers, as though he was touching a mask. With great care, he put on a new plaster. He was surprised that he didn't have more cuts. But the more he moved, the more he understood that Pontus had not just punched and kicked his face and hip. He had beaten him black and blue all over.

He finished up in the bathroom and then drank three cups of coffee at the kitchen table, doing nothing apart from allowing his eyes to adjust gradually to the light that filtered in from outside. He wasn't used to sitting so still; it was actually rather nice.

At around ten o'clock, he rang Lars Indrehaug's office. An efficient, chirpy secretary called Mathilde told him that Lars was out at a meeting, but would be back by lunchtime. Henning was welcome to call again, but should be aware that they were having a fire drill between 12.00 and 12.30.

The mention of a fire drill gave Henning an idea.

And that was why he showed up at the building on Kristian Augusts gate, where Indrehaug Law had its offices, a few minutes before midday. He rang the bell, and while he waited, he looked at his reflection in the glass door and tried not to think about how awful he looked. When the lock clicked, he pulled open the door and walked with determination up to the reception desk, where a uniformed female security guard looked up at him with little interest.

'Hi,' Henning said, giving her a politician's smile. 'Just popping up to see Mathilde on the eighth floor.'

The security guard looked at his face for a few moments. 'Sign here first, please.'

She turned the big visitors' book towards Henning. He looked at the other visitors – the names of the people they were there to meet, the times they arrived and left. Then, acting as though this was the signature he always wrote, Henning grabbed the pen and scribbled something even he had a problem reading. It didn't seem to bother the security guard at all.

As he waited for the lift, he looked up at the sign on the wall and tried to memorise the names of some of the companies that had offices there, so that, in the unlikely event he should meet anyone he knew, he could give a cover story. Judging by the number of companies, hordes of people would have to take the stairs when the fire alarm went off in a few minutes.

The lift arrived, as did two women, carrying with them the smell of coffee and waffles from the canteen. Henning stepped inside, keeping his eyes on the floor. The women pressed the third and fourth floors, and Henning the eighth, and the little box carried them upwards. An oppressive silence surrounded them, and it was hot. Henning felt his pulse rising. His head was still thumping.

He had been to the eighth floor before, after the Henriette Hagerup case in the spring. He'd had a coffee with Lars Indrehaug in his office, having dug up some information that in the end saved the lawyer's client from being convicted for murder. He remembered that all the doors in the building were locked; he noticed that the women in the lift both had key cards.

But Henning had a plan.

He looked at his watch again. Two minutes left. The lift stopped on the third floor, then the fourth, the women getting out. No one else got in, fortunately. He was alone now. One minute to go.

When the lift reached the eighth floor, Henning stepped out into a corridor with a door at each end. As expected, both were locked. He stood where he was, waiting. Looked at his watch.

Then the fire alarm went off.

And at the same time, all the locks clicked. Henning knew that when the fire alarm went off in a building like this, all of the doors would be unlocked to prevent anyone from being trapped inside. To the right,

Mathilde, who he remembered from his previous visit, took off her headset and stood up. Henning went in the opposite direction, hoping she hadn't seen him, opened the door and carried on down the corridor, past some offices. He heard people moving around in some of them, but continued as quickly as he could through another door and into another corridor, where he found the toilets on the right-hand side.

He snuck into one of the cubicles as quietly as he could, pushed the door to, but didn't close it completely. He knew that someone would come round to check that the whole floor was empty, so he took off his jacket, sat down on the seat and pulled his legs up. Then he sat silently.

Moving so fast had made him dizzy and he could feel the sweat on his back, making his shirt stick to his body. He looked at his watch. It would take a few minutes to get everyone out, so he waited, listening to voices pass the toilets, to feet tramping across the floor.

Then everything went quiet. For a long time.

Suddenly the door to the toilets was wrenched open. Henning jumped, but closed his eyes, held his breath and tried to sit as quietly as possible. He heard a foot on the tiled floor, but the door in front of him didn't open. Instead, the footsteps retreated.

Henning released the air from his lungs and looked at his watch again. A door or two slammed, before the noise finally died away and silence prevailed.

He waited for another three minutes before daring to venture out. He didn't have much more than ten minutes, so he hurried back down the corridor, past a meeting room, some more toilets, walls hung with paintings, then more offices. He turned to the left when he got to the end and went through a room with a large photocopier in the corner. Then he slipped down the corridor on the far side, checking that there was no one there.

At last, once he was sure he was alone, he made his way into Indrehaug's office.

OK, Henning said to himself, and looked around. A table, chairs, desk, photographs, diplomas on the wall; he could see the greenery of the Palace Park through the window.

But it was the filing cabinet that interested him.

He closed his eyes and tried to retrieve the memories of his last visit to the office, of what Indrehaug had done when he wanted to double-check a detail from a case he'd worked on some years before. He had got up, gone over to the desk, pulled out one of the drawers, taken out a key, then walked over to the filing cabinet.

Henning opened his eyes again, hurried over to the desk and wiped some of the sweat from his forehead, listening for footsteps and movement in the corridor all the while. He heard nothing.

The top drawer of the desk was open. It contained the usual mess: a marker pen, lots of biros – blue and red – paper clips, some lying loose, the others in a clear box. The next drawer down contained a phone charger, a pack of new batteries, a magazine with a photograph of a celebrity holding a gun on the front. Henning moved it to one side, and there, under an empty toothbrush holder, he found a small, thin key. Could that be it?

Henning looked at the clock on the wall. There wasn't much time left. He went over to the filing cabinet and fumbled a bit with the key before it finally slipped into the lock. There was a loud click, and Henning pulled out the top drawer. There were files and files, but it didn't take long for him to establish that they only went as far as F. He opened the next drawer. It went as far as L. When he opened the third drawer, he ran an eye over the files until he came to M. And there, behind a file that said IVAR MJØNDALEN was the file labelled ØRJAN MJØNES.

Henning snatched it out, put it down on the top of the cabinet and opened it. He leafed through it quickly, checking the clock again. Six minutes to go until half past. He would have to leave soon. He skipped the first page; next was a thick, yellowed page with all the formal details written by hand. The lawyer's brief notes were on the next sheet: short descriptions of Ørjan Mjønes's repeated requests not to give a statement to the prosecution. No explanation as to why.

Henning turned to the next page; a new date; here was a copy of his email correspondence with the public prosecutor. More pages, more notes. He skimmed through more and more pages, and then, when he was almost at the end of the file, he stopped; stared at the sentences in front of him:

Said he couldn't talk because of 'Daddy Longlegs'. When asked directly who Daddy Longlegs was, he said nothing.

Daddy Longlegs? Henning thought. Who can that be?

A moment later he heard something out in the corridor. He realised that the fire drill had finished a few minutes before time and quickly snapped the file closed. Then he put it back where he'd found it, locked the filing cabinet and nipped back to the desk. He put the key back exactly where it had been and promptly left the lawyer's office.

Only seconds later, two men came in through the door by the reception, laughing. Henning quickly side-stepped into the copy room, went out into the corridor on the other side and into the toilets. He closed the door behind him. He hadn't noticed it before now, but his stomach felt like a washing machine.

Henning dropped down on his knees and aimed his mouth at the toilet bowl.

15

Nora stepped out onto the pavement. A chilly autumn wind played with her hair. She pulled her black scarf tighter around her neck and looked left, then right. An old man in a long coat wandered past. His silver, shoulder-length hair was also being blown about. A long queue of cars stood waiting for the traffic lights to turn green. A girl in the passenger seat of a car full of teenagers looked her up and down with disapproval.

I know, I know, Nora thought, *I look like a train crash.*

She took her mobile phone out of her bag and checked to see if she'd received any new emails. She had, reams of them, but none that said 'Hedda' in the subject field. Instead, she went to missed calls and selected the last number, pressed 'Call' and put the phone to her ear, pulling her bag up a little higher on her shoulder.

'Hello, my name is Nora Klemetsen,' she said when someone answered. 'You rang me?'

She moved away from the door.

'Oh yes, hello. Yes I did. I read your article about Hedda Hellberg this morning.'

The traffic lights changed from red to green and the cars started to move. Nora turned into Tjømegaten, where there was less traffic and fewer people.

'I saw her the day she disappeared,' the woman on the other end continued. 'I remember it, because I hadn't seen her for a long time.'

Nora stopped outside an art-and-craft shop.

'OK. Before we go any further, can I ask who am I talking to?' Nora tucked the phone in between her ear and shoulder, slipped her notebook from her bag, pulled the pen from the spiral with her teeth, then bit off the top.

'Oh yes. Sorry. My name is Camilla Wergeland.'

Nora jotted the name down.

'I was in Hedda's class at primary school. Like I said, I hadn't seen her for ages, but then I noticed her at Skoppum Station.'

Nora looked up from the notebook. 'Did you say Skoppum?'

'Yes, the station before Tønsberg when you're coming from Oslo.'

'I know it. What time was this?'

'Just before midday. I was waiting for a train, and I saw Hedda get off on the opposite platform.'

Midday, Nora thought. Hedda's flight to Milan was at 9.50 am.

'Are you sure we're talking about the same day?'

'Yes, I've even checked my diary to be absolutely sure. It was the day I went to Oslo for a job-seeker's course. I didn't know that Hedda was missing until I read the paper today.'

Nora scribbled this down and felt her heart start to race. 'Did you see if she was with anyone?'

'She was alone when she got off the train, but there was someone waiting for her.'

Nora raised her eyebrows. 'Someone was there *to meet* her?'

'Yes, she got into a dark-coloured car, and it drove off straight-away.'

Nora tried to absorb the information she had just been given. 'Did you notice what make of car it was?'

'No, but I think it was a sports car of some sort. The kind where you can take down the roof.'

Nora made a note of this. 'You didn't happen to notice the registration number?'

'Not the numbers, but I think it was an LJ number plate. But then, practically every number plate in Vestfold starts with LJ.'

Nora nodded and wrote down LJ and underlined it twice. 'Did you see if the person driving was a man or a woman?'

'It was a man, I'm fairly sure of that.'

A dog trotted up beside Nora, sniffed her legs. The owner, a woman of more or less the same age as Nora, pulled him back.

'Do you remember anything about him? Hair colour, features; what he was wearing?'

Camilla Wergeland gave it some thought.

'Was he young? Old?'

'He definitely *wasn't* old, I'm sure of that, but I only saw him briefly, and in profile. But I seem to remember that he had dark hair. Shoulder length, I think.'

Nora looked around for a bench, but couldn't see one.

'Can you remember anything else about him?' she asked, and started to walk.

Again, Camilla Wergeland spent some time thinking about it.

'No, I can't remember anything else,' she said at last.

A car drove into the car park, narrowly avoiding a puddle by the pavement. Nora jumped to the side all the same.

'Before Hedda got into the car,' she asked, 'did you notice if she had anything with her? Was she carrying anything?'

Nora slipped between two women who were coming out of City Shopping and carried on up the street. There was nowhere to sit here either.

'Now that you mention it, I think she was pulling a small suitcase. I tried to call her, but she didn't hear me. Or didn't *want* to hear me, I think, because I noticed that she turned her head slightly when I called her name.'

Nora passed a man in dirty clothes who was sitting on the pavement with a plastic cup in front of him.

'What was she wearing? Can you remember?'

'She looked very elegant, as always. Boots, I think; dark jeans, grey jacket. And she was wearing sunglasses.'

Nora chewed her pen.

'OK, thank you,' she said. 'It would be great if you could call me if you remember anything else.'

'I will do.'

'Thank you, once again. It's great that you called.'

'My pleasure.'

Nora ended the call and pushed open the door to Spicy, a café opposite the car park that spoke of late, drunken nights and found herself a table by the window. It didn't take long for her to give in to temptation; she ordered some French fries, which came with too much spice and ketchup, and ate them greedily as she mulled over what the new information might mean and what she should do next.

The obvious thing was to call the police; what Camilla Wergeland had witnessed was sufficiently startling and fresh. Then Nora tried to think professionally. The contents of the follow-up article for tomorrow's paper were now obvious. She could devote a column to quotes from William Hellberg about his sister – what kind of person she was. There were also some quotes from Hedda's best friend that she could use, but she would also have to get a statement from the police at some point.

Whatever she did, though, going back to Oslo now was out of the question. She was not going to just hand this over to the police, she was going to do a bit more investigating herself. After all, it was her friend who was missing and she had a head start on the competition.

When she had finished eating, she took out her laptop and wrote her notes down in a Word file, then started to work on an article. Then she called the head of Home News and told him what he could expect from her in the course of the day. She'd already thought about photographs, and said that she would go to Skoppum Station to take some, but that it would have to wait for later.

Next she phoned Tønsberg Police. She was transferred to Inspector Cato Løken. Nora gave him all the information she had just heard from Camilla Wergeland. She also gave him Camilla's contact details, as well as her own. Løken thanked her for her help and promised he would do his best to answer her questions when she called later to find out how they were getting on with the case.

After Nora hung up, she sat staring out of the window for a while. It was almost one o'clock and she felt that she had managed to get quite a lot done already. But she still felt restless.

There weren't many cars in the car park, but she saw that Camilla Wergeland was right: practically all of them had LJ registration plates. Only Nora's rental car from Oslo and a couple of others were different.

Her eyes stopped when she saw a car parked a few spaces away from her own. It was too far away for her to see the registration number, so she picked up her mobile phone, packed away her laptop and was soon standing by the car, which also had an LJ registration number.

Nora looked around, then went to the rear of the car; there were brown flecks of mud on the tyres and at the bottom of the doors. Nora was still holding her mobile phone, so she typed in the registration number and sent a message to the NPRA, the Norwegian Public Roads Administration. She had no idea how many people drove a cabriolet in Tønsberg, but it couldn't be that many.

Only seconds later, her phone beeped. The name that appeared on her screen made her start.

Nora dialled Camilla Wergeland's number again.

'Sorry, there's just one little last thing,' Nora said. 'The man who picked Hedda up at Skoppum station: you didn't happen to notice if he was wearing a cravat?'

Camilla said nothing for a few seconds.

'Yes, actually he was, now that I think about it,' she said. 'Or perhaps it was just a scarf, I can't be sure.'

Nora realised that it was a leading question, and that she should take the answer with a pinch of salt. But all the same.

'Good. That was all. Thank you.'

It could, of course, be a coincidence, Nora thought, as she put her phone away. There must be plenty of men who liked to wear a cravat. But there were people who used a particular piece of clothing as a kind of signature. Nora had no idea whether Fritz Georg Hellberg was that sort of person or not, but he had been wearing a cravat when she spoke to him not long ago, and he had also been wearing one in the photograph on the wall at Hellberg Property.

And it was his car she was now looking at.

16

You should perhaps take it easy, Henning said to himself as he wiped his mouth then hauled himself up from the toilet floor. His temples were throbbing again now.

Henning rinsed his face with cold water before he went back out into the corridor. He managed to slip out of the locked doors behind a woman who clearly had an errand on another floor. Henning avoided catching her eye; he didn't want to frighten her.

Back at the reception desk, he signed himself out, smiled at the apathetic security guard, and then stepped once again out into day-light and felt the delightfully cool air against his burning cheeks. Even though it wasn't far to his flat in Grünerløkka, he took a taxi, and then tottered up the stairs, knowing full well that he should lie down for a while.

But first he wanted to find out as much as he could about Daddy Longlegs.

He sat down at the kitchen table and opened his laptop. He could clearly see the note about Ørjan Mjønes in his mind's eye. Mjønes was given the Pulli job by Daddy Longlegs, whoever that was. But could Daddy Longlegs also be the man who had given Jocke enforcer jobs?

Henning knew that there was no point in simply searching for Daddy Longlegs on the internet; he would get millions of hits about big, leggy spiders. Smart, Henning mused, to use such a household name as an alias. Not exactly something you could check up online.

He sent an email to two of his regular helpers – Bjarne Brogeland at Oslo Police and Atle Abelsen, an old school friend who was an expert at digging things up on the internet – to see if they could help him find out who Daddy Longlegs was. Then he dialled Geir Grønningen's number.

'Hey,' Grønningen shouted, before Henning had a chance to say anything. 'Good you called. I was going to ring and ask how you were. You didn't look too hot last night.'

'I didn't feel too hot either,' Henning admitted. 'But I'm not too bad now. You busy?'

'No more than usual. What's up?'

'Do you know who Daddy Longlegs is?' Henning asked.

'Yep,' Grønningen guffawed. 'But don't you mean what rather than who.'

'I don't mean the spider. I mean the Daddy Longlegs who gives out jobs like the ones you sometimes take on.'

There was silence at the other end of the line. Then: 'Nope, don't think I've heard of him.'

'It's possible he's a lawyer,' Henning added.

'Called Daddy Longlegs?'

'No, that's his nickname.' Henning shook his head, and immediately regretted it. His brain protested.

'I'll ask around,' Grønningen said. 'See what I can find out.'

Henning thanked him for his help and hung up.

Feeling dizzy, he checked the time. He wouldn't hear from his sources for a while, so he decided to lie down in the meantime, sleep for an hour or so. He'd heard somewhere that the body mended itself while you slept.

And right now that would be a very good thing.

17

Pieces of a life, packed away in boxes.

It didn't seem like a lot, Veronica Nansen thought, and yet there was so much.

She was standing by the door of her storage space in the basement of the building in Ullevål Hageby, where she lived, looking at what other people kept in their cupboards: sacks of wood, bikes, skis; there was even an outboard motor leaning against one of the walls. Stacks of paint tins, brushes, suitcases, clothes, a freezer, shoes gathering so much dust they would be unwearable. Ice skates, flower pots, bags of earth, plastic spades and deck chairs.

Was this all our lives came to – an assortment of everyday objects, worn-out and forgotten in a dim cellar?

Tore had always been a materialist. Loved to adorn himself with expensive, fine things. And he was forever buying her gifts: necklaces, dresses, jackets and suits. He even came home with a car for her once. One of those tiny Fiats. Most probably because he thought it would be easier for her to park in small spaces without denting it. Veronica would smile and thank him for all these presents, throw her arms around his neck and kiss him on the mouth. Sometimes she'd go further, because she knew that was how he wanted her to react. Tore had never understood that what she actually wanted most from him was time.

Tore's life was split between his work and his gym mates; he had her to snuggle up to in the evening when he went to bed. For him, that was perfect. So that was how it had to be. Tore was a *my way or the highway* kind of guy. *Take it or leave it, baby.* She had loved him, it was true. But she'd wanted their life together to be about more than just him.

More often than not there was an apartment showing or a party that he had to go to at the weekend. Sometimes she wasn't even invited. Occasionally, he'd have to rush off to meet a client – no matter whether it was early in the morning or late at night – and, of course, he had a week with the boys every summer when they roared off through Europe on their motorbikes. And then there was the gym. Always the gym. The only day off from working out was Saturday.

Tore's body was his temple, and even though she actually liked that side of him – the fact that he looked after himself – it was always at her expense, at the cost of their time together, just the two of them. But now that he was gone, was not just locked away in a cell, she would have let him travel as much as he liked and train as often as he wanted, as long as he would snuggle up behind her when he came to bed in the evenings.

The people who had broken into her flat a week ago had clearly not been down here in the basement. They'd gone through everything she had upstairs, though. Everything *Tore* had had upstairs. That was why she was down here. She thought that maybe Henning was right, that they were looking for something particular, seeing as they'd only taken the computer and the cameras.

Henning's theory was that Tore had taken photographs of someone or something that had happened outside the building where he lived, on the night that his son died, and that Tore had then tried to use the photographs to get people to help him when he was inside. This meant the pictures might damage them in some way. And that was why he'd been killed. If she could only find the photographs, she might also find out who was actually behind Tore's murder. And perhaps also who was responsible for the fire in Henning Juul's flat. It was worth a try; she owed Henning that much – he had helped exonerate Tore, after all.

Veronica took a deep breath, got out the key to the storage space, unlocked the door and pushed it open. She had put this off for as long as she could, but she knew that she had to clear Tore out of her life. Finally get him out of her system. She took a step inside. The floor was cold.

So, she was looking for photographs.

Photographs of what?

Henning had suggested that it might be people Tore knew – business partners; someone in property with whom he was no longer friends. But Tore wasn't the type to tell her if he'd fallen out with someone. In fact, he wasn't the type who said much at all, and Veronica never asked. The only thing she really knew about his job was that it was about buying and selling, and hopefully, making a few kroner at the end of the day.

Veronica looked at all the stuff they had managed to accumulate, things that they would probably never use again. An old skull-and-crossbones motorbike helmet. Bin liners full of planks that they could burn in the fireplace. Ski wax, even though they never went skiing. An ancient computer.

Veronica took another step forwards, ran her finger along the top of the gun cabinet, then rubbed her hands together. There was a time when she had offered to lend Henning a gun. She had seen things were getting to a point where he might need to protect himself. But he had swiftly declined.

'You could maybe use it for more than just protection,' she had said. 'To get people to answer your questions, for example.'

Veronica was quite tempted by the idea herself. Someone should pay for what they had done. She knew Henning was feeling the same, after what had happened to his son.

Another step. There was a dusty, fusty smell in here. She pulled her running jacket tighter around herself and crossed her arms. Where should she begin, where might Tore have hidden something? The safe was the most obvious place to start.

But how would she get it open?

Tore had never given her the code, not even when he was inside. God knows what was so important that he had to keep it in a safe. Contracts maybe. Keys? Money, possibly. Cash for a rainy day.

Photographs?

She squatted down in front of the safe, wiped off the dust, then noticed a grey smear on her left ankle and wiped that off too. She studied the combination lock. Veronica had a similar one in the office with a six-digit code, 291173 – her sister's date of birth – but she didn't think that Tore would be as sentimental or obvious as that. She tried his date of birth all the same – 190667; the lock remained red. Her own date of birth, 131276, didn't work either. She tried everyone she could think of: Tore's parents and grandparents, his colleagues, his mates from the gym; Geir. She had to look some people up in the tax records to find out when they were born. All to no avail.

Veronica gave up, for the time being at least, and concentrated on other things instead. She went through the bags, looked in boxes, moved everything that Tore had put on the shelves, which he had made himself. She turned and looked around again, and noticed a pile of folders on the floor that looked like it was about to topple over. Bending down she picked them up: contracts, schedules, advertisements – the usual estate-agent stuff.

But one of them caught her attention. There was a photograph of a beach and a housing complex on the outside of the folder. It wasn't hard to work out where the picture was taken, given the accompanying text.

Natal in Brazil.

Veronica remembered what Henning had said about Rasmus Bjelland – the source who had tipped him off about Tore's particular way of doing business. Bjelland had been bankrupt several times and had tried to build up a business and a name for himself in Natal. And he had disappeared.

She sat down on a sack of wood, not bothered by the edges and corners, and started to look through the brochure. She'd just noticed Tore's writing in the margin, when her mobile phone rang.

'Damn,' she exclaimed, when she saw who was calling. She'd forgotten she was supposed to meet her lawyer today, to discuss the details of Tore's will.

18

Nora rushed back to Spicy and sat down at the same place by the window.

So Fritz Georg Hellberg owned a car not unlike the one that Hedda got into outside Skoppum Station. It needn't mean anything, of course, but she was clutching at whatever straws she could find. She took out her laptop and read all the information she could find about Georg.

He was the son of Fritz Hellberg III and Ellen; his father was still alive and lived in an old house in the highly desirable area of Solvang in the centre of Tønsberg. Ellen had disappeared in 1993, only a few weeks after Fritz had suffered a serious heart attack. After the heart attack, he let his nephew William take over as director of the family business. This was a good many years before Georg had even finished school, though he obviously started to work there, too, later on.

Georg was single, as far as Nora could work out, and lived in a flat with a roof terrace in the centre of town. According to the tax records, his income the previous year was impressive – over a million kroner. Nora found him on Facebook as well, and saw that, while he had 1,134 friends, he was not an active user and only changed his status occasionally.

The photos he had posted of himself were not recent, but he hadn't changed much. And in most of the pictures, he was wearing a cravat.

This gave Nora an idea. She called Camilla Wergeland for a third time and found out that she worked in a petrol station on the outskirts of town.

Ten minutes later, Nora parked by the station and went into the shop.

It was easy enough to find the woman who had seen Hedda the day she was supposed to have travelled to Italy, as she was standing behind the counter, serving customers. She was tall, with blonde hair, and looked open and friendly. Nora stood in the queue and waited patiently for the fat man in front of her to pay for his diesel, a newspaper, three different bars of chocolate and two hotdogs. When it was finally Nora's turn, she smiled, held out her hand and introduced herself.

Camilla Wergeland shook her hand and looked over Nora's shoulder to see if it was possible to take a short break. She whispered something to a colleague who was standing beside her then came round to meet Nora by the coffee machine. Nora saw no reason for small talk, so she took out her mobile phone, scrolled to a photograph of Georg that he had posted on Facebook, and asked Camilla if it might have been him who picked Hedda up from Skoppum Station.

Camilla studied the picture, tilting her head. 'I'm not sure,' she said.

Georg was wearing a Burberry cravat in the photograph that Nora had chosen.

'He was so far away,' Camilla continued. 'And everything happened so quickly – a second or two, and then they were gone. And I saw him from another angle.'

She chewed at a nail. Nora looked at the floor.

'But there is a resemblance,' Camilla said.

Nora looked up at her.

'He's about the same age. And his colouring is pretty much the same.'

'Right,' Nora said.

'What's he done?'

Nora hesitated for a moment, then said 'Nothing,' and tried to smile disarmingly, but wasn't sure that she managed it. Once again, she thanked Camilla Wergeland for her help, and then left.

⊙

Not long after, Nora was back outside Hellberg Property. She parked her car a few spaces away from Georg's, and then sat there and waited for him to finish for the day.

When he finally came out, he ran his hand through his hair, looked from side to side and then crossed the road, used his remote key to open his car as he walked towards it and got inside. Nora slid down in her seat.

The engine roared when Georg started his car, and black smoke burped out of the exhaust. Nora waited until he had pulled out of the car park, before starting her own car and accelerating in the same direction.

It was easy to keep track of Georg's car, and Nora made sure there were always at least three cars between them. She soon realised that he wasn't going home, but was in fact on his way out of town. He was driving fast, following Nøtterøveien in the direction of Tjøme. Nora had an inkling of where he might be going, and let the distance between the cars grow. He turned off towards Hulebakk.

She stopped by a bus stop and used her mobile to locate Oscar Hellberg's summer house on Dalsveien. Then she typed the address into the rental car's GPS and pulled away again.

The Vestfold countryside was truly idyllic. The water lapped the shores of the narrow bays, and there were large white, wooden houses with apple trees dotted throughout the gardens. The landscape gradually became less verdant, with smooth rocks surrounded by bushes and low growth to protect the homes against the wind and salt. Some houses lay close to the road, which was asphalted with a broken white line along the edge. At times, she felt like she was passing through a garden, and she drove carefully in case there was anyone walking on the road or on a bike round the corner.

Eventually the trees closed in on the right-hand side. There was a turning that went off into the woods, but it looked more like an unmade track, so she assumed that Georg hadn't driven down there. However, she caught a glimpse of a fence at the end.

Soon, she saw that the fence was high, and ran between the trees and the road, indicating the perimeter of a large property. Nora slowed down, unperturbed by the dark-green Audi on her tail. She wondered what Georg was doing out at his uncle's summer house at this time of year, if that was where he had indeed gone. Summer was long since over.

Nora replayed their short conversation in her head. She would normally have recorded the interview on her mobile phone, but everything had happened so fast, she didn't have time to make any decisions before she was sitting in front of him and they were talking about his missing cousin and mother.

Hadn't there been something quite nervy about the man, though?

You're taking it a bit too far now, Nora said sternly to herself. But all the same, there couldn't be that many people who drove cabriolets, even in a town like Tønsberg, and Hedda certainly wouldn't have got into just anyone's car of her own free will. Nora was tempted to ring Hugo Refsdal, to ask about Hedda's relationship with Georg, but she didn't want to fuel any suspicions or speculation. Not yet.

When she arrived at the address, she saw a drive to the right that led to a high, wrought-iron gate. She turned off to the left and stopped in front of a dilapidated double garage with a corrugated-iron roof. The driveway up to the gate was flanked with dense woodland. It was impossible to see if Georg had actually driven in there, but Nora decided to wait and see if he came back out.

She turned off the engine and tried to think how she might find out whether this was a perfectly ordinary visit or something less usual.

Then she had an idea. She decided to ring Hugo Refsdal after all. It took him a long time to answer.

'How are you getting on?' he asked.

'Um, things are ... fine. There was just something I wondered about. Hedda's father's summer house out at Hulebakk – do you know if they use it all the year round?'

There was silence. Then: 'Why do you ask?'

'No particular reason. I was just curious.'

Refsdal didn't answer straightaway. Eventually, he said, 'They usually close it up for winter after the big crab party they always have at the end of August or beginning of September. It gets too cold there once summer is over.'

'Right.'

'Why?' he asked again.

Nora tried to think of a plausible answer but couldn't come up with anything.

'Who has keys to the summer house?' she asked instead.

'Unni.'

Nora wrinkled her nose. 'Only Unni?'

'Yes. I don't know why, but it's always been the case. That might perhaps be why we don't go there very often any more. She wants to keep an eye on everything.'

Nora thought about Georg, and the fact that he might be there now. Did Hedda's mother know anything about it?

'But I don't understand why you're asking me, Nora. Do you think that Hedda might be *there*? Because she isn't, I went there to check myself.'

Nora's brain was racing. She still couldn't think of a plausible answer.

Luckily, Refsdal didn't persist. Instead, he said: 'But it's a good thing that you called. I've ... found something I have to show you. Would it be possible for you to come out here?'

Nora looked at her watch.

'I'm a bit busy right now, but I could come a bit later this evening, perhaps?'

'Yes, that's fine ... I'm not going anywhere.'

'OK, I'll give you a ring when I'm on my way.'

While she sat there, Nora phoned her boss at Home News and they agreed that she could deliver the final text for tomorrow's article at the last minute. Then she worked a little on the main story, describing how a witness had seen Hedda at the train station in Skoppum on the day that she supposedly flew to Italy.

But why three weeks? Was there a reason why Hedda needed three weeks away? Was the plan that she would return from wherever she was really going after three weeks? Or did she simply want a three-week head start?

Regardless of what her motive had been, the new information gave rise to countless possibilities. And it certainly cast doubt on the theory that she'd committed suicide.

Nora saved the document into the paper's online publishing programme, but she marked it DRAFT so that none of the desk editors would start working on it. She had also arranged with the photo editor that they would find a suitable picture of Skoppum Station, as she had more than enough to do at the moment.

Next, Nora decided to check up on Hedda's finances. She looked in the public tax records and saw that Hedda had earned 417,000 kroner the year before – which was well below the average income in Norway. In 2008, she had made a few thousand more, but in 2007, she had barely managed to earn 390,000 kroner. She remembered what Hugo Refsdal had said – that they had talked about selling the house.

Georg still hadn't appeared, so she also looked up whatever information she could find about Hedda's brother, Patrik. She raised an eyebrow when she discovered that he had a record for drink-driving when he was younger. It was a scandal in the local press, but he seemed to have behaved himself since then and now worked as a sales consultant for a large pharmaceutical company in Oslo, after a few years working as a nurse in a care home in Drammen. He obviously commuted from Jarlsø – a small residential island close to Tønsberg – where he lived with his wife. They had no children.

Nora tried to call Patrik, but only got his voicemail. She couldn't be bothered to leave a message, so instead sent a text to say she would like to talk to him. Nora knew she should also try to get in touch with Unni, Hedda's mother; however, Nora wanted to meet her face to face.

Lights swept over the bonnet of her car, and before she ducked down, she managed to see that they were from Georg's BMW. It swung out onto the road, then he accelerated and it didn't take long before he was travelling at a good speed. Nora pulled herself up slowly, and saw the BMW disappear round a bend.

She was about the start the engine and follow when she stopped herself. She had been sitting here for nearly two hours. What had Georg been doing in there all that time?

Nora started the car and drove towards the gate of the property, not knowing if there was much point. When she reached the gate, she stopped and turned off the engine. The stillness enveloped her.

Nora got out of the car. The wind soughed in the trees. She looked around and then went over to the gate. The summer house was so big that it would be more accurate to call it a villa. There were a couple of floodlights outside, but no lights on inside.

It was impossible to get through the gate without a key and the fence was high. She might have managed to get over it when she was younger and did gymnastics, but now?

The place was no doubt alarmed, Nora thought, finally, and dropped the idea.

But why had Georg come out here?

She spun round, suddenly, looking into the woods, which seemed to be getting darker and darker by the minute. Didn't a branch just snap? Was it an animal or a person?

Nora hurried back to the car and got in.

Chilled.

She felt like someone was watching her.

19

Henning sat up on the sofa. It still felt like his head wasn't properly screwed on, and as soon as he moved, the nausea and grogginess returned.

It took a few minutes before he was awake enough to check his mobile. No messages. He checked his emails; there was an answer from his computer geek friend, Atle Abelsen, to say that he hadn't found anything to indicate who Daddy Longlegs might be. *Someone must know who he is,* Henning thought. *Someone other than Ørjan Mjønes.*

A sudden restlessness assailed him. There were still hours left before he should go to bed again and he had nothing specific to work on. He had to do something. Some kind of activity.

In his head, he went through everything that had happened the day before: the fight with Pontus, Nora's face when she started to cry. Henning tried to shake off these thoughts, and was helped by his phone, which started to ring.

'Veronica Nansen' flashed on the screen.

'Hi,' he said, unable to keep the curiosity out of his voice. 'How are you?'

'OK. Can we meet?'

'Now?' Henning looked at his watch. Almost a quarter past six. 'Yes, of course we can. Where do you want to go?'

'How about the Underwater Pub? It's about halfway between you and me, isn't it?'

In the nineties, Henning had often spent an hour or twelve at the Underwater Pub, which was done out with aquariums and roof beams; there was even an antique bar, in original red marble, from the 1880s. The walls were covered in underwater photographs and ancient diving gear. It looked as though the place had been prepared as a film set.

On Tuesdays and Thursdays, students from the Opera Academy performed here, but no one was singing now. As the door shut behind Henning, he was met by slow, ambient music, which was bolstered by an uninspired rhythm and bass line.

He looked around. Apart from a couple who were speaking in hushed tones over glasses of wine and an old man sitting alone reading the newspaper, his nose nearly buried in the print, the ground floor was empty.

Henning ordered a coffee and went downstairs. He saw a man turning his beer glass, staring intently at the contents. A couple of women, who looked like they might be flight attendants, were sitting opposite each other, having a lively conversation. It wasn't hard to find an empty table, and Henning sat down, looked at the bluish-green walls, the bubbles in the aquariums, the fish swimming around without a care.

Not long after, Veronica Nansen appeared at the top of the stairs and waved to him. Henning stood up and watched her come down.

She's beautiful, he thought. Stunningly beautiful; her tan looked even better now that the cold autumn evening had kissed her cheeks. And she had a body that would turn anyone's head. Long, slim legs. Sublime curves. She had once been a model, of course, and now ran an agency. She was wearing a pair of tight, black jeans, a short, open leather jacket in various shades of dark grey, and a black, polo-neck sweater. A white, soft cotton scarf was twisted around her neck.

The smile she gave him quickly froze and she rushed over to him.

'What's happened?' she asked, her eyes scanning his face.

'Oh, it's nothing,' Henning replied.

'Nothing? Do you think I'm stupid? I can see you've taken a good beating.'

They sat down. Henning looked at her for a moment or two before he decided to tell her the truth. When he had finished, Veronica shook her head.

'It seemed like a good idea at the time,' he concluded. 'And even though I *did* get a good beating, I got the answer to my question. It's a start, at least.'

Veronica sent him a furtive look. One of the flight attendants turned towards them. A waiter came down the stairs and started to clear glasses.

'Do you want anything?' Henning asked.

It took a moment before Veronica replied: 'A glass of white wine, maybe.'

Henning got up, went over to the waiter and asked for a glass of Chablis, then walked calmly back to the table. Veronica had, in the meantime, taken off her leather jacket and scarf and produced some documents from her bag. When Henning had sat down again, she pushed them over towards him.

'What's this?' he asked.

'What does it look like?' she retorted.

It was a brochure for a luxury two-bedroom flat. Henning looked at the photographs of the ocean, the beach, and a new, empty apartment with a tiled bathroom and beautiful, clean surfaces. There was scribble in the margin: *TV in the corner, bar beside it, dartboard*?

'Is that Tore's handwriting?' he asked.

Veronica nodded.

Henning flicked through the rest of the brochure, almost wanting to buy the flat himself. Then he came to the page that contained more information about the residential complex: it was called Sports Park, and it was in Natal, Brazil.

He looked up at Veronica.

'Was this among Tore's things?'

She nodded again.

Henning thought about Rasmus Bjelland, the man who had told him about Tore's dubious business practices. He knew that Bjelland had gone bankrupt and had tried to start a new life in Natal, but after that, all trace of him had dried up. And how he'd got to know Tore in the first place was still a mystery to Henning.

But one thing he did know was that the Swedish League also seemed to like to set themselves up in Brazil – in Natal. In the very same residential complex, in fact.

Henning studied the cover again – the logo and name of the company, *Heavenly Homes*, were on the bottom right-hand corner. It didn't ring any bells.

'So, Tore was thinking of buying a flat in Natal,' Henning said, as much to himself as to Veronica. He put the brochure down.

'It certainly looks like that.'

Henning picked up his cup of coffee, but didn't take a drink.

'And he never spoke about it to you?'

Veronica shook her head. 'Tore loved giving me surprises; he probably planned to wake me up one morning and say, "We're going to Brazil in three hours" – I wouldn't have put it past him.'

'Do you know where he got the brochure?'

'I've got an idea,' she said, pulling the brochure back over and flicking to the back page. She pointed to a name: Charles Høisæther, with a contact number and email address.

The waiter came down with a glass of wine for Veronica, condensation already frosting the glass. The man tried to give Veronica a seductive smile, but she just thanked him, and reached out for the glass without even looking up.

'Charlie was one of Tore's childhood friends,' she explained, lifting her glass and nosing the wine. 'He's from Horten, too.'

'Do you know him?'

She shook her head. 'I know of him, but I've never met him in person.'

Veronica swirled the wine round in the glass a few times before taking a sip, then put it down.

'He was a complete hooligan when he was younger.'

'So was Tore,' Henning pointed out.

'Yes, but Charlie was worse. According to Tore, he had no boundaries. He once gave a boy with cerebral palsy a thrashing.'

She held her glass by the stem and swirled the wine around again a few times.

'Tore showed me some pictures once, of the two of them when they were young.' The memory made her smile. 'Charlie had a very distinctive face, the kind where you can just see that he's trouble. Do you know what I mean? You can see it in his eyes. And he had a slightly mischievous smile.'

Henning nodded.

'He had a really childish face, and it didn't change much over the years.' She took another sip of wine. 'But he got better as time went by; started working in property around the same time as Tore. And they did well, the two of them – until Charlie skipped the country at the end of the nineties.'

'Skipped?'

'Yes, I mean...' She shrugged with open hands. 'I don't know if he skipped the country in that sense, as in ran away. But anyway, it looks like that's where he ended up.' She tapped the brochure with her finger. 'And it looks like he did pretty well for himself.'

No doubt about that, Henning thought, looking at the picture on the front.

'And did they stay in touch?'

'I know that they met up whenever Charlie came back. Played a bit of poker, things like that. But whether it was any more than that, I don't know. I never asked about Tore's business friends.'

Henning thought hard.

'And talking of business,' Veronica continued, pulling her chair even closer to the table, 'there's something strange here. This,' she said, pointing at the brochure, 'was not the only thing Tore didn't tell me about. I always thought Tore was doing well. I mean, it's quite possible that he *was* doing well, but...' she looked around again '...I've come more or less straight from a meeting with my lawyer.' Veronica let out something akin to a sob. 'And it turns out Tore had nothing left.'

Henning's eyebrows shot up in surprise. 'Nothing?'

She shook her head. 'I found some magazines, racing, betting that sort of thing, among his things in the basement. I think maybe he had a gambling problem, but I can't say for sure. And I can't think of any other way he'd manage to spend all his money.'

'Hmm,' Henning grunted, mostly because he didn't know what to say.

He thought about the million-kroner reward Pulli had promised for information that could or would result in him being acquitted of murdering Jocke Brolenius. Where would he have got that, if he didn't even own the nails in his wall?

Veronica seemed to have read his thoughts, and said: 'But of course, we owned our flat and Tore had God knows how many motorbikes, so we would have managed to scrape together some money. But I'm pretty shocked, to be honest. I thought his finances were in better shape.'

Henning, though, wondered what this might mean. Did Pulli owe anyone money, for example? On the other hand, the flat in Natal seemed to indicate that he had capital, or at least thought that he did.

'I'll dig around a bit and see what I can find,' Henning said.

Veronica took another sip of wine.

'And I'd be really grateful if you carried on looking through Tore's things,' he continued. 'In case you can find anything more there.'

She put her glass down.

'I'll see what I can do,' she said. 'If you promise to be a bit more careful from now on.'

Henning looked at her for a few moments, and then answered: 'I'll do my best.'

20

Vestfold is a beautiful place, Nora thought, as she turned into Hans Heyerdahls vei in Åsgårdstrand. These small coastal towns were like pearls on a string; and it wasn't only Tønsberg and Tjøme, where people spent idyllic summers eating seafood, that had something to offer. Nora could perfectly well understand why Edvard Munch had chosen to spend practically every summer for twenty years or so in Åsgårdstrand. The two ferries that shuttled between Horten and Moss had just met halfway across the fjord in the fading evening light. The water was still, and there was only one other boat to be seen, sail folded. Further out in the fjord was Bastøy, the island where young delinquents were sent in the past and which was still used as a prison.

Nora parked in front of the house that Hugo Refsdal and Hedda Hellberg had bought some years ago. An apple tree with long branches full of fruit threw a shadow over the well-tended lawn that surrounded the house like a green carpet. The large windows made it easy to guess where the kitchen was.

A face appeared, Hugo Refsdal waved and then moved away.

Nora turned the engine off and barely had time to get out of the car before Refsdal was there to meet her on the small, slate step.

'So you managed to find it,' he said, and tried to smile.

'GPS,' Nora replied. 'How did taxi drivers ever manage before?'

'You might well ask.'

'What a fantastic house,' Nora said. 'And the view...'

'Thank you. We're very happy here. Come in.'

Refsdal showed her into a hallway with a couple of sizeable cupboards. She pulled off her boots and realised that her feet were very warm; she hoped that her socks wouldn't leave damp patches on the floor. Refsdal took her jacket and hung it in one of the cupboards.

'Thank you,' she said, with a smile.

Explosions and crashing sounds could be heard from the top of the stairs in front of them.

'Henrik has a school friend home with him today,' Refsdal explained. 'We're trying to keep things as normal as possible.'

Nora heard police sirens, skidding tyres, explosions, breaking glass, and loud, malevolent laughter. They walked down the hall towards the kitchen.

'Have you eaten?' he asked.

'No, I...'

'There's some pizza left, if you'd like it. I think it's still warm.'

Nora realised that she hadn't eaten since Spicy and was ravenous.

'I think I'll say yes, please, actually,' she replied.

'Sit yourself down,' he said, pointing to a large, black kitchen table with three candlesticks on it. 'I can warm it up a bit more, if you like.'

'Oh, there's no need,' she said. 'You have no idea how much cold pizza I've eaten in my life.'

Refsdal gave her a wan smile, opened the fridge, took out a bottle of Farris and got a couple of glasses. He then cut two large pieces of pizza, which he put on a plate and placed in front of her.

'Thank you.'

Nora took a bite of the first piece. A crisp base, warm enough and lots of tomato. Simply delicious. But then, everything tasted good at the moment; she could eat anything.

When she had swallowed the first mouthful, she looked at him, waiting for him to tell her what he'd discovered.

'I did as you said,' he started. 'I looked at Hedda's computer again, and I found some searches she made about a week before she was supposed to go to Italy. She had deleted the searches from her log.'

Nora took another bite.

'What was she looking for?' she asked, with her mouth full – it sounded like she was speaking into a cushion. Embarrassed, she put the piece of pizza down on the plate.

'A Swedish man called Daniel Schyman,' he said, glancing at her. 'Do you know who that is?'

The name sounded familiar, but Nora couldn't place him.

Refsdal continued: 'He was shot and killed in his own forest about four or five weeks ago. About the same time that Hedda disappeared.'

Nora nodded, recalling that for quite some time the Swedish online newspapers had been full of articles about Daniel Schyman. It was a while since she had seen any updates on the investigation, but she knew that he had been killed when he was out hunting early one morning. As far as she could remember, the police had not arrested anyone.

'Maybe she was interested in the case,' Nora suggested.

Refsdal shook his head. 'Hedda was doing searches *before* he was killed.'

Nora wrinkled her nose. 'What did she look up?'

'She had gathered various bits of information about him: where he lived, what he did. But he was nearly seventy, so I can't for the life of me understand why she was interested in him.'

Nora didn't know what to say. This put things in a whole new light, and she almost couldn't wait to get back to a computer, so she could find out more about the Schyman case.

She took another mouthful of pizza.

'There was something else as well,' he continued. 'Hedda had looked up information about an address in Tønsberg.'

Nora chewed quickly and swallowed too fast – it hurt her throat.

'Which address?' she asked, as she pulled a face.

'Brages vei 18. I have no idea why; I certainly don't know the people who live there, and can't remember that we've ever had anything to do with them.'

Nora drank some Farris. 'What are they called?' she asked.

'Torill and Jens Holmboe.'

She wiped her mouth as discreetly as possible. 'Have you spoken to them?'

He shook his head. 'It's only a few hours since I discovered all this. I wanted to talk to you about it first.'

'Hmm,' said Nora.

She sat staring at the view as though hypnotised, then she said: 'We'll have to tell the police about this.'

Refsdal didn't react. Instead, he went over to the kitchen worktop, folded up a newspaper and put it on a pile by a bowl containing almost black bananas. He put a dirty milk glass in the dishwasher and threw a half-eaten pizza slice into a green bag in the cupboard under the sink.

'Has Cato Løken, the police inspector, phoned you?' Nora asked.

Refsdal turned towards her. 'No.'

She told him about the article she was planning for the paper for the next day, without going into too much detail, and didn't mention her own suspicions or Georg's two-hour visit to the summer house.

Refsdal's reaction was exactly what Nora had expected it would be; first silence, then anger, then a barrage of questions that all amounted to the same thing: why had Hedda gone back? Who had collected her at the station? He asked Nora whether she knew anything about the car, what the person looked like, where the car went. Nora kept her answers as vague as possible.

Refsdal's interrogation was interrupted by the sound of footsteps running downstairs. Seconds later, a little boy came sliding into the kitchen on his stocking soles and asked, before he noticed that his father had a guest, if he and Mikkel could watch *Harry Potter* three.

Refsdal gave a lame smile and looked at the clock.

'OK,' he said. 'But you can't watch the whole thing – that would take too long. Mikkel's mum will be here to collect him soon.'

'Yeeess,' the boy said, punching the air, then immediately disappeared, his feet pounding on the stairs. Refsdal stood in silence. Then he turned around and grabbed a cloth that was lying beside the sink; he held it under the tap and then wrung it out.

'What a lovely boy you've got,' Nora said.

Refsdal nodded, without turning around.

Then he stood and rubbed and rubbed the same spot on the work surface.

21

Henning said goodbye to Veronica outside the Underwater Pub, and looked around as he tried to decide whether to walk straight home – which would take him about twelve or thirteen minutes, if he went by Telthusbakken – or if he should go the long way round through the centre of town. He plumped for the latter, as he needed to clear his head. He always thought best when he was doing something other than thinking about what he needed to think about.

The pavements were full of people on their way to or from St Hanshaugen; it was a nice evening, though there was still a slight chill in the air, and the clouds had cleared to reveal a pale-blue sky. There was something refreshing about seeing dry streets again.

Henning noticed that he was starting to feel better. His head and hip didn't hurt as much, but every time he took a deep breath, he felt it in his ribs. Walking on asphalt was perhaps not the best medicine, though, and by the time he got to Stortorget, he was getting tired. The idea of walking all the way home was no longer tempting, so he got on a number 11 tram, sat down and leaned his head against the window as he watched the evening traffic in slow motion.

He thought about Nora, and about Iver. At some point he would have to talk to them both, but not this evening. Or tomorrow. He didn't know what to say to either of them. He hadn't spoken to Iver at all since he'd gone on leave.

A man who was sitting further back in the tram, and on the opposite side from Henning, quickly looked away when Henning caught his eye. There was something familiar about him. Hadn't he been standing on the other side of the road when Henning said goodbye to Veronica?

It looked like the same person. He'd stood there, staring in their direction, smoking furiously.

A few seconds later, he met Henning's eyes again. But again, he pretended that he wasn't looking at Henning, and turned his gaze to the window, looking at the evening outside.

The man was small and slim, with dark clothes; he had on a black baseball cap, and a leather jacket with a grey hoodie underneath. He had his hands in the jacket pockets. The tram glided past Oslo Central Station, the shops in Storgata, on past Brugata, where people of all ages and colours stood side by side waiting for a bus or tram. Henning acted as though he was watching what was going on outside, whereas in fact he was watching the reflection of the man in the window. He stayed where he was all the way up to Grünerløkka, looking over at Henning every now and then.

The man was possibly in his late thirties, and looked like he might be Eastern European. Henning wondered if it was perhaps the scars on his face that had made the man curious. In which case, he wouldn't be the first.

But wasn't it a bit odd that he'd been up at St Hanshaugen, then apparently taken the same route as Henning down to the centre, and back up to Grünerløkka, again?

Henning got off at Olaf Ryes plass, which was buzzing with people. Some were still sitting outside under the awning at Kaffebrenneriet, illuminated by the light from the window of the bookshop next door. Henning kept his pace leisurely as he tried to find a window or surface that could act as a mirror. The sign outside Brocante proved perfect.

The man in the hoodie had also got off and was following Henning about fifteen or twenty metres behind.

Henning looked right, then left, before crossing the road. He glanced in the man's direction, without looking directly at him, but could see that he, too, had moved out into the road, and was crossing to the other side. Henning got out his mobile phone and tapped the camera function, then turned the phone and held it by his side as he walked, pressing the screen and hoping that his finger was hitting the camera button and that the photographs would not be too grainy. He might not even get a picture of the man, but it was worth a try.

Henning popped into the supermarket and stood behind some shelves to see if the man would follow. He didn't; not after one, then two minutes. Henning went back outside.

The man was nowhere to be seen.

Henning hurried home, and looked at the photographs he had taken. He'd actually done alright: it was possible to get a fair impression of the man's face. He downloaded the pictures onto his computer and looked at them in more detail.

The man wasn't particularly tall; he had a two-day growth of beard and deep bags under his eyes. Henning was quite certain that he had never seen him before.

He stood up, went over to the door and looked out through the peephole. There was no one there. But he still made sure that the door was locked before he sat back down to study the man on the screen.

Who are you? he wondered. *And why are you following me?*

Nora thought about Hedda and Daniel Schyman as she drove back to Oslo. Hugo Refsdal wasn't a hundred percent sure that they hadn't known each other. He had only been with Hedda for seven years, but she had certainly never mentioned his name in that time. Why would she suddenly look up all this information about him on the internet and then delete her searches?

When she got back to her flat, the first thing Nora did was to sit down with her computer and open the page for the Swedish newspaper *Aftonbladet*. She wrote Daniel Schyman in the search field; there were plenty of hits. It didn't take long to establish that a full murder investigation was still going strong.

Schyman had been found on the morning of 13 August; he'd been shot with a high-calibre weapon, the sort used for hunting. The police didn't think it was an accident. The shot was to the middle of his chest and it had not taken long for him to die.

Two of Schyman's friends were quoted as saying that he was someone who enjoyed his own company; but he was as kind as they come, and they could not believe that anyone would want to kill him. His death remained a mystery.

Hugo Refsdal had taken a screenshot of the log files that Hedda had deleted and had sent them to Nora. She saw that Hedda had looked for information about the forest that Schyman owned, among other things, and had even found a detailed map of the area. She had also found his address.

But what about Brages vei 18 in Tønsberg?

Hedda had typed the address plus 'property history' into Google; but she'd also added her own surname and searched under 'Brages vei 18 Tønsberg sold', which led to a property database. Nora did the same and could see that Jens and Torill Holmboe had bought the property in 2001 for 1,325,000 kroner. There were several other transfers of ownership but the names were not listed. According to Hugo Refsdal, Hedda had never mentioned the Holmboes either, so it had to be the address itself that interested her.

Nora's mobile phone beeped. She reached over for it. Iver had sent her a text message.

Nora took a deep breath before she opened it.

Have you told Henning about the baby?

Nora made an exasperated sound. Not a word about how she was. She just wrote back: *Yes*. A few seconds later, there was another beep.

How did he take it?

Why do you care about that, Nora wanted to ask, and not about me or us? But she didn't, she just didn't answer. If he really wanted to know, he could call either her or Henning. But he probably wouldn't dare do either. Probably hadn't got his head round it yet.

Nora stood up, went into the living room and lit the candle on the windowsill. She sat down heavily on the rocking chair, squeezing the ball in one hand and stroking her belly with the other. Her thoughts turned to Hedda again, and her behaviour in the period before she disappeared. Nora was overcome by a sense of unease. She didn't like the way things were developing.

Not at all.

22

Henning couldn't remember putting his head down on the kitchen table, but he must have done at some point during the night, as that was where he woke up. His cheek was pressed flat, and it felt like his jaw was dislocated – a sensation that made him think of Pontus's punches. The memory was reinforced by the taste in his mouth: dust and metal.

Henning sat up slowly. His eyes were dry and out of focus and it took a few minutes for his head to clear. He stood up, turned on the kettle, went to the toilet, washed his hands and face – carefully – but he wasn't able to think until he'd had some coffee. So he spooned out some instant, poured in some water, a drop of milk from the fridge and then sat down again at the kitchen table where he waited for the day to take hold.

The evening before, Henning had found out that Charles Høisæther was the sole trader in a company called Høisæther Property, which had not earned a single kroner since the end of the nineties. The cash flow had been pretty good up until then, so it was difficult to understand why it had dried up. Whatever the reason, Høisæther had kept a low profile in Norway. Henning had not managed to find even one newspaper article about him on the internet.

Henning tried to call the contact number that was on the brochure Veronica had given him, but was met with a recording telling him that the number was no longer in use. He had tried to send an email to the address provided, to ask if Charlie could spare him a few minutes, but hadn't received a reply yet. He had also rung a number he found on the *Heavenly Houses* website, the company that managed the properties down there in Brazil. He hadn't had much joy there either; there was only an answer machine.

Henning finished his coffee, and realised he was feeling hungry. There wasn't much in the fridge, so he'd have to go out. He called Geir Grønningen as he walked down the stairs.

'Talk about flies and shit,' Grønningen said.

'Have you ever been to Brazil?' Henning asked him. The sharp light outside hurt his eyes.

'Brazil?' Grønningen repeated. 'No. What makes you ask?'

'Did Tore ever talk to you about it?' Henning continued. 'Or, more specifically, Natal?'

'Um, no, don't think so.'

Henning walked past a green rubbish bin. The rank smell of old prawns and cat piss filled his nose.

'So you didn't know that Tore was possibly thinking about buying a flat there?'

There was a short pause. Then: 'In Brazil?'

Henning stepped out onto the street and looked both ways; no sign of the man who might or might not have been following him the evening before.

'I thought maybe you'd want to join him there,' he suggested, and started to cross the road.

'Me? I don't earn ... Seriously, was Tore thinking about moving to Brazil?'

Henning jumped over a puddle and passed in front of Mr Tang's restaurant.

'There are things to indicate he was at least considering it,' Henning said, and looked up Markveien.

Grønningen had nothing more to say on the matter.

'What about Charlie Høisæther, do you know anything about the man?'

'Charlie, yeah, I know him well. What about him?'

A car came racing towards Henning. He darted over to the other side of the road, where Bobby, as always, had his kiosk open.

'How do you know him?'

'Well, he was one of Tore's mates. From way back. Met him here and there.'

Henning passed a car that was parked half on the pavement. There was a picture of a big pizza and a telephone number fixed to one of the side windows.

'What was your impression of him?'

'Of Charlie?' Grønningen yawned. 'Well, he was alright. A bit cocky, maybe. But I don't think him and Tore got on so well at the end.'

Henning stopped abruptly, to avoid walking through some dog shit.

'Why not?' he asked, taking a step to one side.

'Think they fell out about something.'

'Do you know about what?'

'Not a Scooby. Tore didn't want to talk about it. But I kind of had an idea. There was talk about some poker game, so I asked if that meant that Charlie was home. He was, but he wasn't coming to the game, Tore said. He sounded kind of angry, if you know what I mean. Like they'd had an argument.'

Interesting, Henning thought.

'These poker games, did you go, too?' he asked.

'Me?' Grønningen exclaimed. 'Haven't got the nerves for it, me. Even the one-armed bandit on the Denmark ferry makes me anxious.'

A taxi with a series of small dents in the side was driving towards him; it didn't slow down for the speed bumps and the suspension groaned as it hit them.

'So you didn't know that Tore had a problem with gambling?'

Grønningen was hesitant. 'I know that he liked putting money on the horses and things like that, and that he won every now and then. But not much more than that, really.'

'Right,' Henning said, and jumped over another puddle. He was getting close to the tram lines on Thorvald Meyers gate, and the noise was increasing.

'Cheers, Geir. That was all I wanted to know. Speak again.'

'No doubt.'

◉

Charlie Høisæther was becoming more and more interesting, Henning thought, as he finished the call. He wanted to talk to him, hear his voice – preferably meet him face to face.

Henning went into Sultan and bought some Turkish bread, cherry tomatoes, a bunch of bananas and carrots, as well as a small piece of Parmesan cheese. Back out on the street, he did the same as before: looked from side to side, scanning the crowds moving up and down the pavements.

He fixed on a man leaning up against the wall outside an optician's on the other side of the street. To all intents and purposes, he was simply waiting for someone.

It was him.

The same man.

Henning had no doubt; he wore the same baseball cap, the same hoodie. Henning stood and stared at him. The man noticed Henning, but looked past him, down Thorvald Meyers gate and back again.

Henning mulled over the options. It didn't take him long to make a decision.

He started to walk straight towards the man.

The man promptly pushed himself away from the wall, and just then a tram came clattering towards Henning and the driver sounded the horn. Henning jumped back and had to wait for the long, clumsy, blue-and-white beast to snake its way to Birkelund before he could attempt to cross the road. But the tram was followed by lots of cars, so when he eventually reached the other side, all he saw was the man disappearing round the corner onto Markveien. He was walking fast.

Henning knew that he wouldn't be able to catch up with him. Not with his damaged hips and legs.

'Damn,' he muttered to himself, and hurried home.

◉

Back in the flat, he sat down at the computer and sent another email to Atle Abelsen, attaching the photographs of the mystery-man he had taken the evening before. He hoped that Abelsen, in return for a bottle of Calvados, might be able to find out who he was. It was clear now that he was watching Henning; and, in fact, Henning wasn't that surprised by this. What he was more concerned about was just how long he had been following him, and what he might do next.

Henning wondered whether he should finally try, six months after moving into the flat, to use the gas oven, but he decided instead to have three slices of Turkish bread with butter and banana, which he then ate while he pondered how to deal with the situation. He couldn't be any more careful than he was already, so what should be his next step?

Finding the answers to his questions was becoming a matter of urgency.

23

Nora drove straight back down to Tønsberg the next day. She didn't need to go into the office to ask for permission – the way the case was developing, it went without saying she'd get it.

A long night with little sleep had left her with a heavy body and a dull mind, but she forced herself to stay awake by focusing on what she had to do. What she *should* do. The most obvious thing would be to ring Detective Inspector Cato Løken and arrange a meeting, but she didn't want to do that yet. There were still several people in the family that she wanted to speak to first. She hoped, in the meantime, that there was a natural connection between Hedda and Daniel Schyman, and that an outsider like Hugo Refsdal couldn't possibly know all the links in a family as large as the Hellbergs.

Before going into the centre of Tønsberg, Nora tried to ring Hedda's brother, Patrik, again. He surprised her by answering after the first ring. Nora pulled in at a bus stop. As she introduced herself, she took her pen and pad out of her bag.

'Hello,' he said.

His manner was terse and dismissive. She had the distinct impression that Patrik had been avoiding her until now, and had finally decided to answer the phone so she would stop harassing him.

He promptly confirmed her theory.

'I know why you're calling and I have nothing to say,' he snapped.

'Really?'

'I don't know where Hedda is and I have no idea why she has disappeared. OK?'

Nora could tell he was about to hang up. 'Just a couple of quick questions, if I may,' she said.

Patrik breathed heavily into the receiver. 'I've got a long day ahead. What do you want to know?'

Nora could hear the sound of traffic in the background and a door opening and closing. Then an engine starting; even over the phone, the deep bass of the engine told her that it was a car with plenty of horsepower.

'Have you seen today's *Aftenposten*? Read about the most recent development?' Nora pulled the earpieces out of her bag and attached them to the phone.

'Yes.'

She pressed the earpieces in and put the mobile down on the centre console. 'And do you have any comments?'

'Any *comments*?'

Nora steadied the notepad with one hand and held her pen ready in the other. 'Yes.'

'No, I have no *comment*. And what did you think I might say – that I was surprised? Frightened?'

Nora didn't answer. She heard him snort at the other end.

'Was that all?' Patrik asked. 'I'm late as it is.'

'Have you been out to your father's summer house recently?'

There was silence.

'The boat season's almost over,' he then said.

'So you're saying no.'

'Yes. I'm saying no.'

Nora checked in the rear-view mirror that a bus wasn't coming. 'Do you know if Hedda has been there?'

'No.'

A car sped past. Nora watched it until it was out of sight.

'What sort of relationship did Hedda have with Georg?'

The question just popped out; Nora immediately regretted asking it.

There was another silence.

'Your cousin, that is,' Nora added, to prompt him.

'Why do you ask?'

'I was just wondering. From what I've heard, Hedda spent a fair amount of time with him when they were younger—'

Patrik interrupted her. 'Keep Georg out of this.'

Nora raised an eyebrow. 'Why?'

Another silence. Then: 'I don't want to say anything about Georg.'

Nora felt a stirring. 'You don't have a particularly good relationship with your cousin, I take it?'

Silence.

'No comment,' he said, finally.

I see, Nora thought to herself. People who are not used to talking to the media seldom know that saying no comment sometimes speaks volumes.

Patrik took another deep breath. 'Was there anything else? As I said, I'm late already.'

'Yes. Do you know who Daniel Schyman is?'

Yet again, there was a few seconds of silence.

'No,' he said. Then he hung up.

Nora decided to drive out to the summer house again. Everyone was presumably at work now, so she could poke around out there in peace for a while. This time she parked further back down the road and walked the last few hundred metres through the woods towards the property. Even though she was surrounded by trees, she felt a stiff wind blowing in off the sea and pulled up her collar. The smell of the forest enveloped her.

When she got to the wrought-iron gate, she looked around at the trees closest to her. The last time she was there, she'd felt as though someone was watching her from between the trunks. There wasn't a sound this time.

Nora walked along the fence as she thought about what to do. The fence was too high to climb over. She wasn't tall and would need a trampoline to jump it.

It didn't take long before she spotted a branch that reached out towards the fence. Nora was still fairly slim, and the branch looked solid; it might take her weight. Worth a try, she said to herself. She went over to the tree, remembering how much she used to love climbing trees with her older sister: the feeling of the bark under her hands, which scratched and left scabs that she could pick at later when she was in bed. She felt the same joy again as she grabbed hold of the nearest branch. It was an adventure every time. How high would she get? How high did she dare go?

She didn't have to climb higher than a couple of metres before she was up on the branch. It bounced under her feet like a diving board. She held onto the trunk as she slowly inched her way out along it. The fence was about six or seven centimetres thick.

She looked down, then straight ahead, tried to muster the courage she'd had when she did gymnastics as a kid. At her best, she'd been able to do a cartwheel on a beam that was narrower than her own feet. And even though it was long ago now, she reckoned she should be able to land on the fence and still keep her balance. All it required was concentration. She had to look straight ahead. Arms out.

When she jumped, the branch protested, but didn't break. Nora aimed for the fence, touched it with both feet, but the momentum she had from the jump carried her on over the fence. Her knees jarred as she hit the ground, but she managed to roll forwards relatively softly. At least she was able to remember how to do that.

'You idiot,' she said aloud, as she brushed the damp leaves and grass from her trousers. There were wet patches on her jacket as well. And some mud on her boots and knees. She stood up straight and looked around again. She could see the summer house through the trees.

It was a nice, wooded area. There was enough space around the trees for the light to filter down. The trees were mainly spruce, but she saw some juniper bushes dotted around, and a few pine and aspen trees.

What do you think you're going to find in here? she asked herself.

Hedda, of course. She was here; that was why Georg had come here the day before. Was he holding her prisoner? Had the article in the paper made him nervous? Had he been trying to hide her body better?

Nora moved as quietly as she could. If there was anyone here, she didn't want to alarm them. There were cameras above the gate, but they were pointing at the road outside. Nora made her way to the garage and looked around the corner. No cameras on the front of the house. Grey water was washing heavily against the jetty where a boat called *La Dolce Vita* was moored. Nora walked over to it.

This was a fantastic place.

Close to the jetty and boathouse, a big lawn ran down towards the water. There were two annexes, both the size of a normal home, and a big terrace outside the main house with outdoor furniture that was very definitely not bought at IKEA. There was also a fireplace, and gas canisters beside two enormous, covered barbecues, a cobbled path with fine grass between the stones. Everything was well tended.

Nora approached the house. The curtains were open. She had guessed they would be drawn, as the place was not in use at this time of year. Or perhaps Georg had forgotten to close them again when he was here the day before?

She stepped onto the terrace, looking up at the building. There were two smaller windows next to each other – presumably a bedroom – and a glass door. She peered in through the windows first: in fact, it was a study, with a desk and shelves of files, plus cabinets and lamps. There was a neatly made bed in the next room, with paintings on the wall and rugs on the floor.

She moved over to the door, cupped her hands and, putting them to the glass, looked inside. There was a big fireplace and a TV area the size of a small flat; the walls were lined with bookshelves; and there was a solid wooden dining table and chairs.

But several of the chairs weren't in their places around the table. They had been pushed out, and there were scratch marks on the slate floor; like thin lines drawn with chalk. The table was at an angle as well, and the rug underneath it was crumpled. Nora now noticed that some of the books were sticking out more than others, as though someone had taken them from the shelves and then put them back in a hurry.

Then she froze. A shard of glass was lying under the table.

And suddenly it was there again, the feeling that someone was watching her.

Nora turned around and looked down towards the fjord. There were no boats on the water, no faces in the annex windows. And the other side of the water was too far away to see anyone.

The next moment, something banged above her.

Nora jumped, not knowing what it was. But when she turned and looked up at the wall above her, she saw a splintered notch. A bullet hole. And she had no sooner turned round again, when there was another loud bang.

24

The small driftwood cupboard was full of stuff that Henning had kept – mostly receipts he would never actually need, Post-it notes, pens, brochures, menus. He rummaged around until he found the tape recorder he'd used until everyone starting using smartphones.

He'd found his old cassettes among all the junk that 123News had got rid of when they refurbished the editorial offices, in the period when Henning was unfit for work. On one of them he'd found the interview he'd done with Rasmus Bjelland at Huk, one day in autumn 2007.

At the time, Bjelland was a desperate man. All the crooks living in Natal in Brazil, who had been hauled in by the police down there – for laundering drugs money and other illegal activities – thought that Bjelland had been a police informer. With a price on his head, Bjelland had gone to ground. There were even rumours that he had approached Kripos, the Norwegian criminal investigation service, to ask for a new identity. Henning had managed to track him down, though, through a former girlfriend Bjelland couldn't quite manage to let go. Henning had sent a message saying that, if Bjelland wanted to talk about the case, he was happy to provide a channel. A few weeks later, the former girlfriend had contacted Henning. Rasmus had agreed to meet him at Huk.

There, he swore his innocence and said that he had nothing to do with the police operation. At the time, Henning had been most interested in the accusations against Bjelland, which was what he later wrote about. Now, though, he remembered that during the course of their interview, Bjelland had said something about Tore Pulli.

Henning sat down at the kitchen table with a glass of water, put the cassette with the Bjelland interview into the machine and pressed play, only to realise it was at the end of the interview and he had to rewind it. The interview hadn't been digitalised, so it was a slow process, and not easy to find the start. But he got there eventually.

'Thank you for agreeing to meet me.'

'You're welcome.'

Henning could hear the sound of seagulls swooping and chattering in the background.

'You're not an easy man to get hold of,' Henning said.

'For good reason.'

'Are you scared?'

'You would be, too, if you knew what I know.'

'And what do you know?' Henning smiled at his own question. Too direct, too early.

'If I tell you, they might kill you.'

'So, what you're saying, is that I could be killed simply for talking to you. When the interview is published, these people will be wondering what else you might have told me.'

'You're here at your own risk.'

'I'm fully aware of that. So why not tell me everything? Why not share the burden?'

'Because...' Bjelland paused for a beat before he continued. 'Because I don't know you. For all I know, you might be on their payroll.'

'If you really believed that, Bjelland, you would never have come. I'm pretty sure you'll have checked me out beforehand.'

Henning remembered that Bjelland had studied him hard for some time, before a smile started to pull at his lips.

'Yeah, you're right. I know you're a good guy, on paper at least. You've written a lot of good articles. But this is heavy shit, and I know that the more I say, the greater the chances are that I'll be killed.'

'OK, stay in your comfort zone and tell me what you can. Give me your story.'

Bjelland then told him about all the years he'd worked as a carpenter.

The business had gone well for a long time, but then he started to have problems with certain clients. He was fairly vague about why, but when he was offered the opportunity to make a fresh start in Brazil, he grabbed it greedily with both hands. He didn't want to discuss the rumours about him being an informer, but he assured Henning that there was no truth in them.

They talked about Brazil for a long time: how he had managed to escape after the police operation in May; about his wife, Mariana, who he'd had to leave behind, or, to be more precise, he'd sent to an unknown address; about how much he missed her.

'But what do you know that makes you so dangerous to these people?'

Bjelland had taken a deep breath and looked around. Throughout the interview he had always been on his guard, checking his surroundings, and looking away whenever anyone was in the vicinity; he was even wary of women with prams.

'D'you know who Tore Pulli is?' And before Henning could even answer, he continued: 'Of course you do, everyone does. But what most people don't know is that he still has close links with people in the criminal underworld. And that he makes his money through them.'

'Them?'

'Yes...' Bjelland had stopped talking at this point and looked down.

'In what way?'

'You're a journalist, you can find that out for yourself.'

'It would be far quicker if you just told me.'

'Put it this way: Tore has never worried about climbing over corpses to get what he wants.'

'For example?'

Bjelland had smiled. 'Go back to the nineties,' he had said. 'Have a look at his acquisitions, what he was selling. You'll find some pretty dodgy things there if you're prepared to dig a bit.'

Henning then tried to get him to elaborate, but Bjelland countered every attempt. In the end, Henning gave up.

The recording was almost finished. They started to talk about what Bjelland would do next.

'As little as possible,' he said. 'I'm going to lie as low as I can.'

Then they both said their thanks and goodbyes and Bjelland left.

Henning stopped the cassette and sat thinking. The best thing would be if he could find Bjelland again, get him to say more and give concrete examples. But he knew that would be difficult. It was unlikely that Bjelland was still in touch with his former girlfriend, so tracking him down would probably take a lot of time as well.

Go back to the nineties.

Henning had tried this before, but there were no records of the acquisitions and sales companies had made. It was only possible the other way round – if you knew the specific buildings and property registration numbers, as you could then look up the property history. But to go that far back, without knowing which properties you were looking for...

Henning had done some spot checks, without uncovering any irregularities. Bjelland's claim that Tore would happily climb over corpses to get what he wanted was not exactly a surprise, but it was confirmation that the whole business was sinister. And it wasn't hard to understand why Tore wanted to avoid any information getting out.

Henning tried to call Charlie Høisæther again, with the same result as before. He took a drink of water and pondered what to do next. After a while, he stood up and went to put on his shoes and jacket.

Why not? he said to himself. *It's worth a try.*

25

Nora shielded her head with her hands, threw herself down on the ground and crawled behind one of the barbecues. Her heart was in her mouth, the hairs were standing up on her arms and her breathing was shallow as she listened for footsteps.

You have to get away from here, she thought. The person who had fired the gun could easily find her hiding place and shoot her point blank; or they might aim at the gas canister beside her and the explosion would finish her off.

But she heard nothing.

Nora didn't dare lift her head to see if there was anyone there. Instead, she fumbled to get her mobile phone out of her bag, shakily tapped in three numbers, put the phone to her ear, and waited for an answer.

It was quick: 'Emergency services, how can I help you?'

Nora stammered and stuttered, but she managed to introduce herself, say where she was and what had happened.

'Is the person who shot at you still there?'

'I–I don't know,' Nora whispered.

'Can you get to somewhere safe?'

She tried to look around, but the barbecue and trees and walls made it difficult.

'I don't think so,' she said.

'OK, the police are on their way. Just stay where you are and stay on the phone. Tell me what you can see and if anything happens.'

Nora closed her eyes, finding it almost impossible to breathe.

'Are you there?'

'Yes, I'm here,' she whispered and tried to make herself as small as possible. She still couldn't hear any footsteps. But what she did hear was a car starting up in the distance, then accelerating away from the place.

'I think he might have gone,' she stammered.

'OK, just stay where you are until we get there.'

Nora did as she was told. She felt hot and cold at the same time, and realised she was shaking uncontrollably. She looked over at the wall of the house, at the result of the two bullets that had sung over her head. If the intention had been to kill her, whoever fired couldn't be a particularly good shot. The holes were high up on the wall.

Nora tried to work out who might know that she was out here. No one. She hadn't told anyone. So had she surprised someone?

A few minutes later she heard sirens – wails becoming louder and louder. She waited a bit longer, then stood up warily, keeping her eyes on the trees from where the shots had been fired, but she was increasingly certain that she was now alone. Her legs were numb, but her breathing was now more regular and she had the shaking under control. Soon, the sirens were so close that the birds took flight.

And yet she started when the first policeman appeared by the garage. He was armed. A voice behind him shouted, '*Clear.*' Similar messages were called out all around her, and not long after there were people everywhere. Nora was immediately guided round to the other side of the house. Outside the gate, open now, its chain broken, was a row of police cars, flashing blue. And even though it was the middle of the day, the light they gave off was powerful.

A man in civilian clothes, who she guessed was in charge, came over to her.

'Are you OK?'

'I think so,' Nora said. Her throat was dry.

The man held out his hand.

'Cato Løken,' he said. 'We spoke on the phone yesterday.'

'Nora Klemetsen.'

Giving a fleeting smile, she studied the man in front of her. His stomach bulged over his belt like a pillow. His hair was carefully combed over a balding crown. Folds of skin trembled under his chin, where a dull razorblade had left thin cuts. Nora reckoned he must be in his early fifties.

'So, this is what you actually look like,' he said.

Nora pulled her jacket tighter. 'What do you mean?'

'Well, I just ... you look a bit different from your picture in the paper.'

'Oh right,' Nora smiled.

But she was quickly serious again. Uniformed policemen were walking back and forth around them. She could hear the crackling of radios nearby, voices, messages she couldn't quite make out.

'Did you see who shot at you?' Løken asked.

Nora shook her head. 'It all happened so fast,' she said.

An officer shouted for another officer called Trond.

'What were you doing out here?' Løken asked.

It was only then that it dawned on Nora that she was trespassing, and that the people who owned the place would now find out. And might well report her. Nora decided to play an open hand all the same; she couldn't think of any other tactic. So she told him about her suspicions – that she had followed Georg Hellberg out here the day before, because he owned a black BMW cabriolet.

'So you thought you might find Hedda?'

'Yes. Or ... I don't know. I think, mainly, I was curious.'

'And you think that Georg has something to do with Hedda's disappearance?'

Nora thought for a moment before nodding. 'This place is definitely important in some way or other,' she said.

Nora also told him about what she had seen inside the house: the scratches on the floor, the shard of glass under the table. The policeman nodded as he took a *snus* tin from his pocket, and packed two pouches up under his lip.

They stood there and looked around. The patrols were getting ready to leave. Løken waved one of the officers over, then took a step away from Nora. They stood whispering for a few seconds, before Løken came back.

'The person who shot at you probably got in through a hole in the fence at the back, here,' he told her. 'There are fresh tyre tracks.' He pointed into the forest, towards the road.

Nora remembered the track that she had seen the day before, in approximately the same place.

'But perhaps we can talk more about this down at the station,' Løken added.

'Just one thing,' Nora said, taking a step closer. 'Do you know what calibre it was?'

Løken nodded. 'A .308 rifle,' he said. 'Quite powerful. Generally used by hunters.'

26

Nora drove behind Cato Løken into the centre of Tønsberg. She'd refused his offer of a lift, insisting she could drive herself; she needed some time to digest what had just happened.

She thought about Daniel Schyman, who had been shot and killed by someone who could hunt; and about herself – she'd been shot at with a similar weapon, perhaps even the same one. And not only that, the attack had happened at a place that played a central role in Hedda Hellberg's family.

Coincidence?

Nora had worked with crime-related stories for long enough to know that coincidences were rare; she had learned instead to look for connections. In addition, the fact that the shooter had been so wide of the mark led her to think that killing her was not their intention; they just meant to frighten her.

Well, congratulations, she thought. *You succeeded, whoever you are.*

But it still raised a couple of important questions: was the idea to frighten her off the case? Or to stop her from poking around at Hulebakk?

Whatever the motive was, it wasn't particularly well considered. Whoever it was must surely have realised that she would call the police, and that they would come out to investigate. Shooting at her had just drawn more attention to the place.

Nora thought about Hedda's internet searches: the map she'd studied, the area where Schyman had been killed, the gun he'd been shot with. There was one rather sinister explanation: perhaps it was

Hedda who'd fired the shots. Which would explain why she had missed by about half a metre. She didn't want to kill her old friend.

But then, why was she at the Hellberg family's summer house? And why hadn't she given any signs of life for nearly five weeks?

Nora parked behind Løken in a gloomy street, overshadowed by the redbrick building that housed the main police station. They took the lift up to the second floor, where Cato Løken had his office. He indicated that she should take a seat, and then disappeared through the door.

Nora looked around. A messy desk, dusty plants in flowerpots; an overflowing paper basket, a veritable chaos of files and documents. And on the walls, a rather crude picture, clearly painted using a worn brush on curling paper – a winter landscape with mountains in the background – and a large map of Vestfold County. It was a room that would always smell the same, no matter how much you aired it. A trace of stale tobacco, a hint of Løken's leather jacket, spices from many a takeaway eaten when working late.

Løken returned with two steaming cups of coffee. He gave one to Nora. She said thank you and smiled.

When Løken sat down at his desk, his chair rocked and moaned for a few seconds before falling silent. The policeman blew on the contents of his cup, then took a cautious sip.

'So,' he said. 'What do you make of all of this?'

Nora clasped her hands around the cup. She had stopped trembling, but it was good to feel the heat of the coffee.

Nora crossed her legs. 'Can I ask you something first?' Løken opened his hand to indicate she should go ahead.

'Was it Georg Hellberg who picked Hedda up at Skoppum Station?'

The policeman hesitated a moment before saying: 'I'm afraid I can't comment on that.'

'But I know that Georg was out at the family place yesterday after-noon,' Nora said. 'I've no idea what he was doing, and no one tends to go there at this time of year. I've had that confirmed by one of Hedda's family.'

She took a sip of coffee. It burned her lips.

'If it was Georg who picked her up,' she continued, 'and she hasn't been seen since, it's possible that he drove her there – somewhere she wouldn't be disturbed this late in the autumn.'

She watched him closely for any signs of confirmation. There was none.

'Something's going on out there,' she insisted.

Løken put his hand into his jacket pocket and took out his *snus*. Said nothing.

'Have you checked his phone log?' Nora asked. 'His toll tag for that day?'

Løken looked at her for a long time, measuring her up, assessing her.

'Listen, Nora. We're only at the start of this investigation, which would never have been reopened if you hadn't shaken it to life again. We concluded that it was suicide; the family thought it was suicide; but now we're not so sure any more, especially after what happened to you out at Hulebakk. You can quote me on that. But, of course, I can't comment on the ongoing investigation, I'm sure you understand that. So, in terms of our work, it would not be particularly helpful if you were to speculate or write about your own conclusions in the paper.'

'I've never done that, and I never will, either.'

'But what you *can* write, is that we're following up some new leads, and several of them are of interest.' He lifted the cup to his mouth.

Nora sighed. His statement was far too standard and bland, and would hardly raise an eyebrow on the news desk or among the readership.

There was a thoughtful silence. Nora decided to tell the policeman what she knew about Daniel Schyman and Hedda's internet searches. By the time she finished, Løken was sitting up straight, eyes wide open.

'Hedda really did that?'

Nora nodded. 'I haven't spoken to everyone in the Hellberg family yet, so I don't know if there's a natural explanation for her sudden interest in a retired Swede. But so far I haven't found any link between Hedda and Schyman.'

Løken gazed out of the window. Nora sat and watched him for a long time.

'Have you told anyone else about this?' he asked.

She shook her head.

Løken rubbed his chin and muttered something. Nora followed his restless eyes. His mobile rang, interrupting his thoughts.

He answered with 'Yes,' and 'Can you give me two seconds?' Then he put a hand over the phone and said: 'I'm afraid I'm going to have to take this.'

'OK.'

He put down his cup and stood up. 'What we've talked about here – the business with Sweden and all that – don't mention that to anyone. Not a word, is that clear?'

She looked up at him.

'OK?' Løken moved over to the door. He turned, his hand still covering his mobile, and said: 'Not a word. Wait here, I'll be back shortly.'

While Nora waited for him to finish his call, she phoned her editor and asked if she could book in to a hotel in Tønsberg for the night.

'I'm losing three hours' work time every day just driving back and forth,' she argued. 'There's more bubbling under the surface down here, I'm sure of it.'

She didn't say anything about the gunshots, knowing it would only lead to a merry dance in which the editor would order her to come back and she would refuse. It was out of the question, the case was too important and too open now for her just to let it go.

The editor agreed to her request, and said that he would text her the details once they'd booked a room. Nora thanked him and ended the call.

It was another ten minutes before Løken returned.

'My apologies,' he said, closing the door.

Nora waited until he was sitting down.

'So what's happening?' she asked.

Løken didn't reply. He put his phone on the desk in front of him and gave her a hard stare.

Finally he said, 'I don't normally feed journalists information in cases like this.' He straightened up and studied her for a moment or two longer. 'But you do have a rather unique standing in this case, and now you've uncovered yet another clue that pulls things together even more. This is not only a declaration of trust, Klemetsen; it's a one-off. So, don't you dare abuse my faith in you; and don't expect it to happen again, you hear?'

'I do,' Nora said and leaned forwards in the chair. 'So what's happening?'

He took a deep breath. 'We're going to take Georg in for questioning,' he said.

'You are?'

He nodded. 'You can't write anything about this yet, but we know he was the one who picked Hedda up at Skoppum Station.'

Nora looked at him, wide-eyed. 'How do you know that?'

'His car,' Løken said, and picked up his cup from the desk. 'There are a limited number of cabriolets on the road these days, and his was the only one that could have been at Skoppum Station at that time.'

He took a sip, swallowed and pulled a face, then put the cup down and leaned back again.

Nora thought hard. As there were no electronic traces of Hedda after she went into the airport, she must have communicated with Georg some other way.

'Did she have another phone?'

'It would appear so, yes.'

Nora sighed; there was only ever one reason anyone needed a second phone. Hedda only wanted certain people to get hold of her. Her husband, Hugo Refsdal, was not one of them. This raised even more questions, to which Nora didn't have the answers.

'Where did he drive her?'

'We can't say for sure.'

Løken was leaning so far back now that his shirt had slid out of his trousers. Nora tried not to look at the white flesh that rolled free.

'But you know where his car has been?'

'More or less.'

Nora waited for him to say more. He didn't.

'Well?'

Løken leaned forwards again, appearing to weigh things up before he spoke: 'We know that Georg's car crossed the border into Sweden on the day that Daniel Schyman was killed – that is, the day after he picked up Hedda at Skoppum Station – and that it came back again later the same day.'

'So...' Nora couldn't navigate her thoughts.

'We've been in contact with our colleagues in Sweden,' Løken continued, picking up his mobile and pressing a few buttons. 'One of them is coming here this evening. He has some questions he'd like to ask Georg.' He put his phone down again.

Nora tried to process this information.

'We're not sure yet how all the pieces fit together,' Løken said, 'but we're going to put all our available resources on the case now.'

'What does that mean, in practice?'

Løken paused for a moment before answering: 'Among other things, we're going to search Oscar Hellberg's summer house tomorrow, as soon as it gets light. With dogs and the whole works.'

27

Henning had decided to go to Juristen, a bar and restaurant in the centre of Oslo, where the clientele included a lot of lawyers. His plan was to see if there was anyone he knew – someone who, after a beer or two, he could pump for information about lawyers who moved in the grey area between right and wrong. Someone who might know who Daddy Longlegs was. Rumours were as rampant in legal circles as they were in any other professional group.

Henning realised fairly swiftly that it was a bad idea; Juristen wasn't the best place for a confidential conversation – voices and laughter rose and fell in waves, and he didn't see any of the lawyers he knew personally. But it was good to be out having a beer; it was a while since he'd done it, and as he was on the lookout for potential sources, he decided to go over the road to Stopp Pressen, a favourite watering hole for journalists. Maybe there was someone there he could talk to.

In Stopp Pressen, Henning ordered another beer and found himself an empty booth. In the past, there had been gigs, jam sessions and quiz evenings here, but there was nothing like that now, just a song over the loudspeakers that Henning had heard before, but couldn't remember the name of. The beer was going down nicely and the bar was filling up. The lights had been dimmed, which made everything easier on the eye, and he scoured the room for familiar faces, but saw none. The smell of grilled cheese made him hungry, but he managed to resist ordering anything.

The beer here was good; it was a long time since the golden, foaming liquid had slipped quite so pleasantly down his throat. Henning drank three pints faster than he'd intended and soon the hard edges were blurred and the stripy fabric on the chairs became more hypnotic. He also found he had to visit the gents several times. On his return from one such trip, he stopped abruptly at the bar to avoid walking straight into Iver Gundersen.

Nora's boyfriend.

Father to her as-yet-unborn child.

He was standing in front of Henning in his worn corduroy jacket, with his messy, shoulder-length hair, trying to make eye contact with the man behind the bar. They both started slightly when they spotted each other. Henning immediately saw discomfort in Iver's eyes; they told of stories that he didn't want to hear right now; not ever, in fact.

Iver tried to smile, but didn't quite succeed. 'So, this is where you're hiding?' he joked.

'I'm not hiding,' Henning replied.

Iver nodded, looked him up and down.

'What happened to your face?' he asked.

'Roller skiing,' Henning told him.

Iver looked at a loss for a few long, awkward moments, then turned to the bar and asked for a beer. 'Do you want one?' He glanced at Henning.

Henning hesitated, but then nodded. Iver held two fingers up.

When the barman had given him the drinks, Iver turned to Henning. 'Have you got a table?'

Henning was about to point to the booth where he'd been sitting. 'I did,' he said, looking at the three men who were now installed there.

'There's an empty one over there,' Iver said, nodding to a table in the far corner, by the window onto the street. 'Shall we sit down?'

'Think my back would be grateful if we did,' Henning said.

Iver gave Henning one of the beers and headed over towards the empty table. Once they had sat down, he said: 'Didn't think I'd bump into you here.'

'Likewise,' Henning mumbled.

Soon the room would be spinning. A new song blasted out over the loudspeakers.

'Didn't exactly think you'd show up here,' he continued. 'Not now, at least.'

Iver looked down and drank some beer in silence.

'I hear Nora's told you,' he then said.

'Mm,' Henning said and raised his glass. 'Cheers.'

Iver hesitated then clinked glasses with him.

'I've been meaning to talk to you about it,' he said. 'I think I understand how difficult it must be for you.'

Henning put his glass down so hard that the foam sloshed over the edge. 'Difficult?' He stared hard at Iver. 'You think it's difficult for me to hear that you and Nora are having a baby?'

Iver started to say something, but didn't manage to get the words out of his mouth.

'You know fuck-all about how I feel.'

Iver pulled in a little closer, putting his elbows on the table. 'No, maybe I don't, but hasn't it occurred to you that it might be difficult for me, too?'

Henning looked up at him.

'I mean, you and I – well, we work together, and when you think about everything you and Nora have been through...' Iver didn't finish the sentence.

Neither of them said anything for a quite some time. Iver drank some more beer then put his glass down; he watched a woman as she walked slowly towards them, then turned away when she saw there were no empty places.

'And we didn't exactly plan it,' he continued, and pressed his fingers together. 'I'm not sure that I'm ready to be a father. Certainly not now.'

Henning had never seen Iver like this before. He was always the life and soul at work, someone who attracted attention as soon as he came into a room, full of stories and anecdotes, someone who made people laugh and feel at ease. Now he seemed smaller than usual, Henning thought. More frightened. More vulnerable. And it made him like Iver more than he was willing to admit.

Henning picked up his glass, took a drink. The room swayed.

'And Nora, she...'

'I don't want to hear it,' Henning said.

'No, I don't suppose you do,' Iver conceded.

They sat in silence for a few minutes, each with their own thoughts, drinking some more. Their glasses left wet rings on the table. A man at the next table emptied a handful of nuts into his mouth and chewed happily.

'What about Nora?' Henning heard himself ask.

Iver wet his lips. 'She'd perhaps hoped for, well, a bit more enthusiasm on my part.'

More beer. The room got foggier. Aerosmith tried desperately to sing about love in an elevator.

'It'll all work out,' Henning said, eventually.

'Hm?'

'Just give her time, she'll understand.'

Iver wiped the corners of his mouth, then ran a hand through his hair.

'It's like having a gun to your head,' Henning said.

Iver looked at him.

'Being a dad.'

Iver nodded, but Henning could see that he didn't understand what he meant.

'You go around being frightened the whole time,' he explained. 'Frightened that something might happen.' He looked down as he said this, turning his glass round and round.

The volume of the music increased. Henning struggled to hear his own thoughts and words, but he knew them by heart.

'And you think that all the awful stuff you read about in the papers – it won't happen to you and your child; it only happens to other people's kids.' Henning could hear that he was slurring his words. 'And as long as that's true, it's the best thing in the world. Being a dad. You know that only you and one other person can give this little person everything he needs. It's something that's impossible to understand, until you've been there yourself.'

He raised his glass again, tilting his head back.

'I didn't understand it at first,' he admitted. 'In fact, it took a long time before I understood anything. But I am very glad that I did, before it was too late.'

Iver didn't say anything. He didn't drink; he just looked at Henning.

'That sounds pretty good,' he said.

'And when it's gone, then...'

Henning didn't know how to finish the sentence. Or in fact, he did, he just didn't want to.

'I know one thing for sure,' Iver said, a moment later.

Henning tried to focus on him.

'And that is that you're drunk as a skunk.'

Henning picked up his glass, unsure that there was anything left in it. 'You're right,' he slurred.

'And I don't think you'll make it home on your own.'

Henning blinked. Blinked again, when nothing got clearer.

'Say when you're ready to go and I'll make sure you get home.'

Henning put the glass back down, tried to pick Iver out from everything that was swirling around the room. Thought he caught his eyes somewhere between the waves.

'I don't think I can do this,' Henning said.

'Do what?' Iver asked.

Henning waved his hands around. 'Be here,' he said.

'Here?'

Henning's eyes started to roam again. 'Be your friend,' he said. 'See you with Nora. With the baby. I don't think I can fucking cope.'

Iver nodded sagely. Then he emptied his glass and said: 'Come on then, Henning. I think you need some sleep.'

28

Nora was tempted to stay at the police station until the detective from Sweden showed up, but it would take too long; her deadline was looming and she hadn't yet found an angle for tomorrow's piece. Not one they could print, at least. She had no plans to turn herself into headline news.

Løken had reached the same conclusion as Nora – that the shots were fired to frighten her, so he had no concerns about letting her go. But he did advise, even urge, her to go home and lie low for a few days. Nora mumbled an unconvincing 'yes'.

Strangely enough, she didn't seem to be that affected by the shooting incident. Yes, it had been pretty intense at the time, and yes, it had been frightening, but she was calm again now and not just a little curious. She was also aware that any reaction might be delayed. In the meantime, she fully intended to use the energy she had left.

So she set out for Kalvetangen, where Hedda's mother lived. Mothers often knew their children in a special way, Nora reasoned, and she had a whole host of questions she wanted to ask Unni Hellberg. The real question, however, was whether or not Unni would be responsive, particularly now that Nora had trespassed on her property.

⊙

Kalvetangen had been a dumping ground for industrial waste, until the area was redesignated as a commercial zone in the mid-1980s. Towards the end of this redevelopment, applications were submitted to build housing for security guards and support staff, but there were no regulations that covered this, and so, before long, Kalvetangen looked more like a residential estate. And even though Nøtterøy Council had stipulated how many of the buildings could be used for residential purposes – no more than fifty percent – and that no building was to be more than 150 square metres in size, big villas were soon being built, several of them well over 300 square metres, with imaginative descriptions of the businesses that would operate from them. The most common ploy was for the owners to register a sole trader at the address and then rent out parts of the building to themselves.

Nora had no idea whether this was what Oscar and Unni Hellberg had done, but she did know that they had bought into the exclusive residential area in 2007 for the tidy sum of twenty-six million kroner.

Nora couldn't help dreaming a little as she drove slowly past all the villas. It would be fantastic to have so much money, she thought. It would certainly have solved a problem or two, even though she knew that, generally, when you got something you wanted, your worries and problems then just shifted onto something else.

Before Jonas came into the world, Nora wanted nothing more than to have children. Once he was there – living, breathing and growing, and more beautiful than anything she had ever seen – all her concerns were focused on satisfying his needs. And her worries changed as quickly as those needs: how would he get on at nursery, would he make friends, what would happen when he started school? And whenever he got ill, she would worry that it was something more serious than it ever was. It struck her that no matter how fantastic it had been watching Jonas grow up, it had also been difficult.

Could she really face going through all that again?

Could she face filling her life with all that fear, all those niggling concerns?

Nora got lost in her thoughts. She wasn't paying attention and soon realised that she had driven too far, so she had to turn back at the end of the road. The houses closest to the water were the grandest, with shiny, expensive cars in the drives. Nora followed a dense, neatly trimmed hedge until she came to the Hellbergs' home – which actually looked like several houses that had been put together under a single, red-tiled roof. The house included a double garage, but there were no cars parked outside. The closest thing to a neighbour on the right-hand side was a car park for the marina. A crowd of masts stood tall over the water, supported by millions of kroner, no doubt. Nora couldn't see a single basic, wooden boat.

The house itself was painted white, and the pillars by the entrance appeared to be holding up the first floor. The clean window panes twinkled in their glossy white frames. And behind the house, the water lapped against the shore. Nora got out of the car, and walked up the paved driveway, past a floodlit fountain with its soothing tinkle. She had to ring the doorbell twice before she heard footsteps behind the double door with its two oval windows that looked like cartoon eyes. A woman appeared behind the glass; she opened the door warily.

Unni Hellberg was a few centimetres taller than Nora, with short, highlighted hair and square spectacles with thin red frames. She was carefully made up, but the skin on her face looked like it had been over-stretched. She had a cigarette in her hand and the blue smoke spiralled upwards. She lifted her chin and looked down at Nora from where she stood two steps above.

'Yes, can I help you?' she said.

When Nora introduced herself, Unni Hellberg's face changed instantly. Her lips parted slightly, her eyes narrowed. She quickly stepped forwards.

'I've just spoken to my lawyer,' she said. 'He told me what happened. Are you alright?'

Nora was taken off-guard by her concern, which didn't tally at all with the impression that Hugo Refsdal had given of Hedda's mother.

'Yes, I'm fine, thank you,' Nora assured her with a smile. 'But it was a close shave.'

'Yes, goodness,' Unni said.

'I apologise for breaking into your property,' Nora said. 'I'm only trying to find your daughter. That's why I was at Hulebakk.'

Unni lowered her eyes, and took a drag on the cigarette.

'Did you read the article I wrote about Hedda in today's paper?' Nora asked.

Unni continued to stare at the ground. 'Yes,' she said, blowing the smoke out slowly. 'It's...' She shook her head. 'You have no idea how much time I've spent looking for Hedda,' she continued, and lifted her head. 'And then it turns out she came back the very day she...'

Unni looked away. Nora noticed that the hand holding the cigarette was shaking. She took another quick drag on the cigarette, which now had a long tip of ash.

'She must have found someone else,' Unni said, turning back to Nora. 'It wouldn't surprise me.'

'What do you mean? Do you think—?'

Unni held her hand up. 'I have no reason to think that.' She smiled sheepishly. 'But why else would she be picked up by anyone other than her husband?'

She took a final drag on the cigarette, descended the front steps and went over to a marble ashtray that had been discreetly positioned on the ground by the wall. She bent down and stubbed the cigarette out, then carefully put the lid back on the ashtray.

'People are always finding new partners,' she said, putting her hand on the small of her back as she came up the steps. 'All the time, everywhere.'

A great sadness scudded across her face. Then she seemed to pull herself together and smiled at Nora again.

'Please don't say anything about that; it's pure speculation on my part.'

Unni Hellberg spoke with a lilt, and enunciated all her words. Nora wasn't sure whether she was trying to sound grand, or it was simply her natural way of speaking.

'Would you like to come in?' she asked.

Nora smiled. 'Yes, please.'

'Just so you know, I would rather not end up in the papers. It's hard enough for me as it is.'

'Of course not, there won't be any need for that.'

Unni pushed open the door and showed Nora into a hall that was bigger than her living room. The tiles on the floor were black and white, like a chessboard, and a white spiral staircase coiled up to the next floor. Nora took off her boots. She felt like she was stepping into a museum, its rooms stuffed with precious treasures.

'Let's go into the drawing room,' Unni said, leading the way.

The house was quiet, the kind of house where the walls would creak and crack at night, the kind of house that Nora couldn't live in herself. It was too big, too grand, too expensive and would take too much time to look after. She had the feeling that Unni Hellberg had dedicated the last few years of her life to this house. All the furniture had been placed thoughtfully, the chandeliers sparkled, the floor in the drawing room was dark, solid wood – Nora guessed it was oak – the walls were hung with stuffed elk heads, and long, elegant rifles from past generations, as well as ancient portraits.

'Would you like a cup of tea or coffee?' Unni asked.

'No thanks, I drank too much coffee at the police station,' Nora said with a smile. 'But please, don't let me stop you.'

'Given what you've just been through, I should perhaps offer you something stiffer, but I saw that you had the car.'

'Thank you,' Nora said.

Unni directed Nora over to a leather sofa and armchairs, with a dark wooden table in between. Nora could imagine men in tartan trousers smoking cigars, talking about business and exchanging hunting stories over generous glasses of cognac.

Unni sat down opposite her, one leg crossed over the other, smoothed out a crease in her trousers and folded her hands on her lap.

'Do you know if anyone has been out to the summer house recently?' Nora asked.

Unni picked a hair off the sofa. 'Hugo was there one afternoon,' she said, and folded her hands again. 'But other than that, no one has been there for ages. There simply wasn't time for it this summer, with Oscar so ill.'

'But someone has been there,' Nora said. 'There was certainly someone there today. And I have good reason to believe that someone has been there recently.'

Nora told her about what she had seen through the windows. 'What do you make of that?' she asked.

Unni shifted on her chair, wetting her lips. 'I don't know what to say,' she replied, and put a finger behind the glass of her spectacles and rubbed the thin skin under her eye.

'You're the only one who has keys to the place, is that right?'

Unni nodded slowly for a few seconds. Nora thought about Georg, the fact that he had gone there. He had driven in through the wrought-iron gates, so he must have had keys; unless he had stolen Unni's set. Nora didn't want to ask the question; it would allow for too many counter questions, which she didn't know if she could or should answer.

Nora looked around the room, her eyes resting on the guns over the fireplace.

'I see you're a hunting family.'

Unni followed Nora's gaze. 'Yes,' she said. 'It's a tradition: grouse, elk – and Oscar even went over to the west coast to hunt deer as often as he could. If there was something he could shoot, he would.' She rolled her eyes.

'Did Hedda hunt too?'

'Sometimes,' Unni said, clasping her hands again. 'She always wanted to do what the boys were doing, and when she got older she was allowed to; she became quite a good shot, or so I've been told. I never joined them – I've never liked hunting; I think it's a barbaric tradition.'

Nora nodded, more to herself than anyone else.

'What about Georg, was he ever part of the hunting party?'

Unni sent her a swift look. 'Why do you ask about Georg?'

'Just curious,' Nora repeated. 'About family relations and things like that.'

Unni shifted in the chair again. 'I don't know,' she said, hastily, with an edge to her voice. 'As I said, I'm not interested in hunting.'

Nora scratched her temple and studied the woman on the other side of the table. Not a hair was out of place, but she had more colour in her cheeks. A single, stubborn wrinkle had become increasingly visible on her forehead. She plumped the cushions behind her.

'She's always been a family person, Hedda. And I'm sure that if she'd been a boy, she would have joined the family business. But she was the youngest, and always wanted to do her own thing. Stubborn as a mule.'

Nora looked at Unni, waiting for her to carry on.

She started to laugh. 'I remember one time, when Hedda was little,' she started, 'she must have been about two or three. We didn't live in this house then, but we had to keep her tied her to a tree in the garden, almost like a dog. It was the only way to keep a check on her. Otherwise she just ran off.'

Unni smiled – a broad smile that eventually faded. She reached over to a brass box that stood next to the ashtray on the table, took out a cigarette and lit it with a lighter from the same box.

'She was quite a special child, Hedda. Often sat on her own, just thinking. I sometimes wondered what she was thinking about, but she never answered when I asked.'

Unni took a drag on the cigarette and exhaled slowly. Then she shook her head.

'The past few months have been terrible for this family,' she said. 'First Oscar, and then Hedda.'

She pursed her lips, looked away. But Nora could still see that her eyes were glistening. The telephone in the hallway started to ring – a loud, old-fashioned sound. Unni got up, placed the cigarette in the ashtray, and once again put her hand to her back as she started to walk.

'It's probably just my lawyer,' she said, partly to herself, partly to Nora.

She excused herself and went out into the hall. The ringing stopped and Nora could hear her voice, but not what she was saying. She stared at the cigarette burning down in the ashtray; was tempted to lean forwards and stub it out, but she didn't.

A few minutes later, Unni came back. She apologised again.

'Is everything alright?' Nora asked.

CURSED   **159**

'Yes, yes,' Unni said, dismissively. 'Whoever broke into the summer house appears to have got in through a hole in the fence, which I thought had been repaired ages ago. But, clearly not.'

'Did many people know about it?' Nora wondered.

'Certainly, most people in the family. And I'm sure some others, people who go for walks out there and the like.'

Nora nodded slowly. 'Did you have much contact with your daughter?'

Unni didn't answer immediately.

'Not as much as I would have liked,' she said eventually. 'She was so busy with her company.' She raised her eyebrows.

Nora had already considered her next question carefully, and now decided just to ask it straight out.

'Daniel Schyman,' she started, 'was he a family friend?'

Unni sat staring at Nora for a few seconds, the cigarette hovering in front of her mouth. Her lips slightly parted again.

'He's Swedish,' Nora added. 'Retired.'

'No,' Unni said brusquely and shook her head. 'I've never heard the name before. Is that ... someone the police suspect?' She almost sang the question.

'No, not at all,' Nora said. 'He's ... he's just a name that cropped up when I was digging around.'

Unni breathed in more nicotine. Then she stubbed out the cigarette, rubbed her temples and looked at Nora with kind eyes.

'I'm sorry, but I think I'm going to have to call it a day,' she said. 'I'm utterly exhausted by everything that's happened.'

She got up, pressed her temples with her index fingers and smiled apologetically.

'Of course,' Nora said, and pushed herself up from the chair. 'It was very nice talking to you. Thank you for your time.'

Unni didn't answer. She accompanied Nora to the door, where she put on her jacket and scarf and then sat down on a stool to pull on her boots. Unni waited by a table, wiping an invisible layer of dust from the leather cover of the visitors' book.

Nora stood up again, and held out her hand. 'Thank you,' she said. 'I'll ring if I hear anything more about Hedda.'

Unni gave a fleeting smile. Nora recognised the sentiment: gratitude devoid of hope. She squeezed Unni's hand; it was thin and dry.

'Goodbye,' Unni said, and closed the door.

Nora drove slowly away from Kalvetangen, ruminating on the woman she had just met, on the life she led – her sore back, the cigarettes that had become her constant companion, the silence. She might well be rich in terms of goods and gold, Nora thought, but she was struck by the fact that she had never met a more lonely person.

29

Henning couldn't tell which way the taxi driver was going, but he was definitely driving too fast, almost dangerously so. Henning drifted in and out of sleep, looking at the cars and lights and people that flew by as he tried to remember what planet he was on.

They drove over a speed bump and up a hill. The street grew darker, the taxi slowed. Then over another speed bump. They were in Markveien. Henning recognised the red, floodlit exterior of Paulus Church. The car slowed further, and stopped just outside Bobby's kiosk on the corner, which was still open.

The trip had made Henning nauseous and dizzy; he staggered as he got out of the car and ended up in the middle of the road, with cars on all sides. The lights from one shone straight in his eyes. He heard Iver talking to the driver and the receipt being printed.

'I can manage from here,' Henning slurred, when Iver closed the car door behind him. Henning stuffed his hands into his pockets, dug out the keys, then dropped them on the ground. He bent down and tried to pick them up, but failed, as a pain shot through his hips, reminding him that he hadn't taken his tablets for a while.

'Yeah, right. Certainly looks like it,' Iver said.

The taxi drove off as Iver helped Henning up and gave him the keys. Henning stood there swaying, then focused on Iver.

'I can manage,' he said.

'Are you sure?'

'Yes, for Christ's sake.'

Then everything happened at once.

A car that had been parked with its lights on at the junction with Steenstrups gate rumbled into life. There was a screech of rubber, and the engine's thunder changed key as the car accelerated, making Henning turn his head. But all he saw was blinding lights. Then came a deafening roar. Above it he heard Iver shout out his name and felt him slam into his side, forcing the air from his lungs. It was only then that he realised the car was heading straight for them. Time paused infinitesimally. Then he was falling, Iver clasped around him. A dull thud in his head told him they'd hit the asphalt hard. But somehow his body didn't register the impact; he just heard the grumble of the car as it accelerated down Markveien, wheels screaming as it swerved. It was all over in a matter of seconds.

The noise of the engine faded into the sounds of the street.

Henning lay where he had fallen. Iver rolled off him. They didn't move. Henning felt something warm trickle down his forehead; the ground beneath him was cold. Slowly, slowly he turned over and looked at Iver, who was breathing fast and hard, his eyes wide open.

Henning sat up and shuffled away from a pile of glass from a shattered car window.

'Did you get the registration number?' he asked.

Iver shook his head.

Henning breathed heavily. The sharp light had made it difficult to see what kind of car it was. He had only caught the colour – white.

'What the fuck was that about?' Iver said.

Henning tried to take in the colours and sounds around him.

'Someone just tried to kill me,' he said quietly.

'Why?'

Henning got up, staggered a bit, then brushed the dust and dirt from his clothes.

'We have to get away from here,' he said. 'They might come back.'

He ran his hand over his head and felt something in his hair. Grit. He pulled it out, then gave a hand to Iver and pulled him up. A man and a woman passed by, arm in arm, and looked over at them.

'Who's trying to kill you?' Iver asked.

Henning took a deep breath. 'It's a long story. Do you want to come in?'

Iver straightened his jacked. Stopped. 'To your flat? Now?'

'Yes.'

Iver stared at him. 'Someone just tried to run you over and kill you, Henning. They know where you live. What are the chances they'll try here again?' Iver pointed at the building where Henning lived.

'They won't dare try inside.'

Iver threw up his hands in disbelief. 'You never know. There's no way I'm going to let you go in there now. We're going back to my place. You can crash on the sofa.'

Henning looked at him. 'On your sofa?'

'What – you want my bed?'

Henning looked straight ahead; it was a long time since he slept on anyone else's sofa. Then he considered what Iver had just said.

He might have a point.

'OK,' he said. 'But you better have some good food in the fridge.'

30

Nora checked into a hotel in the centre of Tønsberg – a room with a view over the canal, free Wi-Fi and a desk where she could work on her laptop. She didn't have long now to finish her piece for tomorrow's paper, and she still had no idea how to pitch it. She tried to call Cato Løken, but there was no reply.

Perhaps he was busy questioning Georg, she thought. And even though she'd won his trust, he still might not tell her anything.

Nora logged onto the internet and checked what the other papers had written, but none of them offered a new or interesting angle on Hedda's disappearance. She saw that Løken had given a statement to the Norwegian News Agency, but it was neutral and said nothing new.

To keep herself occupied, she decided to do a background check on the other members of the Hellberg family. She discovered that Hellberg Property was established in 1948 by the lawyer, Fritz Hellberg I, who died six years later in a car crash. From 1954 until the yuppie era in the eighties, the company had progressed well under the leadership of Fritz Jnr, before Fritz Hellberg III took over. Following a heart attack, this Fritz had passed the reins to his nephew, William, and that was when Hellberg Property had started to buy up sites and old tenement buildings for new flats and development. It was also when the company really started to prosper.

The Hellberg family appeared to be a fine combination of lawyers, property magnates and trophy wives. Fritz III married Ellen – née Nygaard Næss – in 1975; Oscar married Unni – maiden name Lerche – in 1971, when Unni was only nineteen. Nora decided to draw up a family tree, based on their relationship to Hedda.

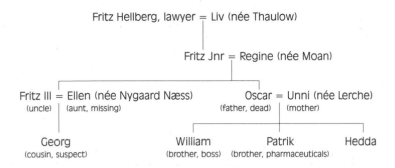

It took her twenty minutes to write a reasonable family history, and she was pleased with the background and context she had created for the story.

Nora tried Løken again. This time, after many rings, he answered.

'Hi,' he said.

'Have you finished questioning Georg?' Nora asked, pulling the earpieces from her bag and plugging them into the phone.

Løken started to laugh. 'You don't waste time on small talk, do you?'

Nora put down the handset with a smile and noticed in the mirror opposite that her teeth looked anything but white. She pursed her lips.

'I've got a deadline in half an hour, and I'm sure that you have more than enough to do, so I don't want to waste time talking about the wind and weather.'

'You could certainly say that,' Løken sighed. 'And no, we haven't finished. We'll probably carry on for the rest of the evening, perhaps even the whole night; it depends. The family lawyer is being obstructive, so it's pretty slow going.'

Nora stood up, picked up the phone and dug her toes into the soft, dark-green carpet. She realised she wasn't going to need her notepad for this conversation. She stopped by the TV, ran a finger over a laminated page that was stuck down beside it, giving a list of channels one to thirty-two.

'Has he said anything about picking up Hedda?'

'No.'

She turned towards the bed. 'Nothing about where he took her? The trip to Sweden?'

'Afraid not,' Løken said, and let out another sigh.

Nora sat down on the bed. The soft mattress bounced.

'And he's free to leave the police station whenever he wants?'

'We can hold him for forty-eight hours before we either have to apply to keep him on remand or release him.'

Nora lay down, the phone on the duvet beside her.

'And it's a right you'll make full use of?' she asked, looking up at the ceiling. A spider was crossing the yellow surface at speed.

'For the moment, yes. But please don't write anything.'

Nora ran her tongue over her lips. 'What *can* I write then?'

'That there are leads pointing in a specific direction and we're questioning everyone who knew Hedda.'

She sat up again. The abrupt movement made her dizzy. 'You think that he's killed her, don't you?' she said.

'I'm afraid I can't comment on that,' he replied.

Nora scratched a spot just above her ear. 'What do the Swedish police have to say? Do they think Hedda's disappearance has anything to do with the Daniel Schyman murder?'

'It's too early to say.'

Outside the hotel window, a boat made gentle splashing sounds as it travelled by on the canal. A seagull cried nearby, and was immediately joined by several others.

'OK, I'll just write that you're working on some very strong leads. Does that sound alright?'

'Yep, you can say that.'

Nora ran through things quickly in her mind. Was there anything else she wanted to know?

'What about the gunshots? Have you got any further with that?'

Løken exhaled noisily. 'No. But we've had some calls from the local press. Some neighbours heard the shots and phoned to see what was going on, particularly after we got there.'

Nora stood up again and wandered over to the desk, where her laptop screen had gone into sleep mode. The screensaver was a picture of her and Iver at Liseberg, on a carousel that had been far too fast for Nora's liking. But it had made her smile, and still did now.

'What did you tell them?' She touched the laptop, the picture vanished.

'That a couple of shots were fired at the Hellbergs' family summer house, but that it was still unclear as to why they had been fired and by whom. I pointed out that it's the middle of the hunting season and that perhaps they were just trial shots. And as no one was injured, I don't supposed it will attract much attention.'

Nora nodded. That sounded about right.

She thanked him for his help and ended the call, then sat down at the keyboard and decided that her angle would be that the police now believed that Hedda's disappearance was a criminal case and they had leads that pointed in a clear direction. It was sufficiently vague, but would still provoke curiosity. Combined with the background story she had written earlier, it could be a good piece, after all.

She lay back down on the bed, exhausted, but her head still full of questions. She squeezed the ball in her right hand, then her left hand, then her right hand, as she stared up at the ceiling. She had the impression there wasn't enough space between her ears and her body felt heavy and sore, as though she had spent an entire day in a shopping centre. She should really go out and have a proper meal, but she felt more like eating some junk and going to bed.

In the end, she raided the minibar for crisps and nuts; she even found a Toblerone, which she wolfed down. She then lay in the bath, splashing her feet and stroking her belly, filled with morbid thoughts about her diet.

She wondered what Iver was doing, if he was at work or out on the town. No doubt one of the two. She could just picture him: quick movements, charming, eye contact. Nora knew that he came across as an exciting and dynamic person. And she had seen his eyes when a beautiful woman came into the room.

They had discussed it intermittently – what was allowed and what wasn't – and Iver had always said that it would be unnatural for him not to indulge his love for women when there were so many of them. But he never actually did anything, he claimed, just dreamed about it, thought about it.

Nora gave herself a good soak and scrub, even though hotel soaps always made her skin so dry. She should have bought a change of clothes or three, and a toothbrush, as she didn't know how long she'd be here. She decided to do it as soon as the shops opened the next morning.

She got out of the bath, dried herself and slipped under the duvet. The spider was still moving around on the ceiling, as if it didn't know where to go.

Perhaps Hedda had gone to Sweden with Georg, and that was where she was now. Maybe they had planned to kill Daniel Schyman together, but then something had gone wrong, so Hedda hadn't come back with him. Or maybe Georg had killed them both. Or perhaps he'd not done anything with her until they got back to Hulebakk, and that was why he was going back there the day Nora had followed him. He'd wanted to hide the body properly. And then he took a shot at Nora when he saw her snooping around; tried to scare her off.

You're taking it too far, Nora told herself, as she felt her eyelids drooping. The greatest mystery was still why they would want to kill Daniel Schyman in the first place.

31

The bacon hissed and sizzled, sending fat up onto the white tiles behind Iver's cooker. Henning sat at the kitchen table and observed Nora's lover.

'What stage is she at?'

Iver turned, leaving the bacon to its fate. 'Fourteen weeks, I think. Or ... oh, I'm not sure.'

The kitchen table was wooden and full of old scratches and dents. Henning ran his finger over the surface, then round his glass and the jug of water.

He remembered that period. Fourteen weeks. The first critical stage was over, and you could talk about it; they had only just started to dare thinking about themselves as potential parents. They had started to plan – where the baby would sleep at night, if they knew anyone with a spare pram, anyone who could pass on baby clothes. They had also started talking about a name. And of course, Nora noticed the physical changes; she never complained, though, just got rounder and more radiant. She glowed. Iver gave the bacon thirty seconds more before taking it out of the frying pan, then cracked four eggs in its place, and stirred a little in the pot on the neighbouring hotplate.

Henning poured a glass of water and drank it. It wasn't the first time someone had tried to kill him without succeeding, but it had been pretty damned close. A small cut to his forehead was the only injury he had to prove it. If Iver hadn't been there, Henning wouldn't be sitting where he was now. He didn't like being indebted to anyone.

Iver put the bacon, eggs and beans on a plate, cut some slices of bread to go with it, and then they ate in silence. It was a long time since Henning had eaten anything so good.

'I don't normally even warm them up,' he said, pointing at the baked beans.

'Your poor stomach.' Iver smiled.

Henning laughed.

When they'd finished, Iver cleared the table and put the pans in the sink.

'OK,' he said. 'Tell me what's going on.'

Henning folded his hands on the table in front of him. Before starting, he thought about what he was going to say, what he should leave out.

Nothing, he decided.

So he told Iver about the tip-off that Rasmus Bjelland had given him; about the fire, and the note on the door that said *first and last warning*; quickly glossed over what had happened with Jonas, and carried straight on to Jocke Brolenius's murder and the phone call Henning had received from Tore Pulli in prison. Then he told Iver about Tore's murder and Ørjan Mjønes's arrest.

Henning held nothing back. He told Iver about the report that someone had messed with, the break-in at Veronica Nansen's flat, the camera that had disappeared and the photographs that appeared to be missing. It was a lot to take in, but Iver looked as though he was keeping up. At least with the important things.

'So you think it's this Daddy Longlegs – or someone who works for him, who's trying to kill you?'

'I'm not entirely sure,' Henning said with a shrug. 'But it's definitely a possibility. I haven't managed to find out who Daddy Longlegs is yet.'

Iver nodded slowly, but then shook his head. 'Fucking hell, Henning, this is crazy.' He stood up, took the jug of water over to the sink, turned on the tap.

'I know,' Henning said. 'And I shouldn't really have told you any of that, because it might put you in danger, too.'

'Suppose so,' Iver said, sticking his finger under the tap. 'But it's what I live for, after all. Stories like this.'

He put the jug under the tap and filled it again. Turned off the tap and sat down, before pouring some water into Henning's glass first, then his own.

'I don't think Nora would be very happy if she found out that I'd told you,' Henning said, taking his glass.

Iver put the jug down. 'So she doesn't know what you're doing?' he asked.

'She knows about Pulli,' Henning said, and flicking some drops of water from the side of the glass. 'But she didn't really believe me. Or that's to say, I think she didn't want to believe me. But what do I know?'

'So what's the key thing you need to find out? What do you need to know first?'

Henning took a sip of water. 'Have you ever heard of a guy called Charlie Høisæther?'

Iver thought about it.

'He used to be big in property development here,' Henning expanded. 'About the same time that Tore Pulli made a name for himself. They were childhood friends. If you want to help me, I need to find out if the two of them ever did business together and, if so, in what way, and if anyone suffered as a result. According to Rasmus Bjelland, Pulli thought nothing of climbing over corpses to get what he wanted, and I'm pretty sure he meant it literally.'

Iver nodded.

'I also need to find out what kind of relationship Charlie has with the Swedish League in Natal, other than that they might have bought apartments from him there.'

Iver emptied his glass.

'Do you think you can manage that?' Henning asked.

'I'll certainly give it a damned good try,' Iver said, and smiled.

Then he was suddenly serious again. 'But you need protection, Henning.'

Henning shook his head. 'I've not got enough to go to the police yet.'

'I wasn't thinking of the police.'

Henning glanced at him.

'I was thinking a gun. Next time, they might be more up-close and personal, and then you'll need something more than my strong arms to protect you.' He made it sound like a joke, but his face was serious.

'I don't like guns,' Henning said.

'Nor do I,' Iver assured him. 'But do you know what I like even less?'

Henning didn't flinch.

'Dead friends. You need a way of protecting yourself, Henning. You need a gun.'

Henning locked his fingers together. Remembered that Veronica had said exactly the same. Maybe they both had a point.

Iver yawned. 'Sleep on it,' he said. 'I'm certainly going to do just that.'

Henning nodded.

'Are you staying up for a while?'

Henning didn't answer at first. 'Don't know that I'll be able to sleep yet.'

Iver took a step towards the bedroom. 'If you need a bit of distraction, my TV is full of bad channels. Not much porn, mind.'

Henning smiled.

'See you in the morning,' Iver said.

He had opened the door to the bedroom, when Henning said his name. He turned around.

'Thank you,' Henning said. 'For...'

He couldn't finish the sentence.

'Ach,' Iver said, and waved his hand. 'Whatever.'

32

Nora started the day by reading all the online newspapers she could find, and quickly concluded she still had the scoop. She was the only one who provided detail about the police having strong leads – clues that they were following up. The other papers had only picked up on the case in the small hours, and all they had managed to do was quote her. It was always fun to be quoted.

At a quarter past eight, she sat down for breakfast in the dining room. The plate in front of her was full: she'd picked up slices of bacon, a mound of scrambled eggs and a couple of pieces of smoked salmon. She also had a large glass of juice and an almost overflowing cup of coffee. It might be a while before she had anything else to eat.

Her plan for the day was simple: as soon as she'd finished breakfast, she would go and buy some emergency clothes, then she would go back out to the Hellbergs' summer house at Hulebakk, take some pictures of the police who were searching the property, then send them over to the news desk with a good, tantalising headline. Then the internet people could add the material that she had already produced. That would make it to around fifteen or twenty lines, and it might even become a top story.

When Nora reached Hulebakk, feeling like she'd eaten a horse, the iron gates were open and there was a row of cars parked outside. There were also cars outside the garage. Nora spotted Cato Løken's car, parked by itself some way off. She was about to take out her mobile phone when she heard dogs barking among the trees.

Nora walked towards the noise. There were no cordons yet, but it didn't take long before she bumped into a uniformed policeman.

'Hi,' she said. '*Aftenposten*. What's happening?'

The man – tall and dark with a beard – looked at her sceptically.

'Have they found anything?' she asked, when he said nothing.

'I don't know,' was his reply.

Nora knew what he was thinking: here already, vultures. That was generally what the police – especially the men – thought of journalists.

The noise got closer. Dogs barking, branches snapping. A voice called from among the trees: 'The dogs have picked up a trace.'

Nora's right hand went to her mouth.

Hedda, she thought. *Poor thing*. And before she could stop herself, she was crying. She took a few steps away from the police officer and tried to pull herself together. *You're at work, for goodness sake*, she said to herself. She pulled out her phone and typed a quick text to her editor: 'Seems body has been found. Will call as soon as know for sure. Will send pictures ASAP.'

Detective Inspector Cato Løken stepped out from the group of officers. He wasn't surprised to see her there. He had his professional mask on.

'We'll have to cordon off the whole area,' he said to the two officers standing closest to him, who then nodded and rushed off to the nearest police car for some red-and-white tape. Nora took some pictures, trying as hard as she could to stop her hands from trembling. She didn't manage it, though, and had to hold the camera with both hands to get a reasonably sharp image. She sent these to the news desk with as high a resolution as possible, using the email function on her mobile phone. The grey, autumn sky and matt-green trees created a gloomy atmosphere that was perfect for a murder case. She began shaking again, appalled at herself for having such a thought.

Løken continued to give instructions. Nora knew that it was only a matter of minutes before the competition showed up, so she walked towards him and called his name. Løken pulled a face and lifted a warning finger, but once he had finished telling a couple more people what to do, he came over to her.

'Is it Hedda?' Nora asked, even though she was certain she knew the answer.

Løken looked deep into her eyes. 'You can't write anything about this yet,' he said in a firm, hushed voice. 'But I can tell you that we're a hundred percent sure it's not Hedda we've found.'

◉

Henning hadn't slept anywhere other than his own flat for at least a couple of years. And before that, he'd only rarely stayed with anyone other than Nora.

Iver's flat was just as he'd imagined it would be. It definitely bore the marks of a bachelor; to be more precise, the absence of a woman was evident. Nora was no doubt here every now and then – he'd seen an extra toothbrush in the bathroom – but the big loudspeakers in the living room said it all.

He looked at his watch. It was late morning. Iver had left for work ages ago. There was a note on the living-room table to say that he would call later.

The events of the previous evening came back to Henning: the car's bright lights, the screeching tyres, Iver's shout, the silence that fell over Seilduksgaten afterwards. It had all happened so fast, been so close. He was lucky to be alive.

Henning went into the kitchen and opened the window to let in some air. He looked out over the grey town – a town that appeared to be at a standstill from this viewpoint, up high; but the chimneys on the horizon were smoking, and, if he listened, he could hear the traffic singing a song about a city that never slept. Not really.

Could he actually live anywhere other than Oslo?

He would prefer to be somewhere where as few people as possible knew him; another country, perhaps. It would be easier that way, and he quite liked the idea of life as a loner – it was appealing. But he knew he couldn't leave his mother. Not while she was still alive. Who would buy her groceries; supply her with alcohol, and with the cigarettes that exacerbated her lung disease? Which reminded him, he should go and see her soon. He dreaded even the thought of it. She never thanked him for all he did for her. And was always ready with some accusatory comment. The old bird might keep going for another twenty years, at least, for all he knew; so, no, moving seemed out of the question.

Henning went into the bathroom, had a piss and splashed some water on his face. It helped to ease the residual puffiness. But he was just as tired and dozy when he sat down and turned on his mobile. He'd received a couple of text messages from Iver. *'Awake?'* and *'Call me when you wake up.'*

Henning couldn't face talking yet, so he downloaded his unread emails – twenty-three in all. One was from Atle Abelsen, his hacker friend.

Hi. The guy in the photo is called Durim Redzepi. He's from Kosovo, did a runner to Sweden because he's wanted for double murder in his own country. Responsible for several jobs in Norway. The police in Oslo are after him. If this guy is on your tail, go hide or get a gun.

Double murder, Henning thought. That wasn't small fry.

He closed the email and dialled Iver's number.

'Hi,' Iver shouted. 'How are you?'

'Fine,' Henning said. 'And you?'

Henning heard Iver get up from his chair.

'Not a good day for news,' Iver said. 'I'm falling asleep here.'

Henning could hear the normal newsroom buzz in the background.

'But I've looked up Charlie Høisæther,' Iver carried on, clearly moving through the office. 'And I've found something strange. Or perhaps not so strange, when you think about it – but a curiosity, shall we say.'

'And what's that?'

Iver closed a door and there was silence behind him.

'Do you know who William Hellberg is?'

Henning mulled on the name.

'He's the brother of that girl who's missing in Tønsberg,' Iver continued, before Henning had had a chance to think it through.

'Oh yes,' Henning said, and then remembered what Nora had told him. 'What about him?'

Iver gently cleared his throat. Then he said: 'Well, his wife owns a flat in Sports Park in Natal. And guess who lives next door?'

33

Nora took a step back as she tried to take in what Løken had just said.

'You mean, it's not Hedda?'

Løken looked around. 'The body we found has been there for a long time,' he whispered.

If it's not Hedda, Nora reasoned, if the body's been here on the Hellbergs' property for a long time, well then it might be Hedda's aunt, Ellen Hellberg.

Nora shared her thoughts with Løken.

'It's far too early to say anything.'

'But is it a woman or a man?'

'Impossible to say.'

Which meant there wasn't much left of the body, Nora thought.

'What about clothes?' she asked.

Løken turned away.

'I can't comment on that.'

'Any indication whether the person was killed or not?'

'That's for forensics to decide.'

Løken started to walk away. Nora followed.

'When will you get an answer from them?' she asked.

'Don't know. We have to get the body out of the well first. And I don't have time to talk to you right now.'

Nora let him go and stood there thinking. It had to be Ellen Hellberg, she told herself. Who else could it be, if it wasn't Hedda? But if you wanted to commit suicide, would you jump down a well?

Some people might, she mused, as it would be impossible to get out.

But wouldn't someone have found her in the meantime? They must have looked for her, after all.

Perhaps not right here, she thought. The wooded area was sizable and presumably the well hadn't been used for years.

As Nora looked at her watch, two cars came tearing down the road towards the gate. She guessed it was *Tønsbergs Blad* or *VG*'s Vestfold team. The broadcasters would be here soon as well, and all attention would be focused on relations in the Hellberg family. Georg was still being held in custody at Tønsberg police station, suspected of being connected to Hedda's disappearance in some way. What would *he* think if it did turn out that his mother had finally been found?

The cars parked nearby. It was tempting to stay, but Nora knew that the police would keep a tight lid on the discovery and would wait until a press conference was called before they said anything. And that could be several hours yet.

The more she thought about it, the more certain she was that there was more to be gained from poking around in the family history. She hadn't done much more than scratch the surface.

Nora rang the office and updated them, suggesting that they should send more people down. The news editor immediately agreed. Nora put her phone back in her bag and started to walk towards her car.

Yes, she thought to herself before she got in, *you have to do it*. But before she pulled out onto the road, she made a pact with herself: this would be the very last time she would do what she was about to.

Veronica Nansen kept the phone tucked between her shoulder and ear as she clicked on the mouse; a calendar covered half the screen in front of her. Her eyes ran through the dates.

'How nice that you want Andrine,' she said to the client at the other end. 'She's already got another job that day, but I'll ask if she can still fit you in.'

'Perfect, thank you.'

'Let's leave it there, then, for the moment.'

Veronica hung up, wrote Andrine's name and RING in capital letters on the notepad in front of her. The VIP girls' evenings were very popular: makeover evenings for small groups, with a fashion show, make-up and styling, and a professional photo session with all the participants at the end; photographs they could use as profile pictures at work or on social media. More often than not the latter.

Operation Self-Confidence. Everyone wanted to stand out in the group picture; everyone wanted to know how to disguise a double chin, highlight their cheekbones, look five kilos slimmer, or ten or fifteen. Everyone wanted to be supermodels and experience a little bit of Hollywood in their living room. And she, Veronica Nansen, could give them just that.

There was nothing wrong with wanting to feel young and beautiful, to relive the glamour of your youth, as you got older, if only for a few hours or days. It was about more than just getting good fashion and make-up tips. Lots of people enjoyed the social aspect, the opportunity to meet others, but what Veronica had come to understand was that it was also about being *seen*, about being pampered. Women often lost any sense of self between the laundry, changing nappies and work. They might have denied themselves any pleasure for years, and for many of them, there seemed to be little difference between a makeover and a confessional. It was incredible the extent to which these women were willing to share their lives and struggles.

And in that way, Veronica felt that she was doing something important. She was helping people to feel better about themselves, giving them tips on how to maintain their quality of life, even improve it. And yet it was getting harder and harder to find the motivation to go to work in the morning; she thought she knew why.

It had taken time to get to where she was now, and she still hadn't completely shed the 'porn' label. The photographs that had been taken of her nearly twenty years ago, when she was young and inexperienced, even a bit stupid and naive, were constantly being pulled out, even though she had put her clothes back on long ago, and had kept them on since. The two favourites were the cover of *Vi Menn* magazine and a job she'd done for a solarium company that had now gone bankrupt.

Fortunately, she not only had a body that appealed to the advertising industry, she also had a face. For several years, she had consciously only taken jobs that showed as little flesh as possible, and gradually she'd become more and more accepted as an ordinary model. At one point, she was even the host of a reality TV show that gave young hopefuls a chance to become models. That was the job that had made it possible for her to start Nansen Models. She had wanted to pass on her experience in the industry to others.

Marrying a man like Tore Pulli had been both good and bad for business. It had raised her profile in the media, which meant the company became even better known; but it had also made it harder to shake off the furtive glances from people who believed she was basically a madam. And it didn't exactly do wonders for her reputation when Tore was arrested and then later charged with murder.

It made lots of clients nervous – they didn't want to be associated with her because she was associated with him; and even though Tore was acquitted posthumously, the original sentence was deeply rooted in their memories. Veronica knew only too well how tempting it was to put it all behind her, to leave this city and even this country and start afresh somewhere new. Her sister Nina had made a career as a personal trainer in Los Angeles, and had said many times that she could do with a good friend to help her with all the celebrities. As long as Tore had been alive, it was simply not an option. But now?

She could sell her business; it was no doubt worth a fair amount. The only thing holding her back was the fear of change – leaving the framework that had somehow held her life together, facing the uncertainty about living in a foreign country. And then there were her parents, who would soon be retiring. Who would look after them when the time came?

Veronica closed the calendar, and clicked onto the *Aftenposten* internet pages to check the news. She often did this when she needed to think about something else. A body had been found, she read. The woman had been lying at the bottom of a well for years. How awful, Veronica thought, and clicked on the link. She scrolled down and saw a photograph of a woman who had been missing for a long time and who lived in the area where the body was found. She was an attractive woman: long legs; slim; beautiful brown hair.

Veronica read the report.

Stopped.

She looked at the photographs taken outside the offices of a property developer in Tønsberg. And a whole host of memories welled up. Painful memories; difficult conversations.

With Tore.

She closed the window, put her elbows on the table and hid her face; she felt her heart trying to creep up into her throat. She swallowed and wondered if she should say anything to Henning.

A moment later, her phone rang.

It was him.

Henning.

34

Solvang was an area of Tønsberg that reeked of old money; full of big houses with even bigger gardens, ancient apple trees and manicured lawns; hedges to stop people looking in, and cars that cost a year's salary or three. Nora had no idea whether Fritz Hellberg III was someone who liked to show off his wealth. She took a deep breath when she came to the substantial, square house at the end of the road where he lived.

The villa was enormous and painted grey with white windows and gables. Nora reckoned it must be around four to five hundred square metres in size; the whole property was at least a couple of thousand square metres and was surrounded by a metre-high, brown picket fence, with a dense hedge inside to block the view further. But Nora could still see the tall, white pillars at the front of the house, the six windows on the exterior – all with old-fashioned, eight-pane frames.

Nora had always hated this part of her job – talking to the family; she'd always thought that people should be left in peace when they had lost someone close to them. At the start of her career as a journalist, she had been forced to contact people in sensitive situations and it had been just as horrible every time. Later she simply refused to do it, but this time she was too curious not to. And she didn't have much time. The discovery of the body was already known across the country, so Nora wouldn't be the only journalist trying to contact Ellen Hellberg's widower in the coming hours.

She drove in through the gate, and parked in front of the house. The gravel crunched under her feet when she got out of the car and walked over to the steps. She rang the doorbell and soon after heard footsteps inside. The door opened. A man appeared on the threshold, squinting into the light.

Fritz Hellberg III was barely recognisable from the photographs Nora had seen online. They had obviously been taken some years ago, when he must have weighed at least double what he did now. The face she was looking up at was thin and drawn. A wattle of sagging, red skin wobbled under his chin.

She'd heard the cliché 'he's half the man he used to be' often enough, but seldom had this description been so fitting. Fritz Hellberg III looked ill. But he smelt good – his eau de cologne made her think of her own grandfather, who was dead now, but had always been good-natured, humorous and kind when he was alive.

Nora introduced herself.

Fritz shrank a little when he heard her name. She had the impression that he had just been crying; his eyes were red and puffy.

'I've come straight from Hulebakk,' she said.

He closed his eyes, tightening his grip on the door handle.

'It didn't take you long, did it?' he said, and opened his eyes again. There was something resigned about his voice, as though he didn't have the strength to be angry or annoyed. But his remark still had a sting to it.

'Have the police been in touch yet?' she asked.

'No,' he said, with a sigh. 'But I've spoken to my lawyer. And he's spoken to them.' His eyes were shiny.

'So it is Ellen they've found out there?'

He didn't move, just stared straight ahead. Then he nodded, almost imperceptibly. 'Her necklace...' His voice, which was thin and whis-pery, broke. He looked away.

'My condolences,' Nora said. 'I can't imagine what it must be like to...'

'Can't you?' His eyes flashed. 'Isn't that how people like you make a living?' His voice had suddenly transformed into a coarse snarl.

Nora couldn't think of anything to say in her defence, so just looked at him with what she hoped were understanding eyes.

'I'm sorry,' he then added, swiftly. 'I didn't mean to...' He couldn't finish the sentence.

'That's quite alright,' Nora said. 'And just so you know, I'm not here to write about your grief, or to get you to express how you feel – I'll leave that to the tabloid journalists.'

'Why are you here then?'

Nora thought for a moment. 'You've perhaps seen the two articles I've written recently,' she tried.

He nodded reluctantly.

'I came to Tønsberg to find Hedda, your niece, and I don't intend to stop until I have.'

'But why are you *here* then?' Hellberg asked again, and looked at her with doleful eyes.

Nora took a deep breath. 'Because I have a feeling that something happened in her family – in your family – which is somehow connected to her disappearance. I know that your son is being questioned at Tønsberg police station, and that they're still considering whether to hold him on remand or not. And I hoped that you might be able to tell me something that might shed light on the whole thing.'

He shook his head. 'I certainly don't intend to share my sorrows and suffering with *Aftenposten* readers.'

He was about to turn his back.

'But you don't need to,' Nora tried.

He stopped.

'Like I said, I'm trying to find Hedda. One of the advantages of talking to a journalist is that we generally protect our sources. Well, I certainly do. If someone is scared of saying something that might be damaging, I don't push it, as the police are duty-bound to do. And right now, your wife's been found dead at Hulebakk, your niece is missing and your son is being held on suspicion of having something to do with her disappearance. If you try to see it through anyone else's eyes, Mr Hellberg, you'll realise that there's something very odd going on here.'

Nora studied the man in front of her. It looked as though he was trying to straighten his shoulders, without much success. His cheeks were even redder. He thought long and hard. Then he lifted his head and said: 'It's cold out. Would you like to come in?'

Nora gave him warm smile. 'That would be very nice, thank you,' she replied.

⊙

They went into the library, which smelt of old leather and cigar smoke. There was an old, dark-oak table in the middle of the room, with a leather chair behind it. And on the table there was a lamp, writing materials, envelopes, an elegant penholder, and a porcelain cup with the Hellberg family coat of arms on it. The same coat of arms was hanging in a frame on the wall behind, beside a picture of the farm that William Hellberg had spoken about – the first property they'd ever sold. Everything about Fritz Hellberg III, everything about the library, spoke of history and money. Of quality.

'It's a bit early in the day,' he said, indicating to Nora that she should sit down. 'But I really need a drink. Can I offer you a whisky?'

Nora put her hand to her stomach. 'I'm driving,' she said, 'but thank you.'

'So be it.'

Fritz went over to a corner cupboard where there were three crystal decanters with amber contents. He got out a glass and poured himself a drink. He swirled the liquid round in a dance at the bottom of the glass before lifting it to his nose, inhaling deeply a couple of times, then taking the first sip. Half the contents of the glass disappeared and he kept his eyes shut. Nora could see the strength it gave him. She also knew better than to interrupt a ritual, and so, instead, she tried to work out what approach was needed to get him to answer all her questions.

She decided to let Fritz do most of the talking. She got out her notepad and put it on her lap.

'My wife,' he started, focusing on a point on the wall. 'I was twenty-three when I met Ellen. She was a nurse and had been hired to look after my mother at the end of her life.'

Nora kept her eyes on the contents of the glass that sloshed around as he walked to and fro.

'They quickly developed a very good relationship. My mother was glad of the chance to tell someone else about everything she'd done for the family business – we'd all heard the story about how she developed the archiving system when Father took over the company in the fifties a million times before.'

He rolled his eyes, and shook his head a little.

'I had a close relationship with my mother, but I soon realised that it wasn't only her I was going to visit.'

Fritz smiled at the memory and emptied his glass, closed his eyes again, then poured some more whisky. He sat down at the enormous oak table, which lent him just the authority he seemed to want. He folded his hands.

'Ellen and I got married a year and half after Mother died.'

He smiled and shook his head gently again. Nora guessed that it had been a spectacular wedding.

'I can safely say that I was the world's happiest man. And the first years of our marriage were wonderful. I don't think even Ellen would deny that. But we struggled to have children, and for a long time, I thought that we wouldn't. But then Fritz Georg was born, in 1977.' He stared at his glass. 'And from then on, Ellen lived and breathed for Georg alone. I've come to understand that it's quite usual for women who have yearned for a child for a long time to then become totally obsessive about the child when the dream comes true.'

Nora thought briefly about Henning. He'd once accused her of the same thing during an argument.

'And that's exactly what happened with Ellen,' Fritz continued. 'She didn't care much about me any longer. I had my own problems, having taken over the company when my father became seriously ill. I worked a lot, ate a lot of unhealthy food. And doubled in size.' He made a gesture with his hand over his stomach. 'And I guess that was one of the reasons why my wife looked on me with increasing revulsion.'

Fritz didn't look at Nora as he spoke, but stared instead at the contents of his glass, which he kept in continuous movement, with small, finely tuned turns of the wrist. The dance of the amber nectar seemed to have a hypnotic effect on him. His voice was a monotone and small pearls of sweat were visible on his forehead.

He carried on with a sigh. 'My brother Oscar was, in many ways, the opposite of me. He was moderate in terms of food and drink; he cycled and ran; he even canoed out at Hulebakk in summer. And there's no doubt about it, women found him devilishly attractive. My wife included, unfortunately,' Fritz sighed again.

He paused. Nora had to stop herself from asking questions.

'Oscar, for his part, had had to marry Unni when she was only nineteen, because he'd managed to make her pregnant. William was born in 1969, and then Patrik arrived three years later.'

And after another three years, Hedda, Nora thought.

'Oscar was outgoing, social, always in a good mood. Ellen always looked forward to the summer, to the crab parties we had out at Hulebakk. We had barbecues, went swimming – or that's to say, the others did. I generally sat in a chair with my face to the sun and one of these in my hand.' He lifted the glass as though to illustrate his point.

It took a while before he continued. 'It was Unni who came and told me one day.' Fritz shook his head. 'I remember it only too well, the day it happened. It was autumn, like now. She came storming into my office, just as I was about to go into a meeting. She'd found one of Ellen's scarves in Oscar's car, and when she confronted him, he admitted they were lovers.' Fritz emptied his glass and groaned. 'And it had been going on for a while, it turned out.'

Nora thought about the woman she'd met out at Kalvetangen the evening before. Having heard Fritz's story, it was easier to understand her sadness.

The memories made him shake his head again. 'But Unni, she's the sort who would rather keep up a façade. She didn't want to do anything about it; she just wanted Oscar and Ellen to stop seeing each other and for all the problems to disappear.'

'Perhaps easier said than done,' Nora commented.

Fritz appeared to start at the sound of her voice. 'Yes, but we kept up appearances, as we'd been taught to do. Our relationship was obviously never the same again. And, naturally, I hated my brother and I hated Ellen for having betrayed me.'

He paused.

'But I didn't kill her,' he said eventually. 'I could never have done that to Fritz Georg. And I'd had a heart attack just a few weeks before she disappeared, so was still pretty much bed-bound. Would never have managed to do it.'

Fritz took out his handkerchief and pressed it against his forehead, his eyes, then put it back in his pocket.

'What happened in the days and weeks before Ellen disappeared?' Nora asked. 'Did the four of you have it out?'

He lifted his head, but lowered his eyes. 'No.'

Nora waited to see if he'd say any more, but he didn't.

'Not even Ellen and Unni?'

Suddenly he looked straight at her. 'Unni had nothing to do with Ellen's death.'

'How do you know that?'

He shook his head. 'Unni was a stick of a woman at the time; still is, for that matter. And I don't know if you've been out there and seen the well, but it has a big, heavy, concrete cover, which has always been there. Unni would never have been able to lift off the cover. It could only have been a man – or several people. And I know that it certainly wasn't me.'

Nora thought for a moment. 'And you have no idea who might have done it?'

'No,' he said.

Nora considered what Fritz had just told her about his brother. Oscar was strong. Had something happened between Ellen and him? Had they argued?

But Oscar was dead and whatever might have happened between them would never be known. Unless that was why Hedda had disappeared. Because she knew the truth. Which meant that at least one other person did too.

According to Hugo Refsdal, Hedda had sat by her father's side day and night in the days before he died. Maybe he had said something to her? It wasn't unusual for people to feel the need to get things off their chest before they died.

'Was she depressed, your wife, in the period before she disappeared?'

He tilted his head to the left, then to the right. 'It's such a long time ago, but I seem to remember she was pretty much as she always was with me – cold and distant; uninterested in what I was doing. But she would light up as soon as Fritz Georg came into the room; it was like flicking a switch.'

He smacked his lips. Then his face changed. As though he had remembered something. 'She did do one thing that I thought was rather odd at the time,' he said, and looked up at Nora. 'And I now think it's even odder.'

Nora waited for him to continue.

'Just before she disappeared, she started a fund in Fritz Georg's name and put in a substantial sum. He was to get it when he turned eighteen. I had no idea she had so much money, but now it seems to substantiate the idea that she committed suicide.'

'You mean the fact that she made financial arrangements in Georg's favour?'

He nodded. 'She must have known she was in some sort of danger,' he said, seeming surprised by the thought.

Nora wrote the word FUND in capital letters on her notepad, and underlined it twice. They both sat with their own thoughts for a while.

'Mr Hellberg, we're going to have to talk about your son, as well,' Nora said, eventually.

He closed his eyes for a moment.

'Have you spoken to Georg since he was taken in for questioning yesterday evening?'

'Only very briefly this morning, via Preben Mørck, our lawyer.'

Nora straightened up. 'I understand that Georg didn't want to say anything about where he and Hedda were going the day he picked her up at Skoppum Station.'

Fritz stood up, picked up his glass and went back over to the cut-crystal decanter. 'No, and he wouldn't tell me anything either.'

Nora was tempted to follow him, but stayed sitting where she was.

'Can you think of any reason why Hedda would tell her husband she was going away for three weeks, when in fact she was up to something with your son?'

He poured himself another generous drink.

'I don't know,' he said, putting the stopper back in. 'But I don't think there was anything going on between them. As far as I know, Hedda was happy with her life. Hugo is a good man.'

So it was still a question of where they were going and why, and what went wrong.

'Did you have much to do with Hedda?'

'Me? No,' he said, shaking his head. 'But...' He turned towards her. And again, he had a rather astonished look on his face. 'She actually came to visit me here not long ago.'

Nora looked up at him.

'I think it was just a few days before she was due to go to Italy,' he continued, and took a step closer. 'It was quite strange really, because she'd never done anything like that before. That's to say, come here to visit me on her own.'

'What did she want?' Nora asked.

'She wanted to talk about Ellen,' he said, and looked at Nora.

The frown on Nora's forehead deepened. 'Ellen?'

'Yes. She asked if I knew what kind of books Ellen liked, if she'd had a favourite author, that sort of thing. Hedda said that she'd caught the reading bug and knew that Ellen had been interested in literature; read at least two books a week.'

Nora thought hard.

'So she wanted some suggestions on what to read? When she was in Italy?'

'That's what I thought.'

There was nothing strange about asking for suggestions about what to read, Nora reasoned. The only thing was that she had never seen

Hedda read anything other than course material when they lived together. But then, you could develop an interest in literature at any time. Why the sudden interest in what Ellen liked to read, though? Especially when Hedda wasn't even going to Italy.

'Things don't look too good for my boy,' Hellberg said in a melancholy voice. 'They've found blood out at the summer house, on the fireplace in the living room.'

Nora's eyes opened wide.

'And at least one shot had been fired too. The police found a bullet in the ceiling.'

Nora didn't know what to say, or what it meant.

Fritz sat down heavily. He looked at her with drowsy eyes. 'And if that's not enough, one of our hunting rifles is missing.'

35

It was busy outside Ullevål Stadium, the national football team's home ground, with hordes of people milling around the building's shops and offices.

Nansen Models didn't quite fit in among the car-parts merchant, the supermarkets and the off licence, but the fact that it was only a kilometre's walk from Veronica Nansen's flat in Ullevål Hageby made it an appealing location. Henning positioned himself by a shop front to wait for the company's founder. When she did eventually come out, she stopped abruptly as soon as she saw him.

'Hi,' Henning said, and took a step closer.

'Hi,' she said back.

'On your way home?' he asked.

She nodded, hesitantly.

'Do you mind if I walk with you?'

She didn't answer for a few moments.

'No,' she said finally, and put her bag over her shoulder and started to walk. They passed a shop that sold Apple products, a sports shop, then the entrance to a hotel.

'Busy day?' he asked. 'You must have seen that I've been trying to call you.'

'Yes, there ... there's been a fair amount to do.'

A boy on a scooter was heading straight for them. Henning had to step to one side to avoid being run over. The boy's mother was not far behind and apologised.

'The last time we met,' Henning said, 'you told me about Tore and Charlie Høisæther. That they grew up together and were friends.'

Veronica glanced at him.

'Do you know if they ever fell out at any point?'

'Fell out?' Veronica repeated.

'Geir Grønningen certainly seemed to think so,' Henning said. 'I thought you might have picked up on something.'

A homeless man with red cheeks was standing outside the off licence, a cup in his hand.

'No, I ... I can't say that I did,' she said. 'But that's not really surprising. Tore never talked to me about things like that.'

'You didn't notice anything from his behaviour?'

Veronica thought about it. 'I don't think so. Tore never brought his work problems home with him. If he needed to get something out of his system, he went to the gym or found a road without much traffic and no police, so he could ride his motorbike at top speed.'

They walked for a few metres without saying anything.

'But it was a bit odd that I didn't see Charlie at Tore's funeral,' Veronica said. 'Then again, if he was in Brazil, it might not have been that easy for him to get over.'

'William Hellberg ... is he someone you know?'

Her shoes, which clicked on the tarmac, faltered, slowed down, then picked up pace again.

'Yes, I ... know of William, of course,' she replied in a quiet voice, looking straight ahead, taking care not to bump into a woman with four bags of shopping.

'In what way?'

Veronica brushed some hair out of her face.

'I've met him socially, at parties and dinners, you know. Him and his wife.' She started to walk faster again. 'They were childhood friends as well,' she said, and adjusted the bag on her shoulder. 'Tore and William, that is.'

Henning studied her as they walked. Her quick, sharp moves and evasive eyes. She sniffed loudly, only lifting her head occasionally.

'What is it?' he asked.

Veronica glanced over at him again and pulled a baffled face.

'You seem nervous,' he said.

'Do I?'

She tried to laugh it off, but it just made things worse. Her smile froze, her eyes continued to dart back and forth, and Henning had to move faster to keep up with her. The closer they got to the ICA supermarket, the busier it got. People were coming out with bulging bags; a man pushed a shopping trolley full of food in front of him, with a gleeful little girl in the seat. Cars were parking and driving off, and the smell of fast food drifted towards them.

Once they had left the stadium behind them, and had walked past the metro station and the first bus stop, there were fewer people on the pavement. Henning made a point of not saying anything, but just looked over at Veronica every now and then, waiting for her to comment on what he'd said. Soon she slowed down again, raised her eyes and looked at the hedges that partially hid the big houses.

'I think Tore and William were in the same class at secondary school, or something like that. Or maybe Tore was a couple of years younger. I'm not sure. They certainly spent a lot of time together as they got older. William came from a rich family, and I think he maybe thought it was cool to hang out with someone like Tore. They came from such different worlds.'

They walked on.

'But then William started to work – was more or less given the family business at a time when Tore...' She looked around again. The nearest people were at least twenty metres away. '...At a time when Tore had started to get a name for himself in quite a different field,' she concluded.

A school class came walking towards them, all the children in reflective vests. Veronica crossed the road; Henning followed.

When the children were at a safe distance, she said in a barely audible voice: 'Not long after Tore and I started going out, I asked him what he'd done over the years. It was no secret that he'd been a real bad ass. I didn't want any shit to come up once we were a couple.' She glanced over her shoulder. 'So I demanded that he told me everything he'd done; who he'd done a job on and why. And Tore was fine with it. He told me about the people whose jaws he'd smashed, about a man who had his balls crushed because he'd done something to a woman Tore knew.' She let out a heavy sigh. 'Tore had done quite a lot,' she said. 'No doubt about it.'

It dawned on Henning where the story was going, but he wanted to let Veronica tell it in her own time.

She stopped walking and looked at him. 'William Hellberg was one of Tore's first clients.'

Henning didn't answer, just held her gaze. She couldn't take it and looked down at the ground again, then everything around them – anything but him. A bus came rattling towards them with a queue of cars behind.

'William was new in the property business at the time,' Veronica continued. 'His business style was probably a bit wild and ruthless to begin with. But whatever the case, I asked Tore if he'd done other things. Worse things.'

Veronica looked at him again.

'You mean, if he'd killed anyone?'

She held his gaze, then nodded slowly.

'And what did he say?'

'He said no. But I don't know how truthful he was being – I definitely got the feeling he hadn't told me everything.'

It was Henning's turn to nod. He thought about Nora. She'd met William.

'So you didn't really believe him?'

Her eyes followed a man who jogged past. 'I don't know. But it does bother me, particularly now when I think about the woman they found out at the Hellbergs' summer place today. She disappeared around the time that Tore did some work for William.'

36

This is getting more and more complex, Nora thought as she left the home of Fritz Hellberg III. There were clear indications that there had been some kind of scuffle at Oscar Hellberg's summer house, and that at least one shot had been fired, but all this had nothing to do with the discovery of the body in the woods. What's more, there were still no fresh clues about Hedda, unless the blood proved to be hers. What Nora did know was that Hedda had developed a sudden interest in Ellen Hellberg's reading habits just before she disappeared.

What a mystery, Nora mused as she got into her car and drove away. The police had announced that there would be a press conference at three o'clock, but that wasn't for another few hours, and Merete Stephans could cover that, anyway.

Nora thought about Ellen's husband as she drove. His eyes had some of the same dullness as Unni's. As though nothing could make him happy.

Grief, Nora said to herself; *a virus you can never quite kick. Not completely.*

She checked her mobile phone; someone from the office had called several times, but she didn't have much more for them to publish right now. The sensitive family secrets would remain secret for as long as possible – that was the last thing she had promised Fritz as he slipped into the whisky haze that looked like it wouldn't wear off for the next couple of hours.

Nora tried to ring Unni, to get her version of the story about Ellen. But, unsurprisingly, her phone was switched off. Nora could perhaps try to find her landline number, or drive out to Kalvetangen again, but after some consideration, she decided instead to pay another visit to Hellberg Property.

She parked in more or less the same place as the last time, and went into the office in the hope that William would still be as positive and willing to help her do her job as he had been before, even though much had changed in the meantime.

One of the staff came to greet her as soon as she opened the door. Nora asked if William was around. The man disappeared into the back, and only a few moments later, the boss himself was standing in the doorway; Big Brother, as Georg had called him. William whispered an inaudible message to his employee, then gave Nora a nod to indicate that he could see her. She walked towards him with a sympathetic smile, and, when she was close enough, held out her hand.

William took it. His fingers were clammy and his handshake weaker than before. He showed her into his office again and they sat down. William's mobile phone rang and he checked the screen. His shoulders slouched ever so slightly.

'Journalists?' Nora asked.

'No,' he shook his head. 'My wife.'

He waited for a second before answering the phone. Nora made a point of looking away, not wanting him to think she was interested in their conversation. A copy of the family coat of arms hung on the wall. She hadn't noticed it last time. It was an engraving in dark wood.

'But can't you...'

Out of the corner of her eye, Nora saw him rolling his eyes.

'...Can't you get someone else to collect him? I'm in the middle of something right now.' William sighed. 'Yes, I know, but...'

He glanced surreptitiously at Nora. She got out her own phone, unlocked the keypad and went to her emails. No new information, only group emails – minutes from past meetings and reminders of others.

'OK,' William said with resignation. 'But I'll have to come back to the office afterwards.'

He put down the phone without saying goodbye, apologising to Nora, who put down her own phone.

'My wife,' he explained. 'She's rather overprotective about our son. As I said last time, he's got a rare illness, so we can all get a bit stressed when he's not well.'

'Is something wrong with him?'

'Now? Probably not; he's just got a bit of a temperature.'

Nora remembered how she had been with Jonas at times – in the first year, particularly. Everything was new, everything was danger-ous, and it took a while before she understood that children needed to be sick every now and then; it was how they built up their immune system. So it wasn't surprising if people were overly cautious, especially when their child had a chronic illness.

'Do you have time for a very quick chat first?' she asked.

'Very quick,' he smiled.

'Could I ask what you think about all of this?' she said. 'The discov-ery of Ellen's body; your sister being missing; the shots that you've no doubt heard were fired at me yesterday?'

'What I think?' he said, with a deep sigh. 'It's not looking good for Georg, that's for sure. And if he has killed Hedda, well...' William balled his fists and clenched his teeth.

'Do you know if he's a good shot?'

'Georg?' William sat up. 'He came hunting with us a few years ago. Shot about four or five grouse a day. I don't think he ever missed. So yes, he's a good shot; was probably the best among us.'

Nora thought about Patrik's dislike of Georg, and the iciness she thought she now detected between William and Georg.

'How was your father in those final weeks before he died?'

Hellberg gave her a puzzled look. 'I'm not quite sure I understand your question.'

'Was he bitter because he was going to die? Did he reminisce a lot about his life? Were there things he felt he had to get off his chest?'

Hellberg looked at her even more keenly. 'Uh, no, I'm not sure really,' he said, then leaned back in his chair again. 'I was told that he cried a lot, which for him, was pretty unusual. He was quite a macho type. But ... well, it can't be that unusual for someone to get sentimental when they're approaching the end.'

'No, not at all,' Nora reassured him, mostly for the sake of saying something.

'But he didn't tell me anything – I wasn't really there as much as everyone else, though. It's possible he said something to the others.'

Nora remembered what Hugo Refsdal had told her about Hedda – that she was a real daddy's girl. Which would lend ballast to the idea that Oscar might have told her something about his life. Something about Ellen, possibly; something that led Hedda to lie to her husband about needing three weeks' recuperation in Italy. Perhaps Oscar suspected that Ellen had been killed and that she might be buried out at Hulebakk. That would explain why Hedda went there, why she allied herself with Georg, Ellen's son.

But it did not explain why a police search was needed in order to find her, and why Hedda was now missing. Nor why Hedda had suddenly become so interested in a Swedish pensioner who had been killed soon after.

Nora asked William if he knew who Daniel Schyman was.

He put his fingers together to make a triangle. 'No,' he replied. 'Who is he?'

'What about Jens and Torill Holmboe? Do you know who they are?'

He squinted up to the left.

'They live in Brages vei 18,' she told him. 'Here in Tønsberg.'

Again, he seemed to think long and hard.

'I've known pretty much all the flats and houses that we've sold over the years,' he said. 'But that doesn't ring any bells. Why do you ask?'

Nora crossed her legs. 'I know that shortly before she disappeared, Hedda seemed to be interested in both Schyman and that address; she did internet searches for them. But I haven't managed to find any reasonable explanation as to why. I thought perhaps you might know.'

He shook his head.

They sat in silence for a few seconds. Then William looked at his watch.

'I really must go now,' he said. 'Was there anything else?' He stood up.
'No,' Nora replied.

She looked at the coat of arms on the wall behind him. An idea struck her and she couldn't fathom why she hadn't thought of it before.

'Not right now, no.'

◎

Out on the street, she found her mobile phone and rang Hugo Refsdal.

'Hi, it's Nora,' she said. 'Have you heard what's happened?'

A heavy sigh at the other end. 'I don't know if I should be happy or sad that it wasn't Hedda they found,' he admitted.

'I can understand that,' Nora said, trying to be comforting, and walking as she spoke. It felt colder now than it had done only half an hour ago. 'But there was something else I wondered about. Oscar's will?' The way she said it was both a question and a suggestion.

'Yes, what about it?'

'You said you didn't know how much Hedda had inherited from her father,' she said. 'But did the family ever discuss the settlement of the will?'

Refsdal chewed something he had in his mouth. It sounded like a carrot.

'There was a lot of discussion the day they went through the will,' he said, and swallowed. 'But I wasn't part of it. Unni took the family and the lawyer with her into the library after dinner.'

Nora stepped on to a zebra crossing just as a car turned into the road.

'The children, in other words?' Nora asked, as the driver slammed on the brakes. She sent him an angry look.

'Yes,' Refsdal replied. 'And Georg.'

Nora stopped in her tracks. 'Georg?'

'Yes, he was asked to come in, too, but later.'

Nora got the car keys out of her bag, and pressed unlock. 'So he inherited something, too?'

'I assume so, seeing as the lawyer wanted him to come in.'

Nora opened the car door, threw her bag down onto the passenger seat and got in. 'But you don't know what?'

'No.'

'Didn't you ask Hedda about it?'

'Yes, of course I did. But Hedda made it quite clear that it was none of my business.'

Nora processed this.

'And you didn't think that was strange?'

'Yes, but I didn't want to push it – not straightaway, at least. It wasn't long after her father had died and I thought she would just tell me in her own time, when she had more of a perspective on things.'

'Hmm,' Nora muttered. It struck her as rather peculiar that Hedda didn't want to share this kind of information with her husband. But then there was a lot about Hedda's behaviour at the time that didn't quite add up.

Nora thanked Hugo for his help and hung up. She knew there was something staring her in the face, but she just couldn't see it. She sat and pondered for a few minutes. Hedda's brother, Patrik, had been the hardest to get hold of since Nora had been in Tønsberg; he was the person in the family that Nora felt she knew least about. But she also remembered the snort Patrik gave when Georg's name was mentioned.

Keep Georg out of this.

Nora decided to pay him a visit at home.

37

Patrik Hellberg and his wife lived out on Jarlsø, a small island about ten minutes' drive from Tønsberg – a place where you could have a terrace and sea view without having to cut the lawn and stain the fence. Most of the inhabitants were from Vestfold, but more recently, some people from Oslo had also moved to the island, and other people had their summer cabins there.

When Nora rang the Hellbergs' bell, a woman answered the intercom.

'Patrik's not here,' she said.

Nora frowned. 'How long will it be before he's back?'

'I don't actually know.'

'You don't know how long it will take from wherever he is, or you don't know when he's coming back?'

'Both, in fact,' she said. 'Patrik's very busy at work at the moment.'

Nora waited a moment before she continued. 'Could I maybe have a few words with you instead?'

This was initially met with silence.

'What about?'

Nora could hear the scepticism in the woman's voice.

'About everything that's happened in the Hellberg family recently,' she said, well aware that it was vague and potentially alarming.

'I don't want to be interviewed,' the woman replied.

Nora sighed inwardly; she hated having to coax people into talking.

'I'm not sure if you know who I am,' Nora started. 'But I studied with Hedda in the nineties. Journalism,' she added, pre-empting the question. 'We haven't had much contact since then, but that doesn't mean that I don't still consider her a good friend. And I would very much like to find out what's happened to her. I just have a few questions, so I can understand the family better.'

The woman didn't answer.

'Just a couple of minutes?' Nora pressed a little more. 'And I promise, I won't write anything about you in the paper. I'm only trying to find out what's happened.'

There was no reply. Not for a long time.

'Oh, OK,' the voice said, eventually. 'Two minutes.'

'Thank you so much.'

The door buzzed.

'We're on the third floor, left-hand side. Facing the sea.'

'OK,' Nora said. 'Thank you.'

Nora went into the hall and took the lift up to the third floor. The woman, who Nora presumed was Patrik's wife, met her in the doorway. She was wearing baggy, black tracksuit bottoms, and a white top under an open, grey cardigan.

'Hi,' Nora said, and held out her hand. 'Nora Klemetsen.'

'Olivia Svendsen.'

Olivia had a baby-smooth face, bright-red lipstick and carried not a gram of spare fat on her body; in fact, she looked like she could do with an extra kilo or two. Nora, who was on the short side herself, noted that Olivia was not much taller. Her hair was the colour of Mediterranean sand with darker highlights. She looked at Nora with icy-blue, guarded eyes.

'Come in,' she said, stepping to the side.

Nora went into the flat, which was lovely and light, with taupe walls and white window frames. A red Persian carpet was on the floor. In the hallway, a glass table stood against the wall, and above it, a square mirror with a glass frame. The reflection from a lamp on either side gave off a warm glow. On the opposite wall was a huge oil painting of a shoreline, with smooth rocks sloping down to the water. An old chest of drawers stood beside it.

'Wow,' Nora burst out, when she went into the living room. The floor was darker, the lighting dimmer, and a door was open to the terrace that overlooked the fjord. The surface of the water shimmered, stirred by a persistent, cold wind. 'What an amazing place you have.'

She made a full turn, taking it all in, and instantly had the urge to open all the doors and look in all the cupboards. Nothing had been abandoned on the floor or left out of place. The sofa cushions were perfectly positioned. None of the surfaces was overflowing with papers, keys, matchboxes or hair bands, as they were at her place. The day's post lay on a table beside the phone: a small, neat pile of envelopes, all addressed to Patrik, as far as Nora could see.

The Hellberg home, Nora thought. Everything just as it should be.

'Thank you, yes, it's not bad,' Olivia said, and straightened her back.

Nora continued to admire the floor, chairs, walls.

'Have you been living here long?'

'We were one of the first to buy,' Olivia said and wandered further into the room. 'We knew that it would become a popular area.'

'I'll say,' said Nora, following her.

'Would you like a tea or a coffee, or anything else?'

'A cup of tea sounds good. But only if you're having one,' Nora added, hastily.

Olivia didn't answer, but carried on into the kitchen, where the white goods weren't white, but brushed steel, the cupboards were white and shiny, and the counter black, with a perfectly integrated hob. One of the Svendsen-Hellberg home's elegant props was taken out of a corner cupboard, filled with water and popped on the hob. Olivia then got out some tea bags that Nora knew could not be bought at any old supermarket, and took down two mugs from one of the top cupboards and a vanilla-white sugar bowl with a silver spoon in it.

Nora looked around for wedding photos; there were a couple on the wall in the living room. She went over to them and studied Olivia's wedding dress, hair, flowers. It made her think of her own big day. Whereas Olivia Svendsen and Patrik Hellberg had no doubt invited hundreds of guests, there were only twenty-eight people at Nora and Henning's wedding. She had wanted to invite the whole world and celebrate for three days on end, while Henning would have preferred a ceremony at the town hall before going to a café for a beer and some food, and then back to work the next day. They ended up with something in between – a garden party at Nora's parents' home, where they danced long into the night.

The water soon boiled and Olivia poured it into a teapot that she had prepared. She then put everything onto a small tray and took it with her into the living room and set it down on a table by the leather sofa.

'Patrik told me that he'd spoken to you,' she said.

Nora wrinkled her nose. 'Did he?'

Olivia nodded, her eyes fixed on the glass table in front of her.

'And how did he feel about the press digging all this up?'

She held back at first.

'Well, I wouldn't exactly say that he was happy about it. Patrik is a Hellberg, after all, and they generally want to keep everything in the family. But I don't think he was particularly angry with you.'

A hint of ginger rose on the steam from the tea and teased her nose. Nora realised she was hungry.

'I hope you don't mind me asking, but how has Patrik reacted to everything that's happened in the family recently?'

Olivia picked up the teapot and gave it a swirl so the tea bags started to swim round.

'Patrik has barely been at home in the past few weeks, so it's not easy to know. But I think it would be safe to say it's affected him. He was very fond of his father. And then the whole thing with Hedda as well.'

She sat back in her seat again.

'Did he have a close relationship with her?'

Olivia shook her head. 'I don't think so. Hedda has never been here for coffee and cake, put it that way.'

'Why not?'

'I'm not really sure, to tell you the truth. We meet once a month at my mother-in-law's family dinners, and then there's the various children's birthdays, as well. But, with Patrik travelling so much for work, there's not really been time for much more. He barely has time to spend with me.' Olivia gave a small smile.

Nora nodded. 'Where does his work take him?'

'All over the place,' Olivia said, and rolled her eyes. 'Poland, Denmark, Sweden.'

Nora looked over at her. 'Sweden?' she repeated.

'Yes. In fact, he's been there quite a lot recently. I think the truth is, he rather likes it. All the travelling I mean. In summer we spend five solid weeks on our boat, only going ashore when we need to.' She lifted her eyes, looking a little dreamy. 'I live for those weeks,' she concluded.

Nora waited before asking her next question.

'Have you ever heard of a man called Daniel Schyman?'

Olivia leaned forwards, and quickly looked in the teapot.

'No,' she said leaning back. 'Who is he?'

Nora didn't answer and decided to tackle the real reason why she was there.

'Olivia, there are a number of things about Hedda and her family that I don't really understand.'

Olivia lifted her chin ever so slightly.

'Like the settlement of Oscar's will, for example.'

Olivia's eyes narrowed almost imperceptibly.

Nora swiftly continued: 'I'm not going to write about it, but I just don't see why Georg should inherit anything?'

She mooted it as a question. Waited for Olivia to respond.

'You perhaps weren't asked into the library that day, either?'

'No,' Olivia replied, picking up the teapot and pouring Nora a cup, slowly. 'But Patrik told me that Georg had got the summer house.'

Nora's eyes grew wide. 'Really?'

Olivia nodded. 'You might say it didn't go down very well.'

Nora could feel that her mouth was open. Olivia put down the teapot, and leaned back among the cushions.

'But...' Several thoughts were vying for Nora's attention. 'But why?'

Olivia looked at Nora askance.

Nora remembered something that Fritz had said: that at one point he'd thought he and Ellen couldn't have children. But then Georg was born all the same. Nora felt a flame shoot up her spine, and explode behind her forehead.

'Was Oscar in fact Georg's father?'

A sheepish smile crept over Olivia's lips. 'My father-in-law was a magnet for the ladies,' she said, shaking her head. 'He had something very special about him ... charismatic.' She looked away. 'I know it's terrible of me to say so, but he was a very stylish man.'

Nora remembered the looks Oscar had sent her the time he came to Oslo and took her and Hedda out for a meal. He was quick to give compliments – both to her and the waiting staff. And she had to admit, she'd been utterly charmed.

So if Georg had inherited the summer house, it wasn't so strange that he had the keys, she thought. She also realised why Patrik had as good as snarled when his name was mentioned. She guessed that the relationship between the cousins was not the best; the interaction between William and Georg at Hellberg Property testified to that.

At this point the front door opened. Olivia jumped and rushed out into the hall.

'We've got a visitor,' Nora heard her say.

There was a tinkling of keys as they hit the table.

'Right.'

'It's a journalist from *Aftenposten.*'

'Have you...' Patrik Hellberg's voice was bright, but firm. 'Have you let a journalist in here?' he asked.

'We're just chatting,' Olivia tried to reassure him.

Patrik came into the living room and looked Nora straight in the eye. She stood up.

'Hello,' she said. 'I hope I'm not intruding.'

'Get out of here. *Now.*' Patrik put his arm out emphatically and pointed to the door.

'I apologise if you think it was inappropriate,' Nora tried. 'That was never my intention.'

'You and all the other journalist scum should leave me and my family in peace,' he growled.

'I'm only trying to find your sister,' Nora said, looking at him, unruffled by his aggression. He was not particularly broad and his arms were thin. His shirt was tight around the midriff and she could see his navel.

Nora was about to slip past him when she stopped.

'Thank you for the tea,' she said, and turned to Olivia with a smile. 'It was very kind.'

Olivia nodded stiffly. Nora went out into the hall and put on her shoes and jacket.

'Should you ever want to talk to me about something, Mr Hellberg, you'll find my card here,' she said, and put it down on the table under the mirror. 'Whether you like it or not, a lot will be written about you and your family in the coming days and weeks. And if you want to have some control over what people are told about you, then I might be a good bet.'

She opened the door and said with a smile: 'Not all scum is bad, you know.'

38

When Nora was halfway down the stairs, the Bee Gees' 'Stayin' Alive' started to play in her pocket. She took out her phone, thinking it was probably Merete Stephans or someone from the newspaper. It wasn't.

It was Henning.

Nora stopped.

She hadn't spoken to him since she told him she was pregnant. He hadn't answered her text messages either, and now here he was calling her.

She put the phone to her ear and answered with a quiet hello, which was clear and deep at the same time.

'Hi, it's Henning,' he said. 'Are you busy?'

'No, not at the moment. How ... how are you?'

'Are you in Tønsberg right now?' he asked.

Nora was startled by his directness.

'Yes, well almost,' she replied, and moved down a step.

'Have you spoken to William Hellberg recently?' he asked.

Nora accelerated. 'About an hour ago,' she said. 'Why do you ask?' Her boots made a deafening noise on the stairs.

'Tore Pulli started his career as an enforcer in Vestfold,' Henning said. 'And William Hellberg was one of his first clients.'

Nora stopped by the door on the ground floor. 'You're joking.'

'What's your impression of Hellberg?' Henning asked.

Nora pushed open the door and a gust of wind hit her in the face. The telephone whined and crackled.

'Um, I don't know,' she said. 'Polite, proper.'

The wind was stinging her cheeks, so she walked as fast as she could towards the car.

'When was this – that Tore and Hellberg worked together?' she asked.

'In the nineties,' Henning told her. 'It wasn't a huge number of jobs, but Tore was a brutal bastard at the time.'

Nora thought about Ellen. Killed and dumped in a well by someone strong enough to lift a cover that must weigh at least a hundred kilos.

'I have to talk to him,' Henning said.

'Huh?' Nora said, distracted.

'I have to talk to William Hellberg.'

Nora was at the car. 'Why?' she asked.

'Because he knew Tore and because he's worked in the property business for years. Whereabouts are you in Tønsberg? I need to get a bit more info on him first.'

Nora hesitated and then suggested they should meet at the hotel where she was staying.

'OK, I'll be there in an hour or two.'

They hung up.

Nora got into the car and thought about what to do in the meantime. She tried to ring Cato Løken, but only got his voicemail.

She sent a text instead: *Is there anywhere we could meet? Have something I want to talk to you about.*

While she waited for an answer, she went online to check what Løken had said at the press conference. He'd confirmed that the body was Ellen Hellberg's. A necklace with her name on it had been found among the bones and had helped to identify her. The police were now treating it as a criminal case, but he did not want to speculate about possible motives or perpetrators, or whether the discovery had anything to do with Hedda's disappearance.

Her phone beeped. Løken's reply: *Can meet you briefly in twenty minutes. Park in a side street by the police station. I'll find you.*

'Weren't you going to lie low for a while?' the detective inspector asked, as he got into Nora's car half an hour later.

'I'm not very tall,' Nora said.

He laughed, briefly. 'How are things?'

She shrugged and said, 'I'd rather ask you the same question.'

Løken's smile withered and he was serious again. 'Well, I have to say that the whole thing with Ellen Hellberg was a bit of a surprise. And it certainly puts the fact that Hedda is missing in a new light.'

Nora nodded. 'And there's no doubt that Ellen Hellberg was murdered?'

Løken didn't answer straightaway.

'After all, she was found in a well with the cover in place.'

'Yes and no. She was killed, yes. Strangled.'

Nora wrinkled her nose. 'How do you know that already?'

Løken looked over at her. 'The lingual bone was broken, which is quite normal with strangulation,' he said.

'Falling into a well couldn't have caused it?'

He shook his head.

'Someone had thrown some twigs and branches into the bottom of the well first, so she would have landed quite softly. And no other bones were broken.'

Nora considered the significance of this. Perhaps her killer regretted the murder?

'Has Georg said any more since hearing that his mother's body has been found?'

Løken took a deep breath and exhaled slowly. His lungs rattled.

'We only had time for a brief interview after the press conference,' he said. 'He was pretty emotional. This sort of thing sometimes loosens the tongues of people who are about to be locked away. But he didn't say much. Claims he has no idea what's happened to Hedda since he picked her up at the train station.'

Nora arched an eyebrow. 'Did he not drive her out to the summer house, then?'

Løken hesitated before answering.

'He says that he lent her his car.'

'And that she drove herself out there?'

Løken nodded. 'That was where she was going, according to Georg.'

Nora thought about Georg's car, and the fact that it had passed through the tolls.

'So that means it was Hedda who drove to Sweden the day that Daniel Schyman was killed?'

'According to Georg, yes.'

Nora followed a passing car with her eyes. The windscreen wipers were on even though it wasn't raining.

'What was she doing there?'

'Don't know.'

'Hedda didn't tell him why she needed his car?'

Løken shook his head. 'He seemed genuinely surprised when he heard that the car had been in Sweden.'

Nora's brain was racing. Then she said: 'He's had plenty of time to think up a cover story. Maybe Hedda and Georg had some kind of relationship at one level or another, then something happened between them – something that meant he killed her. And then, when the fact that she was missing was reported in the paper, he panicked – which was why he went out to Hulebakk to remove any traces of her. And, because he knew I was working on the story, he followed me and fired a few warning shots out at the summer house to scare me off.'

Løken didn't correct her.

'But Hedda isn't there, not in the house or the woods,' he said. 'Otherwise we would have found her by now.'

'What about the water?'

'We're naturally checking out that possibility, too.'

'So you're searching in the water as well?'

He dithered, then nodded.

'Have you found anything?'

He shook his head.

The two things could be unrelated, Nora thought. Maybe William contracted Tore Pulli to kill the woman who was destroying his parents' marriage, and then his cousin killed Hedda sixteen years later.

But, if what Georg had said was true – that he lent Hedda his car but didn't know that she was going to Sweden – that must mean that Hedda had reason to trust Georg, but no one else in the family.

Perhaps she'd found out that William was responsible for killing Georg's mother, and that there was something at the summer house that could prove it. Ellen herself, for example.

But why did Hedda lie to her husband? Was she scared that Hugo Refsdal would tell someone or try to stop her from going through with whatever she'd planned? And how did Sweden and Daniel Schyman fit into it all?

Nora asked if the investigation in Sweden had come up with any more answers.

'Nothing tangible or conclusive,' Løken told her. 'And Georg is adamant that he hasn't been to Sweden for a long time.'

'Hmm,' Nora said, thinking. 'But let's say, for the sake of argument, that Georg is telling the truth; that Hedda borrowed his car, and she was the one who went to Sweden. Where did she go afterwards? Is she on the run?'

Løken scratched the side of his head.

'Georg has his car again,' she continued, 'so she must have come back here at some point. Has he said anything about when and where he got the car back?'

Løken shook his head. 'No. But the car came back to Vestfold the day that Daniel Schyman was murdered – we know that from the data on the toll tag. Georg said he'd tried to contact Hedda over the next few days, without any luck. So he took the bus out to Hulebakk to see what was going on. He says he found nothing, other than his car. According to Georg, Hedda was not there.'

'There's a considerable chance that he's lying,' said Nora. 'Or that someone else is involved; William, for example.'

Løken looked at her. 'William?'

Nora straightened up. 'I've got a theory I'd like to run by you.'

She told him about Tore Pulli and the fact that William Hellberg had given him several jobs in Vestfold in the nineties, around the time that Ellen Hellberg was killed. Løken listened and nodded to himself as Nora talked. He narrowed his eyes when she mentioned the concrete cover over the well where Ellen had been found and described Pulli's strength and reputation for brutality.

When Nora had finished, Løken nodded a few more times. 'The problem with that sequence of events,' he stated, 'is that it's hard to prove it unless anyone confesses. They don't write contracts for that kind of thing, and Tore Pulli is dead. The only chance we have is that William admits it, or that we find indisputable proof in the well that shows he had something to do with it. And what, after sixteen years, would still be intact enough to be used in court...?' Løken sighed and shrugged. 'You don't have anything to confirm any of this, I presume?'

Nora thought about Henning, and wondered how he'd found out about William's relationship with Pulli.

'It would be my word against William's, whatever the case,' she said, stroking her stomach.

Løken looked at his watch and took a deep breath. 'I'm going to have to go,' he said.

'OK,' she said.

The inspector opened the car door and got out. Then he put his head back inside. 'And next time,' he said, with an impish smile, 'bring some coffee with you.'

39

Henning was leaning against the back of his yellow car, playing with his Zippo, when Nora pulled up beside him. She smiled, but his only response was a short nod.

Nora took a deep breath before she got out, uncertain about how to greet him. Recently they'd started to give each other longer hugs than before, but it didn't feel natural now.

'Hi,' she said, and walked slowly towards him. It was only then that she saw the injuries on his face.

'What's happened?' she cried.

As she approached, she reached out a hand to touch his cheek, but he pulled back.

'It's nothing to worry about,' he said.

'Nothing to worry about? Who did this to you?'

He didn't answer immediately. 'Really, don't even think about it,' he said in the end.

Nora felt like she was about to explode, but she controlled herself. She'd never known how to deal with Henning when he was in this mood.

'Is there somewhere we can talk?' he asked. 'Or do you want to talk here?'

She looked at his bloodshot eyes. His drawn cheeks.

'Here? In the car park?' She tried to smile.

Henning looked over her head. A car caught his attention. Then a bird. Then a person crossing the street.

Nora tried to catch his eye, but it was impossible. 'Are you hungry?'

Henning squeezed his nose between his thumb and finger.

'They've got Caesar salad in the restaurant here. And they're pretty generous with the Parmesan, which I've heard you like a lot.' Nora smiled again. Felt that he was relaxing. 'Come on,' she said, and indicated with her head. 'I'm hungry.'

They went into the restaurant, found a table and ordered one Caesar salad, one tomato soup and two glasses of water, then sat in silence, surveying their surroundings while they waited for the waiter to bring the food.

Nora looked down. 'Henning, I...'

'I don't want to talk about it,' he said.

Nora lifted her head. 'Why not?'

'I don't want to.'

She sighed. 'Henning, we're going to have to talk about it at some point.'

He looked up, and for the first time since she told him she was pregnant, he looked her straight in the eye.

'You live your life, Nora, and I live mine. We don't need to talk about it.'

Stubborn as a five-year-old, Nora thought. She felt the anger boiling up again, and wondered if she'd be able keep it in.

'Henning, no matter what happens to you and me, we'll always be connected in some way. You know that as well as I do.'

Henning lowered his eyes. Didn't say anything.

'And not even a baby is going to change that,' she added.

Henning put his hands on the table. Drank some water from his glass.

'So, what's he like, this William?' he asked. His focus shifted to the side.

Nora didn't answer. She waited until he was looking at her again.

'So you don't want to talk about it?'

'I don't want to talk about it.'

An elderly couple came into the restaurant and sat down a couple of tables away. A slow song drifted in from the lobby, making Nora think about dance floors, clammy hands round her waist, a whispered question, could he maybe come home with her?

'He's big,' she said, finally. 'Tall, that is. Dark. Longish hair.'

'I don't mean what he looks like. What sort of person is he?'

She opened out her hands in a shrug. 'Typical salesman. Typical male who's used to getting what he wants, I reckon. I don't really know; I've only met him twice.'

'But do you think he could have paid Tore Pulli to kill Ellen Hellberg?'

'Shh,' Nora urged him, and looked around.

'They're not going to hear anything,' Henning said, and nodded at the elderly couple.

'Yes, but all the same,' she said through gritted teeth.

Henning waited for her to continue. The song, 'Lady in Red', was reaching a climax.

'Was William angry with his aunt? Hard to say, even if Ellen did ruin his parents' relationship.'

Henning put his hand on the table smoothed out a crease in the white tablecloth. 'OK,' he said, and looked up at her. 'Tell me more about the story you're working on. And William's role, in particular.'

Nora took a deep breath, wondering where to begin. There was so much. At the same time, it was always a good idea to talk through the complexities of a story with someone, especially someone as sharp as Henning. So she told him everything she knew, down to the smallest detail, even things she had told him before. Henning didn't say a word the whole time that she talked.

'Seems like you've won the trust of this Cato Løken guy,' Henning said, when she'd finished. 'How did you manage that in such a short time? You didn't know him before, did you?'

Nora shook her head. 'I've opened the whole case up for them,' she said, and looked at Henning. His eyes were intense. He was studying her.

'But there's something else,' he said.

Nora didn't answer straightaway.

'What do you mean?' She looked down; she'd been in this position many times before, and knew there was no point in trying to hide anything from him.

After a moment, she lifted her head again. 'Someone shot at me the other day,' she said.

Just then, the waiter came with their food. Henning stopped with his mouth open, his eyes fixed firmly on Nora as their food was put on the table. He didn't even register when the waiter asked if they needed anything else, just waited for him to leave.

'What the fuck did you just say?' he asked, as soon as they were alone again.

Nora told him about the two shots, that she had called the emergency services, and the police had arrived within minutes, with Cato Løken at the helm.

'And he's realised that I can help them, too,' she said. 'He's not like some of the other policemen that I've dealt with. Isn't it great when you get sources like that?'

She tried to smile again, but Henning didn't respond. He was still staring at her with big eyes.

'The person who shot at me hadn't planned to kill me, Henning. It was a warning. Someone didn't like the fact that I was snooping around.'

'Clearly. And how do you think they'll react when they realise the warning shots didn't work? You're still here.'

Nora started to laugh. 'Look who's talking!'

Nora picked up her spoon, stirred the soup a little, pulled off a piece of bread. Henning didn't touch his food, just sat with his hands on the table.

Eventually he picked up his fork and said, 'It's not just yourself you have to look after now.'

40

After he'd finished his food, Henning drove to the Hellberg Property offices in the centre of town, primarily to see if there was any sign of life. There was, even though it was past seven in the evening. Henning parked the car and settled down to wait, in the hope that William Hellberg was still there. He spotted several journalist colleagues who were clearly there for the same reason.

Just after eight o'clock, William stepped out into the cold autumn wind. It didn't take more than a few seconds before the first journalist was on him. Henning got out of the car, and watched the spectacle. William shook his head, making his longish hair flutter in the wind, waved them off, one by one, and walked as quickly as he could to the black Lexus that was parked nearby, barking out a few aggressive comments before opening the door.

'And please,' he said, before he got in. 'Don't follow me.'

Some of the journalists pulled back. Henning was standing a few metres away, and for a brief second, their eyes locked. William paused momentarily, before getting into the car and driving off.

Henning went back to this own car and started it up; he knew that its yellow paintwork made it easy to spot in a rear-view mirror, and even though he had to jump several traffic lights on the way from Tønsberg out to Nøtterøy, he made sure he was never more than four cars behind William, who he reckoned was on his way home to Kalvetangen, where he lived a stone's throw away from his mother.

After they'd passed Føynland School and turned off into a quiet road, the black Lexus braked suddenly, the rear lights shining straight into Henning's eyes. William got out. Henning turned off the engine and did the same.

'I thought I told you not to follow me?'

'Yes, you did,' Henning conceded. 'But I'm not here to talk about your aunt or your sister.'

He paused before continuing, to see if he'd roused William's curiosity.

'Well, then, it can wait until another time,' William said, and turned on his heel. He was halfway back to his car when Henning said: 'Tore Jørn Pulli.' He spoke loudly and clearly. 'You knew him well, didn't you?'

William stopped, appeared to think for a moment or two, and then turned back.

'You were friends growing up, and you were one of his first clients when he started out as an enforcer here in Vestfold in the nineties,' Henning went on.

William moved closer, his eyes fixed on Henning. Henning pushed back his shoulders and lifted his chin.

'And who says so?' said William as he approached.

'No one says so. I know. But what I don't know, is how much contact you had with Tore more recently, before he died – other than that you were perhaps going to be neighbours in Brazil.'

William stopped about a metre from Henning, his mouth half open.

'I don't think I've ever seen you before,' he said.

'No, because I've never been here before. But the name's Henning. And these,' he said, pointing to the scars on his face, 'I got these on 11 September 2007, trying to save my son from our burning flat.'

'I'm sorry to...'

'At the time, I was working on a story that would expose Tore and his *modus operandi* – about how he'd worked his way up in the property business by illegal means. Obviously, I'd managed to upset him and others sufficiently for them to try to silence me. And they succeeded, for two years. But now I'm back. And I'm going to turn over every stone I can find, to look for clues that will lead me to whoever set fire to my flat.'

William stared at Henning. 'And you think I had something to do with it?'

'Not necessarily,' Henning said, with a shrug. 'But you were a friend of Tore's; you bought a flat in Natal from Charlie Høisæther, or, rather, it's in your wife's name, but I'm supposing it was you who paid for it. And it's not entirely unthinkable that you might know several of the dodgy characters who live down there. People from the Swedish League and the like.'

Henning paused to see if William would react.

'I think someone in your network has ruined my life,' Henning continued. 'The same person, or people, who had Tore murdered when he was in Oslo Prison. I'm trying to find out who they are.'

William put his hands in his trouser pockets. 'So that's why you're here? To find out if I had some reason to kill Tore while he was in prison? And to set fire to your flat?'

Henning shrugged.

William snorted. 'Let me save you the trouble,' he said. 'I had nothing to do with it. Tore was, as you said, a good friend of mine when we were growing up. That's all. And now I have to go home. My son's ill.'

He was about to turn away when Henning said: 'Do you know Daddy Longlegs?'

William took a few seconds to reply: 'Daddy Longlegs?'

Henning nodded.

'Is this a joke?'

'No. I don't hear anyone laughing.'

Henning waited, watched William's reaction.

'Yesterday evening, someone tried to kill me by running me over in Grünerløkka. I suspect that whoever got Ørjan Mjønes to kill Tore in Oslo Prison has more than one person on his payroll. And I wonder if that doesn't take us back to warmer climes again, Hellberg – to your neighbours in Natal.'

William shook his head. 'I ... we ... lead a very quiet life when we're down there. I don't know anything about the other people who live there, or about what they've done, it's none of my business.'

'Mm,' Henning hummed.

'And I can honestly say I know nothing about what happened to you or Tore, Juul.'

Henning tilted his head to one side. 'So you know who I am?'

William stalled a moment.

'You just told me who you were.'

'I said that I was called Henning. I didn't tell you my surname.'

William held Henning's gaze for a few seconds before lowering his eyes. He looked at his shoe, which was stirring the grit covering the asphalt. His hand rose to his face, scratched his cheek.

'How do you know who I am?' Henning asked, and took a step closer. 'I saw you looking at me outside your office back there.'

William still didn't answer.

'Come on, Hellberg, you—'

'I do actually read the papers,' William said, and looked up. 'That's how I know who you are; and what's more, you've got a face that's easy to remember.'

Henning stood there looking at him.

'And I had nothing to do with the fire in your flat. So,' he waved his hand, 'I hope that you will now leave me in peace.'

William turned and walked to his car. Henning let him go. But he kept his eyes on him, on the car, as it drove off towards the ostentatious houses of Kalvetangen.

41

After Henning had left, Nora stayed in the restaurant.

As she was finishing her soup her phone rang. It was Merete Stephans, her colleague from *Aftenposten*.

'Hi,' Nora said.

'They've found a suitcase in the water just out from the Hellbergs' summer house,' Merete said, without even saying hello.

'Is it black?' Nora asked.

'Yes, it's black. Like practically every other suitcase.'

'Does it have a small Norwegian flag on the side?'

There was no response for a few seconds.

'Yes.'

'It's Hedda's suitcase,' Nora said.

Merete didn't answer straightaway.

'But Hedda hasn't been found yet,' she said, eventually. 'They're still looking.'

Nora frowned.

Merete Stephans told her that she had written a headline story for the following day's paper, which was primarily about the discovery of Ellen's body and the ongoing investigation.

'But they're not willing to say much yet,' she concluded.

'She was strangled,' Nora said.

Another silence.

'What did you say?'

'Ellen. She was strangled. Might be good to include that,' Nora said, and smiled to herself.

'Yes, yes, of course,' Merete replied.

'We'll be sharing the byline on our stories anyway, won't we?'

Merete didn't answer; she just hung up.

Nora rubbed her face in the hope that it she could massage some more blood to her brain, then decided to go up to her room. She thought about Iver, and the fact that she hadn't heard any more from him. About her plants at home, how dry they must be. About all the post that was no doubt bursting out of the mailbox by now. She realised that she missed being with someone – just being. Not working, not thinking. It was an age since she'd been to the cinema, gone for a run; an eternity since her head had not been full of things that got her down.

All the same, it helped to think about work.

She sat down and studied the Hellberg family tree that she'd drawn up. She stared at the name Ellen Hellberg, née Nygaard Næss.

Turning on her computer, she searched around on the internet and quickly found a Tanja Nygaard Næss who was born in 1928 and had paid tax to Skien Council and Telemark County, but there was nothing to say where she lived or even if she was still alive.

Nora rang Hugo Refsdal.

'A quick question,' she said, when he answered. 'Ellen Hellberg, Hedda's aunt – do you know if her mother's name was Tanja?'

Refsdal didn't answer immediately.

'I actually don't know what she's called,' he said at last. 'I've never met her.'

Nora wrinkled her nose. 'No?'

'I've not been part of the family for that long.'

Nora thought hard.

'Do you know if she has any contact with her grandson?'

'I'm afraid I don't know,' Refsdal said. 'I don't think so. But she's still alive. Or she was, the last time I heard anything about her.'

Nora stared at herself in the mirror, noticed that her cheeks had got rounder.

'What have you heard about her?'

Refsdal sighed. 'That she went a bit mad after her daughter

disappeared. Wouldn't accept that Ellen was gone, I think. Evidently she didn't throw away any of her clothes, and used to sniff them all the time.'

Nora thought about how she was herself with some of Jonas's things. Like his ball. Some things you just can't let go. But that doesn't necessarily mean you're mad. There had to be another reason why Ellen's mother wasn't in close contact with the family any more.

'Just one more thing, Hugo. Do you know if Hedda was interested in literature?'

'In reading books, you mean?'

'Yes.'

He started to laugh. 'Why do you ask?'

'I guess it's a strange question,' she said. 'But what's even stranger is that I'm not sure what the significance is, whether you answer yes or no. So I thought I'd ask all the same.'

Refsdal exhaled loudly down the phone. 'No,' he said. 'Hedda never read anything other than the paper.'

Nora thought to herself that Hedda's behaviour in the period before she disappeared had been increasingly odd. Then she remembered what she'd seen through the window at the summer house. The books were all higgledy-piggledy in the shelves.

'Was there anything else?' Hugo Refsdal asked. 'I have to put Henrik to bed.'

'No, that was it. Thank you for your help.'

42

As Henning drove back to Oslo, he thought about what he was going to do. The people who had tried to mow him down the night before knew where he lived, and might try a more discreet method next time. This meant his flat was dangerous, and he'd never get any sleep there now. Should he book into a hotel? That could be dangerous as well.

His phone rang just as he passed Holmestrand. It was Nora.

'Hi,' she said, when Henning answered. 'How did you get on with William?'

'Alright,' Henning said, and told her briefly how Hellberg had reacted. Henning wasn't sure if Hedda's brother was a good actor, or if, in fact, he really didn't know about everything that had happened to Tore. How well had they actually known each other anyway? He wondered out loud.

'Sounds like you're in the car,' Nora said.

'Yes,' he replied. 'I'm on my way ... home. And you?'

'I'm in my hotel room,' she said. 'Trying to work out what to do next.'

Henning closed his eyes for a brief second. He'd always liked hearing Nora's voice on the phone. It calmed him down.

'And are you getting anywhere?' he asked, opening his eyes again; he turned the steering wheel slightly to keep a steady course.

'I'm not sure yet,' she said with a sigh. 'I think I'm getting closer. We'll see.'

Henning nodded.

A long silence filled the car.

'OK,' he said at last. 'I better get myself home to bed. Good night.'

'Good night.'

⊙

Nora ended the call, and scrolled to a text message she'd got from Iver, just before Henning had called earlier.

Just been to your flat, but you weren't there. Are you working? Everything OK?

If you really wanted to know, you could have called, Nora thought. On the other hand, she didn't like talking about important things on the phone. And it was good that he'd been to the flat. Then and there, she regretted slightly that she was where she was.

She sent a text to say that she was in Tønsberg, with work. There was no reply.

Her body was screaming for something sweet, so Nora raided the minibar for more chocolate, and then finished off the frenzy with some nuts. She felt like she was the perfect example of what a pregnant woman shouldn't be. To top it all off, she opened a bottle of Coke and took three big gulps that frothed up in her mouth.

Nora walked back and forth across the room, then stopped by the full-length mirror. She lifted up her sweater and shirt, and looked at her belly from every angle. It was visible now, the little bump, low down.

She pulled her shirt and sweater back down, got the ball out of her bag, lay down on the bed and stared at the ceiling. She thought about Ellen Hellberg, and what it must have been like to have to sneak out in order to meet Oscar for a few snatched moments of happiness.

It's strange, Nora thought, *how much sadness we put up with in daily life, just for those few opportunities.* Like Olivia Svendsen, who lived for the summers, when she was out on the water all the time with Patrik. But was life necessarily about being happy all the time?

Nora's thoughts turned to Henning and the walk they'd taken, just the two of them, to Midtbønipa, one weekend when they'd gone to visit some friends who owned a house in a small place called Solheim – a beautiful, narrow strip of houses on the Norddal Fjord in Vestlandet.

Henning had pointed at a cairn and said that it looked like something, but Nora didn't have a clue what he was talking about. Like what? Nora had said, and then taken a few steps closer to study the stones.

Nora had seen Henning draw a heart once, with Jonas. It had looked more like a plucked chicken without a head. The shape of the cairn had been much the same, and when she'd turned back towards him, saw his gentle smile, the tiny twitches in the corner of his mouth – moist with sweat and the fine, west-coast rain – she'd started to cry. When she moved the stones that made up the heart-shaped cairn, she found a small box that he'd put there the day before, when he'd done the same walk alone. A box with a ring in it.

She'd never been happier than at that moment. She wished she could have frozen it, framed it and managed to remind herself of that feeling later when the rain got harder and colder and the days darker.

It had been no more than a brief moment in time, which led to other moments that eventually papered over the idea of the two of them and the life they would live together. And the very knowledge of that made her sadder than she could remember having been for a long time.

43

They make it look so easy, he thought, the boys on the PGA tour. Just select the right club, twist your upper body a little and whack the ball, which then flies for a few hundred metres and lands straight on the green.

It never did that when he played golf. The times when he did hit a shot that would make even Tiger Woods proud, it was generally just luck – a fortunate bounce here or there that meant that the ball landed reasonably well for a birdie putt. Which he then, of course, missed.

He should really stop watching golf; it only depressed him. But he had to do something as the evenings drew in, when the public prosecution offices had closed for the day and only the night remained – his wife having gone to bed long ago.

He downed the rest of his whisky, sucked on one of the ice cubes for a moment then crushed it between his teeth. He put the glass down, lit a cigarette, took a deep drag and blew the smoke out through his nose. Jim Furyk's rubbish, amateur swing made him snort. Furyk's face was as though set in stone – never a smile, never an emotional reaction to what he'd done.

He was a bit like that himself, certainly from the outside. No one could read him. The woman behind the bedroom door thought perhaps she could, but she couldn't, not really. He had a mask for every occasion. His early years in the theatre had taught him that. The ability to improvise. Put on a show.

Those were the days. His parents came dutifully to see every production – applauding with false smiles and stiff faces because the neighbours were there; they always had a look of expectation in their eyes, expectation of more, something else. And the only time he'd ever seen any kind of recognition in his father's eyes was when he told him that he wanted to study law. The thought of having a lawyer in the family. That was a respectable job. Theatre, on the other hand? *Culture?*

Culture was for homosexuals. There was no money in it, either.

He was three years into his law degree when there was a knock on the door one afternoon. The two men standing outside wondered if he knew where his father was. From their clothes, he guessed they were detectives, but couldn't bring himself to answer their question. Instead, he just shook his head and said that he hadn't spoken to his father for months, which wasn't that far from the truth.

Later that day, he heard on the news that his father had been arrested on suspicion of fraud; he'd siphoned off funds from a number of client accounts and then used the money to finance his expensive cars and other extravagant spending.

He could still remember that first phone call from the prison, a voice that said 'Your father is on the line'. He hadn't heard a peep from him for seven months after the trial and sentencing, and all his father managed to say now, before the call was cut off, was: 'Happy birthday, son.'

He'd never been angry with his father for being a criminal.

But he was angry with the old man for getting caught, for being stupid and careless and for tarring the family name. For being so bad at damage control.

He would never be like that. If it was him that found himself in trouble with the law – if he caught even the slightest whiff of anything that told him 'it's over' – then he would put an end to it all. A bottle of pills, a gun to the head, whatever; as long as it did the job.

The question was, who had been with Henning Juul? Who had managed to push him out of the way before the bumper hit him? But perhaps the answer was simple, given who had shared a byline with Juul more than once – someone who Henning might meet for a beer or two at Stopp Pressen.

Iver Gundersen.

Had Juul said anything to him?

The mobile phone on the coffee table started to vibrate. He pulled himself up and reached over for it. He let out a deep sigh. This was all he needed: him calling now.

'Good evening,' he said.

The line crackled. 'Hi Daddy Longlegs.'

'Don't call me that.'

'Why not?'

'I don't like it.'

'You liked it before.'

'No, I've never liked it.'

'Oh, well. Do you know what I've never liked?'

He said nothing.

'Piña coladas, Daddy Longlegs. Rum, pineapple juice and coconut. Coconut!'

He reached for his glass again, shook it a little, so the ice cubes clinked.

'Coconut is nice with white fish, and a bit of chilli sauce. Coalfish, for example – a totally underrated fish, especially when baked in the oven with coconut. But coconut in a drink?'

He got up, went over to the drinks cupboard, took out the bottle of whisky. Poured himself another glass.

'Is that why you called?' he asked, as he went back to his chair. 'To tell me about coalfish and coconut?'

'You know why I'm calling.'

'And we shouldn't discuss it on the phone.' He sat down.

The crackling disappeared, and for a moment he wondered if the line had been cut off.

But then the voice came back: 'Hit and run, Daddy Longlegs? We're back there again, eh?'

He took a drink.

'Damage control, you said. So far, I've seen plenty of the former and not much of the latter.'

'We really shouldn't be talking about this on the phone.'

'You've opened up a wasps' nest, Daddy Longlegs.'

'I know.'

'Well, you better clear up the mess. Solve our problems, once and for all.'

On the TV, Jason Dufner putted a ball into the hole from seven metres without so much as a smile. He made it look so simple.

'I know,' he said, in the end.

After they'd both hung up, he sat there clutching the phone.

Once and for all.

Stronger medicine, in other words. Not that it mattered to him.

He knew exactly what they could do.

44

Henning rang Iver and asked if he could spend another night on his sofa.

'Of course,' Iver replied.

Before Henning parked the car in Fredenborgsveien, where Iver lived, he drove round the block a couple of times, keeping an eye on the rear-view mirror to see if anyone else was doing the same, but there was no one. When he got out onto the pavement, he couldn't see anyone sitting in a car nearby, leaning up against a wall, or sitting on a bench, waiting.

It was ten o'clock when Henning kicked off his shoes and went into Iver's flat. Iver turned down the volume on the TV.

'Fancy a beer?'

'No, thanks,' Henning said.

There were two cans on the table by his colleague. The flat reeked of cigarettes, and Henning felt an acute need to open a window.

'How'd it go today?' Iver asked.

Henning sat down on the other end of the sofa, and Iver turned off the TV. Henning crossed his legs, took a deep breath and told him where he'd been.

'So William Hellberg knew who you were?'

Henning nodded. 'But that doesn't necessarily mean anything,' he said. 'As he said himself, I've got a face that people remember.'

Iver finished off his can of beer. Henning said that he'd met Nora, at which point, Iver lowered his eyes. There was silence. They could hear footsteps in the flat above, something hard falling on the floor.

'How was she?' Iver asked.

Henning shrugged. 'She seemed alright to me,' he said, and decided not to tell Iver about the shooting.

Iver shook the can to check that there was nothing left.

'What have you done today?' Henning asked.

Iver looked up. 'I've argued with the boss about various non-stories, and, otherwise, I talked to some of my sources about Charlie Høisæther.'

Henning sat up.

'Høisæther Property was a property-development company,' Iver said, and put the can down. 'Charlie bought up old, dilapidated blocks of flats, did them up and sold them on. That kind of thing.' Iver gesticulated with his hands as he spoke. 'And Rasmus Bjelland was one of the joiners he used.'

Henning frowned hard. 'Charlie? Not Tore Pulli?'

'Rasmus didn't work for Tore, no. But he hammered and nailed for Charlie up until winter 1996, then stopped. And eventually he went bankrupt.'

Henning got out his lighter, clicked it on and off a few times, and thought about what Bjelland had said – that Tore Pulli had no problems stepping over corpses to get what he wanted. How could Bjelland know that if he worked for Charlie and not Tore?

You have to go back to the nineties, Bjelland had said.

Perhaps 1996 was the year.

'That Charlie guy is quite something,' Iver said, and shook his head. 'According to one of my sources, Charlie got into trouble one time when he was using some Poles to do up flats. Charlie owed them a lot of money, and in the end settled up by giving them a flat.'

Henning listened with interest.

'But what the Poles didn't know,' Iver went on, 'and obviously Charlie never told them, was that the flat was in a joint-ownership building that had a substantial shared debt. And what most people don't know is that, in a situation like that, when a flat gets a new owner, the bank pays back the developer for their share of the debt.'

'So the Poles were left with the debt, and Charlie earned good money?'

Iver nodded.

'What happened to the Poles then?'

Iver showed his palms and shrugged. 'They owned nothing, not even the nails in the wall, so they had to flee the country.'

'Hm,' Henning grunted. 'Was there anything about it in the papers?'

Iver shook his head and coaxed a cigarette out of the packet that was lying on the table.

'That could be a great story, Iver,' he continued.

'It certainly could,' Iver agreed, put the cigarette in his mouth, lit it and exhaled. 'But I'm going to let it lie for the moment.' He leaned back on the sofa.

'Why?'

'Because Norway doesn't have an extradition agreement with Brazil. And because I don't want Charlie to go into hiding. Not now, when you're...' Iver looked away for a moment.

Henning stared at him. 'Sounds like your source is from the fraud squad,' he said, eventually.

Iver turned towards him, took another drag on his cigarette.

'The person who told you this,' Henning added.

'Oh right, yeah. No ... it...' Iver smiled. 'He's called Milo Cavalli.'

'Right, so now we share sources as well.'

'Yeah, for Christ's sake – and you've eaten all my baked beans.' He took another drag.

Henning grinned.

'He's a good guy,' Iver said. 'Catholic. Gets things done then goes to confession.'

'Could perhaps do with some of that ourselves,' Henning said.

'Not me,' Iver retorted, and winked at him. 'I never do anything that bad.'

He got up from the chair, pointed to the beer can. 'You sure you don't want one?'

45

Nora woke up with a thumping headache. She sat up slowly in bed. She had lain awake half the night. The last thing she could remember was the clock showing a quarter past three.

She got up, and took two paracetamol from her bag, washing them down with what was left of the Coke she had opened the evening before. She stumbled over to the computer, turned it on and looked through the stories the internet editors had posted from the paper edition. 'Ellen Was Strangled' was the main story. Byline: Merete Stephans.

Nora shook her head, feeling the urge to ring the internet desk straightaway to get them to add her byline as well. But she couldn't face it, and instead took out her mobile phone and sent a text message to Fritz Hellberg III.

Good morning. You don't happen to know where and how I could get hold of Ellen's mother? Nora Klemetsen, Aftenposten.

It might not be easy to talk to the old lady so soon after the body had been found, she thought, but she had to give it a try.

Nora didn't feel like the big breakfast she'd had the day before, so she ordered an omelette and drank two glasses of orange juice while she waited for an answer from Ellen's husband. It came when she was drinking her coffee.

Why do you want to talk to the old bag?

Nora wrinkled her nose, but answered: *Just want some background information. Who Ellen was, what she was like. You know us journalists, we like to tell stories.*

She added a smiley, even though it made her feel like a teenager.

He replied: *She lives in a nursing home in Skien. Think it's got Gjerpen in the name. But she's very muddled, so I would take what she says with a pinch of salt.*

Nora thanked him for his help, drank up her coffee, ran up to her room and quickly established that there was a nursing home called Gjerpen in Skien.

Six minutes later she was in the car, on her way there.

⊙

The E18 must be the world's most boring road, Nora thought as the car rolled on. Too much traffic, nothing to see by the side of the road and a speed limit that was ridiculous. But it gave her time to think – about the road and life; the choices she had made and would have to make in the days and months ahead.

Sometimes it wasn't even a choice. It was just the way things had turned out. God knows, she hadn't planned on getting pregnant, couldn't really understand how it happened – she'd always made sure to take the pill; hadn't missed a day. But then, all of a sudden, there was another life growing inside her. Which was guaranteed to change her life, just as Jonas had done.

What she was most afraid of was that the new baby would replace Jonas – not just in her own life, but in other people's as well. People would go around saying, 'It's so good that Nora had another baby, it'll make it easier to forget what happened to Jonas.'

But she didn't want to forget.

Didn't want to. Refused to.

Couldn't.

Nora turned off at Junction 48 and continued over a series of round-abouts, to the left, to the right and straight over. One hour and eight minutes after she left Tønsberg, she arrived at Håvundvegen 17, an ugly, red-brick building that looked every bit as much like the nursing home that Nora had imagined. The windows facing the car park had lace curtains and some also had green blinds, which were no doubt pulled

down to keep out the light, but it seemed unnecessary now that the sky
on the horizon had turned a mucky grey.

Nora found a parking space and realised how tense she was as she
walked towards the three-storey building.

Once inside, she grabbed the first nurse she could find, and asked
for Mrs Nygaard Næss. She was told to go to the first floor, where she
had to ask again. A man with a turban smiled and pointed to a woman
sitting alone by a table, staring out of the window.

'How ... is she?' Nora asked.

'What do you mean?' the nurse replied.

'Is she ... is it possible to speak ... normally with her?'

'Depends,' the nurse said. 'She has good and bad days, like most of
the old people here, but I couldn't say how she is today.'

Nora was tempted to ask if anyone from the police had been there
the day before, but took it as a given. She found it more worrying that
no one had asked who she was, nor why she wanted to talk to Mrs
Nygaard Næss at a time like this.

Nora thanked the nurse for his help and went over to the old
woman. She sat down quietly on the opposite side of the table and
looked around. The chairs were empty. All the inhabitants had wheel-
chairs. One man had a visitor who looked about a generation younger,
but shared the same facial features.

The different stages of life, Nora thought, and swallowed hard. She
was worried about a life that was about to begin. In this place, everyone
was concerned with the opposite end of the journey, when every day,
every hour might be the last.

Nora realised she had to get her act together. It helped to look at
the television on the wall, and at the watering, staring eyes that followed the pictures of a large passenger ship cutting through still water
somewhere in the beautiful, far north. The room smelt of food – fish
of some kind – and Nora felt a pang of hunger. Again.

She turned back towards Ellen's mother, who couldn't weigh
more than forty kilos. Her skin hung loose, with deep wrinkles and
furrows. Her jaw was slack, as though her mouth was used to being

open. And even though she closed it every now and then, it soon fell open again.

She reminded Nora of a thin, old dog.

'Hi,' she said, and moved closer to the table, resting her hands in front of her. She watched the old woman for any reaction, but saw none. Mrs Næss continued to stare at whatever it was out of the window. Nora glanced out and could see nothing other than the sky, in various shades of grey.

'My name is Nora.'

Ellen's mother closed her mouth and smacked her lips a little, before her jaw dropped again.

'I work for a newspaper. And I want to write about your daughter. Ellen.'

When her daughter's name was mentioned, the old lady turned her head and looked straight at Nora. Her eyes were glassy, like tiny jellyfish.

'Could I ask you some questions about her? About Ellen?'

Mrs Næss's eyes focused, sharpened. 'They killed her.'

Her voice was frail. Nora had to concentrate to hear what she said.

'I knew she hadn't just disappeared. My Ellen didn't just disappear.' Her voice grew stronger, had more life in it. 'They said she'd gone out into the forest or drowned herself in the sea. But they killed her,' the old lady said again. 'They did!'

Mrs Næss lifted a shaking finger and pointed out of the window, as though the people she was talking about were just outside.

'She wasn't like that. My Ellen. She wasn't like that.'

Nora straightened up, unsure how to continue the conversation. Then suddenly it was as if Mrs Næss disappeared again. Her eyes faded, the muscles in her face lost their grip, and her jaw dropped open.

Nora waited a little before continuing. 'Are you thinking of anyone in particular in the Hellberg family?'

Mrs Næss turned her head again. 'Parasites, all of them,' she said.

'In what way?' Nora pressed her, gently.

Behind her, someone knocked over and smashed a glass. Nora

turned to watch the bustle of activity that followed. A nurse, who had been sitting folding towels nearby, got up and picked up the shards of glass, while one of the patients scolded a man who was sitting at the table, with a long thread of spittle hanging from his mouth.

Mrs Næss appeared to have forgotten the question. Nora decided to wait a while before asking it again.

'What was your daughter like? Tell me about Ellen.'

Hearing her daughter's name seemed to waken Mrs Næss again.

'She was kind and good,' she said. 'Far too good for...' She pursed her lips as though what she was about to say made her angry.

'Too good for who, Mrs Næss?'

'Too good for that drunken husband of hers.'

The sentence was clear and precise. Nora didn't have time to ask another question before she continued.

'She was a nurse, my Ellen. Like an angel, they said. Looked after that old battle-axe until she died. But do you think anyone thanked her for it?' Mrs Næss sent Nora a hard look, as though she was to blame. 'They're parasites. All of them.'

Nora remembered what Fritz had told her about Ellen, how she had looked after his mother until she died. Mrs Næss must be talking about her. The woman with the archiving system.

'You said "they killed her". The Hellberg family. Do you mean that quite literally?'

Mrs Næss expelled a fast, hard snort. Her eyes blazed with contempt, but she said nothing. Nora looked around, making sure that none of the nurses who came in and out of the TV lounge would hear her next question.

'Who killed her, Mrs Næss?'

A pain clouded the old woman's eyes and she retreated into herself.

'I'm trying to find out who was responsible for Ellen's death,' Nora carried on. 'Please help me.'

Nora was begging, she could hear it herself.

'She found out.'

Nora tried to hold her eyes, but Mrs Næss lost her focus.

'What did Ellen find out, Mrs Næss?' Nora leaned as far as she could over the table.

'She found out what kind of people they were.' Ellen's mother's fingers were constantly moving. Scratching, rubbing, picking at each other, at her nails. 'She found out what kind of people they were,' she repeated, more to herself than to Nora.

'What kind of people were they, Mrs Næss?'

She said nothing for a long time.

Then she turned back towards Nora again. 'Ask that drunken husband of Ellen's,' she said, through set teeth. 'Ask him what kind of people they are. Ask him where their money comes from. Ask him about it.'

She looked straight ahead again.

'I'd rather ask you, Mrs Næss, if you know.'

But Mrs Næss made no sign of wanting to say more. Her hands fell to rest. She just stared out into thin air, with an angry expression to begin with, but then this faded and her eyes became distant. She looked towards the horizon again, at the grey sky. She didn't react when Nora reached out a hand and laid it on her shoulder.

But her words pounded like a hammer in Nora's head all the way back to Tønsberg. She drove much faster than she should, while the questions raced around in her mind.

Ellen found out.

Found what out?

46

Henning hadn't changed his clothes for a few days, and borrowing clothes from Iver was out of the question – if nothing else, they wouldn't fit. His colleague was at least fifteen centimetres taller and carried a good deal more weight on his body. Henning could, of course, buy some new things, but it wasn't only his dirty clothes that made him think that he should pop by his flat. He needed his tablets; his laptop was there; there was probably a fair amount of post, and there was some food in his fridge that would be out of date by now.

So he locked Iver's door around midday and drove to his flat. He did the same thing that he'd done the night before: took a very odd route around Grünerløkka, making sure to drive on less trafficked roads, studying the faces he passed, looking in car windows, checking his rear-view mirror at regular intervals, but he saw nothing of the man who had been standing, waiting for him outside Sultan a few days ago – Durim Redzepi. *Maybe I scared him off,* Henning thought.

As usual, it was impossible to park in Seildaksgaten, but that was perhaps for the best. A yellow car like his would draw attention, especially now. So Henning parked in Fossveien, which was no more than a stone's throw from the flat; and he didn't intend to stay long.

Henning got out of his car into a day that had started heavy with grey clouds, but had now lightened to give the good people of Oslo some hope that the sun would break through. It was much needed.

When he got to the junction of Steenstrups gate and Seildaksgaten, he stopped. The white car that had come towards him at speed had been waiting here. It was as if he were reliving it all: he heard the sound of the engine, saw the lights, felt Iver push him to one side, felt his head landing on the asphalt.

Henning's heart started to race as he approached his building. He let himself in the entrance by the rubbish bins and prayed that he wouldn't meet any of the neighbours. Luck would probably be on his side, as most people would be at work. But when he went into the stairwell and opened his mailbox, releasing a cascade of advertising and envelopes addressed to him, he heard heavy footsteps a couple of floors up.

For a second, Henning wondered if he should turn around and leave. The footsteps were getting closer. He looked up the stairs and saw a hairy hand on the banister; he heard the shallow, short breaths, as though someone had a plastic bag over their face, and his shoulders sank. He started up the stairs.

'Hi Gunnar,' he called up when he saw his 78-year-old neighbour, who sometimes tramped up and down the stairs. He'd had a heart attack a few years before and used the stairs for exercise. In warmer weather, Gunnar Goma wore practically nothing as he went up and down, but Henning could see that, thankfully he had his trousers and shirt on today. His feet, on the other hand, were bare inside his old, worn sandals. Dirty, hairy feet.

'Is that you, son?' Goma said.

'Certainly is,' Henning replied.

Goma had clearly not shaved for a few days, and white tufts stuck out from his folds of skin.

'Your foot's alright again then, I see.'

'Yep,' Henning said. 'How are you?'

'Fit as a fiddle and strong as a bear.'

'That's good to hear.'

Goma pushed back his shoulders. 'You should come by for coffee one day.'

'Mm,' Henning said.

The old man walked past him, his sandals slapping on the stairs. Then he stopped again.

'There was a bloody awful smell from your flat this morning.'

Henning looked at him. 'Was there?'

'Yes. Have you forgotten to feed the cat or something?'

Henning shook his head.

Goma shrugged. 'Well, now you know.'

Goma carried on down the stairs. And Henning went up. Soon he was outside his door. He sniffed, could smell something, but couldn't place it.

Henning put his ear to the door, tried to hear if there was anyone inside, but the noise of his neighbour struggling back up the stairs drowned anything else out.

Henning tried the door. Locked. No scratches or splinters on the door frame. Henning waited until Goma arrived at his floor. The old man stopped and sniffed as well.

'Not so bad now,' he said. 'This morning it smelt like dead monkeys out here.'

Henning put his key in the lock and turned it slowly. The door swung open. The flat was dark. A film of grey light filtered through from the kitchen window.

Henning went in. His shoes were standing where they always stood. The bag of empty bottles was exactly where he'd left it, just beside the door. His laptop was even on the kitchen table, with the screen open.

Had he really turned off all the lights the last time he left the flat?

He normally left something on – the light in the hall or the living room. Sometimes, he even forgot to turn off the light in the bathroom. But everything was off now.

Had a fuse blown?

He went in a bit further, looked around and sniffed again. He didn't see or hear any movement – no sign of anyone there. But something was wrong, he could feel it.

The fuse box was on the wall by the kitchen. Henning opened it and looked inside. The main fuse switch was off. He put his finger on the switch and was about to flick it on, when he suddenly thought of something.

He went into the kitchen and looked around again. Nothing amiss. He went into the living room, nothing there either.

Apart from the Hoover.

Henning hadn't used it for a few days, he was sure of that, and he always put it away when he'd finished with it. But there it was. And it was still plugged in. He went back to the kitchen, and took his time examining everything. He spotted a glass on the shelf by the cookery books, to the left of the cupboard over the cooker.

He definitely hadn't put that there.

Henning took it down from the shelf and sniffed it.

Vinegar.

Which you often put out if you want to get rid of a smell. And Goma had said that it smelt of dead monkeys there in the morning.

Henning looked at the cooker. Everything was off. He opened the cupboard under the sink where the gas canister was kept. The smell was stronger there.

Then he saw it.

A hole in the pipe.

It wasn't ordinary wear and tear – the pipe had been fine when Henning moved in. The hole had been made with a knife. Henning reckoned it was around two centimetres wide.

'Christ, it's dark in here,' Goma said, out in the hall.

Henning got a fright and banged his head on the worktop.

'Not so strange, your fuse has blown.'

Goma stomped into the flat, his hand reaching up to open the fuse box, when Henning shouted: 'Stop!'

Goma stopped.

'Don't touch it,' Henning said in quiet, but firm voice. 'There's a gas leak. If you switch on the fuse, the whole flat will blow up.'

It was just after one o'clock when Nora parked behind the small, red car outside Fritz Hellberg III's house. She got out, locked the doors, looked at the car in front with a puzzled expression, but decided that she wouldn't let the fact that Ellen Hellberg's husband obviously had a visitor stop her.

It was still relatively early in the day, so the odds were that he hadn't tucked into the whisky decanter yet. She rang the bell and it didn't take long before she heard footsteps inside.

Unni Hellberg opened the door.

Nora didn't know what to say. And for the first few seconds it seemed the same was true of Hedda's mother; when she looked at Nora, there was none of the warmth she had shown when she met her out at Kalvetangen two days earlier.

'Hi,' Nora said. 'Is Fritz in?'

Unni pushed back her shoulders a touch.

'Yes, he's here,' she said, without showing any sign that she would let Nora inside.

'I'd like to have a word with him. Or actually, as you're here, it would be good to talk to both of you.'

Nora looked up at the woman in front of her. Her chin was defiant, her lips pursed. She didn't blink.

'Primarily about Oscar's will,' Nora explained.

Unni gave her a cold smile. 'We would obviously not discuss that with you.'

'The police will be told of the contents either today or tomorrow, Unni. Can't we just sit down and talk about it? Nothing needs to be printed in the paper, if you don't want it to be.'

Unni was about to reply when Fritz appeared behind her. He was unsteady on his feet, his eyes were blurry, but he still managed to focus on Nora.

'Let her in, Unni. We both know that it's too late for firefighting, so the least we can do is help shape the outcome. You're concerned about that, aren't you?'

He took a step closer and looked up at her. Unni sent him a hard look before he pushed open the door and invited Nora in.

She didn't need to be asked twice. She was about to take off her boots when Fritz stopped her with a wave of the hand. 'Leave them on,' he said. 'Then it won't just be my ghost that leaves a mark.'

Nora smiled and followed them into the library where she had talked to him the day before. Fritz made straight for the crystal decanter in the corner.

'Do you have to? Now?' Unni asked.

Fritz turned with the delay of an alcoholic. His eyelids were drooping, and it looked as though he was making an effort to keep them open.

'My dear sister-in-law, in your house you can deny me a dram or two, but here, in my own house, I will have as many as I like.'

'I'm only thinking about your health, Fritz. It's not good for your heart to...'

'Puh,' he said, with an irritated shake of the head. Then he smiled at Nora, reminding her of Jack Nicholson as he stood there, almost swaying. 'Miss Klemetsen, could I...'

Nora held up her hand.

'As you will,' he said and turned round again. 'Then I'll drink alone. I'm used to that, after all.'

He poured himself a generous glass and took a swig. Sighed happily.

'There,' he said, and walked over to the chair behind the large oak table. 'Oscar's will. Would you like to start, my dear sister-in-law?' The words came singing out of his mouth.

Unni looked sceptical as she sat down in one of the chairs by the table, opened her bag and took out a packet of cigarettes and a lighter. She lit a cigarette and took a drag.

'No, I guessed as much,' Fritz said, sitting down heavily. 'As the good journalist mentioned, Oscar's will has caused a slight problem for both of us. It's no longer possible for me to hide the fact that Georg is not my biological son, and you, Unni, would rather that the world didn't know that your husband has, for all these years, had an illegitimate son.'

Unni took another drag on her cigarette, refusing to look at him.

'But, he became a sentimental old fool in the end, Mr Casanova, and he wanted to Georg to get his rightful share of the inheritance. So Georg got the summer house. It's worth a few kroner, I'm sure.'

Nora nodded.

'That isn't the only reason why,' Unni interjected, leaning over towards the ashtray. 'It's also where they ... met – Oscar and Ellen, that is.' Unni tapped the ash off the end of her cigarette.

'Of course,' Fritz said.

Nora looked at them both, first one, then the other.

'Was there anyone else in the family who knew about the affair?'

Unni shook her head.

'Not even your son William?'

Unni looked at Nora as though she hadn't understood the question. Nora weighed up whether she should share her suspicions with them or not. She somewhat hesitantly concluded that, yes, she should.

'Around the time that Ellen went missing, William was working with someone called Tore Pulli,' she started, 'a well-known enforcer from Horten, who died earlier this year. Ellen was found in a well on the summer-house property; a well that had a heavy, concrete cover, which only a strongly built man could lift without any help.'

Nora decided not to go into any more details – they could fill them in themselves.

Fritz looked surprised. 'William?' he said. 'Is that ... can it really...'

'That's ridiculous,' Unni retorted, and took another drag on her cigarette.

Nora pulled back a little. 'William might not have liked the fact that Ellen was destroying the family,' she suggested, turning away from Unni. 'So he may have had her killed.'

None of them said anything for a while.

'Do you have any proof?' Unni then asked.

'No,' Nora replied, turning back to look at her. 'If William doesn't confess, that is. And there's not much chance of that – he's unlikely to admit to hiring a killer, because he'll end up in prison. But,' Nora continued, looking at them one after the other, 'I'm starting to wonder if this is where Hedda fits in.'

Nora waited until she had their full attention.

'I think she may have discovered that William had a hand in it.'

Unni crossed her legs. 'And how would she have discovered that?' she asked. The greyish-blue smoke from her cigarette spiralled up towards the ceiling.

'She sat by her father's bed day and night at the end,' Nora said. 'Oscar may have shared his suspicions with her.'

Unni gave an exasperated smile. 'That's pure speculation.'

'It is,' Nora admitted. 'But do you have any other explanation?'

Unni took a last drag on her cigarette and stubbed it out in the ashtray.

'Hedda went out to Hulebakk five weeks ago,' Nora continued. 'I think she was going to reveal who killed Ellen; but someone managed to stop her before it was too late.'

Fritz took a sip of whisky. 'And you think it was William?' he asked, in disbelief.

Nora shrugged. 'It's certainly a possibility,' she said.

There was silence. Unni covered her mouth with her hand, the index finger resting on the bridge of her nose. Fritz also appeared to be deep in thought.

Ask that drunken husband of hers.

'Where does the Hellberg family fortune come from?' said Nora quietly.

They both snapped to attention.

'What do you mean?' Unni asked.

Nora looked directly at Fritz. 'What did Ellen discover about the family, Fritz?'

He looked back at her with wide eyes. Nora didn't blink, just waited for him to say something.

His shoulders relaxed. 'Oh. You've been talking to Tanja,' he said.

Nora didn't answer.

Fritz glanced at his sister-in-law and shook his head. 'That old bag of bones. Didn't I tell you she was a little muddled?'

'Yes, you did,' said Nora. 'But she said that Ellen had found out where the family fortune came from, and that I should ask you what kind of people you were. And that's not the sort of thing you say with no reason. She must have heard something somewhere.'

'The reason that we've never invited her here,' he said, pointing his shaky index finger in the air, 'is that she might say something to Georg.'

'So there's nothing in what she says?'

'No,' he said, quickly.

Unni stood up. Fritz followed her with his eyes as she walked behind Nora's back. Nora waited for him to explain, but he didn't.

Nora realised there was one more possibility: Fritz had the strongest motive of them all for killing Ellen. His wife had been unfaithful – with his brother, no less; and Georg wasn't even his son. If Ellen had then also found out something that might tarnish the family name – if it became known – well, then he may have arranged to have her killed. His heart attack meant that he couldn't have done it himself, but he had enough money to get someone else to do the job for him.

Nora looked at the picture that was hanging on the wall behind Fritz. It was the same one that William had in his office. Suddenly she had an idea.

'OK,' she said, and tried to smile. 'I'd better get going.'

Fritz stood up and took a step closer. 'Don't you dare write anything about this,' he said, in a hard voice.

'No, no, of course not,' Nora said. 'Not until I've found out what the truth is.'

She turned and started to walk towards the door.

'Thank you for taking the time to talk to me,' she said. 'I can find my own way out.'

47

Henning managed to get Goma back out into the stairwell, opened all the windows, and quickly phoned Oslo Fire Brigade and Bjarne Brogeland at Oslo Police. Then he knocked on all the doors in the building and got everyone out, before he himself sat down, exhausted, on a pile of stone slabs in the back yard to wait.

A couple of years earlier, he'd covered a case in which a married couple in their fifties, planning to make a claim on the insurance by causing a gas explosion in their kitchen, had managed to blow up their whole house. They'd totally miscalculated how far the gas would spread, and the damage that such an explosion might cause. The husband had presumably thought he was far enough away to light up a cigarette as he came down the steps.

It was the last thing he did.

So Henning knew you had to be careful with gas, and what the intention was here. Whoever had been in his flat wanted him to come home and, finding his flat was dark, think that a fuse had blown; he'd switch the fuse back on, and ... Bang. When Henning had worked on the story about the insurance fraud, someone from the fire brigade had explained that a spark was enough. If he'd flicked the fuse switch, the fridge would have started up again; and if that didn't do the trick, the Hoover had been plugged in and was presumably on, so the gas would have been be sucked into it, and promptly cause an explosion.

It would have been hard to prove what had actually happened – what had caused the explosion. The evidence would be destroyed. And Henning would have burned to death.

Smart, he thought. He also knew that a special smell was added to domestic gas so people would know when there was a leak, which was why they'd put out a glass of vinegar – to hide the smell. Henning hadn't checked, but guessed there were probably more glasses dotted around the flat.

Bjarne Brogeland arrived just after the fire brigade. Henning took him to one side and they went and sat on the steps that led down to the play area.

Henning had gone to the same school as Bjarne in Kløfta, where they grew up. They hadn't had much to do with each other at the time – or even, later on, when Bjarne was in love with Henning's sister, Trine. The policeman was Henning's opposite in every way. Tall, muscular, fit and particular about his appearance, even his fingernails; but he'd proved to be a very good detective.

Henning told him everything – just as he had with Iver; about the story he was working on, about all the things that had happened so far; and that someone had apparently tampered with Indicia – the police shared reporting system – and removed information about Tore Pulli's movements in Markveien in the hour before Henning's flat was set on fire. Initially, everything had pointed to Assistant Chief of Police, Pia Nøkleby, as her user information was registered in the Indicia log, but Henning didn't think she had anything to do with it; he believed instead that someone had somehow managed to get hold of her username and password.

'Yes, she did mention that,' Bjarne said, when Henning had finished.

'Did she?' Henning said.

'Yes, she told me about it. That it had happened, I mean. She wanted me to find out how you knew.'

Henning almost told him that he had a secret source in the police, but didn't know the person's identity, as he'd only chatted with them online.

'You can tell her it's nothing to worry about,' he said, instead.

'Nothing to worry about? Of course it is.'

'Yes, but it's not dangerous in the way that she thinks it's dangerous. Pia's probably scared that I'll write about it. But I won't. I'm on leave, and it's in everyone's best interests that you can sort out your security problems without the rest of the country knowing. After all, the most important thing is that you have people's trust. I'm more interested in whoever managed to do it. How and why they've been allowed to operate freely, as it would seem they have.'

Neither of them said anything for a while.

'Is that why you've taken leave?' Bjarne asked.

'Yes.'

'And it's because of all this – Jonas, Pulli – that someone is trying to kill you?'

'Yep.'

Another silence.

'You should have contacted me ages ago.'

'But I had nothing to give you. And I still don't. What I've just told you wouldn't hold up in court.'

'No,' Bjarne said with a sigh. 'It wouldn't.'

The firemen were busy running up and down the stairs. Gunnar Goma talked to everyone who went past.

'And while we're on the subject of circumstantial evidence,' Bjarne continued, 'we'll need to have it confirmed or discounted, first of all. And that won't necessarily happen overnight. I'll need help. So I suggest I tell the others about it first, and then...'

'No, don't,' Henning said.

Bjarne looked up at him.

'Why not?'

'Because I'm not sure how long these people's arms are, or what size ears they've got. They presumably managed to get hold of Pia Nøkleby's username and password, so I wouldn't trust everyone around her a hundred percent. And that means, everyone around you, too, I'm afraid.'

'So what do you recommend I do, then?' Bjarne asked.

'Only choose people you trust implicitly,' he said. 'Two – max three. And make sure that no one else knows what you're working on.'

'A unit within a unit, you mean,' Bjarne said.

'Something like that.'

Bjarne nodded slowly and looked straight ahead.

'See what you can do,' Henning said, and stood up. 'And in the meantime, I'll try to find out who this Daddy Longlegs guy is.'

Bjarne stood up too. 'How are you going to do that?' he asked.

Henning turned to the policeman and said, with a twinkle in his eye: 'I'll see if I can fight my way in there.'

48

Nora hurried out to the car, got in and started the engine. *That was intense*, she said to herself as she reversed out of the driveway. *I wonder what Unni and Fritz said once I'd gone.*

As she drove away from the large house in Solvang, her breathing relaxed. But the conversation she'd had and everything that Ellen's mother had said, churned around in her head. The old woman had clearly not had anything to do with the family after Ellen disappeared. If what she implied was true, that perhaps wasn't so strange.

Ask him where their money comes from.

Her phone started to vibrate in her bag, so she stopped the car, dug it out and put her earpieces in. Her heart sank a little when she saw who it was. She took a deep breath and kept her eyes on the road.

'Hi, Iver,' she said, the first word loud, the second quiet.

'Hi,' he said. 'Um ... where are you?'

'Tønsberg,' Nora said, braking at a junction and changing down into first gear.

'Are you still working?'

'Mm,' she said, looking right and left.

'Are you going to stay there tonight, too?'

'Don't know. Possibly.'

Nora drove on, waiting for Iver to continue. When he did, his voice was warmer than usual.

'We need to talk, Nora.'

She didn't answer.

'But I don't think talking on the phone is the best idea. Can I come down there?'

Nora was driving slowly, and saw in the rear-view mirror that a car was driving close behind her.

'Now?' she asked.

'Yes, or later this evening, perhaps?'

She put on her indicator to show the driver behind he should overtake.

'I don't know, Iver. I'm working and...'

The car sped past her.

'...I don't know how long I'll be,' she said. 'But sometime this afternoon should be fine.'

'OK, great. Where are you staying?'

Nora drove into a parking place. She didn't really know where she was, but it didn't matter.

'Hotel Brygga.'

'Great. See you later then.'

'Mm,' Nora said and ended the call. She exhaled. *At last*, she thought. But what was there to talk about, really? How was he going to convince her that he really wanted them to be a family?

If that was what he wanted to talk about.

Nora couldn't bear to think about it right now, so instead she turned her thoughts to the picture she'd seen on the wall in William's office and again in Fritz's house – Morsevik Farm. She decided to look it up on the internet, to see what information she could find about the farm. She grabbed her phone, typed in the name, and quickly saw that the owner was a man called Jarl Inge Dommersnes, who was born in 1929, according to the tax records.

Nora wondered if he was still alive.

She decided to find out.

Morsevik Farm was in an idyllic setting, not far from the main road, about halfway between Åsgårdstrand and Tønsberg. Nora turned off onto a narrow dirt road with fields on both sides. Further on, the road split in two, either side of a large oak tree, with one track leading to a barn and the other to the main house, a big white building.

Nora drove up to the house, where there was a kind of roundabout with various shrubs and bushes growing in the middle. An old blue Toyota – covered in mud and dirt all the way up to the windows and its rear more rust than paint – was parked by the front door.

Nora parked, got out and rang the doorbell, then stepped back to look at the house while she waited. The walls had clearly not been painted for years. Some roof tiles had slipped off. She rang the bell again. This time she heard footsteps inside. When the door opened, she was looking straight into the eyes of an old man who had a pair of spectacles on a cord round his neck; they looked more like magnifying glasses. Nora wondered if he was slightly deaf as well.

'Yes?' he said, looking down at her from the doorway. His voice was strong and clear; he sounded like he might sing in a choir. His face was furrowed and wrinkled, and his skin, which was otherwise fair, was given extra colour by all the moles. He had at least fifteen on one cheek alone. His hair was snow white and looked like silk.

Nora introduced herself.

'Yes?' he repeated, squinting down at her.

'I'd like to ask you some questions about your house,' she said. 'Well, about the whole farm, really.'

The old man peered at her even more intently. He was wearing red tracksuit trousers and a matching jacket, open at the neck, his chest hair sticking out.

'Could I start by asking how long you've lived here ... Mr Dommersnes, isn't it?'

He nodded and looked at her for a few seconds more.

'Are you going to write something about my farm?'

'No,' Nora assured him. 'I'm writing about the Hellberg family. I'm just doing some background research, and if I'm not mistaken, Morsevik Farm was Hellberg Property's first ever sale, just after the war.'

'I don't know whether it was the first or the tenth,' Dommersnes said, and came out onto the step. 'But it's true, I bought the farm in

1948. And we've lived here ever since – my wife and I. Or that's to say, there's only me now; my wife died four years ago.'

'I'm sorry to hear that,' Nora said.

He waved it off. 'She was in a lot of pain at the end, so...' he said.

Nora waited a little before she continued. She felt she needed to choose her words carefully.

'Can you tell me what happened? When you bought the farm?' she started.

He peered at her again. His mouth opened and he narrowed his eyes, revealing a long row of uneven, coffee-stained teeth.

'How the transaction was made? Whether it was an easy process? That kind of thing.'

'Of course. There were no problems as such. I'd inherited a reasonable amount of money from my father, who'd died shortly after the war, and I'd always wanted to have my own farm. The man who lived here had no relatives to take over, so we got the lawyer to sort all the paperwork so I could buy it. Would you like to come in and have a cup of coffee?'

Nora smiled. 'Yes, please, that would be nice.'

Dommersnes stepped back and opened the door fully for her. He stooped as he walked down the hall. She immediately felt the cold seeping in through her coat.

'Sorry, it's a bit cold in here,' he said, as if he'd read her thoughts. 'It's a big house, and I can't afford to keep all the rooms heated.'

Nora decided to keep her jacket on for the moment.

'We can sit in the kitchen; it's warm there. Just keep your shoes on, it's already dirty in here anyway.'

Nora did as he said, and followed him through the dark house, its walls looking like they were full of history. The rooms smelt of wood smoke and tobacco – of lives lived. There was a black wood-burning stove in the living room that looked like it might weigh a ton, but it was not lit at the moment. Beside it was a small pile of logs.

They went through two doors that she struggled to close, before they got to the kitchen. She could feel through the soles of her boots that the floor was cold here, too, but the air was definitely warmer. A large table took up a good deal of space in the middle of the room. There was an old stand-alone cooker against one of the end walls, and on the other, a worktop with a coffee machine, newspapers and a radio. Some dishes were drying on the draining board, ready to be put away.

'Please, sit down.'

Nora took a seat and looked around as he got out two cups from one of the top cupboards. There were large windows in two of the walls; the paint was flaking on the window frames and the putty was disintegrating. She could smell burned coffee and she braced herself for the bitter taste when he put a cup down in front of her. She decided to wait a little before drinking it. Dommersnes also put out some biscuits, which she was afraid to eat, even though she was starving.

'They're from the shop, I'm afraid,' he said, with an apologetic smile.

Nora was more concerned about which century they were from, but took one all the same, to be polite. She bit into it; it tasted of caramel and nuts, and the sugar crunched between her teeth.

'Mm,' she said.

Dommersnes smiled. 'My wife's father was from England,' he told her. 'She always used to bring several packets back whenever she went to visit the family. The English know their biscuits. And now they've started to sell them here, too. They import all kinds of things these days.'

'They're really good,' she said.

Dommersnes sat down. Nora tried not to look at his nasal hair, which vibrated every time he breathed. There was long white hair sprouting out of his ears as well. She took a sip of coffee and was surprised at how good it tasted; it was just the right temperature, too, as she had let it stand for a few minutes.

'So,' he said. 'What have the Hellbergs been up to now, then, to make you want to write about them?'

Nora arched an eyebrow. 'What do you mean?'

'Hm?' He took a sip of coffee.

'You said, "What have they been up to now, then?"'

'Did I?' He put his cup down.

'Yes.'

'Must've been a slip of the tongue.'

He let out a brief, forced laugh, and Nora looked at him sceptically, but decided not to follow it up right away.

'Mr Dommersnes, I...'

'Please, call me Jarl Inge.'

Nora smiled. 'There's a lot going on in the Hellberg family at the moment,' she said. 'Ellen Hellberg, Fritz the third's wife, was found dead yesterday, and there's everything to indicate that she was killed. Her niece, Hedda – who I studied with – is also missing, and there are those who wonder if something similar has happened to her. And...' Nora thought for a moment before carrying on. 'And I wondered whether it might have something to do with the family's background and wealth. How they got their money. Which was why I asked about the situation when you bought Morsevik.'

Dommersnes straightened his top, pulling down one of the sleeves. Nora drank some more coffee and took another biscuit.

'Well,' the old man started. 'There were no secrets and irregularities involved when I bought the farm; I know that for a fact. But there were rumours going around in the fifties.'

Nora leaned forwards a little. 'What kind of rumours?'

Dommersnes studied her for a short time.

'At the start of the war, there were quite a few Jews living around here,' he told her. 'Jews who were either deported towards the end of 1942 and never came back, or who simply fled over the border to Sweden. If what I heard was true, then old Hellberg "bought"' – Dommersnes indicated quote marks with his fingers – 'some of their properties, so the Germans couldn't get their hands on them. But not many of them came back, so eventually he sold the properties on and kept the money himself.'

Nora sat with her mouth open. 'And he hadn't paid for the properties to begin with?'

'No doubt he had,' Dommersnes said, and drank some coffee. 'But probably only a nominal sum. Presumably the intention was that they would then buy their properties back after the war.'

Dommersnes took a biscuit as well. A few crumbs fell from the corner of his mouth onto the plate and down his front. He didn't seem to notice.

Nora mulled this over. Could that be what Ellen had discovered and told her mother? Was that why she'd been killed?

'Do you know which properties they were?' she asked.

He shook his head, took another bite of the biscuit and swallowed it down with some coffee. Nora thought about the address that Hedda had looked up on the internet: Brages vei 18.

'I guess there's no proof of fraud anywhere?'

'No ... at least, I very much doubt it,' Dommersnes said, and put his cup down on the saucer with a clatter. 'Unless you were able to find some of the old pro forma contracts and compare them with the sales after the war.'

Nora remembered what Fritz had told her: that Ellen had developed a close relationship with his mother before she died – a woman who had organised the company archives after her husband took over the business in the fifties, and who had proudly told Ellen about her work.

Fritz's mother might have found something, Nora mused. When she was sorting out all the company letters and contracts. Something that could prove all this. Something that she'd told Ellen about.

Nora had heard lots of stories about what some Norwegians got up to during the war – stories that had eventually filtered out into the public domain. It wasn't only in other countries that people had behaved appallingly. She knew about prison guards who had treated their fellow countrymen like animals, simply because they were Jews; who had struck and kicked them, not given them enough food or proper beds to sleep in, ordered them to do almost inhuman tasks at inhuman times. Nora had also read about people who claimed to be helping the Jews cross the border to safety, but who had instead killed them and stolen anything of value they had with them.

People didn't like to be reminded of it – would rather forget everything to do with the war; and that wasn't so strange. It was quite human really, to want to cover up uncomfortable truths. But some things, some stories, couldn't be buried.

Nora decided to ask one of the researchers at the paper to look for more background material. It could provide a starting point for a whole series of articles, she thought. She felt her fingers itching to start writing.

"The Hellbergs are a rum lot,' Dommersnes said.

Nora nodded, more to herself; then it struck her what he'd actually said.

'What do you mean?' she asked.

'One of them knocked on my door one evening recently and asked if I was interested in renting out my barn.'

Nora's eyebrows shot up. 'Your barn?'

'Yes – said he needed some space,' Dommersnes continued. 'Storage space, primarily. And he needed it as soon as possible.'

Nora nodded more thoughtfully this time.

'I don't use the barn any longer, I'm too old to repair things; so I thought, why not? And it's a bit of extra money. Five hundred kroner a month. I almost feel like a crook.' He smiled.

'How long ago was that?' she asked, without smiling back.

Dommersnes squinted up to the left. 'Um, it must have been a month ago. Or thereabouts.'

A month, Nora thought.

Hedda disappeared just over a month ago.

'You said, "one of them". Do you know which one it was?'

He sighed apologetically. 'I'm not very good with names.'

'What did he look like? Tall, short, young, old?' Nora was leaning almost all the way across the table, now.

Dommersnes cocked his head to one side, then the other. Then he met her eyes. 'He was about your age, I think. Maybe a few years older.'

49

Nora couldn't end her visit quickly enough. She thanked Jarl Inge Dommersnes for his help, said goodbye and left. The autumn wind whipped around her.

Maybe a few years older.

Hedda had, of course, found out about all this, Nora thought. William had realised Hedda was up to something and had tried to stop her. But it seemed she had to be certain first, which was why she'd enlisted the help of Georg, Ellen's son – a man who was also interested in finding out why his mother had been killed, and who had the keys to Hulebakk, no less.

Nora was surveying the barn when Dommersnes came down the steps behind her.

'Has he been here since you rented him the barn?' she asked.

He hitched his jogging trousers even higher up his waist.

'I'm not always aware of everything,' Dommersnes said. 'I often sleep quite a lot during the day and go to bed early. But I think there's been some activity down there nearly every day. He must have a lot that needs storing. Or perhaps he's just interested in the bomb shelter.'

Nora looked up at him. 'Bomb shelter?'

'Yes, there's a bomb shelter in the barn. The man who lived here before was the fearful type, I think,' Dommersnes said, with a laugh.

She thanked the old man once again for his help, got into the car and drove off. But instead of driving out to the main road, she swung left towards the barn at the fork, hoping that Dommersnes hadn't seen where she was going.

She parked behind the barn, out of sight of the house, in case

Dommersnes was still on the steps. Then she got out and looked around. The colours in the sky were losing their strength and the wind gusted against her, dulling the sound of her boots squelching on the mixture of sand and wet grass. All around her, she could see tyre tracks. While she couldn't be sure, she guessed they were made by tyres thicker than those on her own car.

The door had a padlock on it. Nora inspected it; it was heavy and new – no more than a month old. She didn't even try to pull at it; she knew she wouldn't be able to open it, and she didn't want to alarm anyone – if there was anyone about.

She went round to the other side of the barn, her boots sinking in the mud along the base of the barn wall. It was the traditional red colour, though there wasn't really much paint left, now; everything was weathered and old. She stepped over an old kick-sled that had found its resting place on the north side of the barn. Nearby, the rusting carcass of an old tractor had driven its final few metres into the long grass, which now grew out from under it. An old, green oil drum had been abandoned alongside it.

There were no other doors into the barn. At the back, the woods stopped just where the ground sloped down to the building. Nora could well imagine that, in the old days, the path down to the water ran along here. The fjord wasn't far away.

She continued round to the next wall. One of the planks here was loose and stuck out like an arm. Nora went over to look. Several other planks beside it were also coming away. She tugged and pulled a little at the board that was sticking out, and managed to break it off. But the hole needed to be bigger; she might still be thin, but a single plank didn't leave enough space for her to wriggle through. So she pulled and wrenched at some of the other planks, then kicked at them until they broke and it was possible to crawl inside, even though it meant going down on all fours.

She felt the damp seep in through the knees of her trousers. The ground was cold and wet under her hands, but she crept in, arms and head first, making herself as small as possible so she could squeeze herself through. Her bag, which was hanging round her neck, got caught on one of the planks, so she had to reverse to unhook it. Then a nail caught at one of her trouser legs and tore a hole.

Great, Nora thought.

Soon all of her was through. Her eyes gradually adjusted to the dark. It wasn't a big barn; now she was inside, she could see that all the walls were of roughly equal length. A beam stretched across the entire ceiling, some heavy, old rope wound around it. A door, which had presumably hung somewhere in the main house a long time ago, stood leaning up against one of the walls. There was a pile of tyres, wrapped in plastic. Nora had no idea what some of the other junk – tools and equipment – was for. The air smelt stuffy and of rotten wood.

She could tell that a vehicle of some sort had been driven into the barn a number of times: there were hollows in the earth floor, and in places the zigzag pattern of tyres was just visible.

She moved further in, looking around. The day outside forced its way in through a crack in the planks and bathed a wheelbarrow in a dull, dusty light. She moved slowly, and as quietly as possible, even though she knew she'd already made a racket breaking the planks in the wall.

A cat shot out from somewhere, making Nora jump. She felt her hands start to sweat and tingle. A chill spread from her neck, down her spine and out to her limbs. She took a deep breath, shaking her head at her reaction. Then carried on through the spiders' webs, dust and dirt.

Suddenly she spotted it.

A trapdoor.

It looked like it had a handle. Hopefully she could lift it up from the floor. She moved closer, slowly, looking around her again. There was no one there.

She bent down, studied the handle and noticed that it was free from dust. It had been used recently.

She grabbed it and pulled the door up towards her. She had to put her back into it, as the door was heavy. She tensed her legs and leaned back, groaning as she did so, but soon the trapdoor was open. She looked down. There were some stairs. She couldn't see anything else in the dark.

'Hell,' Nora mumbled. Should she phone someone?

Henning and Iver were too far away. Cato Løken would also need at least half an hour to get there, if she could get hold of him in the first place.

In the end, she was just too curious not to take the first step down into the bomb shelter.

Then she took another. The damp wood creaked. Nora swore silently, it was almost too dark down there, as though she was about to sink into an ocean without knowing its depth. More stairs, more creaking, Nora stepped as lightly as she could.

Eight steps later, she was down on the floor. She could feel the concrete under her feet. It was pitch black all around. But she heard a noise further in. A kind of breathing noise. Was it a fan?

She waited until her eyes had adjusted to the dark, then looked around for a switch. She got out her mobile phone and activated the screen, which gave a little light. She could see storage spaces with padlocks on the doors, and all kinds of things inside. The place smelt old and fusty. She heard nothing other than that repetitive sound. And her own steps.

'Hedda?' Nora said, tentatively.

Her voice was muffled by the walls, giving her an idea of how thick they were. She guessed there wasn't much mobile coverage down here, should she need it. A quick glance at her phone confirmed she was right.

But there was electricity; she could hear it. It must be some kind of ventilation. With slow steps, she went further and further into the dark. The light on the screen of her mobile phone disappeared. She pressed it on again. Stopped, held it up to see what was ahead.

And what she saw made her gasp.

The next moment, she was aware of a movement beside her.

Then everything went dark. She felt a hand and a damp cloth over her mouth and a strong arm grabbed her from behind, holding her firm. She tried to breathe, tried to break away, but the drowsiness came creeping over her, and everything got darker and darker and more diffuse.

Then her legs buckled.

50

Henning sneaked into the 123News office, avoiding as many looks and hellos as possible. He found himself an available computer as far away as he could manage from the nearest journalist or line manager. He was lucky; there weren't many people at work, and it seemed that none of his bosses was there. He logged in and quickly printed off the photographs of as many lawyers as he could remember.

Slipping out of the building, he drove up to Ekebergssletta, where he sat for while, before driving to Bogstad, on the other side of town. It was a good way to pass the time; he liked driving and seeing Oslo in its deepening autumn colours. If the sun had been shining, the city would have looked like a postcard. The clouds parted every now and then, allowing a glimpse of a tired sky, but soon they were scudding in and out of each other, creating new formations.

Henning decided to get to Bispegata early. He decided he could always go for a wander around the Medieval Park while he was waiting. Even though it was tiring to be constantly looking over his shoulder, he wasn't frightened – just on his guard. And his vigilance had worked; he was now sure no one was following him.

He parked under a large tree that made the falling dusk even darker, and got out into the cool evening air. It was a quarter past seven. He held the photographs he'd printed out in his hand, looking through them again while he waited.

At last Henning walked towards the big brick building at the end. It brought back recent memories, though perhaps memories was not the right word; he couldn't recall much more than being severely thrashed.

But he could remember the smell, the atmosphere, the grunts of the men who punched, kicked and threw each other to the ground.

A man in jeans and wearing a leather waistcoat over a bright-red T-shirt appeared from the road. Henning recognised him straightaway, but stayed where he was, waiting for him to get a bit closer. Then he walked towards him.

'What the fuck?' the man said.

Henning gave a brief nod. 'Hi, Nicklas,' he said. 'Thanks for the other night.'

Nicklas turned, looking around.

'Relax, it's just us here, for the moment. I guessed you might come first, as you're the doorman.'

The Swedish Fight Club's bouncer didn't look reassured. 'You've got some nerve coming here again,' he said.

Henning ignored his comment, and instead pulled out the first photograph from his pile: Lars Indrehaug.

'Is this the guy Pontus was thinking about?' he asked, showing the picture to Nicklas.

Nicklas started to walk past Henning.

'Is he the one who gave Jocke Brolenius work?' Henning had to trot to catch up with him. 'Is this Daddy Longlegs?'

Nicklas walked faster, started to get his keys out of his pocket.

'Please,' Henning said. 'My son, Jonas, was only six years old. He had thin, fair hair and had just learned to read. He liked football and playing with Lego – just like your son will when he gets to that age.'

Nicklas spun round, walked straight up to Henning, grabbed hold of his face – a thumb on one side of his mouth, the rest of his fingers on the other – and squeezed as he pushed him up against a blue container.

There was a crashing sound.

'How the fuck do you know that I've got a son?' he said, with his face close to Henning's.

Henning tried to answer, but it was impossible with the Swede's hand round his mouth. He tried to breathe through his nose and suddenly felt the effect of the injuries Pontus had inflicted on him.

Nicklas let go. 'Scram, before the others get here.'

Henning put a hand to his jaw, and made some chewing movements to check if it was still working.

'No one needs to know that you've helped,' he said. 'You don't even need to say anything, just nod or shake your head when I show you the photographs.'

Nicklas lunged towards him, tore the sheets of paper from his hands, crumpled them up and threw them in the container.

Then he walked off.

⊙

Henning took a few moments to collect himself, then he walked back to his car. Getting in, he rubbed his face, and sat thinking for a while.

What now?

He could ring Geir Grønningen again, see if he'd found out who Daddy Longlegs was; but Grønningen had not proved himself to be a great detective. And if he *had* found out anything, he would have called.

Henning started the car, and listened to the hum of the engine. It was the same pitch as his mobile phone, which, at that exact moment, started to vibrate in his jacket pocket.

It was Iver.

'Hi,' Henning said.

'Henning, have you heard anything from Nora?' Iver asked.

'Not since yesterday,' Henning replied, and put his hand on the gear-stick. 'Why?'

'I can't get hold of her,' Iver told him. 'I've been trying to ring her for nearly three hours now, and it just goes straight to voicemail. I was supposed to be meeting her in Tønsberg.'

'When?' Henning asked.

'We hadn't really decided on a time, just sometime this afternoon.'

Henning thought for a moment. It was nearly seven o'clock.

'She's probably busy with an interview,' he said.

Iver didn't answer straightaway.

'Yes, of course,' he said, eventually, but Henning could hear the concern in his voice. It made him worried, too.

A trailer drove into the yard. Henning followed it with his eyes as he asked: 'Have you spoken to anyone else?'

'I contacted one of her colleagues who's down here, but she hasn't talked to Nora at all today. And none of the hotel staff have seen her either.'

Henning put the car into gear. 'I'm sure she's just working,' he said. 'Or her phone's run out of juice – that happens to everyone.'

But Henning realised he hadn't even managed to convince himself this was true. It was almost unforgivable for a journalist working in the field not to be in regular contact with the news desk. Nora knew that. And three hours was a long time.

He tried to think. Nora had said that she was onto something.

'Are you still in Tønsberg?' he asked.

'Yes.'

'OK,' Henning said. He pulled out into the road and accelerated. 'I'll be there as soon as I can.'

51

Henning tried to call Nora at regular intervals as he drove down to Tønsberg but, like Iver's, his calls went straight to voicemail.

Where the hell was she?

Henning met Iver in the car park outside the hotel where Nora was staying. He parked in an available space and was out of the car before the old engine had stopped turning over.

'Nothing new?' he asked.

Iver shook his head.

'Have you spoken to the police?'

'Yes. But it's too soon for them to do anything.'

Henning stopped about a metre from Iver. 'Who did you talk to?'

'Some officer, I can't remember his name.'

'Was it Cato Løken?'

'No.'

'Get hold of Løken,' Henning said. 'He knows who Nora is; they've been in touch.'

'OK,' Iver said, stepping back as he dialled the number, and putting the phone to his ear.

Henning stayed where he was, deep in thought. Then he looked at his watch; nearly half past eight. What the hell could have happened?

He tried to reconstruct the conversation he'd had with Nora at the hotel the day before, when she told him everything she'd found out so far; searched for any details that might give him a clue.

He couldn't think of anything.

Iver came back. 'I got hold of Løken,' he said. 'He'll be here soon.'

'OK,' Henning nodded. 'Good.'

He ran his fingers through his hair and tried to ring Nora again. Same result. Think, he admonished himself. Where could she be?

Twenty minutes later, a dirty, white Ford came driving in towards them and parked alongside Henning's car. A rather dishevelled-looking man, with at least two portions of *snus* under his upper lip, got out.

'Which one of you is Gundersen?' he asked.

Iver stepped forwards and held out his hand.

'Cato Løken,' said the detective.

Henning introduced himself as well, explaining that he knew a good deal about the case.

Løken peered at him for a moment or two.

'I've heard about you,' he said, and nodded.

Henning didn't answer.

'So you think something's happened to Klemetsen?' the policeman asked.

'Yes,' Henning and Iver chorused.

'I'm inclined to agree with you,' Løken said. 'I've met her a couple of times. Smart lady. Good nose.'

That was Nora, alright, thought Henning.

'When was the last time you spoke to her?' he asked.

'Yesterday,' Løken replied. 'How about you two?'

Iver described his last conversation with Nora, and Henning said that he'd spoken to her the day before.

'Is it possible to find out where she was before her phone stopped working?' Henning asked.

Løken gave Henning a long look. 'Yes, of course it's possible.'

Henning took a step towards him.

'Nora would never just vanish like this, Løken. Something has happened to her.'

The inspector ran a hand over his stubbled chin before taking a phone from his pocket and dialling a number, walking away as he did so.

Henning looked over at Iver. The possible implications of the fact that Nora was missing were inscribed on his face. Deep lines on his forehead. A grim look in his eyes.

'We'll find her,' Henning said.

Iver turned towards him.

'I promise you,' Henning repeated. 'We'll find her.'

Iver straightened his shoulders. Took a deep breath and exhaled loudly.

'We won't get a search party out tonight,' he said. 'It's too late.'

Henning looked around. The evening was dark and heavy.

'Then we'll drive around and look ourselves. She had a hire car, didn't she?'

Iver nodded.

'Then let's go look for it, just drive around – all night if we have to. It's better than nothing.'

Løken came back, slipping his phone into his pocket.

'They're checking her phone location,' he said. 'But, regardless of where her phone stopped working, she could have been taken anywhere by now. If anyone has harmed her, that is.' Løken looked at his watch. 'You can get pretty far in a few hours.'

A car with a foreign number plate drove into the car park and stopped a few spaces away. A family of four got out. The children – a boy and a girl of about the same age: six or seven – looked tired. The boy had a tennis racquet in his hand.

Henning waited until the family had passed before he turned to Løken and said: 'Are you still holding Fritz Georg Hellberg at the police station?'

Løken said yes, they were.

'Løken, I know that it's not normal practice, but would it be possible to speak to him?'

'To Georg?' Løken's eyebrows shot up. 'Absolutely not,' he snorted.

Henning looked around to see if anyone else might hear what they were saying.

'Løken, please. I'm a hundred percent certain that Georg knows something. And he's not likely to tell you. He's probably scared that it would only make things more difficult for himself or the people he loves. I, on the other hand, am a journalist on leave whose only interest is in finding Nora. And as I just said, I firmly believe that Georg can help us.'

'In what way?' Løken asked.

'He knows the family,' Henning said. 'Maybe he knew what Hedda's plans were, given that he picked her up at Skoppum Station and lent her his car. She must have told him something. And we need more than a qualified guess to know where to start looking. You said so yourself – Nora could be anywhere.'

Løken didn't answer. He hesitated, was having second thoughts, Henning could tell. But they had no time to lose.

'Løken, Nora said you were different from the others. Now's your chance to prove it. Deep down, you know we're right. Something has happened to her.'

Løken rubbed his eye as though trying to get something out of it. Then he huffed and puffed a bit.

'We do very occasionally allow unofficial conversations with prisoners in remand,' he said. Then he nodded at Henning's car. 'Come on then, follow me.'

52

It only took a couple of minutes to get from the hotel to the police station in Baglarveien. Løken drove his car down into the garage, but the barriers prevented Henning from doing the same. So he parked on the street, illegally, and waited for Løken to reappear.

The detective then led Henning and Iver into the lift and up to the second floor, where his office was located.

'Wait here,' Løken said. 'And don't make too much noise. I want as few people as possible to know that you're here.'

When Løken had gone, Iver tried to phone Nora again, but cut the call off almost straightaway. He sighed, held the phone in one hand and ran the other over his hair. He paced back and forth, not looking at the pictures, the calendar on the wall, the map of Vestfold, the children's drawings with dates and names in the bottom right-hand corner.

He stopped and looked at Henning. 'What are you going to ask him?'

Henning turned. 'I'm going to *goad* it out of him,' he said.

'Goad him?'

Henning nodded.

'You think we'll find Nora by teasing him?'

'Georg's been in here for a while now, Iver. He can't possibly know what might have happened to Nora. But he might know something else. Something that can point us in the right direction.'

Iver shook his head feebly, sent Henning a furtive glance then paced up and down again, before going over to the window and looking out at the evening sky.

'I don't see what else we can do,' Henning concluded.

Iver didn't reply.

It was a good fifteen minutes before the door opened and a young man came into the office, with Løken right behind him. Henning and Iver turned towards them.

Fritz Georg Hellberg looked more like a boy than an adult, Henning thought. He was short, and his suit jacket hung off his shoulders. He knew the sort: a boy who'd lived deep in Daddy's pockets for most of his life; who bought expensive watches and tailored clothes because it gave him status and attracted a certain kind of girl.

Now, though, he looked like he hadn't slept for days. His shoulders were stooped, his face was pale and drawn, his cravat was crushed and dirty. He looked utterly exhausted and not a little scared.

'Who are they?' he asked. 'More detectives?'

'No, no,' Løken said, behind him. 'These boys just want a quick word.'

Georg turned to Løken. 'Why?'

'Because...' Løken paused. Instead, he looked at Henning and said: 'Perhaps you'd like to explain?'

Henning gave Georg an encouraging smile, held out his hand and introduced himself. Georg tentatively accepted his proffered hand.

'We're here because we're trying to find a journalist who works for *Aftenposten*,' said Henning. 'You met her earlier this week – Nora Klemetsen?'

Henning waited for some kind of response.

'Is she missing?' asked Georg eventually.

Henning nodded, looking over at Løken. The policeman understood.

'I'll be just outside,' he said quietly, then withdrew and closed the door behind him. Iver sat down behind Henning. Henning asked Georg if he'd like to sit down, but he shook his head.

'I know that you're exhausted,' Henning said. 'I'm sure the past few days have been pretty dreadful for you.'

'You can say that again,' Georg sighed.

'I'm sure you've been asked the same questions over and over again, so I hope you can face a few more from me. It won't take long.'

Georg didn't answer, just looked at Henning with dull eyes. Henning decided to cut to the chase; he started by giving a brief outline of what Nora had been up to in the past few days. He finished by saying that it was possible she'd come too close to an uncomfortable truth and, as a result, had now fallen victim to some criminal act.

Henning took a step closer and gave his voice some more warmth. 'And it seems reasonable enough to assume that it might have something to do with your mother, seeing as Hedda contacted you and no one else in her family. She needed someone she could trust.'

Georg lowered his eyes. The seconds drew out before he eventually said: 'Hedda suspected that Mum hadn't taken her own life.' He looked over at the door. 'She thought she'd find the answer out at Hulebakk.'

'The answer?' Henning said.

Georg shrugged and showed his palms. 'Yes, but ... I don't think it was necessarily to do with Mum. There was something else.'

Henning racked his brains.

'She didn't want to say what it was,' continued Georg, 'and I ... well, I wanted to help her look, of course, because I wanted to know what had happened to Mum. But Hedda said no, that I had to act as normally as possible, so that no one suspected that she was out there.'

'No one in the family, you mean?'

Georg nodded.

'Because Hedda believed that someone in the family had something to do with your mother's disappearance?'

Georg took his time, finally murmuring, 'I think so.'

Henning turned round as he thought. 'Where did it all come from? Did she ever say?'

Georg primped his cravat. 'Oscar,' he said. 'Or rather, Dad – because he was actually my father; that's to say, my biological father. Hedda sat with him night and day towards the end. And I think he had his suspicions about what had happened and told Hedda.'

Henning swung round to face him. 'Is that why she borrowed your car?'

'Yes. And then I did as she said for a few days: acted normally, went to work, went to the gym, went out on the town. I was dying to know what was going on.' He looked away for a moment. 'But when I went out there a couple of days later, she wasn't there.'

'And your car wasn't there either?'

'No, it was there.'

'And had apparently been to Sweden in the meantime?'

'Yes, that's right. But I've no idea what she was doing there,' Georg said.

Henning walked around the room, thinking hard. 'What did you do after that?'

Georg put his hands in his pockets. 'I went into the house, obviously; looked for her everywhere. I found my car keys on the mantelpiece in the living room. Her suitcase and clothes were still in one of the rooms. But I couldn't find her, so I went back the next day and the day after that – to see if she'd come back or if I could work out what had happened to her. I looked everywhere.'

'And when the police took you in for questioning, you didn't want to tell them what you've just told me because you knew what they would think: you were the last person to see Hedda; you'd lent her your car, and they'd no doubt be able to find evidence of her in it.'

Henning stood still and looked at the young man, who had once again lowered his eyes.

'But given what you know now, do you have any idea who might have harmed Hedda? And who might have Nora?'

Georg put his hand over his mouth, pinched his nose.

'It has to be someone strong,' Henning carried on. 'Someone who could overpower them. I don't know Hedda, but Nora's pretty strong.'

Georg shook his head.

'Sorry,' he said. 'I've no idea.'

There was a knock at the door. Cato Løken popped his head round. 'The last base station to register Nora's mobile phone was Innlaget,' he said. 'And before that, Ilebrekke.'

'Where are they?' Iver asked, and stood up.

'On the other side of Tønsberg,' the policeman said. 'Out towards Åsgårdstrand.'

'How far apart are the two stations?' Henning asked.

'Not that far.'

Iver came and stood by Henning's side.

'What's out there?' he asked.

'Largely forest, and the main road to Horten,' Løken said. 'A few houses here and there. The Karlsvika and Skallevold camping sites are out that way. And a couple of farms, of course, but not a lot else.'

'Well, at least we've got somewhere to start,' Iver said.

Henning nodded, and then turned to Georg.

'Do you know of anything in the area that might have some connection with your family?'

Georg looked up in astonishment.

'Have any of your family ever gone camping there, for example?'

'Not that I know of.'

'Are there any other places in the area where it might be easy to hide?'

Georg thought about it.

'Cabins, gullies, bunkers – anything?'

Georg pushed his chin out. 'Morsevik Farm is out there...'

Løken came further into the room.

'It was the first property that my great-grandfather ever sold,' Georg explained. 'Everyone in the family knows about Morsevik Farm; it's been mentioned in every single speech I've ever heard about Hellberg Property. It's just off the Åsgårdstrand road, but slightly hidden.'

Henning and Iver looked at each other.

'Let's start there then,' Henning said. 'Thank you, Georg, you've been a great help.'

53

'I suppose there's no question of you waiting for me,' Løken said, as Henning and Iver raced to the lift.

'No,' they shouted together.

'Be careful,' Løken called after them, his hand on Georg's shoulder. 'I'll be there as soon as I can.'

Henning and Iver rushed out onto the street and got into the car. There was a yellow parking ticket envelope under the windscreen wiper, but Henning ignored it and put his foot on the pedal.

'Do you know where it is?' Iver asked.

'No, but we just need to follow the signs to Åsgårdstrand.'

Iver put on his seatbelt, got out his phone and started to tap in the name. He'd soon found the farm.

'A man called Jarl Inge Dommersnes lives there.'

Henning pushed the car as fast as it would go. They quickly found the road that ran between Tønsberg and Åsgårdstrand. Even though the sky was black, the pools of light from the street lamps and from external house lights gave Henning a vague idea of the landscape.

'There,' Iver said eventually, pointing his finger in front of Henning's face.

Henning saw a house number and a green mailbox at the side of the road. He turned then accelerated, sending the dirt and grit flying into the dying autumn fields. The track forked and Henning took the left branch, up towards a house, where he slammed on the brakes, making the tyres spin in the gravel.

They jumped out, ran up the steps and rang the bell.

While they waited for someone to come to the door, Henning and Iver glanced at each other and then around at their surroundings.

Nothing happened.

'There's a barn over there,' Iver said, pointing. 'I'll go over and have a look while you wait here.'

'OK.'

Henning watched from the step while Iver went off down a path with grass standing tall on either side like a miniature avenue. He rang the bell again, holding it down for a long time, but he couldn't hear any movement behind the door. The outside light was on, but he saw no sign of life in the windows closest to the door. It was past ten o'clock, so if Dommersnes was at home, he might well be in bed already.

Henning rang the bell yet again, and still heard no footsteps inside. He sighed and went back down the steps, searching the dimness for Iver, without success. The sky above him was dark. A plane cut through the clouds: it sounded like the sky was being torn open.

Henning turned towards the house one last time before getting into the car and driving off, skidding over the sand and gravel. He drove as fast as he could to where the track divided around a large tree, then turned sharply to the left and in towards the barn. He braked hard, startled by what he saw.

A rental car. Parked up against the wall of the barn. They couldn't have seen it from the road.

Nora.

Henning leaped out of the car and shouted for Iver, but got no answer. He couldn't see him either. He ran over to the car, looked in through the window, saw a packet of menthol lozenges in the mid-console, a hair band on top of a crumpled pay-and-display sticker.

Iver must have gone into the barn, Henning thought, and went over to the door. He pulled and pushed it. Locked. He studied the padlock, it was pretty solid. Shiny, certainly not old. He walked along the wall on the left-hand side. Soon he spotted a hole, bent down and crawled into the dark interior.

Getting to his feet again, he brushed the dirt from his knees and looked around, listening. Then he started and jumped to the side, straight into a rake with rounded teeth, which clattered to the ground.

Iver was standing beside him.

'Shit, you frightened me, you idiot,' Henning hissed.

'Come over here,' Iver whispered. 'Look at this.'

He pointed further into the barn. They came to an open trapdoor.

'It looks like a bunker,' Iver said.

Henning went down a step. It creaked, so he stopped, listened for any sounds. Nothing. He took another step. And another; no noise this time. Henning held onto the rail as he descended, Iver close behind him. They reached the bottom, and found a concrete floor.

They took a few steps in. Henning went first, making sure to lift his feet so he wouldn't make shuffling sounds. A faint light made it possible to see the contours of the narrow passage. It was no more than two and a half metres from the floor to the arched ceiling. Henning felt the sweat on his forehead and noticed that he'd been holding his breath. He gasped.

The passage swung sharply to the right. Henning looked round the corner. No one there, but the light was stronger. And now he could see where it was coming from: there was a room further in; the light was slipping out from under the door. A few more steps and Henning was in front of the door. He tried the handle. It was unlocked.

Henning carefully eased the door open, feeling Iver's warmth right behind him, his breath on his neck.

They were stopped in their tracks.

There was a green military camp bed in the corner of the room, which must have been there since the war. And on the bed lay a woman with long, fair hair, her eyes closed, completely still. Her chest rose and fell steadily. She had a tube in one of her nostrils, which came from a transparent bag that was attached to a small, purplish-white machine on a frame; the label read: *Nutricia* and *Flocare Infinity*. The display showed: 150ml/hr. She also had a cannula in her arm, and the tube was attached to another transparent bag, which Henning presumed contained water. There were two more bags by the camp bed – one with brown contents, the other with yellow.

Henning had never seen the woman before, but it was not hard to guess who it was.

Hedda Hellberg.

In that moment, Henning had no idea what had actually happened, and could think of no plausible explanation why Hedda was there – why she was being kept alive in this way and hadn't been dumped in a ditch somewhere. But there she lay all the same.

'Go back up and ring Løken,' he said to Iver, and nodded to the door. 'Ask him to send an ambulance and explain the situation down here.'

Iver did as he was told. The sound of his hurried footsteps on the concrete floor faded into the distance.

But where was Nora? thought Henning.

He looked around, but found nothing other than some boxes of clear, empty drip bags and plastic tubes, a tin of Vaseline, four 1.5-litre bottles of water, one of them half full, some scrunched-up carrier bags from a supermarket, a chopping board and breadknife on a small worktop, some bread in a bag, two packets of crispbread, a jar of strawberry jam and a plastic spoon.

Henning stuck his head out into the passage. He couldn't hear or see anything; no other room where Nora could be. He went back in and stared at Hedda, lying without moving under the duvet, her face white, her lips blue, her cheeks sunken. Even her eyelids didn't move. There was a suture kit lying beside her.

Henning placed his hand lightly on her forehead. Normal body temperature.

'Hedda,' he said, bending down towards her. 'Can you hear me?'

Her face showed no sign of response. He squeezed her hand, but it felt dead in his.

Only a few minutes later, Cato Løken entered the room, with Iver at his heels. The inspector turned off the torch he was carrying and stared in disbelief at what he saw in front of him.

Henning let go of Hedda's hand, stood up and said: 'I think I've got an idea of who you're looking for.'

54

Cato Løken ran up from the bomb shelter and back outside, so he could meet the paramedic team when the ambulance arrived.

Soon Henning and Iver heard heavy footsteps, and two men in red-and-green uniforms entered the room. They quickly examined Hedda before taking out the tubes and cannula, then used the camp bed as a stretcher to carry her out and up to the ambulance. The whole thing took no more than a few minutes.

Løken, Iver and Henning stayed in the room.

'So, you think that Patrik Hellberg is behind all this?' Løken asked Henning.

'He works for a pharmaceutical company,' Henning said. 'I'm sure he's got access to medical stores. The things here' – he pointed around the room – 'are pretty easy to get hold of. And they're not particularly heavy or difficult to operate.'

Løken looked with interest from Iver to Henning and back again.

'Don't look at me,' Iver said, and put up his hands. 'I don't understand any of this.'

Løken took a closer look at the machine that Hedda had been attached to, and at all the other equipment spread around on the floor, by the wall, on the table.

He scratched his head.

'OK,' he said. 'We know that Hedda was out at Hulebakk, because we found her suitcase in the water just out from the shore. And we also know that at least one shot was fired, as the bullet was lodged in the living-room ceiling. We found blood on the fireplace – not much, but now that we know Hedda's been lying here in a coma, it's reasonable to assume that it was her blood we found. But ... where does Patrik come into the picture?' He turned towards them. 'And why didn't he take her to hospital?' Løken scratched his head again.

'Maybe he didn't dare,' Henning suggested. 'He would've had to explain what had happened then. And the hospital would have called the police.'

'Right. And then?'

Henning moved towards the door, then turned. 'My guess is that at the point when he took her here, there was some possibility that she'd regain consciousness and could squeal on him.'

'For what? Murdering Ellen Hellberg? Or Daniel Schyman?'

Henning let out a long breath. 'I don't know,' he said. 'But we're forgetting Nora. Her car's parked outside.'

Just then, two uniformed policemen appeared in the doorway. Løken nodded to Iver and Henning.

Iver went out first and stopped just outside the door.

'There's another way out from here,' he said.

Løken turned on his torch and shone it down the passage.

'Look,' he said, pointing at the floor.

Henning moved closer. There were two wide streaks through the dust, all the way down the passage.

'He's dragged her,' Løken said.

They looked at each other.

'And there's her bag,' Iver said. A leather bag lay abandoned by the wall. He went over and picked it up.

'Jesus,' Henning said. 'Nora's been kidnapped.'

Since she'd been down in the cellar the last time, Veronica Nansen had given a lot of thought to Tore's safe and the code. She'd come up with a long list of possibilities and alternatives, but none of them had worked. Not the date of their wedding, nor the date he'd established Pulli Property, nor the day he sold his first flat. She'd gone through his parents and grandparents, and every date that was significant for them, but nothing had changed the light from red to green.

She looked around at all the stuff bursting out of bags and boxes. She'd gone through most of it already, but there was no harm in looking again. If nothing else, she might get an idea from some object – anything that might point her in the right direction.

She opened a shoebox; then quickly put it down again – just CDs, DVDs, computer games. She looked in a bag of training gear – boxing gloves, a belt, talcum powder. Down it went. A bag of old comics, *Silver Arrow, Secret Agent X-9*.

She sighed.

She started to look randomly through a Co-op bag full of paper and envelopes bearing the Pulli Property logo. She turned it upside down and emptied everything out. Found nothing.

She wondered about the nagging feeling she'd had since she'd seen the photograph of that beautiful woman in the paper. Ellen Hellberg. At the same time, she thought about how evasive Tore had been when she'd asked him if he'd ever killed anyone.

Veronica got out her mobile phone and looked up Ellen Hellberg's date of birth online. She was born in 1950, on Christmas Eve to be precise. Veronica chewed on this for a few seconds before tapping 241250 into the keypad on the safe; she hesitated before putting in the last digit, but then did so all the more decisively.

Red light.

She breathed out. That was a relief. What a ridiculous thought, anyway. But then she had another one. If Tore really had killed Ellen Hellberg, then there was another date that they shared.

The day she disappeared. The day she died.

It said in the paper that Ellen Hellberg was reported missing on 17 August 1993. Veronica punched in the new numbers.

Red light.

Phew.

What else could she try?

There was actually one place she hadn't looked. After he'd died, the prison had sent back Tore's personal belongings. She'd just signed and accepted the delivery and then taken the box straight up to the loft. It was still there. There wasn't likely to be anything relevant in it, she thought. Tore had practically nothing with him in prison – not that she knew of, anyway; just some clothes and a couple of photographs.

Veronica locked the door to the basement storeroom, went upstairs to the loft and opened the storeroom door there. There were some jackets and suitcases; some wine bottles covered in a film of dust; thick bags with extra duvets in; a sleeping bag; some pans that were too big to be stored in the kitchen cupboard. She saw the box straightaway – she'd put it down just inside the door. It was taped closed. Tore's name was written on the outside.

She took a deep breath, then bent down and pulled off the brown tape. All she needed to do was lift the lid.

She felt a pressure behind her eyes. She had to pull herself together. She took out a jacket, two shirts and some jogging pants, which she reckoned he would have worn nearly all the time. They had an elasti-cated waist – fortunately, she thought, as Tore had lost so much weight in prison.

A clear plastic bag with a zip caught her eye. It contained his rings, chain, watch and dog tag. Veronica took out the wedding ring. It was solid and heavy. She turned it between her fingers. The date they got married was inscribed on the inside.

What was she going to do with it? Get it melted down? No, she couldn't do that. Leave it in a drawer to collect dust? That didn't seem right either. Keep it on a chain round her neck? Too much like a teenager.

Veronica looked through the final few things. A couple of training books, a biography of Arnold Schwarzenegger in English. Hand cream. A packet of ibuprofen, a half-empty packet of cigarettes and a lighter.

That was it.

She sighed again. Earlier in the day, she'd called the company that made the safe, explained the situation and asked for their advice. As it was an insurance-approved safe and Tore had changed the original code and used his own, they couldn't help her. It was then the owner's responsibility.

But it was always possible to contact an 'expert', as the man on the phone put it: someone who was trained to open safes of that kind. Alternatively, she could cut open the safe with an angle grinder or a cutting torch. Apparently drastic measures were needed.

Veronica put the ring back in the plastic bag, and examined the other bits and pieces it contained. When she picked up the dog tag, she stopped. The usual information was inscribed on the front: that Tore was Norwegian, his personal ID number, his blood type. But Tore had scratched a six-digit number on the back: 691499. She remembered immediately what the number was.

When Tore had been in the army, his troop had been sent to the Terningmoen camp, where everyone had been issued with a AG-3 rifle. They'd all had to memorise the issue number inscribed on the side of the rifle, so they wouldn't take anyone else's by mistake. Tore's number was 691499.

Veronica locked the loft door and hurried back down into the basement, the dog tag in her hand. It didn't take long before she was in front of the safe again. It's worth a try, she thought, and punched in the first five numbers quickly, then, again, havered for a moment before punching in the final nine.

She put her hand to her mouth.

Green light.

Veronica's breath was shallow and fast as she slowly opened the door. She peered inside.

The first thing she saw was cash: not a massive amount, but possibly enough for a good holiday or two. She also saw a shoebox.

She lifted it out and took off the lid. On top was a yellowing envelope. When she picked it up, she could feel that it was old and porous. On the outside it said:

Hellberg Law
Markveien 1
Tønsberg
NORWAY

Hellberg, Veronica repeated the name and blew the dust from the envelope as she felt her pulse accelerate even more. This couldn't be a coincidence.

Again, she put her hand to her mouth. Smothered a sob.

She opened the envelope and saw a sheet of paper. She pulled it carefully out. It was a letter written in Swedish, in beautiful, old-fashioned handwriting:

Karlstad, 8 August 1946

Dear Mr Hellberg
It is with great sadness that we must inform you that Robert and Elisa Ulstein, whose house you bought when they were forced to flee the Germans, have died. The circumstances of Robert's death are unclear. Elisa came to us here on the farm and gave birth to the child she was carrying only a few months before she died. The boy's name is Daniel.

We do not expect anything from you in this respect, as Daniel has already become a part of our family, and we have decided to raise him as one of our own. As far as we know, the rest of Daniel's family were deported in 1942 and none of them have survived. Please do contact us if this is not the case.

Daniel is therefore the rightful owner of the house at Brages vei 18 in Tønsberg. And, now that the war is over, we ask that the house is sold and the money from the sale is transferred to an account that Daniel will then be given access to on his eighteenth birthday. We think this would also be a suitable occasion for him to learn about his family.

Please subtract the amount that you originally paid for the house and any costs incurred by the sale, plus interest, as we do not want you to be left out of pocket or lose any money from this transaction.

With our deepest gratitude for the help you gave to the Ulstein family in difficult times. We truly appreciate it.

With our deepest respect,
Gustav and Agnes Schyman

Why on earth had Tore kept this letter? Veronica wondered.

She emptied the contents of the shoebox onto the floor. Among the things that fell out was a black-and-silver USB stick.

55

Patrik Hellberg swore silently. Just finish, he muttered, I haven't got time for this.

It was like lying in wait – as he had done so many times as a child, with William and Hedda. Playing hide-and-seek in the woods out at Hulebakk, jumping out from behind a tree. They loved giving Hedda a fright; she always wanted to come with them, to do everything they did.

To think that it could all go so wrong.

And now he was running away, from himself more than anything, perhaps. Patrik felt hot, unbearably so. He had the air conditioning on in the car and the fan was going full blast but it didn't help. His body felt like it was in an oven.

He'd driven back and forth past the summer house several times, but there had always been someone there. There were fewer of them now, luckily. What else could they be looking for?

It had taken too long. Patrik had been tempted to go somewhere else, but didn't want to pass any tolls or border points, didn't want to leave a trace of himself.

He turned on the radio. A song he didn't know was just finishing. Then the presenter said there would be a commercial break leading up to the news. Patrik listened to adverts about burglar alarms, about an insurance policy that everyone needed, a car that everyone who had ever paid for repairs should buy. He turned up the volume.

'This is P4. And now, the ten o'clock news.'

Patrick's heart started to race.

'Two people have been found dead on *MS Nordlys* following a fire onboard the ship earlier today. It is not yet known where they were found, or whether they were staff or passengers.'

Patrik listened in suspense. A fatal accident in Sogn and Fjordane involving a car and a motorbike; a report had been published that criticised the Norwegian state railways; an autumn storm was expected to hit Vestlandet overnight. Nothing about Hedda.

But why would there be, anyway? There was no reason why there should be.

He turned the radio off and slowly emptied his lungs. He had to get back there. Change her bags. There would be no fluids left soon.

Patrik thought about the journalist. It was impossible to know how much she'd found out; how much she'd said, done, written about or emailed to anyone. But one thing was clear. He was *not* going back to prison again. No way.

He should have let it all lie, should never have gone to Sweden, should have left Daniel Schyman in peace. But it was easy enough to say that now. His father had said the same thing several times before he died – that he regretted a lot of the things he'd done in his life; that he'd never thought they would have the consequences they did. Ellen, cancer, dying far too soon. He said it was karma: you reap what you sow.

Patrik had listened to every word, and had been determined that he wouldn't make the same mistakes. But that was precisely what he'd done.

He drove past the summer house one more time. There was only one car there now. He could see two people – a man and woman. They took off their plastic overalls and walked calmly over to the car. Neither of them said anything. One of them looked up.

Patrik put his foot on the accelerator, the engine revved, and he drove down the main road a little way and parked up. He waited until the dark-brown car had passed him, then turned and drove back to the summer house. He reversed down the narrow track, his body twisting so he could see out of the back window. He went as far as he could between the trees and bushes, and parked up by the hole in the fence. His car was black so it wouldn't be easy to spot.

He turned off the engine, put on some gloves and got out, slamming the door shut. He walked round and opened the boot, looked at her. Her eyes were still closed.

There was no other way, he thought. He would have to kill her.

◎

Henning, Iver and Cato Løken followed the trails in the dust and soon came to another set of stairs, which led them up and out, into the middle of the field at the back of the barn, some thirty metres from the dirt road. It was dark, but the flashing blue lights from the ambulance swept across the field, illuminating the grass and roofs at regular intervals. A light had now been switched on in one of the rooms in the main house.

They saw the ambulance drive off, and hurried back to their own cars. Løken got out his mobile, dialled a number and put the phone to his ear. Iver went over to Henning while Løken was speaking.

'What the hell should we do?' he said, clutching Nora's bag.

Henning ran a hand through his hair and looked around.

'As Løken said,' he replied, 'they could be anywhere by now.'

Iver hunched his shoulders up and then released them, taking a step back. His shoes squelched on the damp ground.

'But Patrik doesn't know that we've found Hedda,' he said.

'That's true,' Henning agreed. 'He may well not have run off, and he'll probably come back here at some point.'

'So, in the meantime, we have to make sure no one knows we've found Hedda.'

Henning's phone rang. He looked at the screen.

'Can you talk to Løken?' he asked.

Iver was already making his way over to the inspector, who was still on the phone. Henning answered the call.

'Hi Veronica,' he said. 'Listen, it's not a good time, we're...'

'I'll think you'll be interested to know what I've just found,' she said.

'OK – what is it?'

'I managed to open Tore's safe. And I found a letter. I think it has something to do with what you're investigating. It's addressed to Hellberg Law.'

'Hellberg Law?' Henning asked, as he wandered around a bit.

'Yes.'

'Can you read it to me?'

Veronica did as he asked. His mind was racing by the time she'd finished. That might have been what Hedda was looking for out at Hulebakk, he thought.

But how on earth had it ended up with Tore Pulli?

'Could you maybe take a photo of the letter and email it to me?' he asked. 'Or text it?'

'Yes, of course.'

'Great. Thank you.'

'But...'

Henning hung up and went over to where Iver and Løken were talking.

He was about to tell them what he'd just found out, when Løken said: 'I've just spoken to one of the last of our people to leave Hulebakk, and apparently a car that sounds like Patrik's has been driving up and down Dalsveien for the past hour.'

'Really?'

'We've alerted all the customs stations, but no one has seen his car yet, and he hasn't gone through any tolls, which he would have done if he'd abducted Nora and driven off at the time that her phone stopped giving signals.'

Henning put his phone back in his inside pocket.

'Maybe he's waiting for the people to finish off out there,' he suggested. 'Then he'd have the place to himself.'

Løken looked at Henning. 'He'd be mad to go there now. He's got no way of knowing if we're coming back or not. Unless there's something he needs out there...'

Henning remembered what Nora had told him about Patrik. He raised his hand.

'His boat,' he said. 'Patrik's got a boat out there!'

56

The sound of an engine starting woke Nora up. Her eyelids were glued together. Her head ached. She was lying on her side. She tried to move but quickly realised her hands were bound; and there was something over her mouth – a piece of cloth that tasted old. She breathed through her nose, shallow and fast. She managed to turn her head. Parts of her cheek were stuck to the leather upholstery; she'd been lying with her face pressed into it. Prising open her eyes, she looked around, but her head was woozy and it took a few seconds to focus.

She was on a boat.

It started to move. The sudden acceleration pushed her backward, and, unable to stop herself with her bound hands, she fell head first onto the floor. She groaned, twisting and breathing into the floor, trying to get out of her awkward position. *What the hell's going on?* she wondered. *Where are we going?*

She had no doubt that Patrik was at the helm. And she knew where they were; she'd seen his boat the first time she went out to Oscar Hellberg's summer house. She even remembered what it was called.

La Dolce Vita.

The boat lifted up on a wave and then slammed down onto the water again. It sent a jolt up Nora's back; she moaned and heard the spray splattering on the side of the boat. Patrik made some tight turns, slowed down, then accelerated again. Nora knew what the Vestfold coast was like. Lots of small islands and shallows. And as it was dark, it wasn't easy to know where there might be small, sharp rocks that could tear holes in the hull. But Patrik was an experienced sailor; he spent five weeks on the boat every summer with his wife. Hopefully he knew these waters well.

Another wave lifted the front of the boat, then dropped it again with a thump. Nora groaned loudly.

Despite her pain, despite the fear, she felt the need to work out what might have happened. It might just help her. If it was Patrik who had killed his aunt, then he might have killed Daniel Schyman, too. According to Patrik's wife, he'd been in Sweden quite a lot recently.

Patrik might have been just as angry with Ellen as William was, Nora reasoned. Ellen had ruined their parents' marriage. And if she also intended to let the world know how the Hellbergs had made their fortune after the war, it would affect Patrik as much as all the others. It wasn't only their reputation that would be damaged, but also their wealth. The family's entire future was in danger.

Somehow or other, Hedda must have found out what Patrik had done. And that was why she went to Sweden. Then she'd gone back to Hulebakk to confront him.

But it was one thing to kill an old Swedish man at a distance. And quite another to kill your own sister, standing there in front of you.

The boat settled into a steady rhythm, rising and falling on the waves. *You can't just lie here*, Nora said to herself.

Then she felt the boat slowing down. And soon it wasn't moving at all. Patrik's shoes appeared on the steps up to the flying bridge above her. Nora curled up into the foetus position. She wanted to scream, but the gag muffled any sound. She snuffled and snorted, but saw, to her relief, that he had nothing in his hands.

He seemed to be angry, though, Nora thought, squinting up at him and trying to shrink away. He came over and lifted her up into a sitting position. Then he paced backwards and forwards in front of her, rubbing his hands on his trouser legs. Nora tried to read his face. He was thinking; it must be about Hedda. He would have to get back to check on her soon. She couldn't be left alone without care and supervision for too long.

And the thought of Hedda unconscious on the bed, made her go over everything again.

In a matter of seconds, everything fell into place.

Of course.

Nora tried to say something, but still the gag stopped her. Patrik glared at her, before he jumped back up onto the flying bridge. Nora tried to work out where they were, but could only see a few lights on land, which looked some way off. There were no other boats, no shadows or the outline of an island.

Then Patrik came back down the steps, he came straight for her, grabbed hold of her arms and picked her up. And pulled her over to the rails.

57

Cato Løken put the phone to his ear.

'Hi, it's me,' he said, and quickly recounted Henning's theory. 'We need to launch the police boat, as fast as...'

Henning and Iver stared at the policeman as he waited for an answer.

'What do you mean?' he said.

Henning took a step closer.

Løken rolled his eyes. 'Tell them to get a move on, for Christ's sake. And not a word to the press. Say whatever you like, but not a peep about finding Hedda. Tell the hospital people too. Not a word.'

Løken hung up.

'What is it?' Iver asked.

Løken sighed. 'The guys on duty can't drive the police boat.'

'What do you mean?' Henning said.

'They don't have a licence to drive the boat. It might take a while to find someone who has the right papers.'

'Shit,' Iver snapped. 'Can't they just forget about all that – we have to find Patrik's boat before it's too late.'

Løken shrugged.

Iver swore again.

'But there's a lifeboat station at Jarlsø, which isn't too far away,' Løken continued. 'There aren't many private boats out on the water at this time of year; and certainly not at this time of night. So if Patrik hasn't decided to scarper, the chances are we'll find him relatively quickly, as he'll be somewhere locally. Especially as he doesn't know that we've found Hedda.'

They stood looking around. Darkness surrounded them.

'As long as we find them before it's too late,' Henning said. 'Nora's pregnant as well.'

Iver looked over at him.

'Well, it's out of our hands now,' Løken said.

Henning balled his fists, without being aware of it. 'Yes, and that's what I don't like.'

⊙

Nora struggled and kicked so much that Patrik lost hold of her. She fell onto the deck; in her desperation, she ignored the pain. She pulled hard, trying to loosen the cable ties around her wrists, but they only dug deeper and deeper into her clothes and skin.

I mustn't end up in the water. I'll die.

Even if she could release her hands and swim, she would die anyway – the water was too cold and they were too far from land.

Patrik came at her again and attempted to lift her up; but she twisted and turned and tried with every muscle in her face to dislodge the gag. She pushed at it with her tongue from the inside, tried to bring her chin up towards her nose, and gradually it worked. The gag loosened, but not enough to free her lips and teeth.

He grabbed at her again and she kicked him in the knee. He screamed with pain, but it only made him angrier, and he lunged towards her with renewed strength, grabbed hold of her jacket and lifted her to her feet. Then he pulled her over to the railing again, kicking a cushion that must have slipped off the sofa out of the way. No matter how hard Nora struggled, he was stronger than her.

Nora could taste the blood in her mouth. She bit and pulled at the gag, trying to get her teeth free. And all the while, Patrik pulled her closer and closer to the railing. They were right at the back of the boat. Nora resisted as much as she could, using her legs and stomach muscles to brace herself, to stop him from throwing her overboard.

And then finally she got shot of the gag.

'Don't do it, Patrik,' she screamed. 'I can help you.'

Patrik didn't seem to have heard. The wind whipped his hair from side to side, his face was wet, his breathing laboured as he tried again to throw her in the water. But Nora had managed to hook one of her legs round a table that was bolted to the deck.

The next moment, he shot a look to the side. Nora heard it as well: the sound of a boat approaching. Patrik let her go, peered out into the dark, then leaped up to the flying bridge again.

Only seconds later, the motor roared into action; the boat rose up and the water churned. Once again Nora was pushed back by the force, but this time she managed to keep her leg round the table and clung on.

Gradually she pulled herself up and watched the distance between them and the lights on the other boat grow.

She struggled to her feet, but it was hard to keep her balance. The boat bounced from wave to wave, cutting through the black water.

As Nora put her foot on the lowest step, another wave lifted the boat, and she lost her balance for a moment, then the hull slapped down again. She made sure she was steady before she took another step. There weren't many so she was soon on the same level as Patrik, only a few metres behind him.

He turned his head as soon as he heard her.

'Don't!' he shouted back at her. 'Don't come any closer.'

Nora turned, and discovered she could no longer see the boat they were fleeing. She could make out some islands nearby, but had no idea where they were. She knew that they couldn't be too close to land, because the shallows stretched quite some way out and even though the islands were marked, it wouldn't be easy to see them when he was going so fast.

'It was you who shot at me!' Nora shouted.

Patrik kept his eyes straight ahead.

'You tried to frighten me off looking for Hedda. I understand, Patrik, I know that you've been looking after your sister for five weeks; you didn't know what people would think if they were to find her.'

She took a step closer.

'It would be hard for you to explain that it wasn't you who killed Daniel Schyman.'

58

Patrik steered east, heading for the lighthouse at Leistein. He listened to what the journalist was saying.

'If you'd killed Ellen back then,' she continued, 'you would never have been stupid enough to shoot at me, because it brought the police out there. You wouldn't have wanted them to come and search the property, would you? That's obvious. But they weren't looking for Ellen, they were looking for your sister.'

Patrik squeezed his eyes closed.

'I don't know what happened between the two of you, Patrik, and tell me if I'm wrong, but I'm guessing it's your fault that Hedda's in a coma.'

He swung sharply to the left, still at top speed.

'It's possible that Hedda won't wake up again, that she'll be declared dead at some point, and then it wouldn't take much for you to end up in prison for murder.'

Patrik still didn't say anything.

'I think I can help you,' Nora carried on. 'I'm so close to getting the whole picture.'

Patrik wiped his face with his hand. He thought about his father, about what he'd said one of the last times Patrik had gone to see him.

Patrik, there's something I need to tell you.

Patrik had pulled his chair closer to the bed.

There are some things about me and our family that you don't know.

Then he told him, in a weak, tired voice, about his relationship with Ellen – that they'd had to stop meeting only days before Ellen disappeared.

But there's more.

And then he told him about the letter from Sweden, the envelope that his mother had found when she was sorting out the company archives; a letter that told the truth about Brages vei 18 and what should have happened after the war. As she lay dying she had felt guilty that she'd never done anything about it, so she had asked Ellen, who'd been nursing her, to be stronger and more courageous than she had been.

Oscar wasn't convinced that Ellen had committed suicide, but he'd never been able to prove otherwise. And he'd never managed to find the letter, even though she had told him that she'd hidden it at Hulebakk – where they used to meet, him and Ellen, for their trysts.

Have you told anyone else this?

Only you and Hedda know.

Why haven't you told William?

Well, William, he...

And then he'd looked away. Patrik knew that they'd never had a good relationship. William had been far too rebellious as a boy, had spent too much time with dodgy friends, not even come to see his father much, now, when he was dying.

Patrik turned to Nora.

'And you could have denied it all you liked,' she shouted through the sea spray, 'but no one would have believed you if you said you had nothing to do with Daniel Schyman's death. And it wouldn't help much to blame someone who couldn't defend themselves. That's why you thought you'd have to get rid of me as well. Because I'd found Hedda. I could let the big secret out.'

She took another step closer. 'But it wasn't you who killed Daniel Schyman,' she said.

Patrik looked straight at her.

'It was Hedda.'

59

Patrik stood looking at Nora with his mouth open. His eyes wide.

He had tried to talk to Hedda about the past, about Daniel Schyman, but she'd made it absolutely clear that she thought they should let it lie.

'It was too long ago,' she'd said. 'It's got nothing to do with us.'

But it did; it had everything to do with them. They had been given a golden opportunity to make amends. And that was why he'd looked up Daniel Schyman – discovered that he still lived in Karlstad. But when he told Hedda that he'd been in contact with the Swedish pensioner, that he'd agreed to meet him in Sweden and planned to give the old man all the money that was owed to him, she was furious.

'Do you realise what that will mean for the family?' she'd shouted. 'What it will mean for me?'

He hadn't thought that she would do what she did – kill the old man in cold blood, and then try to kill her own brother as well. For what? To protect a terrible family secret? Her own inheritance?

'Hedda phoned me,' he said, and stared out into the dark. They were rounding the south side of the lighthouse and following the red sector towards Hollenderbåen. 'I didn't know it was her to begin with, didn't recognise the number. But she said she wanted to talk to me about something. Out at Hulebakk.'

The boat continued to rise and fall on the waves. He turned back; there were no other boats nearby.

'When I walked into the living room, I found myself looking straight down the barrel of a hunting rifle. Luckily I reacted before she had time to pull the trigger. I grabbed the barrel and pushed it up, then we stood there fighting for a few seconds, like we were kids again.'

Patrik closed his eyes.

'Then the gun went off. And in the heat of the fight, I pushed her over and she fell against the fireplace.'

Patrik opened his eyes and looked at Nora.

'I didn't know what to do,' he said, and started to cry. 'My finger-prints were on the gun; I'd been in Sweden myself that day; and Hedda was lying unconscious on the floor. Of course, I knew how dangerous head injuries could be. I panicked. I knew that all fingers would be pointing at me.'

He could just make out the buildings at Fulehuk, like tiny, glittering eyes.

'So I took her and the rifle with me. I couldn't take her to hospital, because then I'd be asked questions that it would be too difficult to answer.'

Patrik looked at Nora again.

'I drove around without any plan, trying to work out what I should do. Then I passed Morsevik Farm, and remembered that there was a bunker under the barn. Everyone in the family knew about it. I managed to persuade the man who lives there now to rent me the barn.'

Patrik swung the boat round suddenly, then it returned to a steady course.

'And you looked after Hedda there.'

He nodded. 'I hoped that she'd wake up, that I'd be able to talk her round, get her to hand herself over. But she still hasn't come round. And the longer I looked after her, the worse it got, the more lies I had to tell. It's...' he shook his head '...unbearable,' he finished.

Nora nodded. 'And then I rang and asked about Hulebakk, so...'

'So I went out there and saw a rental car parked nearby. I guessed it was you snooping around, and I was scared you might find something. Her suitcase, for example. You'd written that it was missing. It hadn't crossed my mind that she'd have some things with her; that she'd intended to stay there for a few days. So I took the gun with me. I had to get you away from the place. Thankfully, the police didn't go into the house that afternoon, so I went back later and got rid of the suitcase. The extra mobile phone.'

Suddenly there was a loud bang from under the boat. Patrik had to hold onto the wheel in order not to fall down. The boat pulled to the side. He saw that Nora had been thrown forwards into the windscreen, smashing the glass. She was bleeding from a gash on her forehead, but she was still conscious. Then the boat was still. There was a hissing noise in the engine room.

'Shit,' he said, and hurried down the steps. There was steam coming out around the door. The water must have reached the hot engine already.

He grabbed two life jackets and ran back up the steps. Nora had managed to get to her feet again. He rushed over to the sticker by the VHF, displaying the lifeboat numbers, got out his mobile phone and rang the lifeboat station at Jarlsø, where *Sjømannen* was ready to launch at a moment's notice.

'It's Patrik Hellberg on board *La Dolce Vita*. We've run aground on rocks not far from Fulehuk, I'm not sure of the exact position. But she's taking in water already. It'll only be a matter of minutes before she sinks.'

◉

'You have to put on a life jacket,' Patrik said, when he'd cut the cable ties from around her hands and properly pulled away the gag.

Nora looked around. She could see land straight ahead. But it was some way off; she'd never manage to swim that far.

'Put it on,' he repeated. 'Now.'

The life jacket he'd thrown at her was lying at her feet.

'You need to put yours on, too,' she said.

'Yes, I know,' he replied. 'I will.'

Nora realised the boat was sinking. It was like being in a lift that was going down very slowly.

She thought about the child she was carrying; about Iver, Henning, her parents, her sister; she thought about salty liquorice and sushi and all the things she loved to eat. About sand between her toes. And about Jonas. She had to fight back the tears.

She did as Patrik said and put on the life jacket, tying it tight around her chest and waist. The water was still rising and soon her feet were wet, and then so were her ankles. It was so cold, so icy cold – it felt like it was biting. Her trousers soaked up the wetness, stuck to her skin, and she breathed in and out fast and hard as the water continued to come in.

'You have to jump,' Patrik shouted.

She stared at him in disbelief, but it was only a matter of seconds now. She clambered up onto the roof of the boat, and saw there was not much more than a metre left of the boat above water.

Nora looked at him for a long moment. He was putting on his life jacket, but hadn't tied it properly yet. The water was up to his knees and soon it would be difficult to jump at all.

She turned round, staring at the great blackness in front of her. She really didn't want to do this; it was the last thing in the world she wanted to do. But she had to.

She gathered her strength. And jumped.

60

Neither Henning nor Iver said anything in the car as they drove back to Tønsberg. Henning stayed within the speed limit; he didn't see any point in racing. It wouldn't help. He had his mobile phone between his legs so he'd feel it if it started to ring.

'Fuck, I hate this,' Iver said.

Only a few days ago, Henning had thought he didn't need anyone, that he would never love again; that he didn't care about anything. But he wasn't made that way. And if he lost Nora now, without...

His phone started vibrating. It was Løken.

'Hello?' Henning said. His voice was shaking.

'Patrik called the lifeboat station's emergency number a couple of minutes ago,' the policeman told him. 'They've run aground on some rocks.'

'Are they alright?' Henning asked.

Løken didn't answer straightaway.

'No, I don't think so,' he said after a pause. 'The boat has disappeared from the radar.'

Nora tried to breathe, but couldn't. And she couldn't move, either.

She lay on her back with her face upwards, floating on the waves, up and down, up and down. She wasn't going to last long like this. It was too cold. If she didn't manage to pump the oxygen in her blood up to her head very soon, she'd faint. If she rolled over and her head went under water, then...

Breathe, she said to herself and tried to gain control over her lungs. She managed a small gasp. The sky was clear and full of stars. A wave hit her unexpectedly and she swallowed a lot of water. She started to cough. Her chest was stinging and burning, but at least it made her lungs work, even if they didn't want to. Then another wave washed over her, she tried to hold her breath this time. It turned her over on to her side and she had to use her arms and legs to stabilise herself. Only just managed.

She shouted for Patrik, but didn't get an answer. She shouted again. All she heard was the sound of the constantly moving water, bubbles rising up from the boat, which had sunk below the surface now.

Nora let out a sob. She'd managed to control her breathing now, to a certain extent at least. She closed her mouth and nose and waited for the icy helmet around her head to disappear. She'd be able to breathe again soon.

Nora thought about giving birth, how important it was to breathe properly. She tried to be aware of her surroundings so she'd be prepared for the next wave.

The sound of an engine made her turn her head.

There. A light, not far away.

But it disappeared again the next moment when the biggest wave so far pushed her to one side. Nora thrashed her arms and legs. It might be the lifeboat, she thought, all hope's not lost; just a little longer. Come on, fight, you've got more life in you yet.

She lifted her hands up as high as she could, waved them around, back and forth.

There, she saw the boat again. It passed about thirty metres in front of her. She shouted and screamed as loud as she could. But the boat carried on by. Another wave took her and she wasn't prepared this time, the water filled her mouth as she shouted. Again she swallowed water, lots of water. She gurgled and swallowed and coughed all at once. Everything was starting to spin round. She didn't have much breath left, but she tried to keep hold of it until the water washed over her face.

She managed, and started to shout for the boat again, mustering every little bit of strength she could, but knew that she just didn't have enough air. And soon she had to hold her breath again.

Another wave, Nora was more prepared this time; she managed to float up and down without her head going under. She saw where she was, could see parts of an island to the left.

The boat had turned and was heading slowly towards her.

They've seen me, she thought, and the next moment she saw a beam of light just to the right of her, like a beautiful white ray of sun. She tried to reach out to it, kicked with her legs, waved her arms, and she heard the dunk-dunk-dunk of the boat's engine as it drew closer. And then suddenly the light was all around her. It hurt her eyes, she squeezed them shut and forgot to close her lips, was too busy shouting and waving, and more water washed over her, pressing her down and to the side. Her whole body went under this time, and she spun round and round.

Nora tried desperately to struggle to the surface again, but everything around her was getting blacker; she couldn't breathe. She knew she mustn't take in any more water, but she was about to burst; she had to gasp for air.

⊙

Henning pulled into a bus stop and turned off the engine. Iver stirred in his seat and rested his head on his hand, with his elbow by the window.

Henning looked out at the darkness. He could see lights in the windows dotted around. Somewhere over there was the sea. Big and powerful and cold.

He normally loved the sea, but right now he hated it. If it had taken her, if Nora was never found...

He gripped the steering wheel, and thought about the evening he'd come home and she'd said those fateful words. Jonas had gone to bed long before. The flat was quiet. It still smelt of supper. She'd lit the candles on the windowsills.

Henning knew straightaway that something was up. There was a gravity in her eyes that he'd not seen before, and a sadness; but she was also wearing a stern mask. She'd decided. Enough was enough.

'This isn't doing me any good,' she'd said. He hadn't understood the sentence to begin with, but the meaning became clear enough when she carried on. 'I think it would be best for me if we lived apart for a while.'

Then she'd pointed out into the night.

Everything was so cold. And he probably didn't react in the way that she had wanted him to. He'd probably got that wrong, too.

He had got angry, hadn't asked for an explanation. Just turned around and walked straight out again. No pleading. No begging. No promises to change and improve. No questions about what the problem was, what he could do to make things better. He just walked out, certain that she didn't love him any more; he'd noticed it for a while now. The resigned look in her eyes, her reluctant footsteps around the flat, how she turned away from him when she slept. The emails with small declarations of love that had stopped coming. The absent text messages.

Henning thought that someone else had captured her heart. So, over the following days and weeks, he didn't try to win it back; he just met her with silence, misplaced pride, and a slow-burning anger...

She wanted to split them up. To ruin his relationship with Jonas. To destroy Jonas. Make him a statistic. Henning threw himself into his work, more fearless than ever. Everything that they'd had, that he thought was so good ... gone.

He'd been the biggest idiot in the world.

And now...

He would have given anything to be out there. He would have done anything to find her, to save her.

He should have fought.

It was too late now, for them, but not too late for Nora. She still had her life in front of her. Henning glanced over at Iver.

They still had their lives in front of them.

The phone rang. Henning picked it up.

◉

The life jacket pushed her up and she managed to get her head out of the water again. The light burned in her eyes.

But she heard something new – a voice shouting, 'To the right, to the right.'

She turned round, splashing with her right arm and hand, trying to do a stroke at the same time as getting air down to her lungs. The pressure in her head lessened and it was easier to see again. And what she saw, only a few metres away, galvanised her that little bit more.

A lifebuoy.

Nora tumbled round and took another stroke, let herself be lifted by the next wave, before tackling the water again. It was heavy work; the wave had pushed her away from the lifebuoy, but she focused on just how close she was, on the baby in her stomach, and pushed back the water with one arm, then the other. She took short breaths, kicked with her legs. Only one metre more.

Nora threw herself towards the lifebuoy, managed to touch it with her fingers, but it slipped away again. Another wave was coming, so she waited for it, let it lift her up and away. She heard the same voice calling from the deck, but she couldn't make out what it was saying, could only think about the next stroke, the next centimetre. She had to do it.

Nora took three deep breaths. Then she put her head down in the water and swam as fast as she could while holding her breath. She closed her eyes and forced her way forwards, stretching out towards the lifebuoy. But she couldn't feel it at her fingertips; she splashed and thrashed a little more.

Suddenly she had her hand on something round and smooth. She held onto it for dear life, threw her arm round the inside of the ring. Then she pushed herself up from the water's deadly hold.

◉

'They've found her,' Løken shouted from the phone. 'They've just pulled her out of the water!'

Henning felt his jaw drop. He swallowed, turning towards Iver, and gave him the thumbs up.

Iver collapsed in the seat beside him.

Henning did the same. He blinked hard several times. He needed to compose himself for a few moments before he could speak.

'Fantastic,' he said, quietly.

'But they're not coming in just yet, they're still looking for Patrik.'

Henning coughed. 'Haven't they found him, too?' he asked.

'No,' Løken replied.

Henning thought about the moment when Jonas came into the world. Up to that point, every second in the birthing suite had been loaded with fear. Nora's pain, everything that could go wrong. And then, when Jonas came out, when Henning heard the sound of his voice – the most delightful scream, so strong already. The relief was tangible and lifted him – them – up. A feeling that he'd never experienced since.

Not until now.

'Thank you for letting us know,' he said, slowly, and then hung up.

He looked over at Iver again. Nora's boyfriend was staring out of the window, rubbing his eyes.

Henning put a hand on his shoulder. Said nothing. Just let it rest there as the seconds ticked by. And he thought to himself that something was right in the world.

The lights from another car hit the rear-view mirror. It was approaching at speed. Henning watched until it had passed. It was actually an ambulance.

It made him think about Hedda and everything that had happened. Everything that Nora had told him.

Henning called Løken back. The inspector answered immediately.

'Where did they take Hedda?' Henning asked, and straightened himself up.

'The hospital in Tønsberg,' Løken told him.

'So the chances are that some of her family are there as well?'

'Yes, I should think so.'

'OK. And that's where they'll take Nora, isn't it? I wondered if you might like to have a chat with some of the Hellbergs first. I've got an idea of how all this might fit together.'

61

The Vestfold Hospital was on Halfdan Wilhelmsens gate in Tønsberg: a modern building made from redbrick and glass. The entrance to the emergency department was paved. And even though it was the middle of the night when Henning and Iver arrived, there was still a row of taxis waiting outside.

Henning dropped Iver off, found a parking space a few minutes' walk away from the hospital and hurried back. When he arrived in the emergency department, he saw a small cluster of people surrounded by police officers; he presumed these must be members of the Hellberg family. A short man with bluish patches on his cheeks limped as he walked back and forth. Fritz Hellberg III, Henning guessed. A thin woman with beautifully cut hair, a sharp chin and her arms crossed couldn't seem to decide which leg to stand on. Unni Hellberg. She straightened her red glasses. William Hellberg was there, too; he was sitting, tapping something into his mobile phone.

Henning remained at a distance, in order to observe the various family members. What astonished him most was the absence of grief and anger – each seemed entirely caught up in his or her own thoughts. Fritz and Unni were standing a few metres apart, but both looked worried. Neither of them seemed to know what to do with their hands.

When Inspector Cato Løken came in, he walked straight over to the family.

He stopped by Unni. 'How is your daughter?' he asked.

She shrugged, palms up. 'It's too early to say, but they've done a brain scan. Is there any news about Patrik?'

Løken shook his head. 'We're using all our resources to search the area, but the conditions are difficult.'

Unni lowered her eyes, put a hand to her mouth, and let out an almost inaudible sob.

Løken gave her a few moments. In the meantime, he caught the attention of Fritz and William and waved them over.

'Mrs Hellberg,' he said. 'I'd like to have a few words with you all, if I may.' He indicated all three of them with his hand.

Unni dried a tear and looked up at him. 'Now?'

Løken nodded.

'About what?'

'What's going on?' William asked when he came over.

'I'd like to have a few words with you all,' Løken repeated.

'About what?' William asked, repeating Unni's question.

A tall man had joined them. 'My clients have been through a lot this evening, officer,' he said smoothly. 'I'm sure you can find another more suitable time.'

Preben Mørck, the Hellberg family lawyer, Henning guessed. He held himself with dignity and authority.

'I'm sure I could,' Løken said. 'But this is a criminal case and I take it for granted that the family will do their utmost to help solve it. I certainly hope they will provide as much assistance as they can.'

Unni and William exchanged glances with Fritz, before looking over at the lawyer, who seemed to be waiting for a decision from them.

'We could also do it down at the station,' Løken continued. 'But we're closer to Hedda here; in case there's any news. As I said, it's just a few words, you're not being questioned.'

Unni lifted her shoulders and sighed.

'In that case, I would like to come with you,' the lawyer said.

'I'll see if I can find a room,' Løken said. 'There are too many people here.'

The Hellbergs exchanged glances again as the policeman walked off. Henning felt William's eyes on him as he wandered over to Iver, who was feeding coins into a vending machine to get some chocolate.

'I'll stay here in case they bring Nora in,' Iver said.

'OK.'

'Good luck.'

Løken soon returned. 'Follow me,' he said, with a nod.

Henning brought up the rear of the family group, listening to the clacking of the lawyer's shoes and wondering if Løken was going to manage this; if he would remember everything.

They went out into a corridor, walked past some chairs and a table with flowers on it, and some trolleys. The patients were asleep; it was the middle of the night, and none of the lights outside the rooms was flashing.

Løken stopped by a door and held it open for them all to file in.

'Please, sit down,' he pointed around the room.

It was a standard meeting room, with a large table. The chairs were scattered about, as though people had had to leave the last meeting in a hurry. Everyone sat down, all except Løken. He stood at one end of the table.

'Why is he here?' the lawyer asked, pointing at Henning.

'For several reasons,' Løken said. 'He's provided the evidence that I'll show you later, and he's here in case I forget anything. I'm not getting any younger.' He gave them a small smile, but none of them was open to charm.

'I object to him being here,' the lawyer said.

'Well, you're very welcome to leave the room if you find it uncomfortable,' Løken replied. 'As I said, you're not being questioned, although that could easily be arranged if you prefer. But we would need to go down to the station, and I'm sure that there will be members of the press hanging around down there and it would take a good deal longer.'

The lawyer looked at Unni.

'Let's just be done with it,' she said. 'The sooner it's over, the sooner we can get back to Hedda. And hopefully Patrik.'

Løken smiled at her and at lawyer. 'Excellent. Thank you. Now, let's do this chronologically. We know that Ellen Hellberg was killed sixteen years ago. She was then dumped in the disused well out at Oscar Hell-berg's summer house.' The policeman spoke slowly and deliberately. 'Only someone who had access to Hulebakk and knew the grounds would have chosen the well as a place to hide a body, and only a strong person could lift the lid, as it weighs almost a hundred kilos. Which excludes most of you; though perhaps not you...' He pointed at Fritz. 'You were big and strong at the time, but then, you'd just had a heart attack. So it couldn't have been you.'

Løken glanced over at Henning, who was sitting with his hands folded, listening.

'We also know that you, William, had used the services of Tore Pulli around the same time; a man who later went on to become renowned for his brutality. You'd known each other since you went to secondary school together in Horten and were part of the same scene.'

'What are you insinuating, officer?' asked the lawyer, thrusting his chin forward.

'I'm not insinuating anything, Mørck, and my title is Detective Inspector, but I'm sure you're aware of that.' Løken sent the lawyer a withering look before continuing: 'And this,' he said, pressing on his phone to produce a photograph, 'is something we found in Tore Pulli's safe.'

He showed the photograph of the envelope addressed to Hellberg Law.

'In the envelope is a letter which talks about a man called Daniel Schyman.'

Løken made eye contact with them, one after the other. The lawyer didn't move. Unni stared back with wide eyes, and then lowered them. William squeezed his hands. Fritz was following everything intently.

'It says in the letter that Fritz Hellberg, a lawyer, bought the house where Daniel Schyman's parents had lived before they fled from the Germans in 1942.'

Løken paused to see if there would be any eye contact. Only Fritz looked at him.

'His parents having died during the war, Daniel never moved back to Tønsberg, and instead became part of the family in Sweden who had opened their home to him. We have not yet clarified exactly what happened to Brages vei 18 – the house that Hellberg bought – after the war. But we do know that the lawyer sold some of the properties he was holding before starting the company that later built the family fortune. And it won't take us long to establish whether Brages vei 18 was one of the properties he sold.'

Løken walked up and down the room.

'If indeed Hellberg did sell Daniel Schyman's house and kept the money himself, I can well imagine that there are those in the family who did not want this to become known. I certainly wouldn't have wanted that if it was my family.'

'Is there a point to this story?'

Løken turned to face Preben Mørck, and took a step towards him.

'Why on earth was this letter in Tore Pulli's safe?'

The detective inspector stopped by the table and in silence looked at each of them in turn.

'Let me tell you why: because he killed Ellen Hellberg. He had been contracted to kill her, because she had somehow got hold of this letter. She knew the family secret. So she was a danger to them.'

'OK,' the lawyer said, standing up. 'You can stop there,' he turned to Unni, William and Fritz, 'I think we've heard enough.'

'I want to hear more,' Fritz protested.

They all remained seated.

Løken didn't need to be asked twice.

'And just before she was killed, Ellen deposited a large sum of money in an account for Georg, her son, when he came of age. It was money she didn't have. She didn't come from a rich family, and she wasn't working at the time; there was no need for that as she was married to you.' Løken pointed to Fritz, and again paused to see if there was any response.

The only person who moved was Unni; she straightened up in her chair.

'So, the question is, where did the money come from?'

Still no one answered. So Løken carried on.

'Our first thought when Henning found out that you, William, had been one of Tore Pulli's first clients around that time, was that you had given your old schoolmate a tidy sum of money to remove a major problem for the family. Not only had Ellen ruined your parents' marriage, she was now also in possession of a letter that contained compromising information – not only for the family, but also for Hellberg Property, the company you had just taken over.'

William looked over at his mother, who was clutching her hands.

'But Tore only did a couple of jobs for you, William, and that was that, wasn't it?'

William didn't answer.

Løken moved closer. 'So the next big question is: who else could have benefitted from Tore's services? Who else could afford to hire him? Who else could have known about the contents of the letter?'

He looked at them all again, one by one.

'Hedda was no more than fifteen at the time, so it couldn't have been her; and, what's more, she didn't have the money.'

Løken continued to circle the table.

'It could perhaps have been Patrik, but he was still at school when Ellen disappeared.'

Løken came to Fritz. 'You had been the head of Hellberg Property for a good while. And you were no doubt very angry that your wife had taken a lover behind your back, and on top of that, given birth to his child.'

Fritz looked straight at Løken, his mouth open.

'But then again, you were in poor health at the time, and were no longer part of the business. Certainly not officially.'

Løken moved on. He came to Unni and waited for some time before he said: 'But you, Unni, were working for Hellberg Property at the time.'

Unni continued to stroke and squeeze her fingers.

'When William first took over, you were in charge of finance.'

She didn't look up at him.

'And I can imagine that relationships were strained, after it had been revealed that Oscar and Ellen were having an affair,' Løken continued. 'I'm sure the atmosphere out at Solvang was not the best.'

Unni still did not look up.

'What happened, Unni?'

'Don't say anything,' her lawyer warned.

'You had the strongest motive for killing Ellen,' Løken said. 'She'd taken your husband; she knew a family secret that you very definitely did not want anyone else to know.'

William twisted round to look at his mother.

Løken leaned down towards her. 'What happened?' he repeated. 'Did she blackmail you?'

Fritz stood up, running a hand through his hair. His face was flushed.

'Or did you offer her a lump sum to forget everything? To give you the envelope so you could burn it?'

When Unni said nothing, Fritz spoke: 'Is it true, Unni?' He took a step towards her. 'Is it really true?'

'Mum,' William said, calmly, and stood up as well. 'Can you not just tell it like it is? For once?'

The lawyer held up a warning hand. 'Unni,' he said, putting his hand gently on her shoulder. 'Come on, let's go.'

She sat with her eyes glued to the table in front of her.

Fritz took a step towards her.

'Do you remember what it was like in the beginning, Mum?' William said. 'After I took over the business?' His voice was gentle. 'You watched over me like a hawk. You were so scared that I might mess up; I was just a young whippersnapper at the time. You looked after me.'

Fritz shook his head, balled his fists. He went over to the window and stood with his back to them, hands by his side.

'And in the beginning, I used Tore a couple of times to get people who thought they could wait forever to pay what they owed us, to cough up. Do you remember, Mum? I know you do, because it was you who got me to stop doing it.'

Unni looked up at him.

'You found out. You said that if it became known that I did business with people like Tore, it would ruin the company, our reputation. Do you remember?'

Unni turned away from her son, crossing her arms.

'And I did as you said; I thanked Tore for the work he'd done and that was that. But no one except you knew about Tore, Mum.'

'William, that's enough.' The lawyer's cheeks were red.

'No way!' Fritz shouted from behind the lawyer. 'No way is that enough! I want to know if what William is saying is true or not!' He approached them with quick steps.

'There's been enough lies and treachery in this family,' William said, positioning himself between his uncle and mother. 'And it stops here.'

'Unni, don't say anything,' her lawyer advised. 'Not now, not here.'

'Let her talk,' Fritz said. 'Let her admit what she's done.'

'Don't do it,' the lawyer said again. 'Don't do it.'

Unni stared at the floor. Her face had been leached of all colour. No one else said a word, they just waited for her to speak.

But she didn't.

Henning thought to himself that there was no doubt that Fritz Hellberg's actions after the war were immoral. But the company could survive that in this day and age; the family could claim not to have known anything about it, or paint it as 'the sins of the father'. The sale of Brages vei 18 may have helped lay the foundations for the family's fortune, but most of the money had been made long after.

But Unni hadn't thought of it that way. She was more concerned with keeping up appearances, and was blinded by hate. So she had killed two birds with one stone: she bought Ellen's silence by offering a large sum of money in return for the letter. And then she had Ellen killed.

Henning decided to say something. 'Did you perhaps suggest that she could put the money in a trust for Georg?' he pushed. 'Did you appeal to her maternal instinct?'

Unni still didn't speak.

'Did you agree to meet Ellen out at Hulebakk, so she could hand over the envelope, but then sent Tore instead?'

There were too many questions, Henning knew that; but he also knew that Unni would never answer. She turned her gaze away from them all. Her breathing was shallow. Everyone was looking at her. He saw her eyes darting here and there. And suddenly it was as if her face, that stiff mask, cracked and fell to pieces. She put her hands to her mouth and started to cry.

She sniffed a little and tried to compose herself, pulling a handkerchief from her handbag and pressing it against her cheeks, her eyes. Then she pushed back her shoulders and lifted her chin.

She stood up. 'Good luck proving that, *officer,*' she said, and gave Løken an icy stare.

'And now, I would like to go and see how my daughter is.'

'We will need to talk to you all about Patrik,' said Løken.

But Unni put her bag over her shoulder and started to walk, without so much as glancing at anyone in the room. *Proud and defiant to the last*, Henning thought.

But questions still remained in his mind. Foremost was: why on earth had Tore Pulli kept the envelope and letter?

62

The lawyer followed Unni, Fritz and Løken out. But William stayed in the meeting room with Henning. He didn't look up, just held onto back of the chair in front of him. Henning watched him, waiting for him to say or do something.

'I guess I should thank you,' William eventually said. 'For finding my sister and ... for piecing all this together.' He gestured around the room.

'It's Nora who deserves the greatest thanks,' Henning told him.

'I'll thank her as well, of course, if I get the chance.'

Henning gave a fleeting smile and nodded. 'There is something you can do in return,' Henning said.

William lifted his head. 'What's that?'

Henning rubbed his hands together. 'You obviously know who I am.'

William nodded.

'And you know that I'm trying to find out who set fire to my flat a couple of years ago.'

William said nothing.

'As I told you the other day, I was working on a story about the property-development industry around that time. And how people like Tore Pulli managed to break through and succeed, in part thanks to illegal means. These are people that I suspect you know, Hellberg.'

William lowered his eyes again.

'And whether you keep a low profile or not when you're in Brazil with your family, you're not blind. And I'm willing to bet that you know Charlie Høisæther; after all, you're neighbours down there and were both friends of Tore when you were growing up. And what's more, you're smart – you pick up on things; you put two and two together. You've just proved that.' Henning made a sweeping gesture with his hand. 'And I realise that you're perhaps afraid to say anything that might have repercussions for yourself; I know only too well how dangerous these people can be. But still, I ask you – help me. Please. If you know anything about this, help me.'

William didn't look up for a long time.

'You've got a son who's ill,' Henning said. 'I'm sure you've thought about how terrible it would be if...' Henning stopped, knew that he didn't need to finish the sentence.

William bit his lip. Put a hand in his pocket, then immediately pulled it back out. He hunched up his shoulders, held them there for a few seconds, then dropped them.

'If anyone asks,' he said, 'then you didn't hear this from me. Alright? I have to be able to trust that you won't say anything.'

'Of course,' Henning assured him, and took a step closer.

William let out a burst of air. 'I don't know if you're aware that Tore had money problems?'

'Yes,' Henning confirmed. 'I knew something of the sort.'

'Tore and Charlie had done a good deal of business together over the years,' William continued. 'Under the table. There was a period when they had no scruples whatsoever. They bought and sold flats from each other, conned the banks into giving them more money than they needed; they had the appraisers on their payroll and God knows what else. But they couldn't keep it up forever. People started to get suspicious – the fraud people at Økokrim among others – and Tore decided that they should keep a low profile for a while. Charlie moved to Brazil and started his own venture down there. It went from strength to strength. And soon Tore wanted a piece of the cake.'

William paused.

'He wanted to buy a flat down there. His wife was about to have her birthday and he wanted to surprise her, that kind of thing.'

Henning thought about the brochure that Veronica had shown him.

'Tore's problem was that he struggled to hold onto the money he earned. The idiot gambled like a lunatic. The last time we played poker together, he was almost desperate, went all in when he had no particular reason to do so, and that meant that he only lost more money. On top of that, his spending was out of control.' William ran a hand over his hair. 'He thought he still had some credit with Charlie, but Charlie wasn't confident that Tore could pull himself out of it, even if business did go well. So he said no when Tore asked to get a flat in Sports Park on credit or down-payments – I don't know the actual details.'

Henning absorbed everything he was hearing.

'Tore told me that he was massively disappointed and angry, and I don't think things were ever the same between them again,' William concluded.

Henning could feel that all the pieces were about to fall into place.

'I've heard that they fell out at one point,' he said. 'Is that why?'

'I don't know. But...' William hesitated. Then he continued: 'I know that they were at each other's throats just before Tore was arrested for murdering Jocke Brolenius.'

Henning narrowed his eyes. 'In what way?'

'Well, what do you think?'

Henning gave William a piercing look. 'Did they fight?'

William waited a beat before he nodded. 'And you can imagine what happened.'

Henning remembered the particular move that Tore was famed for. Elbow in the jaw.

'I think it was the last time they talked to each other,' William said. 'Charlie was seriously pissed off.'

'But you don't know if it was about the flat in Brazil, or something else?'

William shook his head.

But would you really fight about that? Henning wondered. It didn't sound too convincing. Whatever the case, Charlie had decided that Tore was the enemy; they'd done business together in the past, and if Tore had thought about spilling the beans, it wasn't surprising if he'd tried to stop him.

But where did Rasmus Bjelland come into the picture? How had he found out about what Pulli had been up to?

Henning asked William if he knew who Rasmus Bjelland was, if he'd met him down in Brazil.

William shook his head. 'I've never heard of him,' he said.

'What about Daddy Longlegs? Does he give out jobs on behalf of Charlie?'

William shrugged. 'I don't know anything about Daddy Longlegs,' he said. 'I've no idea who he is.'

63

By the time Henning was permitted to see Nora, the eastern sky was starting to turn light.

She'd been examined by a team of doctors and nurses, and he'd seen Løken go in and out of her room several times.

Iver was sitting beside her bed, but they weren't holding hands. Instead, Nora was squeezing a ball that Henning had seen before. He hadn't realised that she'd kept it. Her mobile phone was lying on the bedside table, charging.

She was pale; there were pearls of sweat along her hairline and on her forehead, and her eyes looked sticky. But she gave him a smile when he came in. It looked like her lips were about to split.

'Hi,' she said, in a thin voice.

Henning had so much he wanted to say – various words and sentences battled to be the first, but none of them won.

'How are you?' was all he finally managed.

'OK,' she said, and coughed. 'I think.'

It felt strange and awkward, to be standing looking at Nora in a hospital bed with Iver sitting beside her. He looked around for a chair. Couldn't see one.

'Did Iver tell you about Unni?' Henning asked.

She nodded. 'So he was a murderer, after all,' she said.

Henning looked up.

'Tore Pulli, that is.'

He nodded and sighed at the same time.

None of them said anything for a while. The only thing that broke the silence was the hum and occasional bleep of the machines attached to Nora. Iver slapped his thighs and stood up.

'I'm going to try and find a cup of coffee,' he said. 'Does either of you want one?'

Both Henning and Nora shook their heads. Iver give Henning a brisk nod as he closed the door. Nora tried to pull herself up in the bed, but the effort made her wheeze.

'You're fine lying down,' Henning said.

She lowered herself down again, breathing deeply. Henning sat down on the edge of the bed.

'What about the...' He indicated her stomach.

Nora looked at him for a long time, then a tear slid out from one eye. 'It's fine,' she sobbed. 'It's absolutely ... fine.'

Henning put a finger on her cheek, wiped away the tear, and stroked some unruly hairs back into place above her ear. Then he took her hand, stroked it, down to the nails.

She was warm. She was beautiful. He sat there for a long time; it was hard not to think about everything he felt for her.

'Have they found Patrik yet?' she asked.

Henning shook his head. 'The chances that he's survived are minimal.'

'You know, it wasn't him – who killed Daniel Schyman.'

Henning gripped the rail of the bed, staring at her. 'What do you mean?'

Nora shook her head, clearly exhausted. 'It was Hedda. Patrik told me the whole thing when we were in the boat. I believe him.'

Henning frowned, unsure.

'He did his best to save me, in the end,' Nora went on. 'He gave me the life jacket to wear. And he tried to save Hedda, too; it was an accident that she fell. I've told Løken.'

Henning nodded. He wanted to ask more, but Nora looked too weak to stand up to any more questioning.

There was a long silence. Henning felt her eyes on him. Studying him.

In the end, he bowed his head and said: 'I don't know if I can do this, Nora.'

'Do what?'

'Be here, or there, in Oslo or wherever, when...' He pointed at her stomach again without looking at her. 'I just don't know if I can do it.' Henning couldn't face looking at her yet.

'I understand, Henning. I really do understand.'

He started to fiddle with the duvet cover. 'It's not that I begrudge you it, Nora, or Iver. Or both of you, for that matter, I think it's good, Iver's a...' He looked away again. Couldn't find the words.

They said nothing for a while.

'You don't have to take everything as black and white,' she said. 'Not everything in life is written in stone. I know there's nothing I can do or say that will make it easier for you to live in Oslo when Iver and I and this...' Nora patted her stomach '...when this little thing grows and gets bigger and we move and do somewhere up and go to IKEA. Only you can do that.' She gave his hand a squeeze and then let it go. 'But it would make me so happy if you could still be part of my life, Henning. You'll always be a part of me, even though I might not be a part of you.'

Henning looked down. Didn't know what to say.

The room was filled with a heavy silence.

'What are you going to do now?' she asked, after a while.

'Well, I guess I'll go home,' he said, and shrugged. 'Get on with my leave.'

'Whatever you do,' she said slowly, 'please promise me you'll take care. OK?'

Henning looked at her for a long time, then tried to smile and nod, but didn't quite manage. And then, without having planned it or even knowing where the words came from, he said: 'I love you, Nora.'

Then he stood up and left.

64

Nora watched Henning go. She was left with a peculiar feeling – the feeling that she wouldn't see him again, which was why he'd said what he said.

It made her shudder. And cry.

She thought about all that lay ahead. A new child, a whole new life. The responsibilities and obligations; sleep, lack of sleep, food, nappies, the first smile, the laughter and tears. And she wondered if Iver would manage to take responsibility for anyone other than himself, if she would cope with having him around, if they would both be able to deal with the hurt in Henning's eyes if he did decide to be part of their lives. She so wished she could look into a crystal ball and see the future. There was no set answer. The certainty that there was no certainty made her heavy. Sad. Despondent.

She had to do her best to make it work. With Iver, with the child. With everyone.

There was a knock at the door. Hugo Refsdal popped his head round.

'Hi,' he said. 'Is it OK to come in?'

Nora had guessed that Refsdal might show up, and had hoped that he wouldn't.

'Of course,' she said, and thought about what Patrik had told her before they'd jumped into the ice-cold water, confirming what she had worked out for herself.

'Come in,' she said.

Refsdal had his son with him, who followed a step behind, his eyes on the floor.

'You can sit over there,' he said, pointing to the chair where Iver had sat. The boy went and sat down a few metres away from Nora's bed, clearly not wanting to meet her eye.

There was no way she could tell Refsdal about what Hedda had done – not now; not with the boy sitting there. Løken would tell him soon enough, anyway. It was out of her hands, she supposed.

Refsdal came a step closer. 'I don't know how to thank you,' he said.

Nora gave an embarrassed smile; she never knew how to react to praise or thanks. So instead she asked: 'Have they ... said anything about what to expect?'

Refsdal shook his head. 'It's difficult to say at the moment. She's suffered a major brain haemorrhage, but because it happened some time ago now, they can't operate. We just have to hope that, with time, she'll wake up. One of the doctors said that he had a similar patient once who'd woken up after three months. So there's still hope.'

Refsdal smiled, briefly.

'But she seems to be in reasonable shape otherwise?'

Refsdal nodded. 'The doctors are quite impressed by what Patrik has managed to do. He must have gone there several times a day to change the drips, and move her so she wouldn't get bed sores. The doctor I spoke to said that he must have massaged her muscles as well, to keep them in shape.'

Patrik had taken extraordinary care of her, Nora thought, which was also why she had suddenly understood that he hadn't killed Daniel Schyman. It wasn't in his nature. Hedda thought mainly about herself; and, out of all of them, she had the greatest need for money. And she had always been very protective of her family, never wanted to talk about them.

And when she realised that Patrik wanted to bring everything out into the open, that he wanted to make sure that Daniel Schyman was paid all the money he was owed and should have had years ago, including interest, she took the matter into her own hands. That was why she had told her husband that she needed the break to get over her father's death. In reality, she needed time to plan – and an alibi.

She had allied herself with Georg, persuading him to lend her his car so she could drive to Sweden and kill Schyman. Then she had gone back to Hulebakk to look for the envelope that she thought Ellen had hidden out there – perhaps in one of her favourite books. But she'd also gone there to kill Patrik: the only person alive who could ruin everything for her and her family.

'Anyway,' Refsdal said, breaking the silence, 'I just wanted to say thank you. And I am very glad that you're alright.'

Nora smiled again. He stood up, went over to his son and stroked his head.

It pained her to see how happy Refsdal was now, knowing how awful it would be in the near future, and what might happen to his family when everything came to light.

Happiness was transient; it could never last. Not even having a coat of arms could protect you from that.

65

Henning was in no rush to get back to Oslo. Sitting in the car with traffic all around him was somehow comforting, and he gave his thoughts free rein.

But what was he going to do now?

Iver had given him a set of keys, so he could stay there while he figured out what the next step should be. He had to do something. And even if Bjarne Brogeland had said he would help, Henning couldn't expect others to produce all the results. He had to keep the wheels turning himself.

The question was whether or not Henning should go to Brazil – go straight to the core – or if his chances were better at home. Whatever the case, he was so close now, he could almost see the finish line. He just needed to stay alive a little longer, dig even deeper and get the necessary documentation, then he was home and dry.

Maybe.

They'd tried to kill him twice without succeeding. Who knew when they might try again? He didn't doubt that they would.

His mobile phone started to ring. It was Veronica.

'Hello again,' he said. 'How's things?'

'Henning,' she said, in a very serious voice. 'How quickly can you get here?'

He frowned. 'To your house?'

'Yes.'

'Very quickly, if it's important.'

'I've found something else in Tore's stuff.'

'Right. What is it?'

'I...' She paused before she continued. 'I don't want to tell you over the phone. Can you come?'

'OK,' Henning said, and accelerated. 'I'm on my way.'

⊙

Three-quarters of an hour later, having stopped at a petrol station to buy a red-and-white baseball cap, he parked some way from the street where Veronica Nansen lived. He looked carefully in every direction before ringing her bell. It only took a few moments for Veronica to open the door. She didn't come out, but instead ushered him in quickly. As soon as he was inside, Henning took off the baseball cap and ran his hands through his hair.

'Disguise,' he said, and waved the baseball cap.

Veronica smiled briefly.

Henning took off his shoes, hung up his jacket and followed her into the living room.

'So what have you found?' he asked.

Veronica turned towards him, waited a moment and then said: 'Sit down first.'

'Hm?'

'Sit down,' she repeated.

Henning raised his eyebrows.

'Believe me, you need to be sitting when you see this.'

'OK.'

She pointed to the computer that was ready on the glass table. The screensaver cast a blue light on the white leather sofa.

He sat down and Veronica disappeared into the kitchen. He heard a cupboard door being opened, the clinking of glasses, the tap being turned on. Henning looked at the computer, a photograph of Tore and Veronica on a motorbike somewhere, white cliffs and sea in the background.

He let his eyes wander while he waited for her to come back. The living room was huge and well furnished, with a massive plasma TV.

The flat was full of expensive-looking things. On a small table beside the sofa was a large selection of glossy fashion magazines.

But Henning saw something else that made him start.

A business card. He leaned over, read the name.

Preben Mørck, Lawyer.

The Hellbergs' lawyer.

Veronica came back into the living room carrying a tray. There was a jug of water and two glasses on it. She stopped, looking at him.

'How do you know this guy?' Henning asked, waving the business card.

'Who?' she squinted to read the card.

'Preben Mørck.'

'Preben? He's my lawyer.'

'For how long?'

Veronica sat down. 'He's helped me since Tore died. Why do you ask?'

Veronica poured some water into the glasses. Henning sat deep in thought.

'Why did you choose him as your lawyer?' he asked after a while. 'Did someone recommend him?'

'No. It was actually Preben who phoned me. He said that he knew Tore from before. Offered his services, said that the fact he knew Tore might make things easier.'

Henning felt hot all of a sudden.

He pictured Preben Mørck. Tall, thin. Like a Daddy Longlegs. And Unni wasn't really the sort to go directly to Tore Pulli and say: kill Ellen Hellberg for me. She definitely would have used a middleman.

A lawyer, perhaps.

Henning held the image of the tall man in his mind. It fitted too well. And the fact that he'd become Veronica's lawyer after Tore had died was questionable. Downright dodgy, in fact.

'Why?'

Henning shook off the thoughts. 'Nothing in particular, really,' he said, and put the business card back down where he'd found it.

Veronica handed him a glass. Henning put it down on the table. She held his gaze for some time before she took a USB stick out from her pocket and held it up.

You need to be sitting when you see this.

Henning took the memory stick, put it in the USB port, then double-clicked on the icon that appeared on the screen. There was a folder, which contained several more folders. One of the yellow squares made his skin crawl.

JUUL.

Henning looked at Veronica. She was stroking her chin. He opened the folder, and saw that it contained 213 photographs. He marked them all, then double-clicked again. It took forever to open all the photographs, even on Veronica's brand-new computer. Henning looked up at her while the machine did its work. Her eyes were serious.

The first pictures appeared. Henning saw the date: 09.09.07 16.43. They were photographs of him as he walked up Markveien, alone, with an old bag slung over his shoulder and a carrier bag in one hand. *On the way home from work*, Henning thought, as he felt his heart starting to race. The pictures were taken very quickly, showing more or less the same thing. The camera followed him all the way to the entrance of his building.

The next batch of pictures was from later the same evening, when Henning went out. The time showed 18.58. This time, Pulli had got out of a car and followed him – over the road at the traffic lights and in towards Birkelunden. All the way to the football pitch at Dælenenga, where he always sat high up in the stands, on the warped plank seats. Some hours later, Henning appeared again in Seilduksgaten, on his way home.

The same pattern was repeated the next evening, only from a slightly different angle. Pulli was parked in a different place, and there were fewer photographs. Henning was wearing almost the same clothes as the day before: faded jeans, the same old denim jacket in a slightly different shade from his trousers, a white T-shirt underneath, white trainers.

Henning clicked quickly through the photographs and came to the following day. Then stopped at a photograph that he should have been prepared for, but it made him gasp all the same.

It was a photograph of Jonas.

There they were, side by side, together. Henning was carrying his little rucksack, and Jonas was his usual energetic self.

Henning's eyes filled with tears. He saw them walk up to their building. Jonas looking up at Henning, mid-question. The next picture: Henning with his hands out, mid-explanation. The following pictures were taken from the back, until they went inside.

It was close to silent in Veronica's flat, only the faint humming of the laptop and the distant siren of an ambulance racing towards Ullevål Hospital.

Henning knew that Veronica was watching him. He forced himself to breathe normally.

He clicked on. It was darker now and the first photograph was taken at 19.06. Roughly the same parking place, the same angle. There were people in the street. Cars passing. Pulli had taken several photographs of a car that was parked a few spaces away.

It was a black BMW.

A man got out. He was short and lean, with a distinct, Eastern European appearance. Close-cut hair. The photographs were taken in profile, and there were lots of them.

Henning recognised him.

It was the man who had followed him on the tram. Who had been standing outside Sultan watching him. Who had walked off when Henning looked at him. Who had maybe also tried to run him over.

Durim Redzepi.

Henning clicked on. He saw the short man walking up the street, looking around. Farther down Markveien, he looked up, looked down Helgesens gate, then back again. Henning could see from the pictures that it was close to seven-thirty. About the time that someone broke into his building, his flat.

19.47: the same man still walking up and down, apparently waiting for something. He was talking on the phone, gesticulating. He lit a cigarette. 19.54: he came back towards the black BMW, stuck his head in the window; went back up to Helgesens gate. Stood on the corner, lit another cigarette.

20.01: the man walked towards a car that had stopped on the corner. The window rolled down. He stuck his hand in, took it back out, his fingers clutching something. Then he turned and walked back to the black BMW. The car he had met stayed where it was. The door opened, the driver got out.

Henning sat and stared at the photograph.

No.

It couldn't be; it just couldn't be.

His heart felt like a dry rock in his throat. Henning clicked onto the next photograph to make sure he hadn't seen wrong.

He hadn't.

The photograph was almost identical, just a bit closer. The same was true of the next one, and it was frozen just as she opened her mouth to shout. She looked angry, or anxious – he didn't know how to interpret what he was seeing.

It was too hard.

Too painful.

Henning sat back on the sofa, staring at the image. He felt a burning wind rage up through his body. Up through his legs and arms, to his cheeks and head. He blinked, several times, but the picture did not change.

She was still there.

Trine was still there.

'That's my sister,' he said, and looked up at Veronica. 'That's my fucking sister.'

ACKNOWLEDGEMENTS

God, where should I begin?

To avoid any unwanted knives in the back during the night, I should probably start with Benedicte, my brilliant wife, whose mind scares me half to death sometimes, but also saves my butt when I have dug myself into a corner (which seems to happen quite frequently). Thanks for the support and for being both the best and the worst critic. Yes, you can be quite cruel sometimes ... said the deeply sleep-deprived, anxiety-ridden author.

Thanks, Jørn Lier Horst, for answering all my questions about how to be a cop. As you used to be one, all the mistakes I've put into this novel are on you.

To my super-duper brother-in-law, Tor-Magnus Økstad: thanks for driving me all around Vestfold – not to be confused with the landscape so gloriously described by my BFF, J. R. R. Tolkien in the *Lord of the Rings* trilogy, but the highly scenic county in Norway in which you live. Thanks, also, for telling me what the hell a flying bridge is. Now I know. I think.

I want to thank my sister, Hege, for answering all kinds of questions I have about medical issues. Same goes to you, Kristin Birgithe Jensen, whenever my sister wasn't quick enough to respond. Feel free to take the blame for the medical mistakes I've made in these pages.

To my wonderful editors in Norway, Trude Rønnestad and Kari Marstein: thanks for believing in me, for pushing me (sometimes over the edge; but, hey, it worked) and for lending me your ears whenever I had ideas I wanted to discuss (which seemed to happen quite frequently, too).

I also want to thank Kari Dickson for an excellent translation. Didn't know I could write this good. Which I didn't. You did.

Last, but not least, I would like to express an enormous amount of gratitude to my wonderful, energetic and highly passionate publisher at Orenda Books, Karen Sullivan. I am so thankful to be on your ever-growing team of wonderful and highly talented authors. It truly is a privilege and an honour, and I can't wait to see what the future has in store for us.

Thanks also, West Camel, for doing a marvellous job editing my book. West is the best (I'm sure you've never heard that one before). We'll definitely have a lot of fun in the years to come.

And finally, thanks Henny and Theodor, aged eleven and sixteen, for giving my life purpose when I'm not trying to figure out how to kill people.